a
Stupid Cupid
novel

CUPID'S CURSE

mindy ruiz

Follow your arrow
Mindy Ruiz

Published by A.P. Press, LLC

Cover design © 2017 Regina Wamba of MaeIDesign.com
Cover image by Mae I Design
Content edit: The Paisley Editor, Maria Pease
Copy edit: Hayley Cruz
Book design by Inkstain Interior Book Designing

Text set in Arno Pro.

ISBN-13: 978-0-9904804-6-4
ISBN-10: 0-9904804-6-1

ALSO BY MINDY RUIZ

THE GAME OF HEARTS SERIES

Enchanted Heart

Lying, Cheating Heart

ANTHOLOGY SET

The Peculiar Lives of Circus Freaks

CUPID'S CURSE

JACK

M*y name is Jack.*

Jaquelyn Alcantar might be on my birth certificate, but I wear the nickname that the boy who a-bombed my heart gave me like a medal.

Jack.

Call it my “lemonade out of lemons” moment. Don’t get me wrong. I’m by no means jaded. I love puppies, long walks on the beach, and will even admit to crying to a chick flick here and there. But when it comes to matters of the heart, well, I’m a bitch.

That’s not my technical title.

Officially, I’m a Cupid. Turns out Eros, the God of Love, doesn’t like it when you curse *amore*. He gets downright bitter when you swear never to be a sucker for the swoon. That one phrase, “I’ll never love again!” with the right amount of fortitude behind it will land you cursed.

Yep, I'm totally cursed to play Cupid until I believe in love. If I don't, well, my heart goes all petrified and I become immortal.

Which sounds damn good to me.

I wince as a familiar, painful heat starts in my heart and crawls across my skin. Seconds later, all that energy is concentrating its ire on my left wrist. I don't need to look to see what's causing the radiating pain or the beads of sweat dotting my forehead. The heat is my reward from Eros. A mythological branding of another golden arrow appears on my wrist. It's a physical gold-star reward for my work in getting another soul to fall for Eros and his "all you need is love" way of life. I've learned to embrace the pain, block out the sizzle of my skin being singed. I'm not a masochist or anything.

Quite the contrary.

The shmucks who walk around waiting for love to strike (that'd be me, Cupid) and then think a ring and some hocus pocus "I do's" are the winning ticket combination to their happily-ever-after . . . psh, *those* people are masochists. The heart is made of glass, and it's always a breath away from shattering.

I should know.

I suck in a gasp of air as the last wave of delicious pain strikes.

Anyway, that was then. I look down at my newest golden arrow on my left wrist and wait for the second phase of the branding process. The soft skin around my wrist is puckered and pink, but it's nothing compared to the pain of a broken heart. I run my finger around the edge of the arrow. A smile pulls at my lips. This pain has purpose. To protect the organ that nearly killed me by loving someone who didn't deserve me . . . or my heart.

The strong scent of ocean brine permeates the cold gust of air racing through San Francisco's Pier 39. It mixes with the sweat my branding created and releases a violent shudder that rocks my body.

Phase two.

My fingers dig into the damp wood of the pier. No need to worry, I remind myself. It's all part of the process. Another fierce tremor nearly brings me to my knees. The hair around the nape of my neck dampens some more, and I know I look like a junkie jonesing for her next hit.

It's all for the sweat.

When the branding heat fades and the sweat turns cold, I know another piece of my heart is turning to stone. The first time it happened, six years ago, I thought I was dying from a heart attack. God's way of adding insult to injury. Luckily, I was still on probation and my mentor, Stacey, liked me.

"It's your heart, lovey," Stacey cackled in a British cockney accent. "You'll get used to it, and then you'll love it." After she showed me where my first arrow branding *should* be—something close to a newly inked tattoo, only in gold—on my right wrist, she was recalled to Eros's house.

The sweetheart who'd fallen for love again and had been my first arrow was Stacey's forty-ninth brand.

One away from magic, turn-your-heart-to-stone, fifty golden arrows!

I heard my mentor washed out on the final arrow test. Only the most elite in the Corps achieve fifty arrows. Only fourteen souls have ever attained immortal status. Now, I am one away from joining that group.

After I smoke my final test, I'll have twenty-five gorgeous golden arrow brands encompassing each wrist. Most Cupids are terrified of the golden handcuffs, but not me. When I see the God of Love, I'll gladly toss the last living piece of my heart at his feet and embrace immortality.

Oh, I'll see him.

Eros is not only the God of Love, but he's the Commander and Chief of the Cupid Corps. He personally picks and briefs his Cupids on their last arrow quest. His last effort to make *you* fall for the happily ever after can't be easy. But then again, he never caught the love of his life in bed with his best friend.

I had.

And now, I'm one arrow away from never feeling that pain.

"Jack!" The starry-eyed girl I've been training hollers for my attention. Oh god, she's leaping toward me like the freaking gazelle from Solomon's song—this one *never* had the potential of making it to the big leagues. By the wistful sound in her voice, I know *my* current protégé has gone over the falls of happily-ever-after. Her skin is rosy, glowing with the newfound radiance of love, and the shimmer we're trained to look for is nearly consuming every available surface space of her eyeballs. She looks like a gerbil being squeezed too hard by a love vice.

I'd be jealous if I didn't know this relationship was doomed to crash and burn. No, I'm not psychic. No Cupid crystal ball. It'll fail because they all do. Some make it to the "until death do we part," but then one of them dies and the other is left behind.

Broken.

"Jack! Did you hear me?" she calls.

I stopped trying to remember their names after arrow branding twenty-two. William was with me for two years, almost to the end of his probation, when he fell hard for Kate. Yeah, they had an awesome wedding. Eros and Psyche—Eric and Pam if you're not running with the immortals—attended, which meant I had to tag along. Horse-drawn carriages and an island country went crazy for the next heir to the throne and his happily-ever-after princess.

"Sorry, sweetie. Look at you," I say to my protégé, quickly changing the subject before she asks me what's wrong for the million and twentieth time. "You're absolutely radiating."

"Radiant," she giggles. "You meant radiant."

No, I meant radiating. Love is as toxic as nuclear waste. I need to get my job done and get the hell out of San Francisco. This place is too close to home, even if it is 418 miles to the north.

I plaster on a fake smile, conjure up some enthusiasm, and ask, "Where's the ring?" I barely get the "ing" out before she's got her left hand up and waving her fingers all cheerleader like.

"Look. At. That!" I gasp.

This guy is good. He bought her heart back with a four-carat emerald-cut diamond. "He must really love you," I croon.

"I know!" Her eyebrows crawl up into her hairline while her eyes shoot for the perfect engagement engorgement. "He said he was sorry for calling things off. I spooked him." She sighs like the world is finally spinning correctly, and all it took was an *I'm sorry* and a giant ring. Her eyes flutter and part of me remembers that feeling. That complete faith in someone and something like love.

I wince as my protégé grabs my newly branded wrist— she can't see me brands no one but the Cupid they belong to can— and her eyes lock with mine. "He said it took him two minutes to realize he was wrong to walk away and two months to work up the courage to ask me to give him a second chance and marry him." She flips her hand over and falls further under the hypnotic charm of the engagement ring.

Poor thing doesn't realize that it took him those two months to figure out *her* daddy was the money behind *his* start-up tech company. Didn't take Einstein too long to figure it out once the money started drying up.

"He can't wait to tell my family!"

I fully expect to see a Julie Andrews, *Sound of Music* twirl right about now.

"I'm sure he can't," I say. "Do you love him?" I ask the final exit question.

"Yes," she sighs, but I catch the flash of disdain sweeping across her face. The soft lines of excitement harden, and I know she's starting to see me for what I really am: a high-ranking member of the Cupid Corp.

I swipe my right-hand ring finger across the newly branded arrow on my left wrist and nonchalantly mix some of the Cupid sweat from the back of my neck to activate the toxin from the arrow brand. Then I grab her wrist and press the tip of my pheromone-laced finger to the girl's forehead. Her eyes glaze over, the foggy look of stupid-love swirling like little hearts waiting to dot the "i's" in her future wedding invitation. The girl got exactly what she wanted—she got her man—and I had nothing to do with it. If I had my way, we would have never come back to San Francisco. But her best friend was getting married and . . . bleh. The how we got here from Australia isn't worth reliving. Bottom line when training a Cupid: Never go home. It's like returning to the murder scene in bloody clothes.

Time to erase her memory of me and the Corps. Can't have the fool running back asking for second chances at awesome.

"I wish you and your lover"—I try not to gag on the word—"all the luck in your future together. You've spent the last two months with a life coach. You can't remember my name past it starting with a 'J'—maybe Julie. I'm a typical blonde hair, blue-eyed girl from Southern California who chased the surf to Australia. If it doesn't work out with Romeo"—which I highly doubt it will—"you're going to pick yourself up, dust yourself off, and start looking at all those other losers—ugh, I mean, fish in the sea." The clichés start rolling off my tongue. I usually only add one or two to a wiping, a verbal life preserver reminding them they've survived worse, but with Miss Love Struck, I can't help myself.

I've spent the last two months listening to her drone on and on about how tech-dude was *the* one. How the sun caught his blond curls just right and made them look like gold. And then there was the constant, *"Are you okay?"* that made me want poke out my eyes with a blunt candy cane.

Miss Love Struck stirs, clarity fighting back against the toxin in my branding.

"Close your eyes, count to thirteen, and when you open your eyes again, you won't remember anything except how happy you are." My finger presses deep against her forehead. If I don't hold on to her wrist, she'll topple right over. Thank you, arrow ten, for that helpful hint.

It took me a while to figure out love doesn't happen in your heart, it happens in your brain. Every Cupid has a different method of wiping, but given my recidivism rate being near non-existent, I'm going with the High Jack Wipe. Protégé fourteen dubbed that one. She was a funny bitch.

"Blink twice if you understand everything I've said."

Two blinks, a Kewpie doll pucker, and I know my wiping is solid.

"You've been wiped," I declare. It's Eros's way of closing out a case—a verbal exclamation mark for a job well done.

For me, it's time to grab a bucket of crab legs, a plane ticket back to Australia, and wait for my last assignment. I carefully step away, holding onto my protégé's wrist to make sure she's all balanced out. When I know she's not going to nosedive off the pier, I turn and walk out of her life for good.

Easy peasy.

The wails of the sea lions applaud me as I head to the crab shack. I swear I can hear them keening, *"Well done, Jack!"* Every Cupid handles the end of an assignment differently. I once ran across a Cupid who was jealous of her protégés. She desperately wanted to fall in love again and break her curse.

My lip snarls with disgust.

I guess there are a few Cupids who actually regret the life in the Corps. They're few and far between; most of us can't wait to move on to another assignment. I look at the Corps as proof Darwinism exists, and I'm one of the fittest. Plus, the cover story of working for one of the world's most renowned event coordinating firms, Aiónia Agápi, doesn't hurt. All those wonky letters mean "Eternal Love" in Greek, but to me, it means I'm able to live a caviar life on a soda-cracker budget.

The waistband of my jeans vibrates. Damn, I thought I'd at least have another night at the B&B, but duty calls. I pull off the '90s pager and watch the message from my boss, Eros, scroll across:

I need you in Sunset Beach. There's a ticket at the airport.

My heart drops. Sunset Beach? I fight down the panic and beg the universe, *"Please, be Sunset Beach, Hawaii."* The other Sunset Beach is in Southern California and home to way too many—

Breakfast at Harbor House, 6 a.m., sharp.

My stomach churns, kicking up bile and memories. Yeah, I'm glad I didn't have a chance to eat a bucket of crab legs. If I thought San Francisco was too close to home . . . Sunset Beach is four miles from my own personal hell.

HUGH

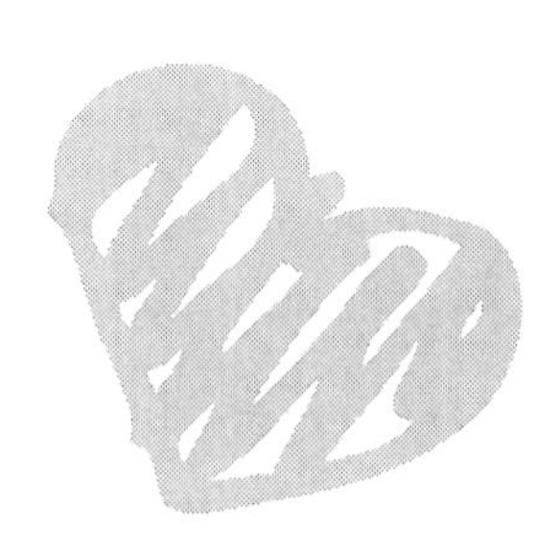

Jack!

Not even the rhythmic *thump-thump* of my feet pummeling the pavement can quiet her name in my mind. Every cell in my body is rejecting the endorphin rush that should have happened three miles ago. I glance at the pedometer on my watch, twelve miles in. Check that, my runner's high should've hit six miles ago.

"Shit," I mutter and start slowing down to a jog.

I'd started my balls-out run the same as every other morning, along the bike path that cuts through the sand from the water tower at Sunset Beach to the Huntington Beach sign on Beach Blvd. I did the obligatory glance at my heart's purgatory, expecting to see the same thing I did every morning: *her* shuttered windows, blocking out the likes of me for six-plus years. Instead, warm light seeped through the edges of the fuck-off window curtains. I nearly ate shit doing a double take.

There was no way Jack was back in town.

Standing instruction and a two-thousand-dollar tip with the property manager to text me, no matter the hour, if she dared to tap a well-polished toe in her father's house said she wasn't back in town. I'd written it off as the cleaning crew getting an early start and continued running into the early morning purple haze. But the gnawing memory of the stained-glass mermaid window winking down at me was haunting.

I was about to run past her house a second time. The first pass by The Huntington Pacific usually only sent a zing of ache to my heart. Normally, the run didn't bother me. Normally, I'd run right past the condo on the sand without a second look. But there's nothing normal about today. My heart smashes against my ribs. Adrenaline that has nothing to do with my run pours into my system. The whitewashed complex comes into sight and my lungs forget how to function.

Six more steps and . . . Ah hell, I'm counting menial things again. I did that when she left.

Seven hundred brushes to clean my teeth.

One hundred and fifty steps to my car from the kitchen.

Four seconds for me to dial her number and hang up.

And one night I can never take back.

My lungs burn from the lack of oxygen, but I don't breathe.

I can't breathe.

Not until I make sure all those memories are locked away, buried deep in the darkness of the house with the bastard I'd been.

No such luck. Every window is lit like a signal to Memorial Day weekends of days gone by.

"Ah, fuck it." My curse hits an older woman walking her dog along the bike path. She gasps, and I can feel Mom's hand from Heaven smacking me upside my head for being such an ogre.

I slow to a walk and finally stand in front of the gated condo complex. It's as brazen as Jack ever was, being the only housing on the stretch of brown-sugar sand from here to Sunset Beach. The first few months I'd started running, Tessa—my best friend even if she thought I was still insufferable—said I was a masochist, a glutton for punishment for altering my route to pass this place. I am far from either. The center of my world is based *on* control. Crafted around me being *in* control. If I'm being honest, the only time I ever *lose* control is when Jacquelyn Alcantar memories seem to rear their ugly little heads.

Sea-salted wind mixes with the sweat dripping off the ends of my hair. I rip my shirt off and wipe the beads from my face, wishing it were perspiration that was making the mermaid window twinkle to life. The curtains are pulled back, and I catch myself stretching on my tiptoes like a kid trying to look at his first Playboy.

The light flicks off, and my heart slows, almost stopping with disappointment when the cleaning crew steps out the front door. It's not like I'd know what to say to her. I can't very well apologize. I rake my palms over my face, half wishing the mermaid window was illuminated or the lady I'd cursed would whack me with her walking stick. Something to snap me out of this stupor. I let go of the rails, step away from the gate, and start jogging home.

I need my head in the game today. Second-quarter earnings were supposed to be in yesterday. They weren't, so I called the pertinent staff in on a Saturday. My staff was pissed as hell that they couldn't leave on a three-day-weekend.

Too bad.

The next time I say I need numbers before a holiday, they'll know I mean business. They'll fear me like they feared my father. Tessa's worked her ass off lining up Tuesday's interviews to tout our earnings. We need to get people excited about Halia Surf again. I pick up my walk to a slow jog. Truth is, Halia needs this boost and I need to redeem myself.

Soon, the rhythmic pounding is back. Sweat trickles down my spine, adding just the right push to make the last three miles the best I've ever run. My nerves settle as I formulate today's plan. Mack, my half-brother, will be at the office. No doubt pushing his "dismantle when dead" program. Our father is still putting up the good fight, but . . . I slow as the Surfside Colony gates come into view. I'm not ready to get behind the idea of dismantling the company Mom loved, the company Jack loved, even if several board members are.

Sand crunches under my running shoes as I pass through the gate, heading to my house on the A strand. The irony hits me square in the chest. My house is a carbon copy of Jack's condo. Both on the beach, both whitewashed pompous structures demanding to be noticed, and both achingly void of life. I kick off my shoes, strip down—not caring about the show I'm giving the neighbors—and slide into the hot tub. Pam knows my routine by now, and if it bothers her or Eric, then they shouldn't look. I push any thoughts of Jack from my brain. The last block in the wall I've carefully built around the space in my chest that used to be my heart locks into place.

I'm Hugh Halia and I'm about to own this world.

I pull my red Tesla convertible roadster into the parking garage, spin around the corner, and screech to a stop.

"Son of a bitch!" I spit. Mack's parked in my spot again. His purple lotus seems to puff up, knowing it's won today's pissing contest of who parks in the CEO's spot. I back up and park in the unmarked stall. The screech of tires on pavement echoes through the garage. Tessa's beamer flies around the blind corner, kicking up exhaust and burnt rubber. She's still balls to the wall. The car's barely parked before her driver's door flies open and mile-long legs spill out. She's rocking another pencil skirt; this one is as black as my mood, paired with fuck-me red stilettos. I hold my breath, wondering what top she's going to shock us with. Yesterday was a silver whisper of fabric with a black bra. Sonia, my personal assistant/girlfriend, went seven shades of jealous on me when she thought she caught me checking out Tessa's backside, which is just wrong and almost incestuous. But a simple Google search later and Sonia had steam billowing out of her ears about rumors from my high school years that refused to die.

"You dated?" Sonia spat at me. "You didn't think telling your girlfriend the P.R. exec you hired was an ex?"

Explaining how Tessa wasn't technically my ex was exhausting, and I didn't have the heart to tell Sonia she shouldn't get used to the girlfriend title. The title kind of came with the personal assistant position, and when my assistants moved on or demanded more, the girlfriend title would still be in my pocket even if they weren't. After Jack, there just wasn't anyone to fill that position.

"What's up, hot stuff?" Tessa croons. She's got a sequined flag top on, minus about four stripes from the cleavage section.

I chuckle and fall into a comfortable stride beside her toward the elevator.

"You should really work on calling me Mr. Halia when we're at work."

Her nose wrinkles up in a cute way that'll make some guy desperate to know how to smooth it.

"You say, 'Mr. Halia,' and my vagina runs and hides, looking for your dad."

"There's a visual I'm never going to bleach out my brain."

I swipe my card and hold the heavy entrance open. Tessa shoots me a grin and steps into the elevator foyer and into the waiting elevator.

"Tell me, why your vagina would be running from my dad?"

"The same reason why your scrotum does"—she throws me a look over her shoulder—"he's terrifying and evil."

A dark chuckle rumbles from deep inside of me. He *was* terrifying. Growing up, I was never allowed to have the girls in the house, so when the garage door rattled the house as it opened, Tessa, Jack, and I were like, *freeze and get the fuck out.* Somehow Dad always knew I'd shatter Jack's heart. I just didn't realize when I blew it to smithereens, most of the shrapnel would lodge in *my* heart.

"We set for Tuesday?" I ask, chasing images of Jack from my mind . . . again.

I watch Tessa's business veneer slip into place. She's always been good at compartmentalizing life. I'm good at smashing and discarding things in mine.

"Absolutely." She reaches into her messenger bag and pulls out a media schedule. The elevator doors pull open and we walk out.

Water trickles down the rocks I'd brought back from Waialua falls. I'd scattered Mom's ashes there. It was where Mom said she lost her heart to Dad. My own heart flops in my chest. I still don't know if the asshole was worth it.

Dad is a Hapa Haole, half white, half Hawaiian. Mom was a local; she gave up everything for him, for love. A familiar knot rolls around in my chest. I'm so glad she wasn't alive to see that Dad wasn't loyal. I guess the apple didn't fall far from that tree.

Morning light filters through the windows lining the lobby. It was one of the few things Dad and I agreed on when we leased the space. We are a surf company; if we don't embrace our love for the outdoors, then how can we expect our customers to?

I keep flipping through the media schedule, barely registering my half-brother sitting at the front desk.

"You got me on 'Morning Joe' and the second hour of *The Today Show*?" I stop short. Tessa nearly runs into me. I forget how tiny she is until she's standing right next to me. My six-foot-five frame towers over her lithe dancer's body. Jack was the same way. Tiny and . . . I chase the thought away with the raise of an eyebrow. I know they're one of my most intimidating features. The way they slant makes my resting face dark and devilish. Most chicks either fall head over heels for the look, or they run for the hills. Jack fell first and then picked herself up and ran for the hills.

Tessa does neither.

She squares her shoulders and pops a hip.

"You're on a plane Monday afternoon. That'll give you plenty of time to schmooze the *O.C. Press* people coming tonight to congratulate you on 'Most Eligible Bachelor' designation and recover from the party after they leave." Her lip twitches with the hint of a smile before she reaches around me and opens the door. She knows Mack's listening, probably fuming I landed the title. I'm still in a pissy mood from this morning, so I'll play along.

"Why the second hour of *The Today Show*?"

"You're the *Press*'s most eligible bachelor. We can parlay this into a bid for 'People's Most—'"

"Why?" I cut her off. "I'm a CEO, not a movie star."

A wry smile pulls across her flawless face, brown eyes sparkling in a way that is reminiscent of the girl I knew in middle school.

"You're the hot as hell, twenty-four years old, fresh out of business school, and CEO of Halia Surf Company. Surf companies not only sell surfboards, but they sell apparel. Women's apparel. We get you, the new head of Halia, recognized as a sex symbol, and we've got the men wanting to be like you and girls wanting to do you. Or at least anyone wearing Halia Surf wear."

"So, you're pimping me."

Tessa steps into my space. Most men go hard when a girl like Tessa says or does something along these lines.

Not me.

There's nothing there.

Never has been.

She straightens my tie and smiles up at me. I know that smile; it's the one that says, "we're still friends even though you made me do the shittiest thing ever and break my best friend's heart with a lie."

"I figured it was about time I got you back."

She steps around me and starts her seductive walk to the boardroom.

The strong scent of "notice me I'm rich" cologne drifts over my shoulder. Mack's new to disposable income. If I liked him, I'd tell him that most chicks love the subtle scent of man filtered through a hint of spice and sandalwood cologne. I don't, so I told him the opposite. Now he smells like he ran the cologne gauntlet of counters at South Coast Plaza.

His hand clamps down on my shoulder, "Congrats on the title, little brother." He lets the jab burrow its way under my skin. Mack is six months and four days older than me. I knew Dad's story that Mom and he didn't think she'd be able to carry a child, but damn, he sure didn't waste any time making sure there was an heir to Halia. Now, there are two heirs to a company that may or may not make it to through the end of the year. I guess I screwed up that plan too.

"Ah, I'm sure you would have given me a run for my money . . . if they'd know about you." I jab back and walk out of his stilled hand. "You coming?"

Mack rakes a hand through his hair. It's not as long as mine. His black curls barely touch his ears, where my waves run down to my shoulder blades. He's got the same intimidating facial features I do: slanted eyebrows and a hard jawline that when pissed as hell, makes our cheekbones look like they could slice a man open. We stand about the same height. It gives me an up-close and personal look at those razor-sharp bones, and I'm certain the man he'd like to slice open is me.

"Wouldn't miss it, baby brother." He forces a smile at me, and I match his grin, white polished tooth for white polished tooth.

The boardroom sits in the back corner of the Halia's corporate offices. We have a small office on Oahu, but here in California is where we run most of our operations. Nine suits and my P.A. sit around the polished Kolohala table. Tessa stands next to my name plaque at the head of the table—no doubt her doing—and Mack is at the far end next to the accountant who smells like Vick's Vapor Rub. Mack shakes his head and leans into Tessa as he walks by. Her back goes ram-rod straight, and I can feel the lid to my temper rattle. She fixes on a plastic smile and pulls my chair out for me.

"What'd he say?" I whisper.

"Nothing I can't handle," she grits through her teeth, then nearly knocks me off my feet when shoving the chair in.

"No worries, Tessa," Mack calls as he picks up his name plaque. "I'll sit here." He walks his name card to the opposite end of the table. "I like the view of the room from here. And in no time, you'll see the view out the windows behind me are much clearer than the view behind Hugh."

I pull in a deep breath. The suits all squirm; they're not used to this blatant call for a power shift, but I am. It's going to be a hell of a long meeting given we're bickering about the seating arrangements.

I steal a glance at my watch: 8:15 a.m.

"What time are the planners arriving at my parents' house to organize the setup?" I ask Sonia. Her melted-chocolate-colored hair is pulled back into a ponytail that does nothing to flatter her face.

"Noon."

I feel the weight settle in between my shoulder blades. I know the staff is competent to set up, but I can't risk it. I need someone there, someone I can trust. I start to suggest Tessa head over there, but Sonia beats me to the punch.

"Maybe you should send Tessa over?"

Out of the corner of my eye, I catch Tessa bristle at the dismissal.

"Tessa." I turn and lay the look I know she can't say no to on her. "It's my parents' house. Nobody knows it better than you do, and we need this to go off without a hitch."

I see her shoulders sag, and I swear I'll make it up to her. She doesn't like being in that house any more than I do. So many memories. So many ghosts.

"Fine." She gathers up her things and shoots Sonia a murderous look. "You can fill me in on the numbers when you get there."

"I promise, no more surprises today."

Ten hours later, as the flash of cameras flicker around me and I'm standing over my half-brother, pummeling him into the ground, those words are haunting me.

One day, I'll live up to the promises I keep lobbing at Tessa.

Three

JACK

I *check my watch one more* time: 6:55 a.m. Eros is late, and I'm either hungover or still drunk. I slide down further into my chair, adjusting my sunglasses. I don't care that the waitress is eyeing me like I'm a Huntington Beach tweeker about to commit felony larceny. If any crime is going to be committed, it's going to be capital murder. And Eros should watch his immortal back.

I have a love-hate relationship with Orange County. I love that my father raised me here. I love that I learned to shoot my first tube about two hundred yards from this table.

But those memories are tainted.

I hate that this place is where I shared my last meal with my father. And I hate that the surf company he and his best friend started in a tiny one-car garage on Toronto Street is what eventually ended up killing him.

I flag down the waitress as she walks by.

“Another cup,” I say, turning away before she can ask if I want anything else. I think I went to school with her. She’s two years older than me and probably wouldn’t remember me unless I was sitting with my former other half. I push away the thought of dark hair and looming eyes. Those black as a shark’s eyes always seemed to hit the deepest recesses of my heart. Eros had better show up in the next five minutes, or I’m—

“Jaquelyn,” a dark voice comes from the back entrance. “I’m sorry to keep you waiting.”

I know he’s not sorry, just like he isn’t sorry he calls me Jaquelyn instead of Jack. He’s a god; they very rarely have that emotion.

Eros stalks across the room. He’s gorgeous as all sin. Sun-bleached hair that curls over his ears and hints of an early summer tan that clings to his flawless skin. Even though I’ve sworn off the excitement of the flutter, I can see how every woman in this world and others would fall for the guy. Thing is, he’s only got eyes for his wife, Psyche, which makes him all the sexier. A faithful hottie, something only an immortal goddess like Psyche can have.

Eros’s look can change from minute to minute. I assume he takes his natural state of being when he’s around his Cupid Corps, but if I look real hard . . . I know I see hints of my dad in Eros, and not just the blue eyes. Eros’s tree-trunk thighs and calves the size of cantaloupes match my dad’s. He has the same chuckle that hangs in the wind. Morning stubble that won’t be touched until it’s closing in on beard status. Whatever your heart desires, your eyes will see when you look at Eros.

My dad was all I wanted when I first met the God of Love. Dad’s death hit me hard—I can still see the charred remains of his car at the bottom of the cliff—but it wasn’t close to the devastation I suffered after his funeral. A vision of dark curls dancing along a tan back that looks like it's sculpted from granite gives way to the same dark eyes I've been trying for years to forget. I kick against the vision, pushing it from my mind.

I'm pretty damn thankful I'm one arrow away from a stony heart. Otherwise, being here, where all those old memories seem to be churned up by the sea, I can only imagine what my heart would desire if my brain is already thinking of the brooding boy I left six years ago.

Eros's blue eyes sweep over me, taking inventory of my emotions and probably my day-old-drunk status.

It was a rough flight.

My palms started sweating when the front desk handed me my boarding pass to John Wayne Airport. My heart that barely registers a thump these days felt like it was going to jump out of my chest when the P.A. system crackled to life and announced they were now boarding elite members to Orange County, California. I'd stayed in my seat until the final boarding call. By the time I sat down in first class, I'd ordered two shots. The perks of first class: they have to cater to you. None of this "when we reach cruising altitude" shit.

I've flown home twice. The first time was six years ago, just after I was recruited into the Corps. I didn't even have an arrow brand, so coach seating, it was. This is the second time I've been home, and it hasn't gotten any better.

My skin alters between feeling so tight, my bones are going to rip through, or so itchy, I wish I could peel it off. Given the fact that Eros is still standing, taking in the sight of me, I'm even more of a hot mess than I think.

"Jaquelyn, are you going to answer me?" His tone is cold, shoulders squared and broad from his arms folded over his chest. I know that look—it's the one before he sends a soul to the—

I sit up in my chair and banish the thought that the look is for me. I value my soul even if I don't cherish my heart.

"Sorry, boss. Rough flight," I manage without slurring, offering him the chair across from me.

His features soften, shoulders rounding, as he disregards my suggestion and sits down into the chair next to mine.

"Have you ordered?"

I shake my head. Grainy pictures of a life I've been trying to forget mix with leftover shots of tequila.

The waitress walks up, and like with most girls taken in by Eros, I completely disappear from her view.

"What a beautiful lady to go along with this gorgeous morning," Eros croons.

I pull my glasses off my face. My head rolls back on my shoulders to check outside. It's a typical May morning in Sunset Beach: cold, the morning fog hasn't burned off (it probably won't), and the only sounds at seven in the morning on Memorial Day are surfers coming in from their early set of waves. But to the waitress (I eye her tag: Morgan. I *did* go to school with her), it's a beautiful summer day. That's the Eros effect. Everything is sunshine and puppy dogs.

"Jaquelyn? You want your usual? Harbor House omelet?" Eros's nose is buried in the menu.

I nod. Something's not right. He's being too accommodating.

The waitress smiles, slips in a curtsy (the Eros Effect again), and sashays off to get our meals.

"San Francisco," Eros starts off. "Great work, Jaquelyn. Record time too. Two months. I think that may be a Corps record."

I swallow hard over the lump forming in my throat. He's being way too kind.

"Are you disappointed with my work, boss?" I hide my paranoia by grabbing a couple of sugar packets before Eros gets at them.

A grin mars Eros's perfect face and then a chuckle. My dad's chuckle. I twitch in my seat, fighting against the urge to rake my hands across my skin and free the memories in me.

"Jaquelyn." Eros leans on the table, hands folded under his chin. "One of these days, you're going to learn to take a compliment for its face value. You do good work, kiddo." He leans back in his chair as Morgan brings him a cup of coffee. She's probably brewed a fresh pot just for him.

"Thank you, darling." He smiles up at her, and the girl floats away in a love-struck haze. "Jaquelyn, I'm here to give you your final assignment."

I sit straight up in my chair—the past twelve hours of inebriation gone. This is it, what I've always wanted, a chance at immortality and a safe heart. Eros empties six packets of sugar into his coffee, stirs, and then reaches into the satchel that wasn't there a moment ago. He slaps a newspaper on the table, and I jump about ten feet out of my chair. Not because of the sound, but because of the picture on the top fold.

"The Halia Surf Company." He points to the picture of two men beating the shit out of each other. "They've reached out to Aiónia Agápi to help them relaunch Halia at the US Open at the end of July."

Morgan's back at the table with a tray full of steaming plates: egg whites for Eros and the Harbor House omelet for me. I grab the hot sauce and start smothering my omelet. Some girls eat chocolate when they're nervous or depressed. I eat hot stuff.

Eros adjusts his plate and picks up his fork. Two bites of egg whites make it past his lips before I realize he's waiting for me to say something.

"That's Hugh?" I point my fork at the partially obscured face. His hair is longer. Down past his shoulders. The picture only shows half his face but damn, if even in black and white print, those stormy eyes don't penetrate me.

"It is."

"And whose ass is he kicking?"

"His half-brother, Mack."

I choke on my omelet but don't miss the satisfied look on Eros face.

"When did that happen?"

"About twenty-five years ago."

I roll my eyes. "I meant, when did Hugh find out he had a half-brother?"

"A year ago, when the old man was diagnosed with prostate cancer."

Something pulls at my heart. Kai, Hugh's dad, is a mean son-of-a-bitch. Hugh was always trying to hang the stars and craft the waves in the old man's eyes. "I hadn't heard about Kai."

"The doctors don't think Kai will make it to the relaunch at the end of July. The old man is tying up loose ends." Eros places another perfectly cut egg white in his mouth.

"So what's my assignment? Why am I in my own personal teenage purgatory?"

Eros wipes his mouth, looks at his watch, and shakes his head. "You're here to train your replacement, who doesn't seem to understand what 'on time' means."

Eros searches the front of the café.

I close my eyes, hoping I've heard my boss wrong. This close to home. All my senses trip at the thought. . .

"No," I whisper, then bite down on my lip to trap any other response. I hear the café door open and nearly bite through my worried lip when I hear the all-too-familiar, ear-piercing squeal that follows. The click-clack of stilettos ricochets off the worn floorboards. I know they're stilettos without opening my eyes. Their slap and the squeal only confirm the writhing knots in my stomach.

This isn't happening. There's no way the gods are this mean. I mean, really? Hugh is bad enough, but . . .

"Oh. My. Gawd!" You can almost hear the blonde in her voice. No wonder

Eros had a shit-eating grin on his face. My replacement is the bitch that stole my boyfriend, and I have to train her with the boy who broke my heart?

"Tessa Saint Cloud," I hiss as I turn in my chair.

She pops a hip and opens her arms.

"Jaquelyn 'Jack' Alcantar!"

"It's Jack now."

"I know." Tessa waves off my comment and wiggles her fingers, but I caught the disappointment they're meant to mask. "Seriously, you're not going to give me a hug for old time's sake?"

"Pretty sure I gave you my last boyfriend—that should count for something." I level a look at Eros. "You're joking, right?"

He merely shakes his head, amusement pulling at the rare dimple in his cheek.

"No one said becoming immortal was going to be easy."

I bite down so hard on the inside of my cheek, I'm certain there's blood.

"Tessa," Eros points to the empty chair. "We've already ordered. You'll find I'm a stickler for punctuality."

Tessa slides into her chair; her easy-going look is unmarred. She either still thinks the rules don't apply to her, or she's so damn new, she doesn't realize the deadly power Eros commands. I'm going with the latter. How she dresses hasn't changed either. Clothing is an accessory like a necklace or a watch. Her barely-there pink skirt hits about three inches south of her hoo-ha, and the black top has a V-neck that hits about three inches north of the same hoo-ha region. Dirty blonde hair pours down her back in beautiful ringlets that I've always been jealous of. She owns every inch of who she is and isn't running from anything. Which makes me wonder—who broke her heart and landed her in the Corps?

"I don't really do breakfast." She adjusts her skirt, completely missing the annoyed pull of Eros's eyebrows, before flagging down an unsuspecting busboy.

"Hi, sugar. Some sourdough toast and fresh squeezed orange juice."

"I'm . . . I'm the busboy." The poor kid nearly drops his bucket of dirty dishes.

She lays a hand on his forearm, and you can see the kid's eyes fill with lust. It's a sleazy trick and has nothing to do with the Corps. In fact, I'm surprised Eros hasn't banished the backstabbing hooker's heart.

Cupid rule number one: No dumping PEA in the mortals. As Cupids, we're a step below a demi-god, and our ability to dump phenylethylamine, aka the Love Drug, are increased to a dizzying level. Any fooling around with a mortal's PEA is strictly forbidden and punishable by a mark. My spine steels at the thought of Eros's mark on your heart.

"I'm sure you'll get my request to the right person," Tessa croons before releasing the boy.

"Tessa," Eros voice slices the air. "You know PEA has a distinct sugary smell."

The girl smiles like the God of Love couldn't smite her where she slutted. "Didn't know that."

"That's your official warning."

I squirm in my seat as if the warning's been issued to me. In the Corps, you get two warnings. Fuck up a third time and your soul is banished. Given the fact that it looks like someone's jammed a steel rod down Tessa's back, she gets the severity of the warning.

She clears her throat, pain pinching her eyebrows together. "I understand." All the giggle and bounce is gone from her voice.

Which Tessa is the farce: the stereotypical beach blond bimbo or the seductress who knows how to use every arsenal of her body?

Absentmindedly, Tessa rubs at the mark we all know is burning into the skin over her heart. I've never known a Cupid with a mark on their heart. I've only heard it's more painful than the arrow brandings . . . and those hurt like a son of a bitch. Not even my mentor, who toed Eros's protocol line like she was Johnny Cash herself, had been marked. *"Keep away from the lightning bolts, deary. Two of them and your soul will wish the only thing you suffered from was a broken heart."* That was the last cockney warning before she put me on a plane to Australia.

Eros folds his hands in his lap, eyes focused on the steam billowing from his cup of coffee that never seems to chill. "I'd hoped to have introductions before issuing warnings. Luckily, you two know each other." He pulls in a deep breath and shoots me a look, daring me to test him.

I know better.

I've watched Eros operate from half a world away, and not even that was enough distance for my liking. The dude may be the God of Love, but he has no qualms about banishing hearts that mock him or his purpose in life.

"Tessa's been undercover for the last year at our P.R. firm. She fielded the call from the reporter from the *Register* that this was going to run. And she's the one who made the suggestion for the Halia brothers to reach out to A.A. for their relaunch."

Eros picks up his fork and points a tine at the front page. "You were there last night. What happened?"

Tessa nods at the paper, asking for permission to pick it up.

"This was at the summer kick-off party last night in the marina. Mack and Hugh had come in from a board of directors meeting. Quarterly earnings are due the fifteenth of June, numbers came in late Friday, and Hugh called the emergency meeting for Saturday." Tessa hands me the paper and smiles at the busboy dropping off her order. "Hugh's P.A. sent me on to the Marina House to schmooze the investors and hold down the house until they arrived."

Tessa looks at Eros and nods at her plate, again asking for permission.

We are all Eros's children, no matter how old or long we are in the Corps. We are his prisoners, and he is our warden until we are freed or his equal. The thought sits in my stomach. I have no desire to be freed from my curse, and when I'm immortal, he will respect me as his equal. I'll run my region the way I see fit.

"Jaquelyn, you have any questions?"

I have a ton of questions, none of which are pertinent to my assignment.

"Yeah, did they come in guns blazing? Are they always at each other's throats? And how long have you been with Hugh?"

The twitch in Tessa's lip means my jab didn't go unnoticed.

"I've been with Halia Surf for eleven months now. Hugh brought in E.A. Public Relations when he found out about Mack. Needless to say, things have always run hot with Hugh and Mack, but with Kai's condition deteriorating and what I can guess are less-than-favorable earnings, Halia Surf not only needs the numbers to go in their favor, the company's life depends on the relaunch going spectacularly and flawlessly. I recommended E.A.'s sister company, Aiónia Agápi, to handle the event planning."

I push my sunglasses up on top of my head and lean forward. "When I left, Halia wasn't at the top, but it wasn't circling the drain either."

"No offense, Jack, but you left six years ago. Things change."

I bite my tongue. Now isn't the time to rehash the way my former best friend shredded my heart. Not with Eros watching.

"I get that, but something had to have happened to tank the company."

Tessa shoots a look at Eros. He nods, and it feels like the whole room closes in on us.

"Mack wasn't the only reason I was brought in. Two years ago, before Kai came clean about his one-night affair, Halia was hit with a sexual harassment case. The girl was an up-and-coming surfer when Hugh signed her four years ago, but after she won back-to-back-to-back titles in Australia, Hawaii, and Huntington Beach, her stardom skyrocketed. Everyone was trying to buy out her contract, low to mid seven figures. But Sandpiper from Long Beach came the hardest. They offered Halia a hundred million to buy out her contract. Promised the girl half of that as a signing bonus."

"I remember reading about this. Randie something. She's a local girl, right?"

Tessa nodded.

"Hugh saw her at the beach on a waterlogged short board. She wasn't even an amateur when he signed her."

"Hugh always did have an eye for raw talent," I muse. "So what? She claimed Kai came on to her?"

"Not Kai," Eros interjected. "Hugh. She claimed Hugh took her out to dinner to discuss the contract, slipped her something, and somewhere during the course of the evening, she signed a ten-year extension on her contract and . . ." Eros's words trailed off.

There was only one ugly thing that made my boss go tongue-tied, and I couldn't even reconcile that with Hugh.

"It's a lie, right?" I scanned the table. Nobody would make eye contact with me. "Tessa, you and I know Hugh. He would never violate a woman. He's never had to."

"The girl went straight to Kai, who promptly paid her an extra two million, plus a percentage of Halia's earnings, to keep it quiet and go away. When Kai was diagnosed, Randie came back, thinking she could tap the CEO well twice with the threat of a rape charge. We had the baby she claimed was Hugh's tested—".

"He didn't rape her," I cut Tessa off with a little more passion than I should show in Eros's presence.

"No." The hint of a smile pulls at Tessa's lips. "Randie jumped the gun, though. Kai is still alive, and the board is acting as a collective governing body until Hugh is confirmed, some outstanding qualification or other."

"But that confirmation came in after the damage was already done. They ran scared, didn't they?" I ask.

Tessa's eyes lose a little of their sparkle. "Yeah. The board decided against fighting the lawsuit and paid the girl fifteen million in exchange for a non-disclosure agreement stating Hugh didn't touch her, and releasing Randie from her contract at the end of this season."

The chili omelet stirs in my gut. Hugh Halia was a heart-breaking bastard, but there was no way in hell he was a rapist.

"Tessa, how much working capital does Halia Surf have?"

Her brown eyes meet mine, and I know it's bad. If quarterly earnings were bringing the two brothers to blows . . .

"Two million. That's enough for payroll and to see them through the summer."

I sink back in my chair. How is this my assignment? How is any of *this* the Cupid Corps' concern?

"I'm confused, Eros," I start. There isn't any good way to ask this without sounding like a cold-hearted bitch. "Our assignments are about love for another person. And while I loved Halia Surf as much as my father did, Halia Surf isn't a person, and companies go bankrupt all the time. Why are we here?"

I stay focused on Eros, because if I see the disgust I know is in Tessa's eyes, then I'll crumble. And I'm one damn arrow away from never feeling anything again.

"Your assignment is a rescue. After Kai's infidelity was revealed and Mack laid a claim to Halia, Hugh's given up on love. The girl he's seeing now is—"

"A bitch," Tessa interjected under her breath. "Sorry, Eros, she is."

Eros clears his throat. "The girl Hugh is dating now is his personal assistant. Neither is in the relationship for love. You both know how I feel about that. I know where this can go. I see where it is going, and I won't have my name made a mockery in such a public forum. Fix it or I will."

Tessa's gaze slides to mine. We both have issues with Hugh Halia, but even I'm not sure he deserves to have his heart banished. At least, not yet.

Four

HUGH

M*y eyelids flutter as soft* hands trace the side of my face. The scent of sea salt and femininity flood my senses. It's that wonderful moment where reality and fantasy mix, and I can't remember if I'm dreaming about the only girl I've ever loved or the painful moment before I open my eyes and realize my mind won't let go of the past.

I hiss as pain shoots down the side of my face. God, it's a hateful bitch of a morning.

"Does it hurt?" the distinctly female voice asks.

The hint of southern accent makes my insides churn. It used to be sweet, but now it's just grating on my last nerve. If Sonia didn't have a way with the board of directors, I'd have found a new girl to hang the PA/girlfriend title on.

I know Sonia's only trying to nurse the stitches over my eye, but damn if that isn't the most sensitive skin on my body.

"Only when you touch it like that." I grab her wrist and try not to shove it and run. She's not coyote ugly, cute actually, but she doesn't hold a candle to the girl who's been haunting my dreams as of late. Sonia's pretty in that small-town-cute kind of way. Jack, though. She was equal parts of girl next door and vixen. She was perfect—I cut the thought off before I allow the memory of her to ruin another day.

Sleep scrapes my eyeballs like angry fingernails as I blink them open and closed, trying to wake up from the nightmare my life has become.

Rays of sun filter in through the white gauzy curtains, bathing Sonia in the glorious early morning radiance. Sonia's been my personal assistant for almost two years. We've been together for a year and half, and not once have we had a morning-after at my house. It was a rule I've lived by up until last night. I vaguely remember getting shit faced at the Hula Grill on Main Street. I think Harry, the bartender, was calling me a cab when Sonia walked in. The rest of the night is a painful fog only made worse by a killer hangover. Sonia sits back on my bed, arms already folded in a pout that's going to cost my pocketbook dearly.

"You were talking about that guy in your sleep again."

I pull myself up against the headboard.

"Jack?" I ask.

Sonia bites down on her lip, brown bangs falling over her cautionary eyes. I know that look too. We're going to have the "are you sure you're not gay" talk again. The plump flesh of her lip pulls free of her teeth, and before she can start, I hold up a finger.

"I'm not gay." I push back the comforter and remind myself not to sprint to the bathroom. "And I don't want to talk about who Jack is." I pull open my nightstand drawer and grab a pair of running socks.

"You're going running?"

"I need to clear my head." For more reasons besides Tessa canceling today's media junket. I pull up my running shorts and head off to the bathroom. "Tessa's got the rep from Aiónia Agápi coming this morning to help clean up Saturday's disaster. A.A. for my business life." I listen for the giggle but there's nothing. Just another way Sonia isn't like my Jack. I squirm at the thought.

"I don't think you need another outside firm sticking their nose in family business."

"Noted."

I hear the huff and know Sonia's figured out that's my go-to dismissal. Yeah, this relationship is on the last mile of running its own course. Sleepovers and pouts are usually the signs of a good assistant planning more than my day. They're planning our walk down the aisle, and that's a walk I promised I'd never take the day Jack walked out of my life.

I toss her a smile before jogging down the steps, out the back sliding door, and into the cool morning. A haze has rolled in off the ocean, and the sun's trying to break back through the fine mist hanging in the air. The temptation to abandon my run and dive into the ocean with a board is back. I swallow down the fear. I love the ocean, but after the night I shattered Jack . . . it just not the same without her board next to mine. A memory of her all-consuming smile, the kind of smile only the ocean, a surfboard, and I could put on her face, ripples to the surface. I know what comes next, the gut-punch memory of her walking out of my bedroom and out of my life. I push the thought away and run the opposite direction of Jack's condo.

It truly is a hateful bitch of a morning.

By the time I pull into Halia's parking garage, I'm running thirty minutes late. Somewhere between Seal Beach and Second Street, my run turned into a jog and then a sit-and-ponder fifty-minute moment.

"Good morning, Mr. Halia," the front desk greets me. "Tessa wanted me to let you know they're in the board room waiting for you."

I nod and grab the mug she's got waiting for me. I pull a sip of Kona coffee into my mouth, and for the first time this morning, my body feels like it's doing the right thing. I'd tried on three different suits, four different shirts, and . . . ah, fuck. I'm counting again. I wind my way back to my office, drop off my things with Sonia, and wave her off from joining Tessa and the A.A. rep in the boardroom. This initial meeting needs to be completely candid. No girlfriends with agendas listening in, because if Sonia really knew how bad off Halia really was, I have no doubt she'd be gone, taking the last few holdout board members with her. In their eyes, me with the prospects of being married is more sellable than my most eligible bachelor title. Despite what Tessa thinks.

I push the heavy Kolohala doors to the boardroom open, when my world stops. One breath and I'm pulled under by the waves of my past.

"Jack?"

A muscle ticks along her jawline. It's the strangest thing to notice first about the girl who's been marching circles through my mind the last few days. I've officially lost it. I suck in another breath of air. My God, she's even more beautiful than I remember. I devour every inch of her and her suit that's all business and femininity. Sweet Jesus, she's wearing black-patent pumps. She wore black-patent pumps and only black-patent pumps the night we spent together after my Senior Prom. I know those sheer stockings only climb up three-fourths of her long, lean legs, even though they disappear under a black skirt that could be a second layer of skin. She has a red silk top on, and I can't help but wonder if she's rocking the same color undergarments. Jack always was tough on the outside but soft underneath. She had a love for intimate wear, and at one point in time, I was the benefactor of all her adoration. Her hair's a lighter shade of blonde than I remember. It's pulled back in a ponytail that makes her face look like it's been carved out of marble. It's the same ponytail Sonia had tried to pull off Saturday, but on Jack, it's breathtakingly beautiful.

"I thought you were in Australia?" I hear the whisper leave my lips and look behind me to make sure someone else didn't hurl the accusation. A tiny breath catches in my throat, waiting to hear her voice. I need to know if it's still smooth as whisky. Does she have a hint of the Australian accent from her time there?

"I was."

Two words and I can feel every cell in me wake up. Six years. I haven't heard her voice in six years, and two words have me going—imagining all sorts of wicked deeds.

"When did you get back?" I ask. Tessa steps forward, and before she can say anything, I throw every ounce of betrayal at Tessa in my own two words. "You knew?'

Tessa's eyes flare with indignation before she nods her head. I know Tessa doesn't deserve the way my lip curls into the snarl I'd rocked in high school. I know Jack doesn't owe me any explanations after what we did to her, but goddamn it, they both were about to be on the wrong end of my short fuse today.

"Jack works for Aiónia Agápi," Tessa interjects.

There she goes again, protecting everyone even if it costs her the most. My feet shuffle toward Jack. It's like my body knows that's the direction to kick to get out of the hellish rip current that's held me under for the last six years. Jack's eyes widen when I step into her personal space. Her pulse jumps along her neck, and it's everything in me not to lean forward and lick it into a frenzy.

Jack steps away from me, her hand an inch from my chest, and I just want to walk into her palm. Feel her hand on me again.

She clears her throat and says, "Hugh, I work for Aiónia Agápi. Turns out you're lucky that I was the closest rep available." She digs into her father's black messenger bag, and I remember the promise I made to the man, why I made

Tessa do what we did. After all these years, my head says it was the right thing to do, even if my gut never really did get on board.

"You're still using your father's bag?" I reach for the worn leather, and just like everything that is, or was, Jack, she pulls out of my reach.

"Yes." There's shock in her voice.

Like nature or the universe knows we're supposed to be together, my eyes find hers and the world blurs. There's only the two of us, and for a brief nanosecond, everything is right. A strand of hair pulls loose from her strict and proper ponytail. I want to reach up and pull the hair tie from the base of her neck. Free all the other strands of hair from captivity.

But I can't.

There are promises to keep and actions that can't be undone. Instead, I tuck it behind her ear and hear the small gasp of shock when I touch her cheek. The ache I've spent all morning trying to push away comes roaring back, but the feel of her—even if it was just her cheek—on my skin makes it worth every agonizing moment I'll spend reliving the moment.

"Please don't," she whispers and steps out of my reach again. Walking around me at a wide berth, she stops at the front of the room and props a hip up on the boardroom table, her skirt inching high enough to distract me.

"Like I was saying, you're lucky I was the closest rep." She pulls Sunday's paper out and slaps it on the desk. "What the fuck were you thinking?"

A chuckle rips from deep in me. There's my girl. All fight and sass.

"I was thinking I'd like to pound my half-brother's face into the consistency of surf wax."

She smiles, and my heart does a weird little flip into my stomach.

"Yeah, well, I'm sure your board of directors and Tessa wish you'd chosen a different path."

"Ain't that the god's honest truth," Tessa chimes in. I'd completely forgotten she was in the room, but that was the Jack effect.

"Tessa had media lined up," I mutter.

"I know." Jack hops up onto the table, and I can think about a million things I'd like to do to her on that table. "You're lucky to have her, Hugh. Now, let's see if we can salvage some of Tessa's hard work. Tell me what happened and then, Tessa, you tell me what everyone heard. Knowing you, you probably know what Mack's thinking as well."

"You know about my half-brother?"

"Hugh, I can tell you what I know, which isn't going to do you or your position any good, or you can tell me what happened. Trust me, the latter is going to get you a lot further than the first." She chews on the end of her ballpoint pen, waiting for me to answer a question I still haven't finished formulating.

"What happened?"

I sit down next to her, fighting every need to touch her.

My head falls forward into my hands. "I wish I knew, Jack." I look up into her eyes. And for the first time in six years, I let someone see how weak I really am.

Five

JACK

I'*m not usually a nurturing* person, but when Hugh hung his head and then looked up at me with those dark eyes filled with pain, it was instinct to reach out and soothe the only boy I'd ever loved. But I wasn't here to make him feel better. I was here to finish training Tessa. And the reason I was training the backstabbing tramp was so I could earn my last arrow and run my own territory. I hop off Hugh's table, pull out the chair next to him, and grab hold of my pen like it's a lifeline to immortality.

"Start with the earnings report and go forward until I tell you to stop, Hugh."

He nods and starts recalling how the directors are finding Mack's idea of dismantling more appealing. That leads to a call to table the motion for the relaunch of Halia at the US Open in Huntington Beach. I lose myself watching Hugh recall the events of Saturday. Not because of what happened, but because of him.

He's changed.

And not just physically.

His hair is longer, the angles of his face sharper, the ferocity of his eyes deadlier. He looks like his father, and a part of me mourns the loss of the idealistic boy who could spend a summer floating in the ocean looking for the perfect wave.

"Jack, do you want to take a break?" Tessa asks, but she's kicking me under the table.

"No, I'm good."

"Are you sure?" Hugh's gaze falls on me. "You're not jetlagged or anything?"

"Thanks for your concern, but, no."

"Good, because I need *Cut-Throat Jack* if I'm going to save Halia from the chop shop." I don't miss the way his knuckles turn white as they try to break off the end of the table. "By the way, you're gonna need to tell me who added the 'cut-throat' to my Jack."

I paste on a fake smile and make no such promise. Hugh may have kept his distance over the years, but he sure as hell has been keeping tabs on me too.

Tessa shuffles her paperwork, giving me a chance to think of all the reasons I love my job. "Event planner" is a blanket title to cover all sorts of sins, not just my Cupid Corps sentence. I earned the "cut-throat" title when I took on the asshole farming company that thought it was okay to use the ocean, up current from the barrier reef, for their personal fertilizer run-off. I'd started training a heartbroken vice president by planning an event for the Great Barrier Reef Foundation until we stumbled across the multi-millionaire farmer and his daughter. The daughter now runs the farming company, which is now the GBRF's biggest contributor, and is married to arrow number four. Not bad for five months' work. The newspapers snagged a picture of me gripping a knife in a precarious position at the fundraiser when I was "explaining" how the farmer dipshit dad was going to be handing over the reins of the company to his daughter or facing global scrutiny. They labeled me Cut-Throat Jack and . . . I kind of like it.

"So why were you and your brother late to the party?"

Hugh rams a hand through his hair. There's a new scar on his forehead that slices through his left eyebrow. His head rests in the palm of his hand, and I can see the strain cutting through the warrior façade. He's tired, he's beaten, and despite the dime-sized warmth in the pit of my stomach, he's not mine to comfort.

"They don't add up, Jack—what my people predicted and the numbers reported . . . there's a four and half percent difference. Jack, if we release these numbers, not only will it put a halt to the relaunch at the Open, it'll cause serious investor pull out before we even go public. Halia will be dead before our feet hit the water."

"So which numbers are accurate?"

Hugh and Tessa exchange a quick glance. There are still secrets between them. I shut my notebook, fold my hands, and try desperately to get a handle on the temper the two of them always seem to kick to explosion level in me.

"Here's the thing, Hugh. I can't do my job unless you tell me all the facts. Yes, I'm an event coordinator. It's a harmless title with very small teeth, but that's because I need the people I'm taking on for my clients to feel lulled into a sense of security. Now, here's the good thing, piranhas are often mistaken for harmless schools of fish until they smell blood in the water. I need to know where the blood is, so I can use my very small but powerful teeth to annihilate them."

Hugh's lip ticks up into a small grin—the same small grin that used to send my heart racing and my girly parts giggling. I lean back in my seat and curse my heart for adding an extra beat.

"Did you just compare yourself to a piranha?" Hugh leans back in his chair, mirroring me. I try not to notice how his biceps pull against the fabric of his shirt, only to be distracted by the buttons straining against his chest. He's so much more than what he was six years ago.

But so am I.

Silence rushes back into the room. This awkward is as consistent as the waves beating on the shore.

"Mack thinks I'm skimming off the top."

"But your people found the mistake." I lean forward and don't miss the way Hugh's eyes dart to the deepening V in my blouse. "Why would you tattle on yourself?"

"He thinks I'm scuttling the ship before the board votes to sell it off."

"Are you?" The flash of heat across his eyes tells me he isn't. My heart would have never asked the question, but I don't listen to that traitorous organ anymore. I push away from the table and start pacing. "And Sandpiper still has interest?"

"Sandpiper knows about all of Halia's dark secrets."

That stops me mid-step. I shoot a look at Tessa who's been church-mouse quiet since we started this meeting. She's good at sitting back and watching the sides even out and then picking the winning one.

I'm not.

"They know the details about the settlement? How?" I find my seat again. Just like everything Hugh is involved in, this is more complicated than two half-siblings duking it out for control of daddy's company. This is corporate espionage, and that can lead to all sorts of trouble.

Hugh quirks an eyebrow, and it doesn't take an Einstein to figure it out.

"If Mack can deliver Halia to Sandpiper, dismantled or alive, then he's guaranteed fifteen percent ownership."

"What's his ownership here?"

"Nothing. He sits on the board and draws a salary. He's taken that 'salary' and purchased a few thousand shares of Halia. You own more of Halia than he does."

"And you really think he's going to tank daddy's company for ownership?" I push away from the table and start pacing again. "Is he that bitter?"

Hugh shrugs his shoulders. The less verbal the Hawaiian giant is, the deadlier he becomes.

"How is your dad?" I watch every muscle in his body tense before Hugh pushes back from the table and stalks to the windows. The corded muscles in his back ripple to life as he braces himself against the pane of glass. Hugh is as devastating coming as he is going. Wide shoulders V into a waist that's perfect for holding onto during . . . I shake the thought from my mind. I don't need to be thinking about holding on to any part of Hugh Halia.

For the past eight years, it's just been Hugh and Kai. With the buffer of Hugh's mom gone, dying in a diving accident off the coast of Catalina, the two Halia men nearly destroyed each other. Explosive, volatile, philandering Hugh—that's what I need to focus on. Not the boy who captured my heart with a seashell and a broken promise.

"He's a stubborn ass." Hugh seeks me out through my reflection. "Even on his death bed, he'll probably outlive all three of us."

"He's at Hoag Hospital," Tessa says. Her voice is cold and distant; in fact, since the conversation started, she seems to have erected a giant frosty wall around her. Love has a way of either burning so hot, you're charred in bliss, or turning frigid to the point that all you can feel is the painful ache of all the memories you used to share.

"Yeah, well I'm not going to be visiting Kai anytime soon," I mutter. He was my dad's best friend, and when it came time to take H.A. Surf to the next level,

Kai dropped the A (my dad) and turned corporate. Dad could have taken the payoff and started his own company, but he always said he loved surfing, not the money that muddied the water.

Hugh chuckles, and my girly parts remind me what his laughter does to them, as well as his brooding.

"All right." I slap the table, hoping to chase away the flutter in my stomach. "So, we can't take back the fight, and we can't alter the numbers, so we'll shift the focus to the future. We need something big and distracting. Something that screams fun, love, and surf."

Silence fills the boardroom. You can practically hear the ideas rising and flattening out before they have time to take form. Hugh's back against the window, hip cocked in a way that his pants pull tight over the curve of his backside and . . . I push my focus past the Hawaiian hottie with a rock-hard ass.

It really is a great office. Right on the corner of Main Street and Pacific Coast Highway. You can see the people milling around down below, wishing the sun would come and chase the gloom away. And when it does, the sun glints off the water and you're certain this is what heaven must look like. My gaze falls back on Hugh. The similarity between the two, the view and the man, floors me, making my mouth run dry with the aftertaste of all those sweet summers we spent under the pier. We had so many plans and not just for Halia.

He'd wanted to marry me.

"A wedding," Tessa pipes in, like she's read my mind. Her eyes glitter, and there's a flush to her skin. "Halia hosts a beach-themed wedding."

"What are you talking about?" The bitterness leaves a rancid flavor in my mouth.

Tessa nearly sticks her head in her bag before surfacing with a notebook. She waves it around like a sparkler on the Fourth of July.

"A wedding. Don't roll your eyes at me, Jack. It's perfect. We do a huge PR push about new beginnings and the new direction Halia is taking. We have couples submit their stories on why they should be Halia Surf's couple." She flips open the binder and papers spill across the table. "The second week of June, we announce the couple. Week three, we let visitors pick the rings and the cake. Week four, we let visitors pick the wedding dress and tuxes. Week five, we let them pick out the honeymoon destination."

"This has all been done before, Tess."

"I know, but it's never been done by Halia or at the Open."

"They're not going to go for it, Tess." I push the papers back at her.

"If Hugh agrees, then you let me sell it."

"Then what the fuck am I here for?"

"Damn, Jack," Hugh drawls. Arms that scream *look at me* flex under the weight of his body. Admiration makes his eyes twinkle like rubbed onyx as he stares me down from the head of the table. I look across the table at Tessa; her arms are crossed, and the two of them have never looked more like a matched set than now. I swallow, forcing the calm to spread throughout my body. I'm here to train Tessa, not lose my cool. I'm not here to save Halia. My heart throws itself against my ribcage in protest.

Once the calm has reached my toes, I look at Tessa. There's something twinkling in her eyes that makes me want to kick the calm I've achieved in the balls and let the fire that was raging a few seconds ago consume me. These two have no clue how they decimated my heart six years ago, and I'll be damned if I give them an inkling now.

"You want to run with the wedding idea?" I ask Hugh. He matches my stare even though his fingers wrap against the table. His jaw ticks while a smile tugs at my lips. God, I've missed sparing with someone of Hugh's caliber. I turn my scrutiny toward Tessa. "And you think you can get the people at the Open to bite?"

She nods her head.

"Looks like my job here is all done." I pick up my notebook and walk to the door. Tessa's eyes flare, and the smirk that's crawling across Hugh's face isn't lost on me. The smart girl in me would take a wide berth around the Hawaiian giant, but the daredevil that just stood toe-to-toe edges up to him for one last look. One last dive into the memory of him. His fingers wrap around my arm, pulling me into his side. Even in my heels, Hugh's a good foot taller than me. His size used to intimidate me, then it made me feel safe—now it's a challenge to make him miss me.

"We need you on this project, Jack."

"No, you don't, Hugh. You never needed me."

His eyes flash, and the silver ring around them that only burns when he's good and pissed is lit up like neon.

"You keep selling yourself that bill of goods, Jack," he bites. That small muscle along his jaw flexes. He did that when I'd hit him too close, too hard. He pulls in a deep breath, and I know I've done more than that.

"You know I'll always need you," he whispers.

Even this close, I'm certain he thinks I haven't heard him. For the first time in six years, I'm speechless. The room collapses in on us. Every sound beyond the tenor of Hugh's voice is muffled and insignificant. The scared little girl in me clamors for the badass I've become to step in, push him away, knee him in the junk. But none of that happens. Instead, I'm rooted to the floor, held by the way his warm palms sear into me. The way my lips tingle at the proximity of tasting all the sweet memories I know sit on his. I know he feels it too; the soft pucker of his lips was always so damn tempting.

Somewhere, a door opens, and was that a gasp?

"Nod your head if you're in, Jack," he commands. His eyes bear into me, demanding I comply. But I don't. I won't ever give Hugh Halia the satisfaction of complying with his demands.

"That's Jack?" The incredulous tone breaks the spell Hugh has cast. We both turn to find a pouty girl with murder in her muddy brown eyes.

My *"You must be the assistant,"* is matched only by Hugh's, *"I told you I wasn't gay."*

Six

HUGH

W*atching Sonia's mouth hit the* floor of the boardroom is almost as sweet as feeling Jack's fingers threading possessively through mine. It's a dick move, but the raw caveman in me wants to fucking pound on my chest when I pull Jack even further into my side. She's practically straddling my leg, and all that heat coming off her taut body, damn, what it does to me. I almost don't care that the warmth I'm feeling is fueled by her fury. The tiny bit of me that does care is quickly pacified when she turns those baby blues up at me.

"Gay?" Jack snorts. "Your girlfriend thinks you're gay?"

My shoulders inch up, and I can't help the smile spreading across my face even if I am going to pay for it later tonight.

"Apparently, I've been saying your name in my sleep."

Jack steps away from me. Two seconds, one sentence and—bam! Like that, the sparkle in her eye, the moment of time we'd found, granted at Sonia's expense, is gone.

Long legs that used to wrap around me carry Jack across the room. One look of disgust is cast my way before she extends a hand to Sonia and says, "I'm Jacquelyn Alcantar. You should get used to the crapload of excuses he's about to hurl your way. But, a little girl-to-girl advice, don't believe a single word that comes out of his lying, cheating mouth."

Jack pushes through the Kolohala doors, leaving the boardroom, and my heart triples its beat. She's pissed at me, which is nothing new, but that cold frost that hardened her eyes—I'd seen that look one other time, and it had cost me not only the girl I loved but almost ten thousand dollars' worth of repairs to my car.

The room tilts when Jack leaves. The girl still does it for me. I know she doesn't think she wants me, but the old man is dying. My heart flips with the thoughts of maybe. I hardly know that I'm starting after her until Sonia wraps her fingers around my arm and stops me.

Cold, dull brown eyes try to slice through me. "We should talk."

"I know." I place my hand on top of Sonia's, willing the words to come out slow and steady, and, given the softening around the edges of her pursed lips, just my touch seems to be doing the trick. Even though I want to rip her fingers off my arm and toss them in the air like confetti. She doesn't deserve my wrath, but god, I need to let it loose on someone. Where's my half-brother when I really need him. "I need you to let me handle the A.A. rep, and then we'll talk until I see the gorgeous smile light up your eyes." I run the pad of my thumb over her cheek and watch those brown eyes soften. I know she's expecting me to bend down and sweep my lips across hers, but I can't. And it has nothing to do with Tessa gagging herself behind Sonia's back.

Sonia rises on her toes as I turn my cheek to receive the impact of her lips. Her eyes flare, and I know this charade is either going to need my full attention or need to end. My heart wants the latter, but given what she knows about Mack and Sandpiper, I'm going to have to man up and take one more for Team Halia.

"Pack a bag and stay with me this week. It's going to be crazy at work, and I need to know I have you at home." The words taste like acid leaving my mouth, but Sonia's a loose cannon, and I can't have her nursing a smoldering fuse.

"Really?" Her eyes light up in a way that makes me feel like shit.

I pull her into me and place a kiss on her forehead. "Do me a favor," I whisper into the crown of her head. "Take the day off and my personal card to Fashion Island. Have a wild one on me."

Sonia squeals, confirming I've bought her forgiveness while she throws her arms around me and pulls me down for a hug. I feel every bone in Sonia's rail-thin body and secretly wish for the womanly curves that I now know firsthand that Jack's sporting. Before I can feel any lower, Sonia lets go and heads for the doors, leaving me and Tessa and all the baggage of our past in the room.

Tessa plants her hands on her hips. "What the fuck just happened there, Mr. Hyde?"

"Before you judge me—"

Tessa holds up a finger, cutting me off. "No, I judge no one. You know that about me. You need to go find Jack. As much as she is a pain in my ass, I can't pull this thing off without her."

"I'm supposed to meet with Mack about the media junket. He thinks he should take lead."

Tessa spares me a look before focusing back on her red nails. "I can handle him."

"And the junket."

"I can handle them both." She lays her hands on my chest and pushes me toward the door. "Please, go get me my Jack."

A chuckle releases from somewhere deep inside of me. It's like high school all over again. The running joke: where's my Jack and coke. Jack never helped the pun because she practically lived with a Coca-Cola IV drip her junior year. She was bound and determined to graduate with Tessa and me. She doubled up on classes and worked straight through the summer before her junior year before she told us what she was doing.

"You two are going to go off to college, and I'm going to be stuck here in teen purgatory waiting for breaks and stolen moments when I can jump on the train and ride down to see you both at the U.C. San Diego. It's not fair." Her lip jutted out just enough for me to capture it between my teeth. She hated that I loved biting her. I loved that after her eyes flashed with fury, they'd settle into a soft haze of love. I never bit hard, just enough to get her attention focused on what mattered.

Us.

"I'm not going anywhere without you here, Jack." I pointed to that spot in my heart that Jack had claimed back when we were kids.

Pain rockets down my chest as Tessa cranks my nipple.

"Damn, Tessa."

"Dude, Jack waits for no one. Move your ass," she snaps.

"Wasn't cute when we were sixteen and is even less amusing as your boss." I don't wait for her response as I rub my offended nipple. The smug look that's plastered on her face says I'd lose another bout this morning. With the women in my past, I was being shut out before my own feet hit the water.

The office is humming now, and not just with the normal gossip buzz that was obviously going to happen after Sunday's news post.

This is different.

This is Jack back. The girl always left a wake the size of Moses parting the Red Sea when she wasn't pissed. I push through the doors and find Mack leaning up against the receptionist's desk with eyes focused on the closed doors of the elevator and try to wrestle down the primal caveman in me knowing exactly what's going through my disgusting half-brother's mind.

"When I'm running things, I'll be sure to leave you in charge of hiring."

It takes everything in me to ignore Mack. Instead, I focus on punishing the down button.

"I thought Tessa was hot, but damn . . ." His innuendo whizzes through the air like a fist at my face.

I feel the small thread break a second before I'm across the room with my hands fisted in Mack's shirt. I have him pinned up against the wall next to the elevator.

"Drop whatever thought you have floating around in that head of yours."

"Easy, brother." His fingernails dig into my wrists, and there's something hiding in the recesses of his eyes. Fear. I could only be so lucky. "We have an audience."

I glance over my shoulder and see every single body in the office is now watching firsthand a recreation of Saturday night. Bodies ebb like a ripple in still water as Tessa makes her way through the spectators.

She pops a hip and points to her watch. "Hugh, really? Take him to Marina's moat after you've dealt with Jack. M'kay?" Tessa doesn't wait for my response before she wades back through Halia's employees, and I don't have time to explain that the moat is where I used to kick everyone's ass who dared to glance Jack's way to my half-brother. Not when the elevator is waiting for me.

I step in and hit the button for the parking garage level. Steel doors shut, and for thirty seconds, I'm taken back. There wasn't a day that went by in high school that someone wasn't sniffing around Jack. She was an innocent beauty back then. Fresh-faced and wide-eyed. She was a beacon for every sleazeball and good guy to muss up. When I'd catch wind about some douche canoe's plan to ask her out or worse—and yes, there were some who had some pretty sadistic plans that included my girl—I'd take them to the moat and "school" them on why Jack Alcantar should never cross their minds. The moat was a storm channel that ran around the perimeter of Marina High School. Jack and Tessa loved that you had to drive over bridges to get to the parking lot. It was their own personal Camelot, and somewhere in that scenario, I was their chivalrous knight. Tessa always could take care of herself, but Jack . . . Jack was mine.

The elevator doors pull open, and I see her tiny frame staring at my red car. I can't help but watch. Her hands flex and release little fists. Anger rolls off her curvy frame in waves of heat that's usually saved for late August summer heat sizzling off the pavement. Another small strand of hair has worked its way loose from her ponytail, and she's alternating her focus of fury between it and the hood of my car. I slip my hands in my pockets and inch forward.

"Pretty sure the last time you looked at my car like that, it cost me half a year's salary to fix."

Jack jumps at the sound of my voice.

"Only half a year?" she quips back, her hands forming tiny little fists again. "I'll have to do better next time."

I run a hand through my hair and watch the effect I have on her when I do. It's good to know some things, even if they're on a pure chemistry level, never change. "Let me make it up to you, Jack."

Her eyes flare, and I can't be sure what I'm asking to make up, the past six years or the last six minutes. I realize either one will do if she'll let me. I walk right into her space, forcing her to look up at me. I've missed her. I've missed how alive fighting with her makes me feel. Which means if I've missed the worst part of our relationship, then I know the best parts (the parts that made me want to be that chivalrous man for her) have been in mourning for the last six years.

"Tessa's got you." She steps away from me, but before she can, I snag her waist and pull her into me.

"I don't want Tessa to handle me."

The pulse under Jack's delicate neck jumps at my words. "I'm not sure that's your call to make anymore."

That little piece of hair I tucked away up in the boardroom has broken free again and is back in her eyes. The urge to free all the other strands from the strict hold Jack's placed them under kicks me in the balls. It would be so easy to take charge, remind her how we used to be, but we're not there yet. If I move too fast, she'll bolt. I can't blame her. I'd run from me too if I knew only the truth we'd allowed her to see. But the old man's on his deathbed, and freedom is so sweet, I can't wait to taste it on her lips. Instead, I step closer and leave that strand of hair behind her ear and revel in the way her breath catches in her throat.

I can wait.

She's worth it.

"Help me," I whisper. Her eyes soften to that sea foam blue that always had a way of pulling me under. "Help me save Halia."

She nods before her brain catches up to her body, and when it does, she goes stiff in my arms. Her eyes frost over, and a small piece of me grieves the loss. Jack steps out of my grip, and for now, I let her go.

"I'll help Tessa help Halia Surf. I'm only here for her."

I lean down, rest my forehead against hers, and watch the chips of ice melt away under my gaze. "I'll take what I can get."

The moment stretches between us. Neither of us is willing to move, either from fear or regret. Her sweet scent hasn't changed much, and I know if I stay any longer, I'll ruin everything. Pulling every moral fiber I have in me, I step away and head back to the elevator, casting a quick glance at her over my shoulder. Her arms are wrapped around her waist like they're the only things that can keep her held together.

I did that to her.

Broke her.

And I'm the only one who can put her back together.

Even if she won't admit it, I know we need each other.

JACK

T*he door rattles on its* hinges, echoing my frustration throughout my dad's condo.

"Tessa," I holler. "I know your skinny ass is here." I toss my purse and keys on the entryway table, kick off my heels, and fight the urge to call for my dad.

"In the kitchen," she sings at me. "I'm making your favorite."

Fish tacos and tortilla soup, I mouth along with her voice. After Dad died and before my world fell apart, we lived here together. It was three bedrooms and I was alone. Dad died on Independence Day . . . my eighteenth birthday. I was so mad at him not allowing me to follow Tessa and Hugh to UCSD. He'd found out I was planning to graduate early and put a stop to it. I chase the thoughts away. Tessa deferred her freshman year and stayed home with me while Hugh went down to San Diego. At the time, I was too numb to see what was going on. I felt all sorts of guilty with Dad dying and Tessa deferring, and then all I could feel was the shift in the universe as my world crumbled all around me.

I pad down the cold, hardwood floors into the kitchen. Chilled evening air that only happens with the season change blows through the kitchen, stirring up the smells of Baja cooking. Tessa's an awesome cook. An only child of a flight attendant meant by the time she was fifteen, she was deemed able to fend for herself. Tessa was a permanent fixture at my house growing up. Her mom lived across the street in the pink condos on PCH and Main Street. When we were teens, Tessa, Hugh, and I would terrorize the tourists during the summer and make fantastic plans during the winter. Part of me feels like I should have always known they were making plans without me.

I plant my hands on the counter so I don't grab for one of her homemade tortilla chips. The girl knows food is my underbelly. Warm chips and—I sniff the air—homemade salsa. She's pulling out all the stops.

"Why are you in my house?" I eye the chips. They're so fresh, the salt is melting into them.

"There's a peach mojito for you. Drink up, buttercup."

I eye the deliciousness and wonder if I'm that predictable or if Eros has clued her in on all the things that have stayed the same. One thing's for certain, she's going to make a hell of a replacement after I survive this last assignment.

The clamor of cooking utensils dies down, getting my attention. She mirrors my stance and nods at the drink.

"It's a peach mojito. I promise. Not hemlock." Tessa winks at me, and I can't help the smile pulling at my lips.

I push the drink away, despite wanting to make nice. I'm not here to fix my past. I'm here to secure my future. And that future means I'll ultimately be

Tessa's boss if she can handle not falling for Hugh again. He has to be the reason she was drafted to Cupid Corps. He's why I'm here.

"We need to clear the air."

"We do?" She picks up a giant ladle and walks over to one of the three pots simmering on the stove. She lifts the lid, and the steam permeates the air with chicken tortilla soup. God, the girl is good.

"Tessa, I think we've lost sight of our task."

"We have?" She pours some soup into a bowl and looks at me. "You still like sour cream and diced onions?

I nod. I need her to know that a walk down memory lane, despite all the good times, is always going to have an ending with me as her boss and her as my protégé. I take the bowl and stir the soup around. It's everything in me not to dive head first into her tortilla soup and all the good memories.

"Still good, girl." I smile around my spoon. "Define our purpose here."

"Stop Hugh and his jackass assistant from giving *love,* and by default, Eros, the middle finger."

I spoon another bite of soup into my mouth. "What happens if we fail?"

"I don't get an arrow, and you don't get a promotion."

I nod, not ready to admit the third consequence tied to Hugh's soul. "Nowhere in there is 'save Halia,' got it?"

Tessa chews on her lip, and I can tell this doesn't sit right with her. I gotta admit, it sits a little hard in my stomach as well.

"Welcome to the big leagues, girlfriend." I shovel another spoonful of soup in my mouth and send a swig of peach mojito chasing after it.

"You really have given up, haven't you?"

I don't answer her. I can't because that would have me digging in places that I've long since abandoned.

"How did the wedding pitch go over with Mack?" I ask instead.

Tessa eyes me a few more seconds. I see resignation wash over her body a moment before she turns back to the pots on the stove. If I know my former best friend, there's rice in one of those pots and homemade beans in the other. Tessa takes off the lids and I see I'm still right about the girl.

"Mack's on board. I walked in on him and two of the hold-out board members going toe-to-toe over the dismantle program." She nods to the pot of beans and then scoops a hefty serving on a plate. "He doesn't have the votes to move forward with the dismantle, so we're all in for the Open." Tessa pulls open the oven and takes out the tortillas and the baking dish that has, hands down, the best-cooked fish north of the Baja Peninsula.

"And the people at the Open? Thanks." I take the plate and wait for her to dish up hers. "When do we meet with them?"

"Already have. One of my first arrows serves on the New Sponsor's Board. He still has a sweet spot for me even if the wipe didn't last."

I giggle around the bite of taco. "Did you wipe him on the forehead?"

She shakes her head. "The heart, why?"

I tap to the spot in the middle of my forehead where the High Jack Wipe happens. "Love happens in the head first. The heart is just the first thing that reacts."

"I'm going to have to disagree."

"Disagree, but I've only had two relapses. One who went back to the Corps."

Tessa hops up on the counter and grabs the other mojito and takes a sip. "I'll have to try it next time. So, Eros—he's pretty intense."

"Yeah, have you met Psyche? Kind of hard not to be passionate about love when you had to fight another god and risk your life to love that one person."

"You think Eros always knew Psyche was the one for him? I mean, it's kind of hard to overcome someone burning you with oil and willing to kill you if they saw whom you truly were. 'Vile winged serpent' doesn't necessarily scream love interest." Tessa leans back and grabs the bowl of salsa. "Talk about the ultimate betrayal and yet, there they are." She shoves a chip in her mouth and casts me a knowing look.

Tessa's random thoughts always have a hidden meaning. It's part of her life game plan: confuse them with the random stupid and then hit them with your smarts. I consider her words, matching her chip for chip, before I finally say, "I think every relationship has to start with a tragedy. What makes a great love story is when two people find their way through the tragedy and despite themselves and all the obstacles against them, still love each other."

"So, the greater the tragedy, the bigger the love?"

"No, the greater the love, the bigger the tragedy." I shove the last of my fish taco into my mouth and put my plate in the sink. "Leave the dishes, I'll clean up when I'm done with my shower."

I start down the hall when Tessa calls out, "I know you still love him."

The answer catches in my throat; it burns because it really doesn't matter what I do or don't feel for Hugh. What he did, what Tessa did, makes it impossible to feel anything ever again.

"I have forty-nine arrows that prove I'm not." I turn down the hall ignoring her last-ditch efforts to taunt me.

"But you're still one away from immortality."

My stomach sinks. Yeah, and it'll be the hardest one yet.

Eight

HUGH

The wrong girl is tangled in my sheets. That's what I've been thinking every morning for the two weeks Jack's been back. I know Sonia's my girlfriend for all intents and purposes, and she's a great girl. But everything's different now.

Jack's back.

And she's not only back in Huntington Beach, she's back at Halia. I'd be lying if the last two weeks have been both agonizing and blissful all rolled into one. But the dance I'm doing with Sonia, trying to keep her satisfied and sated . . . It feels so wrong.

Sonia stirs on top of me. Her lips skim across my chest, and I know it's meant to be delightful, but the shudder rolling through me has nothing to do with pleasure.

"The girls are still on for dinner tonight?"

"Hmm," I grunt and brush a kiss across her forehead. Sonia is fully embracing the "keep your friends close and your enemies closer: motto these days. She's also been sleeping at my house the past two weeks, reminding me why I don't do sleepovers, let alone extended stays.

"You sure you don't want me to cook?" Sonia turns and looks up at me with those puppy-dog eyes. She's a sweet girl, and one day, she'll make some guy really happy. I'm just not that guy.

"No, I think Villa Nova is perfect."

"It really isn't a problem."

I kiss her forehead again and peel out from under her. I know what she's doing. She's pissing on a tree to let the girls know I'm hers.

But I'm not.

And the gnawing feeling in my gut says I never will be.

"I really need you in the office today." I grab her fingers and press my lips to them. "You're my right-hand man." Her fingers tighten around mine before I step away and trudge off to the bathroom. I ram a hand through my hair, fighting the urge to see if there are daggers flying at my back.

I paid for the right-hand man statement all day long. All my ladies are good and pissed. Tessa came in muttering something about Jack giving mules a run for the money in the stubborn department. I earned a scowl and middle finger send off when I told her that was the pot calling the kettle black. Jack blew into the office not too far behind Tessa, and from the fury churning in her eyes, even I knew to batten down the lines and stay away.

I was going to suggest we postpone the final wedding meeting with the US Open people, given everyone's mood, but like the rock stars they are, Sonia, Tessa, and Jack pulled it together and dazzled the suits pretending to be surf lovers.

The sun was just dipping into the ocean, setting the horizon on fire with pinks and purples—by far, my favorite part of the day—when a soft knock sounds behind me and my door opens. My body already knows its Jack. She electrifies the air around me. Even though I'm suffering with Sonia, everyone in the office can tell there's something different about me. One of the interns actually remarked that my normal piss-off scowl looked more welcoming. If Halia survives, I may have to hire him.

"Come on in, Jack," I call out, not wanting to let go of the sunset just yet. The door clicks shut and silence fills the room. If anyone can appreciate my fascination with an everyday occurrence like the sun setting, it's Jack. I love the way her crisp scent fills my room. It's a mixture of flowers and ocean breeze, and it's a scent I've searched long and hard to replicate. But just like Jack, no woman can compare. I turn and lean up against the window. She's in a black dress today. It wraps around her and is tied together with a bow like a present waiting to be opened. Her legs are bare and accentuated by the silver stilettos that put her at just the right height for my mind to wander down all sorts of wicked ways to bend her over my desk.

"The US Open people can't do the final lunch tomorrow and won't be available for a week after that." She riffles through some papers on her clipboard, but it's the silver heart hanging in between her breasts that has all my attention. The way it lays on the voluptuous curves. I don't remember her being this . . . woman. My fingers press into the warm window behind me, wishing they could explore all the other ways Jack has changed.

"Did you hear me, Hugh?"

I nod.

"So you're okay with it?" Her fingers still, and her gaze pins me up against the window.

"Okay with what?"

An exasperated huff leaves her lips, and I want to chase after it with mine.

"You're okay with US Open people joining us for dinner tonight? We really need them to sign off on this proposal." Her hip juts out, and I can feel my lip tick up in a smirk. "Or I can take them to Dukes, and you and Tessa can have dinner tonight."

I push off the window and stalk my way over to her. I love watching her pulse pick up along her neck. The sweet blush that crawls up her neck only encourages me. In no time flat, I'm in her space and she's backing up. My hands fall on either side of the wall behind her, trapping her in between my arms. All I have to do is bend down and capture what's always been mine.

Only mine.

"Hugh," Jack whispers. I know that jagged little line between her eyes only comes out when she's terrified. And I hate that I'm the one putting it there. I want to stroke it away, make her eyes haze over the way they used to when we were this close.

"I don't want to have dinner with Tessa or Sonia or the US Open people." I skim my finger along the side of her face and watch her turn into my touch. I don't even think she realizes she's done it, but that minute gesture does more to turn me on than a room full of Victoria Secret models. And I've experienced them as well.

"Please, stop," she whispers. Her eyes close; her chest rises and falls with an extra breath. I should listen to her. I should back off, respect not only her wishes but her father's, as well. I swallow hard and harness everything in me and step away.

"Did you clear it with Sonia?" I turn and start back to the window. I can't look at her. The flush of desire staining her cheeks might just be the final straw to breaking the promise I made to her father six years ago.

"No, um, no. I'll do that now," she stammers. I hear her fiddling with the door and rejoice in the fact that I'm having the same effect on her as she is on me.

"We should take separate cars," I throw out and hear her grunt of approval.

Villa Nova is a bad idea. It didn't hit me until we walked in the door and the owner spotted Jack and me together.

"Oh, my goodness, look at this! *Le anime gemelle* have returned!" The round owner waddles over to us. Gino Mario's owned this place since the turn of time. Even when I was seven and Mom would bring me here for Sunday dinners, he still had the silver hair comb over. Only now, there are more rolls around his neck than there are on all the tables combined. I brought Jack here for dinner my senior prom. I'd completely forgotten, but the light in his eyes when he sees Jack and me makes me feel seventeen all over again. Hell, Jack makes me feel seventeen all over again.

I lean into Jack and whisper, "I'm so sorry." By the way she's grinding her teeth, maybe Sonia's offer to cook would have been the better option. Jack's Italian isn't as rusty as I'd hoped, and Gino's "soulmate" reference makes her spine straighten like steel has been poured down it. She swallows hard and I feel like shit. There are so many memories here. This wasn't fair. Not to either of us.

"I swear, this isn't what I wanted," I whisper into her hair, inhaling a quick scent of all things Jack. I extend my hand and shake Gino's. His eyes dart between Jack and me, twinkling like he's a kid on a Christmas morning high. Olive skin creases into a smile that makes even the harshest cynic believe in happiness.

"Hi, Gino," Jack says as she's pulled into the folds of Gino's arms. When he's done squeezing her, he wraps an arm around me as well and marches us back into the restaurant.

"I saw your name on the reservation list and saved the best table for you and your party. The suits are here and drinking." He leans into me, Chianti mixing with his words. "I heard about the old man. My thoughts are with you." Gino turns his attention to Jack and I barely make out, "He's going to need your strong shoulders soon, *la mi bella*."

Jack swallows hard over the awkward and kisses Gino on both cheeks, whispering something in his ear before walking over to greet the US Open reps.

"Hi," Sonia's voice grates out. Gino takes her hand, but all the welcome is gone from his eyes. "I'm Sonia, Hugh's girlfriend," she manages before Gino curtly nods and walks away. I love the Italians; you always know exactly where you stand with them.

"He's rude." Sonia slips an arm through mine. I want to pull the same Gino move, but given I'm already paying for this morning's brushoff, I pull Sonia further into me.

"Hugh," one of the execs calls out. I excuse myself from Sonia and head over to the skinny dude with bad acne. I think his name is Dick. Poor guy. He comes up to my armpits, and you know he was the boy who found himself staring at the bottom of a trash can more times than not.

"Hey." I shake his hand and offer to get him a drink. He waves me off with a nod to his glass of clear bubbling liquid. Given his uptight demeanor, it wouldn't surprise me if it were straight up seltzer water.

"I wanted to commend you and your team on the wedding idea. All the girls at the corporate office are swooning."

I chuckle. "It seems to be catching. The same thing is happening with Halia's female staff."

"That's the demographic we're going for." He turns his focus on Jack and Tessa. Like usual, they're off in a corner at each other's throats. "They're quite a team."

"That they are."

"Have you worked with them long?"

I nod and accept the drink Gino's sent over. "We grew up together. I've known the girls since kindergarten."

"Lucky guy."

I chuckle. "We've had some good times."

"I'd love for our press team to do an exposé on the three of you. The team behind Halia."

"Sadly, they're not Halia. They're consultants under Aió̱nia Agápi̱'s flagship and my time with them is limited." The impact of the statement hits me square in the chest. I don't want to even fathom how dull life is going to be when Tessa's gone. And Jack—emotion thickens at the back of my throat to the point that breathing is impossible. I can't let her get away a second time. I signal to Gino and watch his eyes light up when I say, "I need a favor, and it has to do with Jack."

Nine

JACK

Gino pulls me into a hug that makes me wish I were seventeen and starry-eyed all over again. But then I remember how the next chapter of the Hugh and Jack story goes, and I want to throttle the Hawaiian with book-cover-model hair and killer good looks shooting suggestive glances my way.

I escape up the flight of stairs into the best room in the restaurant. It's dimly lit, intimate, with a hint of sweet music from mandolins playing. An old mahogany table that seats twenty sits in the middle of the room like this place is in someone's home and not a restaurant. The room can hold a hundred people, but Gino knows about mood, and he's turned the lights down around the edges and created a special glow around the table. There's a wall of windows overlooking Newport Beach, showcasing the full moon out tonight. The way the moonbeams dance on the waves brings back so many memories.

The first time Hugh kissed me was with my toes in the sand and a full moon showering us in silver light. We were in middle school when our friendship turned to something so much more. Heat flashes across my face as I think of the other first that happened under a full moon. The celestial pull on the waves had nothing compared to the effect it had on Hugh and me.

A waiter asks if I need anything, and I fight back the urge to say a stiff smack of reality, and order a peach mojito instead. I'm watching the waves ebb and flow when I feel Hugh's gaze fall on me. I turn and watch his eyes sear a path from my toes to my lips, pausing at all his favorite stops along my body.

His dark eyebrows dance against olive skin, making my insides swirl with warmth. We were really good together. And then we weren't.

"Somebody's making goo-goo eyes at you," Tessa sings. "But then again, you and Hugh never could be in the same room and not have the wallpaper peeling from the heat you two conjure up."

"What are we doing here?" I adjust the collar line of my dress, realign my heart necklace, and before I can shift on my heels, Tessa levels me with a knowing look.

"You're fidgeting."

"I'm not."

"All of that." She holds a finger up and wiggles the air up and down and all around me. Tessa's eyes twinkle with amusement and then widen into saucers as her mouth falls into a little "o." "You're not still . . . ?" Her words trail off and form an all-knowing smile.

A different kind of heat races through me, but before I can protest, the soft, soothing music of the mandolins are replaced with Dean Martin and the opening bars of "That's Amore." Adrenaline pours into my system as I search the room, looking for the quickest escape because what accompanies this song is . . .

The room spins, and I land with my hands sprawled against the hardest pair of pecs known to man. Hugh looks down at me. The shadows of the room caress his face, and the world seems to fade away. His midnight eyes are sparkling like the moon dancing on the dark ocean waves behind us. My breath catches. A tingle I'd long since given up on dances up my spine as Hugh moves us into an intricate waltz step. I try to step out of his arms, but he pulls me in closer. His hair falls forward, shielding us from the onlookers. Wicked intent dances across his face before he says, "The suits aren't sold on the wedding idea."

"You're lying."

His lip ticks up in that devilish grin I've always been a sucker for. "Could be, but are you willing to risk it?"

I push against his chest, but his fingers dig into the fabric of my dress. Dark eyes search for something in my face, and when he finds it, he smiles, and I know I'm not willing to risk a bigger scandal for Tessa to clean up.

"Be glad it's not the tango," he whispers in my ear, releasing a whole new set of tingles.

The room spins again as Hugh picks up the Viennese Waltz that Gino taught us for prom. Faces fly by as we circle the room. Dean Martin encouraging us that this is all good and fun in the name of love. Gino's ear-to-ear smile spins into Tessa's knowing grin, which spins into the US Open execs' admiring head tilts. The air twirls around us, creating a time capsule, and for a brief moment, I feel like that wistful seventeen-year-old girl who thought her future hung in Hugh Halia's eyes and her heart was freely given to him. A giggle floats up from that same place that girl's been hiding, and I'm rewarded with a full-on smile that lights up all the dark and tortured planes of Hugh's face.

"There's my girl," he says as we pick up the spin around the room again.

Gino, Tessa, the execs, Sonia, and . . . I stop suddenly. The motion rips me from Hugh's arms.

"What are you doing here?" The room is still spinning, and I can't be sure if it's from the dance, my partner, or the son of the god who holds my future in the palm of his hands strolling toward me. Panic claws up my throat, and my hand absentmindedly rubs at the missing arrow on my wrist.

One dance.

I couldn't have ruined everything for one dance.

No! This mission isn't about me. It's about Tessa. My nails drag across the incomplete circle of arrows. I'm one away from running my own territory. This mission is most certainly not about saving Halia. It's about saving me. Halia's had its fair share of Alcantar tears, sweat, and most certainly, blood.

And Hugh can't have my future.

"Jack?"

Hugh comes up behind me, bringing all the questions I know he wants answered—questions I can dodge but will eventually have to answer. Heat radiates off him, doing nothing to chase away the cold fingers of fear.

When I don't start the introductions—how does that even go? *Hugh, here's the God of Love's offspring. I've been moonlighting as a Cupid ever since you destroyed my heart*—Hugh's thick arm shoots past my face, hand extended out. "I'm Hugh Halia."

"I'm E.J." Eros's son shakes Hugh's hand and smiles down at me. "I work with Jack."

"And Tessa," Hugh adds.

E.J. glances around the room for Tessa, only, she's gone. Figures she'd leave me holding the bag of broken hearts. I worry my lip, wondering what E.J.'s going to say, or worse, what he's going to do. It's no secret he's as thrilled about the whole aspect of love as I am. It's ironic too, given his parents are the creators of the whole happily-ever-after sham.

"Mostly Jack these days." E.J. is just like his dad. He's breathtakingly beautiful, and I know what I'm seeing is only a projection of what my heart wants. Which is why his normally alabaster complexion has more olive in its tone, his blond hair is longer, with a dark shade of brown running through it, and his blue eyes now look like midnight.

"Do you mind if I steal her for a moment?" E.J. asks.

I'm already moving before Hugh can answer. Nobody denies E.J.

"Actually, I do." Hugh wraps his fingers around the top of my arm and pulls me back into him. I clamor to gag my inner teen from squealing with delight. I've never heard of anyone standing up to the power E.J. puts off, let alone witnessed it.

E.J. runs his thumb along his jaw and cocks his head. Is that admiration I see in his eyes?

"You do love a challenge, don't you?" The question is directed at me, but Hugh takes it as a personal affront. I spin around; the palms of my hands splay against Hugh's chest, and both of us feel the connection.

"I'll be right back," I whisper. I swallow hard over the fear stuck in my throat. I can feel everything I've worked for slipping away—melting under the intensity of Hugh. I caution a few steps backward, hoping Hugh won't follow. When I spin around, E.J.'s smirking. He loves watching the chaos emotions create. Deep breathes, calm words. I know I have to end this. I can't take even one step down this path with Hugh again. No matter how tempting he is, my heart always will be the one shattered, and I won't risk that hurt ever again.

I know what I have to do.

I spin back around and walk right up to Hugh. I risk one touch, knowing it will be my last, and place my hand on his chest. His heart hammers against my palm. His fingers wrap around my wrist, and I know by the twitch in his lips, he can feel my pulse matching his. He just doesn't know my heart is racing because I'm about to annihilate his.

"Please don't make a scene in front of my boyfriend," I plead.

"Your what?"

"My boyfriend. It's pretty serious, actually." I steal a glance at E.J. and watch the waves of admiration roll off him. I'm not going to leave any doubt in his or Eros's minds that I'm ready to handle my own territory. I'm a Cupid, and it isn't a curse, it's my salvation. "I've moved on . . . and you should too."

Hugh's fingers fall from my wrist. The play in his eyes flicker and die. And for the second time in my life, my heart breaks because of this boy, this man.

HUGH

“*Your boyfriend.” The words taste* bitter on my lips. “He’s your boyfriend?” Jack nods. She doesn’t even risk a look back at the douche from down under.

“I wasn’t expecting him.” She looks up at me, eyes filled with a sheen that I could mistake for tears if I didn’t know her better.

But I do.

This is the girl who ran and never looked back. Never thought I was worth the fight. Cast me off as quickly as when she found me with Tessa.

A cold film of sweat coats my back, reminding me why I have girls like Sonia playing the part of my lovers. I don’t have time for wooing or chasing. And I most certainly don’t have time for Jack and her games. I don’t answer her, just turn on my heels, and walk back to the bar Gino’s opened for the suits.

I love the man.

He's busy making drinks and schmoozing, but I know he's watching me, watching to see if I slide off into the deep abyss like the last time. He had to dive in deep to get me before I was a complete and utter lost cause.

"Is there anyone you don't know, Hugh?" the skinny exec with bad skin asks.

"How do you mean?" I smile at Gino and take the Corona, a fresh lime bobbing in the suds.

"How the hell did you get E.J. Speaker here?"

"You know him?" The cool froth of beer slides down my throat but doesn't have any effect on the heat coursing through me.

The exec shoots me a look like I should before he says, "He's the new A.S.P. board member. He chaired the sponsorship committee before his promotion. You didn't invite him?"

"No. He's on the board of the Association of Surfing Professionals?"

"Well, whoever did has some pretty powerful fingers. He was in Australia two days ago and told the US Open governing body he wouldn't be out west for the rest of the year."

I pull another sip of beer through my teeth. "So why the change of heart?"

The exec looks around me and I know I'm going to regret looking, but I do anyway. E.J. has his head down, listening to Jack probably feeding him an earful. He catches us looking, raises his drink (wine, what surfer drinks wine?), and wraps his arm around Jack. She starts, looks over at us, threads her fingers through E.J.'s hands, and tows him out on to the balcony.

"You two have history?"

Sonia slides next to me, and I can feel my future locking into place. It isn't hot and fueled with passion, but it's doable. It's . . . sweet, like too much candy sitting on a cavity.

"Jack may have been in my past, but Sonia is my future." I place a kiss on the top of her head. I regret the words the minute they leave my lips. The way Sonia looks up at me—she has wedding bells and white-monogramed towels in her eyes. She doesn't know it, but when the Open is over, she's good as gone. Cold wind blows into the room, and I know Jack and her ass of a boyfriend are back. I can feel her proximity, and part of me bristles at the fact this girl has this great of an effect on me.

"Dick." Jack's voice is smooth and in control. Of course, she'd know the exec with bad skin's name. She knows how to work all the angles. "I see you've met Hugh's better half, Sonia."

"I have." Dick's gaze darts between Jack and me. I'm not sure what he's expecting, but I know for a fact he can sense the electricity arcing off the two of us. It's like someone's flipped us, and we're no longer magnets that can't be pulled apart. Quite the opposite. She's lightning, and all she can seem to find is the water that surrounds my soul. With every stolen glance and worrisome way she tugs at her bottom lip, she lights me on fire and denies me the chance to revel in the pain.

An uncomfortable silence descends, and Jack is quick to snatch it up and fix it. "I was filling E.J. in on the wedding idea."

"Yeah?" Dick the pimpled exec's body perks up. "Mr. Speaker?"

"E.J.," the Aussie lilt drifts over my shoulder. "Call me E.J."

Dick fluffs up like an ugly peacock being shown some interest. "E.J.," he tests the name, and by the way his shoulders straighten, you can tell he likes the confidence they provide. "E.J., what do you think of the ambitious undertaking?"

E.J. pulls Jack into his side and mirrors the kiss I put on Sonia's head. Jack's fingers ball up, and I swear I'll pay her a bonus if she knocks out one of his veneered teeth.

"I think if anyone can pull off a stunt in such a short timeframe, my Jack can."

Sonia's grip on me tightens. I want to tell her there's nothing to worry about, she should relax, but before I get a chance, Tessa slips in on the other side of me. E.J.'s eyes widen as he takes her all in, and I want to deck the guy myself. He's got Jack in one arm and eye-fucking Tessa in the other. Dick.

"Hugh." Tessa wraps herself around my arm. "Can I steal you for a second? Dinner seating, you all understand," she explains while prying me loose from Sonia's clutches.

We pad across the room and out on to the balcony. I'm not sure how she does it, but the crisp floral scent of Jack is still floating on the air, and I'm certain if I run my hand along the railing, it will still be warm from her touch.

"What the fuck do you think you're doing?" Tessa's words shake the lovestruck fool out of me.

"Do I need to remind you I'm your boss?"

Tessa plants her hands on her hips and searches the wall behind me before she answers. "Technically, I'm a consultant on loan, but whatever. Why did you invite him?" She points to E.J.

"I didn't. Your partner must have."

"Oh, hell no. Jack wouldn't have invited E.J. here."

"Why not? They're dating."

Tessa chokes out a giggle. "What kind of game is she playing?" she asks more to herself than me.

"They're not dating?"

"Ah, fuck me, I don't know. I haven't seen Jack since the night we . . ." Her hand fishes the air for me to finish the sentence.

"It seemed like such a harmless promise when I made it to Jack's dad." I rake the palm of my hand down my face. "Six years later, and I'm still paying the price of doing the right thing."

"Do you still love her?" Tessa asks.

It's my turn to bark out a laugh. "I'm with Sonia."

"That's not what I asked."

A gust of sea breeze winds its way down my collar. "I never stopped, but it doesn't really matter since she's busy with the douche from down under."

"Douche from down under," Tessa giggles. She crosses her arms and leans up against the railing. "You really don't know how far off the mark you are with that one."

"Sounds like you have some personal experience."

"Only with douches. Present company excluded, although your girlfriend, Sonia, could qualify as one."

I slip off my jacket and wrap it around her.

"Thanks."

"No worries. Give Sonia a break. It can't be easy being the third prettiest girl in the room." I lean up against the rail next to Tessa and nudge a smile out of her.

"Still sporting that silver tongue, I see."

I feel the mischief dancing in my eyes about the same time a blush crawls up Tessa's neck. She's everything that was easy in my life. Living with Dad was hell after Mom passed. I was only twelve when she died. It was like a heavy fog of misery rolled into our house, and all Dad and I could agree on was fighting over Jack and her dad. The summer we turned thirteen, Tessa seemed to blow in, push out all his negative bullshit, and clear a path for me and Jack to find each other. "How'd all those best laid plans turn into life sentences, Tessa?" I don't have to catch her up to speed. She knows exactly what I'm talking about. We were protecting Jack and in turn, damning ourselves.

"I wish I knew, Hugh. But there's got to be a way to fix it all."

"I think Jack and I had our time."

"Love doesn't have an expiration date, Hugh. It's not like a gallon of milk."

"Was there a reason you pulled me out here, Tessa?" I growl.

"Don't take that tone with me. I still know you're afraid of the dark, and butterflies send you screaming like a little girl." She pushes off the rail and heads back to the door. "I have this and lots more information at my disposal. Don't get me started on the reasons you avoid dairy. Lactose intolerance may be tolerated now, but you and I both know the real reason you avoid the white nectar." She puts a hand on the door, and I know we're about to have a Tessa moment when she levels me with a look that makes the full moon pale next to her eyes.

"Don't give up on it just yet, Hugh." She steals a glance over her shoulder. "Some love stories are worth the gut-wrenching middles." My stomach falls when I see Jack cozied up at the bar with Sonia. Long legs veiled by fishnet stockings (How the hell did I miss the fuck-me stockings, and whom was she wearing them for?) dance back and forth from one heel to the other. I know that dance. I know everything about her, and I'd pay with my life if I could forget them all.

"And some love stories are just fairytales told to little girls, Tessa. Come next month, if you're really good at your job, we're going to pull off another hoax and call it a wedding."

"Bitter doesn't look good on you, Hugh." Tessa pushes through the door and leaves me in the summer's breeze. Bitter may not look good on me, but it sure as hell tastes like heaven on my lips.

Eleven

JACK

T*essa seriously has the worst* timing. I'm not even sure she knows who E.J. is. Screw a Cupid! I've got to keep this assignment on the rails. I steal a glance at Hugh and feel that familiar flutter in my gut. Yeah, keeping this disaster on the track, let alone moving forward, is going to be a lot harder than even I imagined . . . and I always imagine the worst.

"You've known her for a long time?" Sonia asks, pulling me from my thoughts. She keeps sneaking peeks over her shoulder at Hugh and Tessa out on the balcony.

At first, I thought Tessa was saving Hugh from a Greek god smack down. Then when Hugh slipped off his coat and tucked Tessa into it, those old feelings of no good started tangling up my gut. I knew the feeling—it was the same one I'd had just after Dad died. I'd find Tessa and Hugh in some sort of heated discussion that always stilted when they noticed me or see stolen looks when they thought I wasn't watching. Toward the end, the unsettling feeling that started out as a nagging pull in my gut became all-consuming. I felt bad for Sonia. It's one thing not knowing anything is going on. It's an entirely different lick of humiliation to watch it all go down.

Hugh left her standing in the middle of the room with all eyes wondering the same thing: who's the girlfriend and who's the shmuck.

I'd been both, and now, it looked like Sonia was going to be the shmuck.

"Yep. We were all best friends growing up. The three musketeers in grade school, and by the time we made it to high school, the names had grown up too."

Confusion flashes across Sonia's face.

"Kids are mean. Hugh and I were the assumed couple. Tessa was our third."

A little "o" forms on Sonia's lips. "I kind of know how that is. Trailer trash from Kentucky moved to California my senior year of high school. There wasn't anything I could do right, except give . . ." A blush stains her neck. "I don't know why I'm telling you this." She peeks up at me through dark eyelashes.

"I have that effect on people."

Sonia spins the umbrella on her drink, steals another peek, and then looks back at me. "I know you don't like me."

"Don't take it personally. I don't like anyone."

She giggles. "You like Tessa."

"We work together, and our boss is always watching. On a good day, I tolerate Tessa."

Sonia shakes her head, searching her drink like the amber liquid is going to reveal some sort of wisdom. "I watch you two together. When your guard is down, the two of you slip into a rhythm that has the whole office in awe. When Hugh joins in"—her voice wavers—"anyone can see how much the three of you mean to each other. It's beautiful. And if I weren't already the jealous type, I'd appreciate the rarity of it all."

I don't know what to do with that. This is truly the admission of a woman who's fallen head over heels for a man I should want to shank with an arrow. Maybe Eros had this wrong. Clearly, one of the two is in love.

"I like you, Sonia."

The admission is like cold water on her face.

"You do?" she whispers.

"Yeah, so I'm going to give you some advice from a girl who fell hard for your guy."

"What's that?" A blush crawls up Sonia's cheeks and into her hairline. She's not Hugh's typical type, but she is the kind of girl you grow old with.

"Keep your eye on Tessa and your hand securely in Hugh's palm."

Sonia's features fall.

"I only wish someone would have given me the same advice about Tessa." My heart lurches at the raw reality of it all. How different I would have done things if I'd known the blissful happiness I'd found with Hugh would end up with an irreparable broken heart. Sonia's muddy brown eyes search mine, looking for the humor in them, but I know all she'll see now is the cold hard truth that loving Hugh Halia with a woman like Tessa around means you better be prepared to fight to the bitter end to keep him by your side. Now, we'll see if the girl has the chops to stick around and earn her happily ever after.

I swivel the seat of my bar stool around as Hugh walks through the door. He fills the frame—hell, he fills the room with his presence. And when those black as night eyes fall on me, it takes every ounce of hurt I've felt for six years to keep the fury I have for him churning.

"Go get your man, Sonia."

She slips off the stool and pads across the room to Hugh, but his eyes are firmly locked with mine. A small tick of a grin pulls at his lips. I answer it by turning my back to him. Just like I should have done all those years ago. Unfortunately, I turn from the snake and meet the charmer who loves all of us.

"What happened to you three?" Gino clucks. His disappointment is nothing compared to the hurt churning in his eyes. "Tessa is off flitting around, you're cold as an ice cube, and Hugh looks like he's dancing on the edge of a very dangerous cliff." His fingers wrap around my hand, warm whiskey eyes impaling me with every ounce of sincerity. "Jack, he was really bad when you left. Then Tessa left . . ." He bows his head like the weight of the memory is even more insufferable than the actual moment. "He was so close to being a tombstone."

"What?" My blood runs cold. It's one thing to wish a person dead, but that's just wishes. I don't think I could handle—

"Just be careful with the pieces when you leave." He pats my hand, cutting off my thought. A gentle smile ghosts across his lips before Gino rounds the bar and ushers our group to our seats.

When I left, I didn't look back. I threw all *my* broken pieces into a bag and headed back to Oxford. I dove into my studies, and six weeks after my declaration of distrust, I was paid a visit by mentor Stacy. She was all pixie hair and bad attitude. She was everything I wanted to be. We'd walk into a pub and every eye would find her. Every guy wanted her and she wanted none of them. She'd let them buy her drinks, fawn all over her, and then turn them down with a simple wave of her hand.

Under Stacy's tutelage, I reached four arrows my first year, which was totally unheard of. But I wasn't happy. I wanted it all. I wanted the power to control love and the ability to take it away. I wanted the full circles of arrows on both my wrists, and I most certainly couldn't be bothered with the two people who'd started me on my path.

"Jack." E.J.'s voice cuts into my thoughts. He pushes my chair in and takes the seat next to me. The fact that he's at one end of the table and Hugh is at the other isn't lost on me, and by the look on Tessa's face across from me, it wasn't lost on her either. E.J. grabs my hand, bringing my fingers to his mouth. The loud exhale from the other end of the table would have been funny if Gino hadn't just dropped the precipitous bombshell in my lap. E.J. and I had better watch ourselves, or we'll end up on Eros's list of wrongs to right.

Twelve

HUGH

The *waves match my mood* this morning. I watch another curl crash and rip up the shore on my way into work. The weather is California beach perfect, and there are a couple of depressions in South America that, if they keep their form, will provide killer waves for next month's Open. It should make me smile, but then I turn into the parking garage.

Son of a bitch.

Mack in my parking spot only adds fuel to the fire Jack and her Aussie boyfriend started last night. I stare at the radio station, listening for Jack's voice. Strangely, the very woman who set me off seems to be the only one who can calm me down. She's pimping Halia's wedding idea this morning. We need to find the perfect couple to put on Halia Surf's Welcome Back wedding cake. The website went live this morning and already we've had a thousand entries.

I turn off the car, race up the five flights of stairs, and turn up the speakers in my office in time to hear the last of a commercial, and then Jack's voice lilts over the airwaves. She's on the hottest morning radio show talking up Halia and the wedding. Tessa was her backbone, which made me laugh. Tessa was never a hide in the shadows kind of girl, but after last week's dinner with the suits and meeting her moon doggie—oh, God, I'm using Jack's Sally Fields's sixties' surfing lingo—she found her place.

"We're back with Halia's representative, Jack Alcantar. So, Halia Surf is hosting a US Open Beach Wedding? What does a couple have to do to enter?"

"All you have to do is log onto Halia's website and upload your video or written statement as to why you feel you deserve the Halia wedding. Voting for the five couples starts next week, June twenty-first." My dick jumps at the vixen-like play in Jack's voice. She is a knockout in person *and* over the airwaves.

"June twenty-first. First day of summer?" the DJ teases.

"It's the first day of summer, and for one lucky couple, it's the first day of an amazing adventure into happily ever after."

"You have a special someone you'd like to add to your wedding cake topper?"

I glare at the speakers. The DJ is totally flirting with *my* Jack. If I can hear it through the speakers, who knows what's happening in the booth.

Jack giggles.

I eye the speaker and feel my smile slip.

"She sure can dish it, can't she?" Tessa says. Leaning in my doorway, she looks like sin on a stick, and if she weren't my best friend, she'd tempt the hell out of a man like me.

"What can I do for you, Tessa?" I turn down Jack's voice.

"You going to this?" Tessa holds up an invitation. "Don't pretend you don't know what it is. Jack got one at the house three days ago."

She tosses the high school reunion invite on my desk.

"This goes on every year. Reunions are supposed to happen every five or ten years . . . like a prison sentence."

Tessa's spine straightens. "They're our friends."

"No, they're not. They're the kids who talked shit about us behind our backs. Or don't you remember the threesome innuendos or the boys who tried to go too far with you because of them?"

Tessa hauls her backside up on my desk, crosses her legs, and leans forward. "I remember every dreadful day of the ordeal. Don't you want to go back and see who got fat? Who's bald? And if Amanda Hickman still gives "U" shaped hickeys?"

I chuckle. "No, I don't."

"C'mon, Hugh. It'll be fun. You can bring Sonia and get the final seal of approval before you put a ring on her finger."

My turn to lean forward. "What makes you think there's a ring?"

She rolls her eyes, hops off my desk, and flips her dirty blonde hair. "The act is dumb, not the girl." Tessa stops in the doorway. "Is she your happily ever after?"

"I don't believe in happily-ever-afters, Jack."

A smirk pulls at her lips. "Tessa. I'm Tessa, not Jack." She pats the door and wiggles her fingers as she leaves. "Your 9 a.m. is here."

"Send him in." I grab my cell from my pocket, pull up Sonia's contact info, and type: **You want to go to a bonfire this weekend?**

I wait for Sonia's reply. It's the first time I've really asked her out on a date, but I didn't think it would take this long. Not when she's all but moved into my house.

Are you asking me on a date?

Yeah, I guess I am, Sonia.

I would, but . . . I have plans.

I shouldn't smile at the text or feel relieved, but I do. I shoot one last text off so I don't feel like a total douche.

I'll be thinking about you.

Speaking of douches, E.J. steps into my office. His Armani suit rivals mine. We stand about the same height, but he's got nothing on me when it comes to looks. Yeah, he's got blond curls that probably knock the girl's bad-boy radar off kilter, but I've got his number. His bright blue eyes size me up, and unlike other dudes, this guy has the gall to think he can stand toe-to-toe with me and then walk away. I bet he's never stepped foot in the ocean he represents, let alone pitted a tube, or worse, worshiped the gentle crest of a wave . . . or my woman.

E.J. folds his arms over his chest. "We gonna stand here like wankers, or we gonna to lay it all out and move on?"

"I'm all for laying you out."

He chuckles, and I swear he's about three steps and an Aussie "g'day mate" from meeting my fist.

"I can see why you were so hard for her to get over." E.J. nods to the chair in front of my desk. I hitch a hip up on the corner of my desk as he slides into the chair. The dude has balls, I'll give him that, but not much more. Few men would let me take the higher advantage given the stare down we just had. I hate to admit it, but I can totally see why Jack fell for this guy too. He's a dick, but he's a dick with confidence to spare.

"What can I do for you this morning, E.J.?"

He steeples his fingers under his chin and admires the view behind my desk for a few moments before speaking. "Your company intrigues me."

"Glad to hear it. Maybe you'll keep that in mind when our sponsorship request comes across your committee's desk."

His eyes cut into me, and a shit-eating grin pulls at his lips. "Jack hasn't told you?"

I shake my head. This is either fabulous news or she is figuring a way to fix the shit storm before I find out.

"Jack probably wanted to share it herself," E.J. offers. I know this guy, though; nothing is ever offered up without a price.

"My girls have been pretty busy with the Open event."

"Yes, I heard. I'm glad Jack and Tessa are doing such a banger job for you." He stands and walks over to the window behind my desk. "This is a magnificent view."

"Glad you like it." An uncomfortable feeling starts to spread through me. I'm not sure what it is. Maybe it's how smooth this guy plays the game. Could be the fact that he feels at liberty to move so freely around my office, which was set up by absolute design to intimidate the hell out of anyone who walked in. But most likely, it's because he has the one thing I still want and can never have.

"I've got a hell of a day, E.J., do you want to tell me the news, or was there another reason you felt the need to drop in?"

E.J. shoots me a look over his shoulder. I know it's meant to slice and dice me, but I'm not in the mood. Haven't been sliced or diced in a good six years.

"First, I've approved your sponsorship, provided you and 'your girls' pull off this wedding event. The A.S.P. loves your enthusiasm and the fact that you're a family-owned business. You have A.A. on speed dial, which doesn't hurt." E.J. pulls out my chair and then sits down on it.

My blood boils.

The balls on this guy have gone from impressive to garish. I temper my reaction. Most people who know me—*hell,* anyone who picked up last month's newspaper—knows I tend to lose the lid on my temper from time to time, and here this guy is turning up the heat on purpose. I slide off the corner of my desk and counter his move by sitting in the chair he just occupied. Back me into a corner and offer me the floor, I don't care, because when the time comes, I'll be staying and he'll be the one walking past the reception desk with my name on the wall.

"Glad to hear it. I know my girls won't let you or me down, E.J."

"Second, I'm not sure if you know my connection to Aiónia Agápi?"

I shake my head. A Greek billionaire owns it, but what does that have to do with a pissy surfer sporting an Australian accent?

"The owner is my father." He lets the words sink in a moment. "He wants to retire, feels that I've had enough life experiences, plus my mother's been begging him to take her on an around-the-world cruise." E.J. rolls his eyes. "What can I say? The man is still head over heels for his wife, all these years later."

"Congratulations, but what does this have to do with me and Halia?"

"It doesn't. It's about Jack. My father wants to promote her, but I'm not sure how I feel about giving her free reign of her own territory."

"Jack's a competent, kickass lady. A.A. should count their stars they have someone like her. So should you."

"I like my ladies a little more docile. Your Sonia is more along the lines of what I'm looking for."

I want to offer Sonia up, but even I'm not that big of a dick. This guy is revolting. What the hell does Jack see in him?

"Again, I'm not sure what this has to do with Halia or me. Jack's happy where she is. If you're asking if I see a future for her here at Halia . . ." The thought blossoms and explodes in two seconds, sending shards of shattered hope billowing into my soul. "Even if I wanted her here, there's no way she'd be happy here."

"So you don't want her?"

I shake my head because I know my voice isn't strong enough to carry the resolve that's needed to convince E.J.

E.J. rises to his feet and starts to the door. "Well, then, I guess I need to figure something else out."

That "something" from earlier in the meeting starts thrashing around in my chest.

"You're not seriously thinking of canning the girl, are you?"

"I don't see what everyone else seems to be going on about."

"Then look harder."

"Says the bloke who slept with her best friend. G'day, mate."

Thirteen

JACK

The sand is still cool even though the early morning sun and monsoonal flow is heating up the air. I'm not sure how Tessa talked me into going to the reunion tonight. Could be the three days of persistent hounding finally wore me down. I'd forgotten how she was when an idea rooted in her brain. Last night—or was it this morning? Really, what is two in the morning between friends?—Tessa sat herself on the edge of my bed and refused to leave or let me sleep until I agreed to go with her to the bonfire. I was so tired, I'd do anything if it meant she'd let me go back to sleep. But after her visit, with the house quiet enough, my thoughts became like little children screaming and running through my mind. Four hundred and seventy-two sheep into my insomnia fest, I threw back the covers and headed to the kitchen to start sifting through the thousands of couple responses we'd received on Halia's Wedding

Couple contest.

I'd sorted them into three piles: not a chance, hopeless romantic, and epic love story. Focusing our concentration on epic love story made the most sense. It would make for better print, and if the couple was good looking, we'd win both the event and the PR lottery.

By five in the morning and three trips to the Keurig, my eyes were crossing and the walls of my sandcastle home were sliding in on me. I slipped out of the condo, not wanting to wake Tessa, and headed down the beach to clear my head. An hour later, I'm at the Seal Beach jetty and my mind is no clearer than when I started.

Just the opposite. Too many emotions and what-ifs and what went wrongs are churning around

I start back; the sun is peeking in between the harbor and the rooftops of the Surfside Colony. Surfers are suiting up for their early morning sets, and an itch I haven't felt the need to scratch in years starts to tickle. Surfing. I was far from noteworthy, just a girl on a board trying to keep up with all the guys. Tessa wouldn't put a toe in the water without charts and reports backing her up, but me—in true form—I dove head first into the waves. Hugh always seemed to end up right by my side.

I walk to the ridge where the dry sand slopes down and transforms into wet silt and the shore. Surfers dot the horizon, bobbing and waiting. It's such a clear representation of my life, bopping from city to city and working toward arrow fifty. Warm sunlight cascades over my face, and I can't help but feel every muscle in my body instantly relax. This place has always been my refuge—even when it was my prison. There is something about a coast sprinkled with surfers that makes you sit back and realize the world is much bigger than you and whatever problem you're wrestling. The sand behind me swishes under someone's feet. A hulking shadow blocks out the sun, and my heart drops before I hear the first tenor.

"I have a spare board up at my place if you're interested," Hugh's voice is full of hope and a hint of question.

Of course, he'd end up by my side. Fate always did have a bitchy sense of humor. I shield my eyes and look up. "I thought you were living in the harbor."

Hugh plants his board and settles down next to me. A black wetsuit clings to every inch of his legs, leaving little for the imagination. The latex arms hang off his waist and all that bronze skin is now on display. Sculpted abs and a chiseled chest rope off into biceps you could lose yourself for days exploring. His hair catches in the morning breeze. Hugh is the epitome of a surf god.

Corded arms rest on his knees, giving me an amazing view of his triceps and abs. All those girlish fantasies of licking homemade ice cream off every inch of Hugh come racing back with the whoosh of the waves.

"I haven't lived there since college." He spares me a look and then focuses back on the ocean. "Should have known fate would've sat your cute little ass on my strand of the beach."

I want to object, but I'm thinking fate didn't have anything to do with it; a Greek god named Eros who was hellbent on me proving my immortal worth is more likely the culprit.

"Had a heart-to-heart with your boyfriend, E.J., yesterday." The ropy muscle that runs down Hugh's neck revolts at the name.

E.J. has that effect on people.

The girls love him, and the boys want to pummel him. It's a good thing he has that don't-fuck-with-me godly air about him, or some guys would actually entertain the idea of walloping the dude.

"Sounds like it went stellar," I say.

"He didn't tell you?"

I shake my head.

"He's stepping down from A.S.P after the Open. That's why he's here." Hugh lets the unspoken *not because of you* catch on another breeze headed out to sea. I'd be hurt if there really was something happening between E.J. and me. I lean back in the sand and dig my toes in further. The crashing waves fill the silence between us.

"Did he say why?" I finally take Hugh's bait and ask.

"Says your boss, the head of A.A., is stepping down."

I sit straight up. "What?" Now he's got my attention. Eros hadn't hinted at retiring. I didn't even know gods could retire.

"Don't you guys talk?"

"Not about business." I let my own inference hang in the air. E.J.'s been off playboying it up since before I joined the Corps. The only thing we really shared was a Sydney zip code and the occasional publicity-fueled run-ins.

Hugh gives me a sideways glance. The hints of a smile that could get a girl like me in serious trouble pull at the small lines around his eyes. Time has been way too kind to this man.

"He say anything about timeframes?"

"Jack, I really don't feel comfortable cluing you in on your man's business."

"Yeah, well, that's not a first for you."

"What's that mean?"

"Nothing," I sulk and dig my toes back into the sand.

Hugh goes back to searching the horizon for swells. Growing up, we could spend hours on the shore searching the horizon for our future and running from our parents' past. The moon would pull the currents. The ocean would pull Hugh. And Hugh would pull me. He was my gravity and at one point in time, I thought he was my future.

"What's bothering you, Jack?"

"Who says there's anything bothering me?" I go still. Hugh always knew when I lied. He said I could only sit still when I had a problem or a lie brewing in my gut. One way or another, he'd always get it out of me.

"You're on the beach, in front of my house, staring at waves like a girl jonesing for a hit of rebellion, at six in the morning. You may have been gone for six years, Jack, but that doesn't mean I don't know you." He reaches out and snags my chin between his fingers. His touch is like fire rekindling all the embers of him I'd long thought had turned cold.

My pulse thunders in my ears as his black as night eyes search mine. I was a fucking fool to think I could breeze in here, do my job, and leave. I swallow over the scared-shitless lump in my throat.

"What's going on, Jacquelyn?"

I blink hard at the sound of my full name on his lips. He only ever used it when he knew I was dancing too close to an edge.

I missed that safety net.

I missed this life.

I missed him.

Hugh wets his lips, sending my pulse skittering. "God, you're beautiful." His fingers holding my chin turn soft and trail along my cheek.

"Come surfing with me," he pleads, pulling me closer to him, and my rebellious body follows his lead. My heart thrashes against its cage. It would be so easy to let go for old time's sake. But where would that lead me? He hasn't changed. He's got Tessa flirting around the office, Sonia in his bed, and me on the beach. Nothing about Hugh Halia has changed. I'd chase him down the tunnel of love and wind up falling off the cliffs when I found him in bed with someone else. Only this time, there'd be no Cupid Corps to save me. I pull away from the warmth of his palm.

"I've been in those waters with you before, Hugh. I can't afford to paddle out there again."

The fire behind his eyes dies along with a piece of me.

"You sure you don't want a board?"

I roll my eyes and point to my now sandy sweat suit. "No suit."

"Go naked."

I choke out a laugh. "Yeah, I know how you wax your boards. Although, it would get me out of the bonfire tonight."

"Ahh, you got talked into the reunion too?"

"Yeah, Tessa get to you?" What was the girl up to? This was my training ops, not a chance for her to showboat for the bosses. But if she knew Eros was stepping down . . . Oh, Tessa. Shimming up to the new boss isn't going to get you your arrows any faster.

"No, Sonia. She found the invite."

A pang of jealousy lets loose as I look back at the A-row of homes in the Surfside Colony. I lick at the question on my lips. I don't normally want to know anything about our clients, but Hugh's different, and part of me can't stand not asking, "Sonia living with you?"

A full-on grin consumes Hugh. Those devilish eyebrows crawl up his face in amusement.

"You're not the only one with pretty serious significant others." He stands up and dusts of the sand. "The board's up at the house, there's a wet suit your size in the outdoor shower. You won't be totally naked . . ."

Those delicious muscles that form a v and dip into his wetsuit ripple as the thought tempts him.

"I can drive you home after." He slips his arms into the suit, pulls the cord to zip up the back, and shoots me an *I dare you* look that's so hot, it could turn the sand around me to glass.

"It's the whitewashed house with black shutters." Hugh nods to the row of houses, plucks his board from the sand, and slips it under his arm. "Might wash away some of those demons you look like you're fighting." He shoots me a boyish smile, and despite every resolve I ever vowed, that piece of my heart that will always be dedicated to Hugh Halia starts to melt.

Fourteen

HUGH

It was a shitty set this morning. Mainly because I was busy watching the coast, waiting for Jack to get pissed enough to paddle out and shove my dare down my throat. I could see her contemplating it while I waited for my first set to roll in. I took out my frustration on a small breaker. By the time I got back out to wait for my second set, Jack was gone, and I was left with the three words that have been banging around in my head for the past eight days. *He's my boyfriend.* That along with her *and it's pretty serious* comment had me paddling in after my third set.

I didn't know words could dropkick a guy in the balls, but that's exactly what her velvet-laced syllables with barbs did. Jack's cocky boyfriend was so lucky the US Open people were watching, or I'd have pummeled his pompous smirk all the way across the pond and back to the land of down under.

Prior to this morning, Jack's made herself pretty scarce in the office since our disastrous dinner eight days ago. Every time I schedule a meeting with her, Tessa shows up. The excuses started off pretty convincingly.

Jack's meeting with the vendors.

Jack's evaluating the site.

Jack's running logistics with the people at the US Open.

The capper was when Tessa said Jack was pitching Halia to the A.S.P. for their World Championship Tour. I had to buy that one when E.J. showed up and gave me the verbal confirmation that Halia was going International.

A small piece of me thought for sure the dude was slinging bullshit and Jack was going along for the ride so she didn't have to face me. I pick up the letter sitting on my desk where Tessa left it. It was from A.S.P confirming their interest in helping take Halia International with a spot as one of their main tour sponsors. Now, I'm the one with shit on my face. Tessa handed me the slap to my ego after I threatened to "Open" a can of my own whoop-ass on Jack's boyfriend if she couldn't be bothered to make a meeting. I'm not sure if she had laughed at that pun or at me. It was as surly as I was, and I'd meant every single syllable of the threat. If I couldn't get Jack to meet me on a business level, then you could be damn certain I'd threaten the man she was dating.

Then, this morning happened.

I walked down to the ocean, thinking I could wash away my own set of demons, and walked right into the lady who seemed to be creating them all. I had to ram my palms into my eyes to make sure I wasn't hallucinating when I saw her long blonde hair waving in the wind. Sitting against a backdrop of early morning purple skies and pink clouds, she looked just like she had when we were growing up. All fresh-faced and full of possibility. All those harsh angles and pursed lips business was gone, and it was just Jack.

My Jack.

I'd contemplated sitting down where I was and watching the enigma for as long as possible. I knew if she'd looked back and found me staring, I'd not only lose the small strides of not having her sneer when I walked in a room, but I could see her saying "fuck the job" and leaving all together. She'd been back in Huntington Beach for three weeks, and every day, I kept expecting that ice casing she walked around in to crack or at least start thawing.

Her back went rigid the moment the sand announced my arrival. I wasn't prepared for the way she whirled around on me, though. Skittish and ready for a fight had me wondering what the hell was going on with my girl.

What was she up to?

The waters churned in her eyes when she saw me take a few steps closer and plant my board. Hey eyes calmed for a bit when I sat down and let her be quiet, but that wasn't for long.

"You ready?" Tessa's voice interrupts my thoughts. "Jack's in the boardroom."

"Nice of her to join us," I mutter, scooping up the file of potential candidates for the wedding fiasco.

"Be nice; she had a long night." Tessa leans up against the doorjamb and examines her nails.

She's up to something too. I know that casual look means trouble, just like I know Jack on the beach before daybreak means distress.

"Her email this morning was time-stamped 4:30 a.m. What's got her all churned up?"

"Bonfire." Tessa turns her attention to the files in her arms, but I catch the quick peek gaging my reaction.

"Hmm."

"You're going, right?"

"Tessa, between you and Sonia, man. This thing happens every year; why is this year so special?"

Indignation crawls across Tessa's furrowed eyebrows. "It's the first time we'll all be there. Jack hasn't been back in six years. She's missed all the reunions, even the fancy holiday five-year at the Hilton. You know how she loves that place at Christmas time, so . . . big deal."

I chuckle. "Yeah, did it ever occur to you that you and I aren't the only things that have changed over the past six years?" I walk to the front door and tweak Tessa's nose. "She's different, Tessa."

An expression that proves my point purses Tessa's lips. "I know."

I take a minute and think about what I'm going to say next. Not because the weight of the words are so bad, but the fact that I'm asking the question is. It means all those reassuring promises I'd given Tessa six years ago were bullshit.

"You think letting Jack catch us in bed was a mistake?"

The words hit Tessa hard. If she was worrying her lip before, she straight up starts chewing it now. I don't get to hear her answer. Not over the loud gasp next to us.

Sonia's eyes are the size of saucers, and her hand covers her mouth like she's about to throw up. "She was your best friend. How could you?"

Tessa flinches as the accusation and judgment fall solely at her feet. Every bad thing has always been chalked up to Tessa. When word got out about Jack finding Tessa and me in bed at my dad's house, everyone assumed it was Tessa who was the aggressor.

She'd taken it like a champ.

"Sonia," I caution. "That was six years ago and there are explanations."

"It's okay, Hugh," Tessa interrupts. "It's not even worth the explanation. It wasn't then and isn't now."

Tessa steps around me, heading toward the boardroom. I reach out to stop Sonia, but she has other plans.

"Jack warned me about Tessa." The heat coming off her wants to burn me, but I'm immune. She's good and pissed, and all that fury is going to end up directed at Tessa unless I man up.

"That was my past." I tighten my grip on Sonia's arm and haul her up onto her toes. "You knew who I was before you jumped into bed with me. I'm still that man. Something you should think about if you want to continue this relationship."

Her nostrils flare. "Is that what this is?"

"What?"

"Are we in a relationship?" I hate the way her eyes search me. "This is what you call what we're doing?" She does a judgmental flip of her hair like she's got me nailed and ready to crucify. "Because this morning, I roll over and find you, not only gone, but on the beach with Jack, holding her face like you're contemplating all sorts of sordid things. Then I find you and Tessa all cozied up in a doorway reliving bedtime memories." Her lip quivers but I don't fall so easily. "So please, tell me, Hugh. Is this how you do relationships? If it is, I'm not quite sure I want to press on with you." Sonia yanks her arm back, stumbling back when her heels touch the floor. She scurries down the hall, casting a disgusted glance over her shoulder before she pushes into the boardroom.

A hard smack on the back shakes me out of my stupor. We need to tie a bell around my half-brother.

"I'm not sure if I'm impressed she had the gumption to stand toe-to-toe with you, brother, or if I'm turned on that she admitted to spying on you and Jack this morning."

Mack's frame is identical to mine. There is no doubting he is my father's son. Right down to the arrogant way he's considering Sonia as a new challenge.

"Given the guilty look on your face, I'd say Sonia wasn't far off the mark with her evaluation. Were you contemplating sordid and wild things with Jack in the sand?"

Stepping around Mack, I don't answer but that doesn't stop him.

"C'mon, little brother. We're family. It's okay to kiss and tell. Didn't Daddy teach you that?"

Yeah, he taught me all about kissing and telling. Which was one of the reasons I agreed to Jack's dad's promise and asked Tessa to do the unthinkable to her best friend.

Salt air and burning driftwood fill the coastline. Given the day I've had, it's about the only thing that can calm me down. The wedding meeting with all my exes went about as well as could be expected. It was bitter cold. Full of curt nods and quipped answers. Nobody cried, nobody pointed fingers, but there was a threatening undercurrent flowing through the room. We stuck to the agenda, and at the end of the hour, we'd narrowed the wedding choices down to six couples. The couples weren't spectacular. In fact, they were downright boring. When I'd asked Jack to see the other file and then scoffed at the label—hopeless romantic—I'd thought all three of my ladies were going to attack. I took the file anyway. This was my company, not a democracy and certainly not the hallways of Marina High School.

Mack was no help. He sat in the corner, watching all the drama unfold like a teenager instead of a man who had his undergrad from Harvard and MBA from the University of Southern California. I was an only child growing up, so the concept of sibling rivalry was completely lost on me. To me, Mack was just as big an asshole as E.J.—who came to pick up Jack for lunch.

Tessa said she had location meetings the rest of the day. Jack overheard Sonia at the front desk tell me she was feeling sick. I'm certain she didn't miss Sonia's declaration that she was heading to *her* house, not mine. Part of me was overjoyed I'd found a way to reclaim some of my personal space back. Jack clocked me with a stupid boy look of her own and told me to send the girl some flowers. After two hours, I sent some flowers over to Sonia's apartment to prove I'm not like Jack's boyfriend. Tonight, I'm well on my way to satisfying my own plans of burying my women troubles at the bottom of a bottle of Fireball Whiskey.

Fiddler on the Roof's "Matchmaker" makes my phone jump on the desk. I eye the dancing phone, knowing its Tessa; the girl keeps hijacking my phone and changing all the ringtones. Sonia's "Sex and Candy" ringtone nearly got me a pan to the back of the head when it went off while I was asking her to call my lost phone. It was my skull or my pocketbook, so I had to come clean about Tessa programing my phone, which made this morning even more awkward. Add to that a text from Tessa saying she agreed with me and we should come clean to Jack. I rub at the headache between my eyes. Sad thing is, the only thought that keeps circling my slightly intoxicated brain is: I wonder what Jack's ringtone is?

I swipe the dancing phone and bite out, "What?"

"Really? That's how you answer your phone now? How many shots of Fireball have you put away?"

"Hi, Tessa. How are you this evening? Better?" I pour shot nine of the amber liquid.

"How many?" Tessa enunciates, and I can all but see her hands on her hips and her irritated toe tapping for me to hurry up with the right answer.

"What do you want, Tessa?"

"First, I want to know how many shots you've done. That'll let me know how to proceed with number two: What time are you going to the bonfire?"

I throw back shot nine and nearly spit it across the room. "Ha! There's no way in hell I'm going to the bonfire of girlfriends past."

Tessa sighs. "You didn't answer my first question, so you forfeit the right to answer the second."

"Tessa, you live in chaos. Your entire life is out of order. If anyone needs to be asking how many shots someone's done, it's me . . ." My rant trails off.

Tessa's mom, the hot-mess airline attendant, held it together when she was taking care of other people, but when it came to Tessa, she'd touch down three sheets to the wind and expect her daughter to clean up whatever chaos Mommy Dearest left behind.

I listen to the silence and crackle of whatever she's cooking on the other end of the phone.

Please, God. Let her say something.

She has to know I don't mean it.

Damn, I really am a douche.

"I'm sorry, Tessa," I whisper. I mean it.

There's a few more seconds of silence. I know the girl well enough to know there's a tear chasing a well-worn path down her make-up perfect face.

"How many, Hugh?"

I'm just as bad as her fucking alcoholic mom. I swallow hard over the word. "Nine."

"That's better than nineteen."

Leave it to Tessa to find the silver lining.

"Can you make it to twenty-six, or do I need to pick you up?

I know she means lifeguard station twenty-six, not the age and sure as hell not the shot count. That's the thing about real friends. It doesn't matter how much shit you throw at them; they're always there, ready to take more and be by your side. Distance may have kept us apart, but time is insignificant when you have the right friends by your side. Tessa knows this. And I know there's no way I'm getting out of the beach reunion tonight.

"I'm good. I'll see you at eight." I reach for the jug of whiskey and then put it down. Tessa, the girl who takes everyone's shit and asks for nothing in return. One of these days, she's going to find someone who's going to come and collect all the favors she's owed. He'll probably sweep her off her feet in the process.

"Beach closes at ten, so I'll see you at seven," she says, disconnecting before I can answer . . . before I can wiggle off the hook.

Fifteen

JACK

The smell of bacon and fresh-baked bread means Contessa Maria Saint Cloud, aka Tessa, isn't playing fair. She's probably even got a freshly sliced pineapple all chunked up and waiting for me to devour on the kitchen bar. I kick off my high heels and toss my keys into the seashell container.

"Pizza'll be ready in fifteen. I pulled an outfit for you. It's on your bed."

"Why do I need an outfit? And why do I need you to pull it for me? My clubbing days are long gone. You weren't even in the same time zone to witness them."

Tessa's blonde head pokes around the corner. "We're going to the bonfire tonight. And the only reason I didn't witness your club ho-ing days is because you wouldn't let me explain."

I pick up my briefcase and head down the hall. I know Tessa; she'll stand her ground and stare down a charging bull. The girl's got an iron spine.

"You, my best friend, slept with my boyfriend—"

"You didn't catch me sleeping with him, Jack." Marinara sauce from a wooden spoon splatters to the floor as Tessa pops her hip. "You caught me in bed with him."

"And there's a difference?"

Tessa shifts her weight to the other hip. "Yes!" She unfolds her arms and sends another spray of marinara sauce onto the wall. "Open your fucking eyes, Jack!" She turns on her heels and disappears around the corner. "Don't worry, I'll clean up this mess too."

"I'm not going to the bonfire, Tessa." I stand in the hall, waiting for her to answer.

"Tessa," I call out, knowing full well she isn't going to answer. "I know you can hear me, and I'm not going to the bonfire. I don't need to see the people who tormented me the three years you were there and then decimated me the year you and Hugh were gone. I don't need to be reminded of the humiliation by my classmates. I've got you living with me, and if it wouldn't earn me a lightning bolt on the heart, I'd fucking disobey Eros and kick your slutty ass to the curb." My angry words bounce off the rafters. Sweat trickles down my back, and I know the bitch won't come defend herself. The melody of "You're Addicted to Love" accompanies the soft vibrations of my cell in my hand. Tessa and her damn ringtones. The day just got fucking worse.

"Hey, Boss."

Bonfires suck.

Sand in your jeans sucks.

Plastering on a smiley face to make nice to those you know for damn sure are going to be talking behind your back sucks.

I follow Tessa up the sand dune as we make the hike to lifeguard station twenty-six. Given the packed free parking lot, my classmates are still cheap, despite the six-figure spoons they grew up with in their mouths. Tessa's ear-to-ear smile is genuine, though. I don't know how she does it. These people were horrid teens; I can only imagine how heinous they are as adults. We near the bonfire rings; a scene shockingly similar to how I imagine *Lord of the Flies* went down seems to be happening. Adults reliving their misspent youth by downing beers hidden in brown paper bags or hard alcohol in red solo cups. Yep, I've reunioned enough.

"Oh. My. God!" The squeal from behind me rattles the fillings in my teeth. I thought for sure the high-pitched voice would tone down once Marina's Social Queen graduated. I don't want to turn around. I'm not sure I can take the assault. Delilah Reynolds was high school perfection. A hundred pounds of perfect skin and blonde hair that screamed school spirit. You'd think with all that pep, she'd be a captain of the cheerleaders, but no, she was so picture-perfect perky, even the cheer squad couldn't contain her. Unfortunately, she had a thing for Hugh, and that made all that pep sour when she looked at me.

"Jaquelyn Alcantar!"

I turn around ready to embrace the daggers, but where a hundred-pound pile of pep should have stood is the shadow of the girl we once knew. She isn't overweight. Just the opposite—she's a waif, a whisper of the girl she'd been in high school and well under her barely hundred-pound, high school weight. Her skin is tanned to the point of leather, and that luxurious blond hair all the girls dreamed of is dry as straw.

"Delilah? Wow." I look at Tessa, dumbfounded. "Wow."

"I know, right?" She twirls in the skirt that looks like she manhandled it off a thirteen-year-old. "Some of us haven't changed a bit." She places a hand on her hip like she's the prime example of the statement. "Some of us have." Delilah rakes her eyes over me (finding me lacking, as usual) before shifting her glare. "Tessa." There's frost in her voice.

"Delilah, glad to see all the surgeries went well." Tessa nods to the obvious implants.

I giggle.

Delilah attempts her signature hair flip, but all that processed hair barely flits over her shoulder. "How's your mom?"

I feel Tessa go rigid next to me. Tessa may have broken every best-friend, decent-person rule there was in the world, but she doesn't need to be crucified for her mother's sins. If anyone is going to publicly shame Tessa, it's going to be me.

"Her mom's doing just fine, Delilah. How's your dad?" I lob back for Tessa. Yeah, I haven't forgotten *Beach Talk*'s (the online tabloid Delilah now works for) exclusive on how the mayor, Delilah's daddy, got caught with his suit pants around his ankles and a hooker attached to his mayoral gavel.

The color that isn't fake-and-baked on drains from Delilah's face. "Drinks are by the sign-in table. Not that either of you will need a 'Hello My Name Is' tag. Everyone knows your names. The threesome scandal you left behind is still whispered in the halls of Marina High. Kind of like an urban legend. Then there's your family's contribution to the gossip mill, Contessa Saint Cloud."

Tessa's shoulders sink under the condemnation, and that small vault in me that's locked away the last remaining friendly feeling I had for Tessa springs free.

Delilah's eyebrows crawl up her face, daring me to say something.

Say anything.

I look around. We've drawn quite the crowd now. God, it really is like high school all over again. The gossip-hungry hyenas circle us, just like they did six years ago. And just like six years ago, Hugh Halia is nowhere to be found.

I step in front of Tessa and hear her pull in a small breath of relief. My hand fishes for hers. This doesn't change how I feel about her, I remind myself. Six years of vitriol bubble up from the dark places that only a teenage girl who suffered through high school knows—that place where every judgmental look, every rotten comment, every hurtful judgment is stored. It's garbage waiting for the woman to come and not just take it out but light it on fire for all to see. I had been that girl, and now I am that woman, and I'm going to light up Delilah with the heat of her own rubbish. I step into Delilah's space, my cheek next to hers so only she and I can hear the truth I'm about to tell.

"Momma Saint Cloud wasn't the only one doing the principal, now was she, Delilah? And Momma Saint Cloud wasn't the only who got knocked up with the principal's baby. She just happened to be the one who got knocked up and *kept* the principal's baby," I caution.

The air around me disappears. The muscle in Delilah's cheek ticks. That may be all the retribution I'm going to witness, but that slight tick in her tan-and-weathered face is enough.

"Now, you're going to apologize to Tessa. You're going to give her one of those famous fake hugs. And you're going to tell the rest of the pariah at the bonfire both Tessa and I are fantastic people and you can't believe you didn't see how cool we were in high school."

Delilah's body starts to pull away, but my hand snakes out, grabbing her upper arm and stopping the movement. "Do it now and for the rest of your life, or I swear to all the gods in this world and beyond, I will air *all* your dirty laundry."

Delilah's breath hitches.

"Nod that you understand." Power surges through me. It has nothing to do with Cupid powers and everything to do with finally taking back the control this girl, this group, held over me. Held over Tessa. I give a slight shake to Delilah's arm when she doesn't answer and then smile when her head bobs in agreement.

"Go."

I push her away and turn on my heels. Too much of that could go to a person's head. Besides, these are Tessa's demons more than mine. I could leave tomorrow and know that my name and what just happened will be on the lips of every Marina grad for years to come.

Ocean waves roar their approval in the distance. Vindication pounds in time with my pulse. I give Tessa a wink as I walk by her. A second later, I hear the "umph" of Tessa landing a solid Delilah hug and the start of public admittance into the in-crowd. It's not the whole school, but it's seventy-five of the biggest gossips our classes have to offer, so I know by morning, news will have made its rounds.

I look back; the red and orange glow of the fire pit casts its inner circle, and Tessa is finally inside. I walk down to the ocean. The quarter moon is doing its best to tip the waves in silver light, but it's nothing compared to a summer full moon. I kick off my sandals and let the cool sand squish in between my toes. I find myself at the small drop where the dry sand lets loose and tumbles down into the shore.

It's my favorite spot.

The crest of sloping sand was where I'd sneak out and plan all my fabulous adventures. When I was a kid, six or seven, my dad would find me at all hours of the night here. The first couple of times, you could see the worry lines etched in his forehead. Looking back, he should have hauled me back to the house, screaming *you're grounded*. But that wasn't my dad. Instead, he'd sit by my side and listen. When I turned twelve, Hugh found me on the crest. He'd planted his surfboard in the sand and sat out the morning set. I didn't think much of it then, but now I know it was him choosing me over the thing he loved most. I turn my head into the breeze and let the memories mix with the air. Both are cold, and only one is soothing.

The sand behind me crunches, and I'm surprised Tessa's given up on the fabulous life so soon. Growing up, it was all she wanted. I never understood it, but then again, my eyes were always firmly focused on Hugh. The memory squeezes my heart and I hate the pain. This was why I'd left. This was why I'd sworn I'd never come back. I guess returning to the scene of the crime was just as dangerous whether it was your first arrow or your last.

"Jack," the deep-timbered voice startles me.

I don't dare look up. Hugh and moonlight were a deadly combination when I was a girl. I can only imagine what the duo would be like now. Instead, I focus on the missing arrow on my wrist.

He shuffles his feet next to me in the sand. At twenty-four, Hugh's a savvy businessman; he knows how to play the game of people, but then again, so do I.

Tan feet sink into the sand. The muscle in his calf flexes, catching my eye, and my lungs tighten. *Who has that reaction to a man's a calf?* My gaze travels up his leg, over the khaki cargo shorts, and stop a moment to admire the bulge in his shorts. My cheeks heat up, and my gaze quickly skitters to Hugh's waist and up the washboard stomach I was treated to this morning. Tan arms are folded over a crisp black t-shirt with Halia's logo on the chest. A cord in his neck flexes. By the time I get to Hugh's face, he's looking down at me with amusement in his eyes. The twisted smirk disappears as he says, "That was pretty amazing what you did back there."

"Delilah had it coming." I pull my eyes from him and stare out at the ocean. There are some moments time can't erase. The memory of Hugh and me on a beach . . .

"That's not what I'm talking about."

I crane my neck and risk another look. I know it's a mistake when Hugh looks back at me, all the amusement replaced with the heat of summers past.

My heart thrashes against its cage, begging for me to allow it loose again.

"Yeah, well, if anyone's going to publicly trash Tessa, it's going to be me."

Hugh shifts his weight.

I know he's searching the waves. We'd done a couple of night surfs when we were sixteen and seventeen. Glow sticks, moonlight—we'd only ride one or two sets before all that slick heat and tension would get the better of us. Another flash of heat races up my face. This one from my very core. *God, what's wrong with me*?

As if he knows what I'm thinking, Hugh sits down next to me. His leg brazenly brushes up against mine. He rests his arms on his knees and links his fingers.

"We had some pretty great times in this water." He nudges me with his knee, and my pulse kicks into overload.

"Yep." That's it. I'm reduced to one-word answers.

Hugh runs a hand through his already-combed hair. I know him well enough to know that's his signal for a subject change. I also know when he sends a second hand through his mussed-up hair, the subject isn't one he's looking forward to.

"She's a good girl, Jack."

Yeah, I don't like this subject either.

"You would know," I toss back.

"Goddamn, Jack. At some point, we get over this."

"*We*?" The indignation chokes me. "*We* get over this? *We* didn't get into this. You and Tessa did! You and Tessa crawled right on into bed and cozied up behind my back. You. You." I force the next words out. "You shattered me, Hugh." I scurry to my feet and start to leave before I shatter all over again. Hugh snags the waistband of my jeans and pulls me back down, landing hard in his lap. My fists look so tiny against his chest, but then again, I was always an insignificant spot against the colorful Hugh.

"Jack," he whispers. His tongue wets his lips like my name on them are a delicacy. It sends my stomach flipping, memories careening back in time. All I have to do is lean forward, press my lips to his and—I cut the thought off. Where Hugh and I were concerned, time didn't matter. What we had. What he and Tessa destroyed. It would always haunt me.

The bite of tears fills my eyes. I would have followed him anywhere. Done anything for him. I search his eyes and I need to know.

"What did I do to deserve that, Hugh?"

The tip of his finger skids along my cheek. His eyes search all the familiar planes of my face like he's discovering me all over again. But when his gaze latches on to mine, a spark arcs through us, and I can't help but hope that he has an answer that makes sense.

"It wasn't what you thought, Jack." His eyes search mine. The heat of him surrounds me, consumes me.

"Why?" I press.

His fingers dig into the fabric of my sweater. For a moment, I think he's going to answer that one question that's haunted me for six years. That moment that sent me spiraling off into space.

"You won't like the answer, Jack. You either hate Tessa and me, or you hate the answer I can give you. I'm asking you to trust me. Trust that what we did, it was for you." Hugh hangs his head. It's everything in me not to give in. To tell him it doesn't matter.

But it does.

"I can't live with that answer." I push against him to stand and leave, but his grip around me tightens.

"And I can't live with you leaving. Not again, Jack."

"That's the thing, I never came back. Not for you." I push against Hugh again. Part of me rejoices in the fact that he won't let me go. The other part of me knows this is Hugh. He wants what he can't have. I'm only a chase, and once he's done with the ride, he'll leave me in pieces. "I spent the afternoon with Sonia."

Hugh's gaze snaps back. The hard, cold look in his eyes returns. "Why?"

"I was worried about her. She didn't ask to be dragged into this nightmare of exes." His grip loosens on me, and the silver ring of fire around his eyes flickers.

"And you did?"

"She's a good person, Hugh. And I get the distinct feeling that despite all your bags of shit, she really does care for you." I shift in Hugh's lap, trying to slide off, but his hands keep me firmly in place.

"You're adding love expert onto your resume?"

If he only knew.

"You feel that way about the douche from down under? He deserves a shot with you but I don't?"

I chuckle. "Don't let E.J. hear you call him that. And you had your shot."

"I could take him."

"I'm sure you think you could."

Hugh pulls me closer to him. His cinnamon-whisky breath swirls around me, sending all those good senses I have skittering.

"I'd fight heaven and earth for you, Jack."

"You'd be fighting for a memory," I whisper. "Sonia's a good girl. She deserves your effort."

"You can push me away, Jack. But you and I both know that what we had . . . it hasn't gone away. I can feel your body coming alive just sitting in my lap. Don't you want to see where we can take this? Don't you want to come home?"

He's right. My heart is pounding in my chest. My thighs are on fire, and the deepest part of me is wet with anticipation. I could give it all up and dive head first into the memory of us. Unleash it from its watery grave.

But where would that leave me?

Eros would strip me of my curse and send me on my way.

No Corps.

No purpose.

And vulnerable to the next time Hugh tripped and fell into someone else's bed.

"I've seen where this takes us." I push off his lap, and this time, Hugh lets me go. "And this hasn't been my home for a very long time."

I grab my shoes and pause a moment. The words sit on the tip of my tongue. The words that will let him go forever. "All those memories, I've long since burned and buried them. If you're feeling anything, it's one-sided. I've moved on, Hugh. Maybe it's time you do the same."

Hugh's spine straightens. The emotions rolling off him are palpable. Even as I walk away, my heart sinks its fingers into the thought of Hugh and me together again. It's a bastard of an organ that's only purpose is to keep you living until the next time you shatter. I scratch at the missing arrow space on my wrist. This mission is off. I'm supposed to be training Tessa, and instead, she seems to be doing everything in her power to get me and Hugh . . .

"That little bitch." I fish out my cellphone from my purse and dial the only number that holds the key to my future. "Eros, we need to talk."

The sounds of steel drums tinkle in the background.

"I'm sorry, sweet Jack. I'm not in the country. Psyche surprised me with a Caribbean cruise. How is everything in Huntington Beach?"

The knowledge Eros is floating in a different ocean than I am fuels my response. "Not good, Eros. When did my final mission become a test?"

"Jack." There's caution in Eros voice. A warning that tells me I'm tiptoeing very close to a line that I don't dare cross. But that doesn't stop me.

"I deserve this promotion, Eros. I've been loyal to the Corps. I've executed every mission you sent me on with speed and precision."

Like he knows what I'm going to say next, Eros cuts me off. "Stop." The air around me stirs. A slice of the beach begins to shimmer and crawl up into the night like a branding iron on plastic. Before my eyes, the fabric of reality is cut. The two sides of existence flap in the air like curtains waiting to be drawn. Eros steps through the rip in time. Fire rages in his eyes, lips pressed into a thin line, probably as thin as the line I'm teetering on. A calculated step into my space makes me look at him. He's six inches taller than I remember. "There is nothing deserved in my corps of Cupids, Jaquelyn. There are only things I deem reward worthy. Behavior that either pleases me or doesn't."

"And you don't think my actions are reward worthy?"

His lip ticks up into a grin, sending shivers down my spine. Eros has always been warm and inviting. The god that stands before me now is neither of these things. He's cold and condemning. "You know I like the work you do, Jaquelyn."

Cold dribbles of sweat streak down my spine at the sound of my proper name.

"Then why did you send Tessa here to tempt me with Hugh?"

"Is he tempting you?"

I shake my head.

"Then why am I here, Jack? If you aren't tempted, then why the phone call? I gave you a simple assignment. See who is using and making a mockery of love. And save Halia Surf if you can."

"What's Tessa's assignment?"

"There's the girl I recruited. The girl who can see past the veil of obvious and search in the depths of the uncertain for the treacherous."

I square my shoulders and feel the surge of moxie dump into my veins. "You didn't answer my question."

Eros's eyebrows climb into his hairline. "Contessa Saint Cloud is here to see if you're not only fit for promotion but if you can banish a heart if need be."

His answer punches the air out of my lungs.

"Hugh?" I whisper. "You want to see if I can banish Hugh's heart, not save it?"

Eros tips his chin. "You wanted answers, Jack. Are you happy with the ones you received?"

I shake my head. It's one thing to hate the boy who broke my heart, it's another to banish the man's heart.

"Your assignment stands, and if you can't get Hugh Halia to respect the bonds of love and matrimony—which I'm quite certain we both know you can't—then you must be prepared to banish his heart."

"Hugh's not engaged. He wouldn't."

Eros bends down and wipes his hand over the sand, instantly turning it to glass. Hugh sits on the shore where I've just left him. He digs in his pocket, punches in a few numbers, and then rubs his hand back through his hair and then forward again. Shit, this is bad. What's he doing?

"Sonia?" His voice is barely audible. "Hi, babe." He runs his hand through his hair, once, twice. And my stomach drops. "I want to do a relationship with you. Let's see where it goes." He smiles, but it doesn't reach his eyes. It's his courtesy grin and that line . . . it's nowhere near the panty dropper doozies he's capable of. Shit, the girl doesn't know he's giving up and she's his consolation prize.

Eros wipes the sand back over the glass. His eyes are inches from mine.

"I won't have people making a mockery of love. If you are going to be a lead, then this will appall you. You *will* banish his heart if and when the time comes. Do I make myself clear?"

I nod. Eros snaps his fingers, disappearing into the fabric of space as it knits back together. And I'm heading back to the bonfire. Hugh Halia needs me . . . again.

Sixteen

HUGH

"Ladies!" I holler. When they don't stop with the high-pitched bickering, I let loose an ear-piercing whistle. "Can we exercise some control here? We have less than forty-eight hours to compile the five couples we want the public to vote on. There is one spot left. Please, I only need you to agree one more time." I turn and put my hands on the window in my office. I'd pay anything to rip off this suit and strap a board to my feet. This has to be my own form of purgatory. The ocean is so close, I can sink my feet into the sand in five minutes or less, and I'm stuck up here.

"Hugh," Jack's silky voice calls me back to the office. "I really think we should go with Derrick and Elizabeth."

The slit on Jack's skirt goes mid-thigh, and takes all the blood from my brain down south. Jack's words make her Ferrari-red lips move, but I can't stop thinking about what they could be doing instead. I can't stop thinking of all the ways I could mar those perfectly polished lips . . . if she'd let me. And she's made damn clear that vision will always be only a fantasy.

"What do you think?" Jack pushes.

An unsettling silence washes into the room. What I'm thinking isn't what any of these women want to hear. Hell, it isn't even something I want to address. My eyes dart back and forth between the three women: one who believes every word I've said, one who wants me to believe in us, and one who can barely believe she has to work with me.

Sonia closes the file folder in her lap. Her head hangs low. "He didn't hear a word you said." When she looks up, the fire in her eyes nails me to the wall, daring me to say she's wrong, wishing I'd prove her wrong.

"You're right, Sonia. I didn't hear a word Jack said. I was too lost in the way the sun was hitting your thigh." A blush races up my girlfriend's neck, staining her cheeks, and climbing into her hairline. "You know I'm a sucker for a thigh, and the way your dress is hanging. . ." I leave the unfinished sentence dangle. It's all a lie, Tessa knows it, Jack hopes it's true, but Sonia's buying all of it. At the end of the day, that's really who needs my attention. Tessa will hustle off to wherever E.A. sends her next, and Jack never really came home.

I was hoping . . .

Well, it didn't really matter what I was hoping.

"Derrick and Elizabeth are a great couple. Elizabeth stuck by Derrick's side when he came back from Afghanistan with a traumatic brain injury. Jack, why don't you leave the file for me to review? Formality, really, but I think it's safe to say Derrick and Elizabeth are definitely our magic couple number five."

Tessa stands and leaves as quickly as she came.

Jack leaves the file on my desk. Something races across her eyes and forms on her lips, but the girl's too damn stubborn to let loose the words.

I love her.

I will always love only her, but I can't keep paying for sins that her father asked me to execute. Turpitudes that kept her safe.

"You did good work, Jack." My eyes stay locked with hers as I call out to Sonia, "Babe, you want to go to Villa Nova tonight?"

Jack's eyes widen, her nostrils flare, and her gorgeous sky blue eyes take on a shine that means I'd proven my point at the cost of hurting her . . . again.

"Um, yeah," Sonia says from the door.

"Excuse me." Jack's voice cracks around the last word. She doesn't rush out the door, just strides out with her pride chasing to catch up. She's right, we both owe it to the people we're seeing to move on. She doesn't even spare Sonia a predatory glare. She leaves as unceremoniously as she had the last time.

"Babe, make the reservations for nine and close my door. I really need to review this and get it over to the legal team."

A smile that should warm my heart breaks like a sunrise across Sonia's face. "Sure, I'll, um, I'll let the web designers know and make sure Legal has the releases from the other for couples." She holds on to the door a moment. "I didn't know you were a leg man." There's a shy, flirty way about her that makes me want to try as hard as she is.

The door clicks shut and I'm alone with my thoughts. They tumble around like a ball caught in the whitewash. Sonia's sweet and kind. The lazy southern drawl can turn a solid man weak. It should have been turning me. I wasn't lying about being a leg-man. Unfortunately, the leg that had held my attention like I was a man clinging to the last thread of life was attached to Jack. I was always attached to Jack. Tessa was a team player in not outing me in her usual no-bullshit way. She always called a spade a spade and hated the lies people hid behind.

I pick up the phone. "Jack, when did the Open people say we could start construction on our booth?"

Papers rustle and Jack's raw voice says, "Four days before opening day. A week from Wednesday."

"And how many days does the team need for set up?"

"Two." Jack's one-word answers are terrifying. I know they're an extreme effort in control. Control not to kill the person who's receiving them. The girl hates me. Again. But that's what she wanted. What I need.

"Where's our construction team right now?

"I don't know, Hugh, I don't keep their schedule."

"Jack, I need your head in this."

"You say that like my head isn't. I wasn't the one panting over a girl's leg when I should have been listening to the pitch."

I ram a hand through my hair and back again. "Find out where the team is and then walk the site one more time."

"Fine."

"And Jack, stop answering me like that. I know you're pissed but—"

"You're taking her to Villa Nova?" The hurt in her voice is so palpable, my chest collapses around my lungs.

"Why does it matter? You don't love me anymore."

"I can't believe I ever did." The phone line goes dead. My heart stutters a moment. This wasn't how things were supposed to go. I usually know the outcome of every venture before I take the first step. With Jack, it only seems to go from bad to worse. This was what she wanted, I remind myself. This was what she said we had to do. Emotions jam the back of my throat, choking me with feelings that I've long since buried. How could God be so cruel? He took the purest thing the earth had ever known and put her under enough heat and pressure to make her sparkle, and God, did Jack shine like a diamond, but fuck, she's as cold as a rock.

"Damn it." I push off my table, sending the file on Derrick and Elizabeth flittering to the ground, papers streaming like a ticker-tape parade.

A small rap on my closed office door has me hollering, "What?"

"Easy, brother." Mack walks in, and my day goes from worse to *fuck me*. My half-brother can take a beautiful day and deface it with his presence. There's something devious about him, something I can't put my finger on. He stalks the room like my father did in his prime. He even has a laser look in his blue eyes, another thing he shares with my father that I don't. Mack's two parts conman with just the right amount of charming. He circles the chairs in front of my desk, eyeing my temper tantrum, and then sits with his feet kicked up.

"Closed door means I don't want to be bothered." I hold the door open, knowing full well the ass won't take the hint.

"I know." He leans his head back and sends me a look that says shit's going to get even more real. "We need to talk, brother."

I push the door closed and temper down all the things I want to say with all the ways I need to be politically correct. He doesn't wait for me to take a seat before digging into his breast pocket and pulling out a folded document. I can tell by the blue backing that it's a legal document, which means not only is shit going to get real, it might get bloody too.

"Did you get one of these?" Mack tosses the paper on my desk. I meet his eyes, then look at the paper like he's thrown down an electric eel on my desk and asked me to stick my tongue down its throat.

"What is it?"

"Mine came to my suite at the Hilton this morning."

Before I pick up the paper and waste any of my time, I pick up my phone and call Sonia.

"Hey, was anything delivered to the house this morning after I left?"

Mack holds up nine fingers and mouths, *"Nine a.m."*

"Around nine?"

"I'm not sure. I left home just after you did. I needed to pick up a few more things from my apartment. We can grab lunch at home and check. It's almost eleven."

Home?

More things?

Shit, she's really moving in. I know I all but asked her to after my run-in with Jack at the bonfire. There are so many landmines in Sonia's answer, but I have to deal with the nuclear bomb sitting on my desk first.

"No, I've got an appointment in Long Beach at noon. I'll swing by and check if there's a notice on my way there."

Sonia's disappointment is tangible even through a phone line. My mind's telling me that Sonia's a nice girl. And everything about her screams safe and long term, but my body is clearly craving something more wild and perilous. Probably wrapped in a tan little figure with blonde hair and ice blue eyes.

I hang up the phone and start reading. Mack's taken an interest in the Newton's cradle sitting on my desk; Jack and I made it when we were in seventh grade. I hadn't realized how intertwined she was in my life. Even if my conscious mind had given her up six years ago, my subconscious refused to let her leave.

So did my heart.

"The old man's got a foot in the grave and is still dicking with our lives."

That grabs my attention. "What do you mean?"

Mack pulls his feet off my desk, leans forward, and flips to one of the last pages. We have the same sharp angles in our faces, the harsh slashing eyebrows that can make girls wet and guys piss themselves. His skin is fairer than mine, and his eyes are a cold, unforgiving blue. I've only met his mom twice, but I know while her eyes are a soft sky blue, Mack's eyes are the same hue only when they have the same pissed off rage hardening them.

"Old man wants his sons married if we're going to stake a claim on Halia. You get first dibs on Halia, but that means you have to put a ring on some girl's finger by your next birthday. Labor Day, young man. If you're not married by Labor Day, then controlling power in Halia reverts to me. I have a year from your forfeiture to make some lucky lady's dream come true."

"That can't be right."

Mack stands up, plucking the paperwork from my fingers. "I'm starting to see why you're such an asshole, Hugh. I'd have probably turned out just like you if I'd grown up with the bastard pulling the rug out from under me every chance he got."

"I got news for you, Mack. Not only are you an asshole—exactly like me—you're a dick and a legit bastard as well."

Mack stops at the door and looks back. "And here I thought we were bonding." He's all calm and poker-faced, but the way his knuckles are turning white as he grips the edge of the door tells me otherwise. "Jack just left, so should I let Sonia know you've got a question to pop?"

He shuts the door and it's everything in me not to throw my chair out the window.

I try for an hour to work after Mack's visit, but all I can see is my old man's snicker as he puts me in another impossible situation. Another fucked up choice that makes me choose between my heart and my soul. I can only hope the devil has carved out a special nook in the ninth ring of hell for the bastard. I swipe the file of Derrick and Elizabeth off my desk, and lose it when I see Jack's handwritten note:

Epic love knows no limit to its endurance, its hope, its trust.

It is, in fact, the one thing that still stands when all else has fallen.

I wasn't a religious man, but I was a boy who could recite 1 Corinthians 13:7 to his girlfriend and watch her abandon all the reasons why they should wait for marriage. Something explodes inside me. I throw the door to my office open, nearly ripping it off the hinges. Sonia's chocolate eyes are so wide, they're on the verge of popping out of her head and rolling around on her desk like Cadbury eggs. I don't lose my cool often, but when I do, everyone knows to clear a path. I storm through the office bullpen, past some clients in the reception area, into the elevator and down. When the doors pull back, I turn and nearly steamroll Jack and her sexy pencil skirt into the floor of the parking garage lobby. With her in my arms and that perfect, startled little "O" her mouth makes as I catch her just before she hits the floor, it all clicks. The reason my world won't spin right, the reason my life has been off kilter for the last six years.

Jack.

"Hugh," she lets out in a rush of air. It's like a match to the kerosene flowing through my blood.

I grunt, right her, and then decide Jack needs to feel as out of control as I do. I dive head first into the roughest, angriest kiss I've ever planted on a girl. I may have growled, "Tell me you don't feel that." By the way her cheeks stain that delicious red, I know my answer was she felt everything I was feeling.

I don't know what I'm thinking.

I'm not.

I'm reacting with raw emotion, and I know that's never a way to handle any situation. Not in the water or out of it, and never with Jack. I all but manhandle her into the elevator after I'm done mauling her lips and storm into the parking garage. I'm still not sure if the crack I hear behind me was the glass door to the lobby breaking from the way I shoved it or Jack throwing her phone at me. Either was a toss-up, but I'm leaning to an irate Jack. Which just makes me smile and feel complete.

I slip the Tesla into third, peel out onto PCH, and fly down the coast. Wind pulling at my hair like an angry lover, I maneuverer around a minivan full of kids and then drop into fourth gear to make the yellow light before it fully commits to red. I quickly check my rearview mirror, totally expecting to see Jack's car behind mine, and feel a familiar pang when it isn't.

A few minutes later, I'm turning into the driveway of my house.

I love living in Sunset Beach, but today, it's not far enough away from the memories of Jack and all the wrong things I did for the right reasons.

I push open the picket-fence gate and feel my blood cool for the first time this morning. The ocean does that to me. It's like the waves set the pace and my body follows.

"Hugh," Pam's melodic voice calls out through the Hawaiian wedding flowers separating our walkways. Beach living means you're practically living in your neighbor's lap. I lucked out; my neighbors are pretty damn cool. Pam lives in her kitchen, cooking and bringing over her latest for me to taste test. When she and Eric aren't traveling, I'm over there for barbeques or drinks. They can't be much older than me, but I always get that parental feeling when we're sitting around the fire pit discussing my plans for a future outside of Halia.

"Yeah, Pam. It's me. Came home to check if a package was left."

"You moving that secretary of yours in?"

I'm glad the wedding flowers are blocking the disappointed, judging look I know is in her eyes. Pam believes in love at first sight, epic romances, and love never failing.

I didn't.

Pam's a lot like . . .

Anyway, I think she knew Sonia was a placeholder for the real thing. But the real thing and me may not get a shot at wrestling out happily ever after if the paperwork Mack dropped on me today is accurate. If I have to be married by Labor Day to keep control of Halia, Sonia's role as placeholder/personal assistant may become more permanent. And that makes my stomach all sorts of queasy.

"Would that make you happy?" I ask.

"I already found what makes me happy. I'm wondering if your mousy little lady does that for you."

I chuckle. "Mousy? Tell me how you really feel, Pam."

She giggles and it sounds like wind chimes. "I always figured you for a bold, confident, in-your-face kind of girl. Someone who could stand toe-to-toe with you and probably walk away with your heart if you let her."

I close my eyes and see the girl she's talking about. She's all those things, except the most important one . . . available.

"I'll let you know if I find her," I say. God, I'm a chicken when it comes to my neighbor.

The hedge rustles, and a FedEx package comes through the green leaves.

"I signed for it," Pam's voice drops. It's the first time I've heard the frost in her tone.

"Thanks, Pam." I grab the package and feel obligated to tell her I'll keep looking for that one, but before I can, I hear her slider close and the air changes. I'd never noticed the sweet fragrance when she was around before. I guess I haven't noticed a lot of things while Jack was gone.

I walk down the narrow path, past the front door, and push the gate to the backyard open. The pool man's been here. The driftwood fence that's up during the winter is gone, revealing the Plexiglas fence with its unobstructed view of the sand and surf of the Pacific Ocean. A small infinity pool runs the length of my backyard. It isn't anything special, but when I feel the need for water on my face, it can handle the countless laps I put in. Closer to the covered deck and outdoor dining room is a rock fountain, similar to the one in Halia's corporate office, spilling into the spa. I don't waste any time shredding the FedEx package. The same blue-backed paper is in there, letting me know I'm running out of options. I pull up a wicker lounger and lie down. I'm nothing but contradictions today. Stretched out in the sun in a suit, the company my mom begged, borrowed, and sold her soul to finance for my dad is slipping through my fingers, and the only way to save it is to marry the wrong girl.

Seventeen

JACK

I *know something's off when I* pull back into Halia's underground parking. Call it Cupid skills, sixth sense, or just female intuition, but whatever it is, the minute my toes touch the slick garage floor, I feel the energy rippling off the walls. I push the sensation away, chalking it up to the tension running between Hugh and me.

My phone buzzes. A text from E.J. I roll my eyes.

If we're "serious," does that earn me the right to round first base and maybe go straight for a steal at third?

"What a dick," I mumble as I type my reply:

Hit the showers, dude. You've totally struck out.

I hit send when the elevator pings and barely have time to see the doors open. Hugh's gaze, eyes glittering like heated lava rocks, lock on to me. Six feet, five inches of angry Hawaiian comes at me like a tsunami of emotion, and there's nothing I can do but stand and let him wash over me.

"Hugh," I let rush out, but it's too late. The walls tip, the world spins, and I'm flying through the air, wishing I'd had enough sense to have worn slacks instead of trying to torture the guy with my pencil skirts. I know what they do to him. I see the lust roll into his eyes like a fog in the harbor. His arms wrap around me, plucking me from my freefall, and again, we're face to face, inches apart. I focus on the thin set of his lips as they curl into a sneer. It doesn't take a love doctor to figure out what's setting the rims of his eyes glowing hot silver. It's me. I've always done this to him. And if I'm being honest, he's still doing it to me.

His lips uncurl from the sneer and then come crushing down on mine. He rakes the stubble on his upper lip across mine, punishing them for all the years we've been kept apart. His tongue sweeps against the seam of my lips, and even if I wanted to, I can't help but open up and let all that is Hugh Halia pour into me. Urgency floods his eyes and bleeds into his lips like a madman searching for something that he lost, something I hope he won't find in anyone but me.

A whimper wiggles loose from the back of my throat at the thought of Hugh and anyone besides me. It always has. There could never be anyone to replace Hugh, and I stopped trying to find a man to satisfy me the day I said goodbye.

A guttural moan pulls from deep in his throat, scattering every logical thought I have to the wind. My free hand skids across the stubble as I resurrect all sorts of memories. Fingertips slide along the sharp angle of his cheek. His breath hitches when I thread my fingers into his hair. It's as soft and silky as it was six years ago. I feel the dump of PEA in my system and abandon all my thoughts for a hit of love's euphoric high. Before I can weigh losing everything and let my heat match his fury, Hugh pulls me upright, smacks one more kiss on my whisker-burned lips, and grunts, "Tell me you don't feel that," before shoving the lobby door off its hinges. "And Jack, the next kiss . . . you're going to have to ask for." A mischievous chuckle rips from inside him. "Maybe even beg."

My wrist, my back, my heart—they all burn from where Hugh held them. And there's a warming sensation over my heart that has nothing to do with the assault Hugh's just laid down. The warmth intensifies until it feels like there's a hot branding stick driving through my chest.

"No," I mutter. "No, no, no." I'm pulling at the fabric of my blouse, but it's too late—my skin is marred with a lightning bolt. Eros doesn't have to be present to know when one of his Cupids is not just having second thoughts but flat out breaking the rules.

"No!" I scream and throw my cellphone at the glass door. I crumple to the floor, fingers retracing the path of destruction on my lips. I'm not sure what hurts more, the lightning bolt warning from Eros or the way Hugh just used me.

I leave my phone. Given the multiple pieces that are scattered on the floor, I'm going to need to pick a new one up anyway. I step into the waiting elevator, and the doors close, bouncing back a version of me I hardly recognize. One kiss from the boy who sent my world spinning out of control has parts of me humming, and if I don't get it together, that same boy's going to get my heart banished, as well as his.

Upstairs, the office seems to be reeling from the wake of Hurricane Hugh. Mack's trying to settle down the receptionist, although I'm not so certain his concern is in her eyes, so much as it is on her breasts.

"What set him off?" I ask Mack.

"Paperwork from Dad's attorney." He nods to the mess on the floor.

I shift my briefcase and walk over to the paperwork. "What's it say?"

"Your golden boy has until Labor Day to put a ring on a finger or he loses control of Halia."

I eye the legal confetti like they're sleeping scorpions. Kai's still trying to control Hugh. Maybe it's about time I go visit the old man, but first, I need to have a heart to heart with Tessa. Looks like saving Halia just became our mission too. He's going to need something to hold onto when Tessa and I go.

"Tessa in the boardroom?" I don't wait for the answer; if she isn't there, I'll hunt her down. This training exercise is over. Yes, I can banish a heart. But this isn't fair. Despite the delicious assault downstairs, someone's got to cut the guy a break . . . even if it's me. Hugh has to marry someone? Then at least it should be someone he cares about. The world needs his passion, needs the spark that love puts in his eyes. I scratch at the warning bolt on my chest. Eros is just going to have to understand this is part of the mission, and Tessa's going to have to man up.

I round the bullpen of desks, my heels clicking on the hardwood floor, and push open the Kolohala doors. Idea boards line the walls. Wedding cakes and dresses, rings and tuxes. My breath catches. I know Tessa's been working her ass off on this at home, tucked away in my dad's old bedroom, but this is the first I've seen of the boards side by side. It's elegant and timeless. The warm sunset theme screams beach, love, fun, and ever after.

"Tessa," I whisper.

"Yeah?" she asks, and I forget the betrayal that ended our years of friendship. Tessa was always talented when it came to pulling things together. Where I like neat and orderly, Tessa always was able to pull the strings of a chaotic mess and weave them into something that was beyond everyone's wildest imagination. She started by stepping in and saving our abandoned homecoming dance my freshman year, her sophomore year. By the time her senior prom came around, everyone knew Tessa would come up with something magical.

I run a finger along the board with the stage and then turn with my arms crossed. Her eyebrows climb her face, because she knows this is my dead-serious look.

Tessa clears her throat. "You heard about Kai's marriage experiment." All the play that normally bounces around Tessa's voice is gone. She sits down and nods for me to take the seat next to her. I've never met this cool, calm, take-charge Tessa. She's someone I'd trust. Tessa reaches into her bag and pulls out a file. I recognize it immediately. It's a Cupid's Case File. The see-through vinyl shimmers with a vein of gold running through it. I meet her eyes and something familiar passes between us.

"Is that this assignment?" I open, then refold my arms; they seem to be one of the few things holding me together after Hugh's kiss.

Tessa nods. Her fingers skid along the clear vinyl, releasing a ripple of gold.

"You show me that, with a bolt already on your chest, and you know what'll happen."

Tessa's lips twist up into a daredevil grin before she says, "I know what'll happen if I don't."

I put my hand on her file, and it transforms into a normal manila folder. Safety devices. Eros thinks of all the cool things.

"Jack, I know you're forty-nine arrows in, but this is Halia." Her fingers wrap around mine. "This is Hugh."

"Tessa, your assignment was me?"

She nods.

"My final assignment isn't to train you?"

She shakes her head.

"How long have you been a Cupid?"

She searches somewhere over my head.

"Seems like a lifetime." When her eyes meet mine, there's a sheen—a sadness that I don't think has ever been there. Not even when Tessa's single mom gave her a positive pregnancy test for her birthday and asked if she was excited for a baby brother or sister. Not even when I caught her with Hugh.

I swallow hard, hoping to chase away the last taste of Hugh. "Then it's time for you to fall for the guy we both know deserves you."

Tessa shakes her head. "He doesn't want me, Jack." She runs her hand over the vinyl folder, and a picture of Hugh, Tessa, and I floats to the surface. Hugh's younger; his hair is cut into a flat top. Freshman year. He has his arms wrapped around Tessa and me, but his lips are firmly planted in the crown of my hair, and that sparkle in his eye could easily be mistaken for the camera's flash. It's not. I've done this job too long to not know that's the glimmer we look for. That's pure love.

"He never looked at anyone this way, Jack. Not while he was with you. And most certainly not after you left."

Heat streaks through me, stirring up emotions that have no business being unleashed, not when I am this close to immortality. Not with a fresh mark on my heart.

"Tessa, I caught you sleeping with my boyfriend. I won't ever trust love again. What about Sonia? She loves him. He could be happy with her."

Tessa shakes her head again and taps the folder. Another picture swims to the surface. It's Hugh and Sonia at last December's Christmas tree lighting ceremony. Hugh has his arm around Tessa and Sonia. His lips pressed into the crown of Sonia's hair. It's a mirror image of the previous photo only I've been replaced. And there's no glimmer. There's nothing but flat black eyes in pain looking at the camera.

Something twangs in my chest.

Jealousy?

Sadness?

"It's always been you, Jack. Why can't you see that? There—" She pulls the picture of me and Hugh up and zooms in on his eyes. "The shimmer is right fucking there."

"I know what I'm looking at. The glitter we're trained to look for before we ask the question, '*Do you believe again?*'"

I swallow hard over the emotions in my throat, ignoring the pull of a thrill-ride forever and focusing on the feeling of a secure eternity.

"Tessa, if you won't do it, then we need to get Hugh to fall for Sonia."

Tessa grabs both my wrists and pulls me toward her. "Jack, there's only one way this will work."

"I can't." The words rip from somewhere deep and damaged in me. They roar to the surface on a sob. "You don't understand what that did to me."

"You're serving a sentence as a Cupid. I have a damn good idea what that did to you." Tessa lets go of my wrists, leaving the statement hanging in the air, and starts to pace the room. She's muttering to herself. I know better than to try and make it out. When Tessa starts speaking in tongues, it's anyone's guess as to when she's going to surface and make sense.

"Tessa, we don't have time for one of your meltdowns. Hugh's moved Sonia into his house."

Tessa's pace picks up, as does the muttering.

"It's a logical step," I push. "She's already fallen. I know you've seen the shimmer in her eyes."

Tessa changes her direction mid stride and walks over to the table. Her hands slap down on the polished wood. "Stop. It."

"Stop what? Stop trying to save Halia? Save Hugh?" I stand up and match her threatening stance. "Stop trying to point out the obvious? Sonia is our best bet. We just have to make Hugh see—"

"Jack, we didn't sleep together."

"What?"

"We didn't sleep together. Hugh asked me to help him make you give him up."

Hot tears well up. I bite down on my lip, willing them to recede. I didn't cry six years ago—I'm not going to cry now.

"Why?" The word comes out shaky and so miserable. "Was I that bad?"

"It wasn't you." Tessa knows better than to try and comfort me. I'm like an injured animal. Worse. I'm a broken girl whose heart just shattered all over again.

"Your dad." Tessa looks up to the ceiling, says a silent *I'm sorry,* and then trains her eyes back on me. "Your dad made Hugh promise to give you up when he died. You don't know how demented Kai is. That wedding stipulation, that's nothing."

"My dad?" I sink into the chair.

"Your dad knew without him here to protect you, Kai would've found a way to get his hands on you."

"I sold Dad's shares of stock to pay for the medical bills, there wasn't . . ."

"Not just the shares of stock." It isn't until Tessa sits down that I notice her hands are shaking. "Kai's not a good man," she continues. "Your dad thought the only way to protect you from Kai was to make sure you not only didn't fall for Hugh, but that you hated every fiber of his being. He saw the way Kai watched you. I saw the way Kai stalked you."

"You're lying. That makes no sense." Even though it makes perfect sense. Kai always made my hackles stand on edge.

"Trust me. It does."

"And you went along with this? You didn't think I could handle Kai?"

"I never wanted you in a situation where I had to entertain the thought." Tessa follows my gaze to her hands; she folds them in an attempt at control.

"Sonia isn't Hugh's match. You are. Kai's no longer a factor."

"I can't." This is all too much. I knew my dad. He wanted me happy. He knew Hugh made me happy. This has to be just another one of Tessa's tricks. I'm not going to fall for it, or Hugh. I wipe the tears away. "I know you what you're doing, Tessa."

Her eyes flare.

"You're obviously not newly cursed, which means you're a ladder climber. I've heard about the rewards for dethroning a niner. If you think some bullshit story about my dad, the man who knew how much Hugh meant to me, is going to make me question all the years I've spent protecting my heart, then you're a damn fool as well as a . . . a hooker. I hope Hugh paid you well. For this time and the last." I grab my things and fish out my car keys. "You focus on your assignment. Focus really hard because when I don't fall, I want a front row seat to see you explain to Eros why *you* failed and why *you* revealed your mission." My voice sounds like a wild woman, but it doesn't stop me. I'm far from letting Contessa Saint Cloud off the hook. "And then I'm going to cheer when he brands that last bolt on you and damns your heart to oblivion."

Eighteen

HUGH

"Hugh?" *A warm hand skids* down the side of my face. I mumble, curling back into the dream I was having.

"Hugh?" the voice persists. I smile at the hints of irritation in it while another palm warms the other side of my face.

I grab the fingers and pull them to my mouth. "I love when you're good and pissed, Jack."

Silence.

"I'm not Jack, Hugh."

I peel open my eyes. The horizon's disappeared into the blackness with only the sound of the ocean in the distance. Silver rays of moonlight fight with the fog that rolls in every night. The lights in the garden have kicked on, casting a warm glow behind Sonia's head. Her eyes are hard and full of accusations.

"Sonia." Even I hear the confusion in my voice.

"That's me." She's dressed in a killer red dress with a neckline that plunges almost to her belly. Her chocolate hair cascades down around her shoulders, and her eyes are good and pissed.

My jaw ticks. "I'm sorry."

"No, you're not." She moves Dad's legal papers and sits down on the lounge chair next to me. It all comes rushing back.

Sonia.

The marriage stipulation.

Jack.

"I waited at the office until eight thirty. Then when I didn't hear from you, I went to Villa Nova, where I waited another hour."

"What time is it?" I right myself and look at my watch.

"It's ten o'clock, Hugh."

"I'm sorry, babe."

"Don't." Sonia fishes her hands out from mine. "You probably called her babe too."

I don't ask who the "her" is. We both know it's Jack. And Sonia isn't wrong; I did call Jack babe. She loved Babe Ruth and the pig movie, and I loved her.

She twists her lips like's she reading my mind. "That's what I thought. Look, I'm going to pack up my things. You clearly don't want me here, and I have an inkling of self-respect left in me to walk away. I'll stay on through the Open, but after that, I'm gone." Sonia stands and hands me the papers. The papers that tell me my best bet for keeping my company is breaking up with me.

"Sonia," I call out, but she doesn't stop. The click of her heels disappears into the house.

"Fuck." I lie back down on the lounge and catch fireworks exploding off in the distance. "Is it really this goddamn hard?" I yell up at the sky. I don't know whom I expect to be listening because nobody has answered in the past. My mom would tell me to clean up my own mess. I doubt she'd lift a finger to intervene for anyone but Jack. The soft click of heels on travertine tiles echo from inside. I strain to hear Sonia's next move. Does she have the balls to follow through with her threat to leave? I listen for the heavy Brazilian wood front doors. They softly shut, and the click of heels on cement carry her away from me.

A heavy sigh, somewhere between relief and regret, breaks from deep inside of me.

Way to fuck it all up.

I reach over and grab my briefcase to dig out the file on Derrick and Elizabeth. Two pages into their story I pick up my phone and call Derrick's cell.

"Hey, Derrick."

"Hugh? *The* Hugh Halia is calling me?" The playful tone in his voice forces a grin on my face.

"Yeah, it's me."

"Holy shit. Hold on, yep, world is still spinning."

"I know, I know. I couldn't get enough of your awesomeness at the bonfire, so I'm wondering if you'll meet me tomorrow."

Silence fills the phone line. Derrick and I were friends in grade school, back when everyone was picked on a team and stellar athletes like Derrick had yet to distance themselves from the crowd. He went to West Point on a full-ride scholarship. There were talks of him going pro after he served. Those talks ended Derrick's first year of active duty courtesy of a roadside IED. He was the only one to make it back home. That is if you count making it home with only with half his memory, no recollection of his fiancée, Elizabeth, and half his left leg gone. Based on their submission essay, even with seventeen surgeries and a traumatic brain injury, Derrick seems to have a better grasp on relationships than I ever will.

Derrick clears his throat. "Can you do breakfast? Or we can chat out in the water like old times? Take the girly aspect out of the equation."

"You're surfing again?"

"They took my leg, Hugh. Not my heart. Didn't you see *Dolphin Tail*? I have something a little more awesome." He chuckles. "Yeah, I can do breakfast."

"Sugar Shack?"

"You choose. You're paying."

"Sugar Shack, a corporate card, and 7 a.m. work?"

"Works."

The phone line goes dead, and I thumb through Derrick and Elizabeth's application. I don't need to review this. This is the epic romance Jack is looking for. The epic romance she deserves.

The sun is just breaking over the buildings on Main Street. Water glistens on the road from last night's sprinkling courtesy of the monsoon sitting off the coast of Mexico. From my table in front of the Sugar Shack, I can still see the waves pummeling the pier. They're easily seven-foot breakers. I loosen the knot of my tie that all of a sudden seems far too constricting. Owning a surf company, you'd think I'd have more time in the water.

Just the opposite.

I'm usually up in my glass prison, yards from one of the things I love the most. Saltwater on my skin, toes gripping the surf wax, and my board skimming along water smooth as glass. Thirty seconds of pure heaven before I pull out and paddle back out to repeat the freedom all over again.

"I know that look." Derrick shakes the saltwater from his hair before pulling the hood of his sweatshirt over his blonde crew cut. "Dude, you own a surfboard company. Change one suit for the other."

I smile and reach for my cup of coffee. "I was just thinking about my jail cell."

The metal legs of Derrick's seat scrape against the concrete. A small grimace mars his face as he eases himself down.

"Still hurt?"

He shakes his head and absentmindedly rubs at the prosthetic leg. "Nah, phantom pains. The brain forgets there's nothing there. You hurt long enough, even when the ache is gone, your heart still clings to the familiar."

"You've basically summed up my last six years without Jack."

Derrick cocks his head and runs a hand across his mouth and down his chin. "The brain and the heart—they may not be located in the same place, but they might as well be the same organ, dude. I have to say, seeing you, Jack, and Tessa all in the same place"—a smile blossoms across his face—"it felt like old times. You three fighting again?"

I chuckle and direct my attention to the waitress hanging out inside. She nods when I get her attention and heads our way.

"Something like that."

"I don't mean to start our little reunion breakfast off on the wrong foot, but I never did understand what went down between you three. You were so sprung on Jack, hearing you boned the bestie kind of . . ." His words trail off. Every muscle in my face is contorted into a snarl. My fingers have balled up into my palms. I take a deep breath and consciously restrain every wild impulse that's flowing through me.

"Sorry. I guess I'm not quite ready to talk about that part of my past."

Derrick leans forward as the waitress shows up to the side of our table. He eyes me and then looks up at the waitress. "Two Main Street breakfast burritos and two orange juices." Derrick looks back at me. "Sound about right?"

"Sounds like old times."

The waitress leaves and Derrick leans back in his chair. "I know all about bad memories, Hugh. I'm lucky if I go three days without a nightmare. But here's the thing—just because they occupy my brain doesn't mean they rule my heart. You won't ever be ready to move forward until you let go of the past. And just because you let go of the past doesn't mean it won't tag along for the ride into your future. You just have to mute its voice."

"How'd you get so fucking smart?" I lean my elbows on to the table.

Derrick taps the side of his head, the side where an angry pink scar runs from his temple into his hairline. "Had some sense knocked into me."

I chuckle and start to tell him the secret only one person alive knows.

"Jack's dad had me promise to give her up when he passed away. He said he didn't trust my dad with her."

"What does that mean?"

My shoulders pull up. "I don't know, but at the time, on his death bed, Joaquin Alcantar was certain of one thing: Kai Halia wouldn't only hurt his daughter, he would destroy Jack if she became a Halia. Given the shit my dad's pulled in the past couple of days, I can't say Jack's dad was too far off base. Lord knows Dad always made Tessa go rigid and docile whenever he walked in the room when we were teens. Even now, with him laid up in hospice, you mention his name, and it's like a zombie's walked in the room and sat in Tessa's lap."

"I'm sorry about your dad."

It's the obligatory apology, the kind that has very little sympathy behind it. Derrick had firsthand knowledge of how ruthless my dad could be when it came to something he wanted. Kai'd wanted Derrick to give up football and sign with Halia. But Derrick only wanted three things in life: to marry Elizabeth Wright, play football, and serve his country.

I shrug off the apology as the waitress brings out our breakfast burritos. In typical male fashion, all conversation ends until we've eaten half of our burritos. Derrick takes a swig of juice and then says, "So what can I do for you, Hugh Halia?"

"I read your story."

A blush splotches Derrick's cheeks. "Yeah, well, Jack is pretty damn persuasive, plus, Tessa got a hold of Elizabeth, and by sunrise, we'd . . . you know, filled the application out."

"I read your story and it moved me. I wanted to let you know I signed off on you and Elizabeth making the top five couples and I'm going to do my damnedest to make sure you guys get the votes."

"You planning on rigging an election for me, man? I'm touched."

I laugh. "I'll toe the line as far as Legal will let me."

Derrick wipes his hands and then shoots one out. "Thanks, man. Elizabeth is going to be thrilled."

I shake his hand and can tell by the look on his face he knows I'm not done.

"Kai has a clause that if I'm not married by my next birthday—Labor Day—I lose control of Halia. It reverts to my half-brother." The omission rushes out of my mouth so fast, I'm not sure Derrick's heard it all.

He folds his arms and evaluates the bomb I just dropped in his lap.

"Given the cold shoulder and heated glare Jack was givin' you at the bonfire, you guys aren't close to marching down the aisle?"

"I'm dating my secretary."

A roaring laugh rips from Derrick. "Dude, you're worse than a fucking soap opera. What the fuck are you thinking?"

"I'm thinking I'm screwed. I can marry a girl I don't love to save the company I do. Or I can bet big on the girl I do love and kiss the company goodbye."

"You don't love Halia Surf?"

"I didn't say that."

"Yes, dude, you did. Look, I don't the details of why you have to choose—call me a hopeless romantic—but I think you already have your answer. You always bet big on true love. You and Jack, with Kai out of the picture, you guys have a shot at the real thing."

"I wish I had your faith, Derrick." I look at my watch and pick up the bill. "Let's do this again."

"Only if you promise to surf with me first."

"Deal." I stand and clap him on the shoulder. "Give Elizabeth my love."

"Only if you pass along my love to Jack."

"Not all of us have brass balls and a purple heart, but for you, I'll let you know which hospital she ends up putting me in."

"Some things are worth dying for, Hugh. Jack's always struck me as one of those things."

Derrick doesn't know how right he is.

Nineteen

JACK

The smell of antiseptic makes me want to gag. It takes me back to the worst day of my life. The day Dad died. They'd just mopped his floors and the wet, medicinal smell was everywhere. It hung in my hair and on my skin for months after . . .

Dad turned his head, told me the room smelled like hell and he wasn't going to be hanging around for the next mopping. I'd thought he meant he was going to be well enough to come home.

I was wrong.

Dad was saying his goodbyes. A few hours later, he grabbed my hand, looked into my eyes, and told me he loved me and to be brave. He said he knew I wouldn't understand what was going to happen next, but it was the only way he could keep me safe. The light danced in his blue eyes, flickered, and then . . .

then it was gone. Just like that, everything I was, was gone.

I was alone.

I close my eyes, and the charred car at the bottom of the cliff at Pacific Coast Highway and Seacliff flashes like a bad grainy movie. I lean against the wall and dig the heels of my palm into my eyelids, trying to erase the memory. When I know I'm not going to hurl, I pull in a breath and start again for Kai's room. But each click of my heel on the sterile tile unearths memory after memory, like the dead rising from their grave.

The day after Dad's funeral, I went over to Hugh's house. I knew Kai was home when I called to talk to Hugh. I never called the landline, but Hugh wasn't picking up his cell. Tessa's hadn't been home all night, which wasn't completely out of the ordinary, but I thought she'd be there for me. Despite my promise to my dad to never go over to the Halia's when Kai was home, I snuck up the trellis of Hawaiian Wedding flowers. The flowers crumpled under each grasp of the trellis, releasing an overpoweringly sweet scent.

I needed to feel the warmth of Hugh's arms around me like a druggie needed a hit. Once I landed on Hugh's balcony, nothing could have prepared me for what I saw. My best friend and my boyfriend . . . The memory still brings tears clawing at my eyes.

They rolled around in Hugh's bed like familiar lovers. The bed he shared with me. White sheets pooled around Tessa's waist as she straddled Hugh. They were so in the moment. Tessa still had her bra on. I couldn't bear to think what Hugh didn't have on. I always thought I'd be the girl to storm in and make a scene. Turns out, I was the girl who slid open the balcony door and stood there—tears streaming down my face—watching. When Hugh came up for air, he noticed me. His face paled, and Tessa dropped her head on his shoulder. She didn't turn around. Maybe Hugh whispered my name. Whatever it was, she couldn't look at me, and I'd never look at her the same.

Hugh didn't scramble out of bed. He didn't even chase after me as I walked out of his bedroom, through his massive house, and out the door. I left as quietly as I came and no one followed after me.

Now, Tessa wants me to believe nothing happened?

Not a chance.

I take another antiseptic-laced breath. I knew Kai was bad when he hadn't tried to contact me after a week of my being back in Huntington Beach. When I received the phone call from the hospice nurse, there was no way in hell I was going to come. Kai'd been asking for my dad or me. The nurse said during his lucid moments, which were few, he was adamant he needed to speak to one of us. Seeing that dad had been gone for six years, the duty fell on me, again.

Whatever Kai wants to get off his dying chest, I expect he'll have six years' worth of cruel and caustic mind games to play. I push open the door to Kai's hospice room and gasp.

Kai's a whisper of the giant man he was the last time I saw him. His skin is a jaundicing yellow. I expected tubes all over the place like Dad. But Kai wasn't in an accident, he was dying, and according to the hospice nurse, that could happen any day.

"Who's there?" Kai's voice labors as he sniffs the air. "Jaquelyn, I'd know your scent anywhere.

I shudder as he licks my name on his lips but stay firmly affixed in the doorway. "It's me, Kai."

"Come in."

"I'm fine where I am."

Kai rolls head toward the door, yellowed eyes stare right through me. "But it's not what I want."

"Tell me you had the wedding clause drawn up long before you got sick. Tell me you wouldn't dare make your son choose between a loveless marriage and the company he adores."

"Jaquelyn, please, come in." Kai struggles to move in his bed. "I can barely see you."

"Answer my question and I'll step in further."

His face contorts (or was that a smile?) and then relaxes.

Game on.

My heart pounds in my ears as I wait for him to make the next move. Time stretches, and the adrenaline that had dumped into my bloodstream when I first walked in here has started to fade. Kai hasn't moved, and part of me hopes he's dead. Hugh would finally be free. For as far back as I can remember, Hugh could never do anything right. I used to think it was Kai's way of forging steel through fire. I don't think that anymore. Kai's pure evil.

"Come in, Jaquelyn."

I jump at Kai's voice.

"I promised your dad I wouldn't touch you."

My heart scurries up into my throat. "What?"

His hand trembles as he waves me in. "Please, Jacquelyn, I have to—" A fit of coughing shakes his entire body. I waiver between going to him and getting a nurse. The coughing dies down and tears trail down his face, mixing with the spit dripping from his mouth. If I didn't know all the ways he'd hurt my dad, took the company away from Dad, I might feel sorry for him.

My heels click on the sterile white tile as I hesitantly walk toward him. The closer I get, the more there's something about this man that makes every hair on the back of my neck stand straight up. He's always had this terrifying effect on me. I thought it was because he was this crazy, larger-than-life Hawaiian, but now I'm not so sure.

"What do you mean you promised my dad you wouldn't touch me?"

His jaundiced blue eyes lock onto mine, and I think a smile tries to pull at his dry, cracked lips. "Your dad was always protecting you."

I shake my head. "What did you mean you promised my dad you wouldn't touch me?" The words break syllable by syllable from my lips.

"Look at you." Kai changes the subject. "You look like your mother. She didn't like me either. I tried everything to get her to see me, but she only had eyes for your dad."

My stomach falls away. "You better not have laid a hand on my mother."

"HA!" The laugh is overtaken by another bout of coughing. "She wishes. She turned your father against me. Told him what she saw and thought it was disgusting." Kai tries to roll toward me but his body barely moves.

I'm by the side of his bed. Close enough that he can reach out and touch me, but I know he won't. Not because of some promise to my father, but because he couldn't muster the strength even if he wanted to. Kai's so weak, his skin so translucent, it looks like tissue paper. Death is crawling across his skin, consuming him inch by inch.

"What did you mean you promised my dad you wouldn't touch me?" I ask again.

Kai's lip snarls, and like a jolt of lighting to his body, the fire in his eye rages. "Your mother ruined everything. She couldn't mind her own damn business. I told her I was taking pictures of the girl in the new line of bikinis. But she ran off and told your dad I was touching the girl. Your mother was a prime example why pregnant women should be home barefoot and not in the corporate world."

Bile rises in my throat. "What?" I whisper, afraid anything else will make me vomit. "What did you do, Kai?"

"I was helping her change. That's it."

"How old, Kai? How old was the girl?"

"You sit there judging me?" He spits, but in his condition, there was no longer any bark or bite in his words. "You're no better than your pregnant mother. She trapped your dad. If she hadn't gotten pregnant with *you,* then Joaquin would have never known."

"I'm going to ask you one last time, how old was the girl? Think before you answer, because if you don't give me an age, I don't care if you are on your deathbed! I'll make sure you die in a prison cell."

Kai's nostrils flare; his eyes dart back and forth, probably searching to see how serious I am. "Sixteen. Plenty old enough to tell me to stop if she wanted me to."

The room twirls, all the blood rushing from my head. I don't want to believe what I'm hearing, but given what Tessa told me yesterday and Kai's all-out admission, he is a pedophile.

"Does Hugh know?"

Kai tries to roll away from me, but I grab his arm and pull him back to me. "Kai," I spit. "Does Hugh know what kind of monster you are?"

"I love women. If that makes me a monster then, yes, because he loves them too. Ask your friend Tessa."

"Hugh's nothing like you, Kai. My father was nothing like you."

I turn on my heels, and despite Kai's taunts of being a bitch like my mother and no stronger than my father, Kai pulls out one last admission.

"The best thing I ever did was rid the world of your father."

My knees buckle, and I brace my weight against the doorjamb as a wave of nausea rolls through me. I don't dare turn around. I know this is exactly what Kai wants. He didn't want to make peace with Dad or me. He wanted to rock my world one last time. The man is so sadistic, I'm not even sure he's telling the truth.

A jagged breath echoes across the room, and I know Kai Halia is far from done with me. His last moments on this earth, all the evil he's stored up—I know it's coming my way.

"I cut his brake lines, just like your mom's, only this time, I did it myself. Had the ex-con who did your mom's show me how to do it so it looked like they were damaged in the crash. I thought it fitting they both go out the same way."

Warm tears skid down my face and plink on to the sterile tiles. I fight every natural instinct in me, gripping the doorjamb like it was Kai's neck and squeezing until my knuckles turn white.

Don't turn around.

Don't move.

Don't give him any more satisfaction than what he's already taken.

He wants me to lose it, give into to every urge to take his life. Me behind bars for his death, it would be the ultimate revenge. It would kill my Hugh.

I hear the bed squeak.

"Your dad"—he spits the words—"he wouldn't take Halia to the next level with me as CEO. Told me I had to turn myself in after Tessa."

Oh my God, what did he do to Tessa?

How am I still standing?

I could kill him. Push a pillow over his face and the world wouldn't know any better. The world would rejoice. My chest heaves.

"I did what had to be done, Jack. And I added the clause to the will the moment you left. I needed to be damn certain Hugh kept his eyes focused on the prize, and if he can't, then Mack can. That boy is cut from the same cloth as me. Ask his mother."

I don't answer. I walk out the door, fingers trembling and dial.

"Where are you? We need to talk." His maniacal laughter chases me down the hall. "Jack, I have more secrets. You know you want to hear them all. Tessa won't tell you. Hugh doesn't know them. You know you want. . ."

I race through the corridor, my breath chasing after me, and break through the hospice doors and into the warmth of the sun. I bend over and throw up my breakfast. This is why I want to be immortal. I don't want to feel any of this. Ever.

The coast is flying past me. I want to call Hugh. I should call Tessa. But what I need is to never feel helpless again. The only way to do that is with fifty arrows around my wrists, and to do that, I call Sonia.

"I need you to meet me at Duke's in thirty minutes. We need to chat." I don't wait for her answer before I hang up the phone. I'm going to save Hugh Halia from making a mockery of Eros's purpose, even if that means he has to spout the big L word to someone besides me. Despite what Tessa thinks, Sonia is my best bet, because I'm not an option.

Forty minutes later, Sonia is shredding a napkin, and I'm waiting for her to give me an answer. I look at my watch again. Five minutes. This question isn't that hard to answer, but I ask it again. "Do you love Hugh?"

Her doe eyes look at me, and I know the answer before she opens her lips. The shimmer is gone, or it was never there to begin with. This assignment has left me so twisted, I'm second-guessing everything. That twisted-up feeling ended about an hour ago, after I left Kai Halia.

"He doesn't want me, Jack. I'm pretty sure you know why."

I lean back in my chair with a huff. I'm one away from becoming immortal, and I'm dealt with the hardest case ever. Usually one person is willing to help me out.

"Let me ask you, if you could have one wish that you knew would absolutely come true, who would you wish for?" I wrap my fingers around her wrist and toe the line of using any powers to sway her answer. I'm not dumping any phenylethylamine (PEA love drug) into her system. I'm gaging at how much isn't there. A clammy sensation sweeps down my spine, and I know Eros is watching.

Sonia's eyes are downcast, searching the pavement for either the right answer or the answer she wants to give me. Given the erratic thump of her pulse against my fingertips, I'm going with the latter. Which totally isn't going to help Hugh or me.

"Don't worry, Sonia. We'll figure something out," I say more for my benefit than hers.

"Sonia, I want to pull you in and have you help me with the overseeing of the site. I think it'll be really helpful for you to have the hands-on knowledge, so you can replicate an event like this after I leave."

"That's really kind of you, Jack, but after this event . . . I gave my notice. I hope you understand what I'm about to say, because it isn't directed at you, but I can't compete with a memory of someone. I also have a little bit of dignity to let Hugh go when I'm clearly not the one he wants."

I reach across the table for Sonia's hand again, but she pulls it away from me. The comment may not have been directed at me, but her reaction to it surely is. "I understand that more than you can imagine. Still, I'd love for you to work with me on this, whether you're here at Halia—which I hope you change your mind and stay on—or you go on to bigger and brighter things in life, this is still great experience."

"It's kind of you. Thank you." A blush creeps up Sonia's cheeks.

After lunch, we walk the site. The team I've assembled is top-notch. They're going to transform our spot of sand into a Hawaiian paradise. In four weeks, Derrick and Elizabeth—I'm willing them to be the couple chosen—will be getting married in front of Halia's version of Paradise Falls.

"Ms. Alcantar," The foreman unravels the plans we've approved. "I'm Sid. Nice to meet you in person." He shakes my hand as we walk over to the hood of his car. "This is by far one of the most aggressive temporary sites we've undertaken. The waterfall itself is no easy feat. The water-return system is state-of-the-art and completely green, running entirely on solar energy. Your US Open rep about wet himself when he heard we were environmentally friendly."

I smile at the foreman and then turn to Sonia. "What questions would you ask?"

Her eyes flare. Clearly, no one's ever taken the time to ask her opinion. Not even Hugh.

"Um, how long—"

I hold up a finger, cutting her off. "Not me. Ask Sid, the foreman."

A smile pulls at her lips. Confidence seems to straighten her shoulders as a sea breeze picks up the ends of her hair. "What's the timeframe from breaking ground to test run?"

"Good question," I whisper, nudging her shoulder to ask more.

Sid is accommodating. Most construction men have a problem being questioned by a woman. Hell, most men have the problem. It's what makes the chase so fun. Keeping them off kilter.

"A week," the foreman answers.

Sonia takes a step closer to the foreman. I knew she had leadership qualities in her; she just had to be brave enough to take that first step.

"What potential problems do you foresee?"

Sid adjusts his stance, then turns and points at his plans. "If anything's going to go wrong, it's going to be with the waterfall. The minute we turn it on, it's going to need to run continuously. Once it's on, it's on. Turn it off and that's the end of the show."

I don't wait for Sonia to pick up on the potentially devastating problem. "That leaves a huge margin for error. Are you planning on leaving a staff member here to safeguard the site?"

"We're construction, Jack. Not security. I can recommend a firm."

"Can you call it into Sonia? She's going to be my second on this project."

Sid grabs his clipboard and flips back a few pages. "I have Tessa Saint Cloud as the second."

"I'm changing the contacts." I fish out one of Sonia's cards that I swiped from the office and hand it to Sid. After the Open, Sonia's not going anywhere but down the aisle. I may not see the glimmer in her eye yet, but I know this girl is the best option we have to save Hugh.

Even if she isn't me.

An hour later, I can see Sonia's had all the overseeing she can take. I send her back to the office to confirm our seats at the Vendor's Ball this weekend. We're going to be announcing the winning couple at the event.

"Make sure you get the extra pair of tickets and then text me the current results for the couples," I call out to Sonia and send up a silent prayer that Derrick and Elizabeth held on through the end. There are a few more things I should have her run down, but she's already slipped into her ancient Honda and has the engine on.

"She seems a little green," Sid says.

"This is her first project. She'll be fine."

"I'm not talking about the project. I have six kids, and the missus sported that same blow-chunks look every time."

"Really? No." My stomach drops, making me feel queasy too.

"I could be wrong. You look a little sick too."

I wave off the water bottle he's offering and force a smile. I know it's a fact of life. At some point in time, Hugh would find someone and start a family. I never thought I'd be around to witness it.

"Maybe we both ate something off at lunch."

"Maybe." Sid shoots me a sideways glance while he rolls up the plans. "We'll be ready to break ground two weeks from Saturday. You make sure you get us a couple that'll do this site proud."

"We'll know next week. I think we have the perfect couple." The voting for the couples went live today, and just as I predicted, Derrick and Elizabeth shot to the top. "I just hope the public get them the votes they need."

Twenty

HUGH

I'm certain I'm going to have to refinish the wood floors in front of the legal department's office. Voting for the Halia Couple closed an hour ago. I've spent about fifty-eight minutes of that hour waiting for Legal's door to open up and verify what should be a foregone conclusion. Jack skidded around the corner about a minute after I did. Her eyes went all shocked and uncomfortable before she ducked into the legal department's office, muttering she'd call me with the results. She and her eyes have been doing that for about a week now, and it's starting to piss me off. I caught her alone in the hallway before everyone showed up for work one day. She wouldn't look or talk to me.

When I asked Tessa what crawled up Jack's butt and decided to rot, she said she didn't know. I was going to call bullshit until I received a call from Sid, our foreman, wanting verification that Jack could change the second contact on our

US Open event. I okayed the change and have spent the last week trying to get an explanation from Jack.

"Any word?" Tessa pokes her head around the corner.

"Not yet."

"I don't know if that's good or bad. Before legal shut the website's administrative backdoor, Derrick and Elizabeth looked like they were going to walk away with this by a landslide."

I stop and lean up against the wall, restraining myself so I don't laugh right in Tessa's face. I'd received a call right after Legal told Tessa no more updates. She apparently had not taken the dismissal too well. Legal let me know they wouldn't tolerate threats to their genitals, and Ms. Saint Cloud would no longer be allowed in their office unattended. The last warning threw me. When I asked why, Legal said Tessa was looking in Sonia's confidential personnel files. I didn't know if I should throttle Tessa or kiss her for looking out for me. I assured the department Tessa wouldn't be bothering them or their family jewels. But between Jack's cold shoulder, Tessa's undercover snooping, and Sonia's new obsession with saltine crackers, I had to admit all three of the ladies in my life were rocking crazy to an art form.

"Hugh, you own the company. Can't you go in there and demand they tell you?" Tessa walks around the corner and leans next to me.

"I can, but if we're ever sued, Legal can't say I didn't know until the results were verified."

"Plausible deniability?" Tessa mutters.

"You've been watching *Independence Day* again?"

"It is the Fourth of July."

"A week ago, Tessa. July fourth was a week ago."

"You say that like there's a time limit on patriotism, well-made movies, and Will Smith." Her eyes take on that dreamy Hollywood crush state that accompanies any mention of Will Smith.

"Duly noted. Quick question. Is there a time limit on bosses asking why their consultants are digging around in employees' personnel files?"

Tessa's body goes rigid, arms crossed, and a purse on her lips appears, so severe it should make me fear for my safety. But this is Tessa, and that reaction means she's more mad that she's caught than worried for her job.

"I haven't a clue what you're talking about."

"Sadly, you don't have Will Smith or plausible deniability on your side." I wink at her.

Tessa pushes off the wall and goes to the other side of the hall. "I don't like her."

"Still not an answer as to why you were digging in her personnel file."

"I wasn't digging. I was fact checking."

Silence stretches between us. Tessa's a master at the game of words. It wasn't until sixth grade that I finally was able to see her traps coming. Still couldn't avoid them.

"And?" I prod.

She shoots a look my way and then goes back to searching the hallway. "Shouldn't Jack be here?"

"Probably not."

Tessa snaps her head back at me.

"Jack seems to be in the 'avoid Hugh' phase of her stay." I shuffle my feet. "I'm thinking it has to do with the visit she paid the old man."

The color drains from Tessa's face. "Why would she visit him?"

"Not sure, but when I checked in on Kai, the nurse said Jack only stayed for five minutes."

"There's a whole lot of secrets Kai could spill in five minutes."

"Yep."

The door to legal opens, and Jack steps out with a smile on her face. "Derrick and Elizabeth are our couple."

Tessa kicks my foot. "What about her plausible deniability?"

Tuxedos are women's way of making a man feel inferior. I don't care what "who wore it best" lists say. You stick a guy in a tuxedo, and he loses every shred of identity he has, fades away into the backdrop, and merely becomes a prop. I pull at the bowtie, stilling when Jack walks up the stairs of the Waterfront Hilton. Women, on the other hand, seem to become goddesses when they're in formal dresses.

The universe punctuates my thought when the woman I can never have climbs the last stair. Jack's black gown clings to every curve I knew she had and some I never would have imagined. My palm tingles with the memory of how my hand used to travel her hourglass figure, how her naked skin felt like warm silk. The roar of my pulse in my ears only encourages the memory of how I could rouse her from a deep sleep with the softest squeeze of that place where her hip dipped. She'd push her round bottom into me, and give me that sleepy *I love you* look that had us both ready and raring to go.

God, she was heaven.

Every inch of her was mine. Every soft moan that escaped her lips when I pushed into her were because of me. And those soul-shattering moments when she completely came apart, I claimed.

"You ready to go in?"

I jump at Sonia's voice. Or maybe it was getting caught while thinking about loving Jack. Whatever it is that's causing all the memories of Jack and me to bubble to the surface, they'll need to find a watery grave and bury themselves. I pull at the bowtie again and will my pulse to calm the fuck down. Sonia is whom fate has chosen me to be with. Sonia is the girl who gets to hang a monogramed towel in my bathroom. I push away the why and embrace the girl. Leaning in, I place a small kiss on Sonia's temple and wrap my arm around my future. It does nothing to loosen the knot of guilt wound in my gut. I love Jack, but Sonia holds the key to my life. A small bead of sweat trickles down my back, and I chase it away with a compliment.

"Have I told you how beautiful you look this evening?"

Sonia smiles up at me; her brown eyes are framed in a harsh black liner, and if there was no Jack to compare her to, she would be the most beautiful girl in the room.

"Thank you." Sonia threads her arm through mine and we head toward the ocean ballroom. Halia has only one table, and while I'm trying to commit to this whole Sonia-is-my-future thing, Jack is going to be sitting right across from me, drawing my gaze all night. Her pigheaded, asswipe of a boyfriend, EJ, really doesn't deserve her. What he deserves is to be beaten into a spot on the carpet. My hand flexes and then balls back up into a fist. Sonia squeezes my arm. Her face pales.

"Are you feeling okay?" I ask, ready to whisk her out of the room. This is my job. Sonia is mine to protect now.

Sonia nods.

Truth.

How I feel for Jack can't be an issue any more. Not after I found Sonia curled up in my personal bathroom at work this afternoon. I didn't think anything of it at first. Figured she was still fighting the flu or something. I couldn't have been further from the truth. Her red-rimmed eyes went wide like an animal caught in trap. My heart lurched as I bent down. She was trembling. Hands tight in her lap, I had to nearly pry her fingers open. The stick with two pink lines tumbled into my palm, and it was my turn to feel sick.

"I don't expect anything," she said. "I know. . ."

I cut off her sentence with a good hard kiss. I knew how that sentence ended. She knew I was in love with Jack, but none of that mattered now. What mattered was, she was going to be a mother, and despite the fact that I couldn't be the father due to a nearly non-existent sperm count, I had better get my head around the fact that Sonia and her baby could be Halia Surf's only hope for a future. If I were a father, it would definitely show the board that I am vested in running Halia like an adult and not the wild child they all think I am.

I hold the glass door open for Sonia. She steps through and abruptly stops. The upstairs ballroom usually did that for first timers. The only solid wall in the room holds the door we just walked through and an exit to the kitchen; everything else is plate-glass window. At night, the pier is lit up, and while it's only a half-moon, the ocean is surreal—like you've left reality and stepped into a fairy tale. The fountains that spill into the pools have an effervescent glow to them. Birds of paradise sit at the base of tall palm trees swaying in the soft ocean breeze. At night, the Waterfront Hilton is as close to Hawaii as I can get.

"This place is amazing," Sonia whispers.

"That it is." Jack's voice drifts in from behind us.

My spine straightens, as does Sonia's. I slide my hand up Sonia's back, taking possession of my future, and given the small gasp behind me, I'm clearly letting go of my past.

I give Sonia another kiss on her temple to make sure Jack knows I've made my choice, and it can't be her. Sonia leans into me as I say, "Our table is in the back, darling."

We have the best seats in the house. Our table is in the corner. Look to your left and you can see the lights of Long Beach; to your right is an unobstructed view of the Hilton's grounds. I pull out Sonia's chair and drop another kiss on her cheek before asking, "Can I get you anything to drink?"

"Um, club soda," she stammers. I smile and watch her eyes light up with a look that transforms her from pretty to gorgeous.

"I'll be right back." I say, running a finger along the side of her cheek. I've never noticed how soft her skin is. I push away from the table, sparing a quick look back at Sonia before slipping my hands into my pockets. Maybe we could be happy. I know one thing, though: if I can't have the person I love, then I'll be sure to make Sonia feel adored. My child deserves that much. Sonia deserves my effort.

Twenty One

JACK

I *wasn't looking forward to tonight.* When I'd heard the Open Sponsor Appreciation Dinner was in the Ocean ballroom, I'd nearly called Eros and told him I gave up. Then Tessa came home. She was ranting and raving about needing a few more minutes in Legal's paperwork to have the proof she needed. I was torn between the inappropriate remark of her being in anything of Legal's and the throbbing headache Tessa wasn't helping. I didn't know what proof she was trying to dig up, and every clinched fiber in my gut said when I did find out, I wouldn't want to know.

I escaped Tessa by renting a room at the Waterfront and getting ready there. By the time I'd slipped into my dress and headed to the ballroom, I'd had a firm plan in place to make Hugh fall for Sonia. That plan went flying out the plate-glass windows of the ballroom when I saw Hugh claim the small of Sonia's back.

Given the shocked look on Sonia's face, she is equally stunned and delighted at the new interest.

I could have stood there slack-jawed all night if E.J. hadn't put his hand on my back and grumbled for me to get my shit together. Three deep breaths later, I finish weaving together the last strings of my dignity and composure and head to Halia's table. It's the best fucking table in the place, of course. Hugh had brought me here the night he told me he loved me. He obviously doesn't remember any of that night, given the way he's leaning into Sonia, arm draped on the back of her chair. His smile touches her cheek, killing a little piece of me, while he points out the lights in Long Beach. Why not polish me off and suggest they take a drive over the Vincent Tomas Bridge and make a wish at the apex too.

"Jack, you don't wear 'jealous' very well," Tessa quips in my ear.

I straighten my spine and take the seat directly across from Sonia and Hugh. Hugh continues to whisper in Sonia's ear, not paying attention to anyone at the table. Not Tessa and her date, not the tubby guy from Legal and his model of a wife. I don't think he even acknowledges when Derrick and Elizabeth join our table, and he sure as hell doesn't know I'm dying a million deaths in front of him. All of Hugh's actions reaffirm my decision to give this all up. I don't need love. I'm better as a stone-cold bitch with a Cupid's arrow at my bidding.

E.J. leans into me. He smells like warm cookies and hot coffee on a cold day. Despite the anger coursing through me, my body relaxes at the scent. E.J. is picking up some of Eros's traits.

"Hurts like hell, doesn't it?" His whisky-tinted voice whispers heat in to my ear.

I instantly search the other side of the table for Hugh's reaction, but he's still enamored with whatever Sonia was saying.

My attention turns to the demi-god on my left. E.J.'s sun-kissed skin sets his blue eyes ablaze. We're so close, we can easily be mistaken as a couple whispering sweet nothings.

"What's that, E.J?"

"Realizing you can be replaced." A smile rips across his face but he isn't done yet. "Welcome to the world of immortality. All the world will know your name, but they won't have a flying fucking clue why they should care." A heartless chuckle shakes his shoulders. As if to prove his point, he nods to the people at the table. Derrick's smiling like a love-struck fool at Elizabeth. Martin, from Legal, grabs the breadbasket for his wife. Tessa's feigning interest in whatever her cover model date is saying, which brings me back to Hugh and Sonia. I lean into E.J., searching for a hint of glimmer in Hugh's eyes as he presses a kiss to her temple. If it is there, then I can get the hell out of here.

"I'll be right back," Hugh whispers to Sonia as he stands. But I can hear him. I guess I'll always be conditioned to melt at the warm timber of his voice. Hugh strolls away with his hands in his pockets. A quick glance back and I know my time here is coming to an end. Hugh's gaze lands on Sonia . . . not me. "Hurts like a bitch, don't it?" E.J. drapes his arm across the back of my chair.

"You could be a gentleman and get me a drink, E.J."

"And miss any of this? Get it yourself."

I push away from the table and walk the opposite direction of the hosted bar. I'll be back before the announcement, but I can't sit here through dinner. It's one thing to know what you're giving up. It's another thing to have a front row seat and watch it slip away.

I ride the elevator down and find the real bar, the one that sells shots, keeps 'em coming, and doesn't ask why.

Two drinks and three shots of fireball in, Tessa finds me.

She *always* finds me.

The girl should give up.

I gave up on her a long time ago.

"What are you doing?" She picks up my fourth shot and downs it. "Fireball? Fuck, Jack? If you're going to nurse a broken heart, then do it properly." She pushes the shot glass to the back of the bar and flags down the bartender. "Four shots of tequila. Two limes." She looks down at me. "Loser goes for the lime?"

"Sounds good, loser."

"Ha. Ha," she chortles. "I've never lost this game, and you're already one, two, three, four, five drinks in?"

"I'm numb, Tessa, that plays in my favor." My barstool tilts a little.

"Whoa." Tessa grabs me by the waist and heaves me back up onto my righted barstool. "Don't get ahead of me. If we're going to go down in flames, then we're going down together. Just let me catch up."

A wave of warmth washes over me. "Why are you still trying to be my friend, Tessa?"

She grabs the four shots from the bartender and then digs in her clutch.

"My treat," he says.

Tessa smiles. "Thanks." But the smile is gone when she looks back at me. "I don't have to try to be your friend, Jack. I've always been."

"I'm not yours." I prop my head onto my hand, but someone's moved the bar.

Tessa catches and rights me again. "I wouldn't be my friend either."

"I paid a visit to the old man. *Bastard.*"

"You're going to have to be a little more specific." She smiles but it doesn't reach her eyes. The way her eyebrows pinch together, she already knows I mean Kai.

"What did he do to you?" Somehow, that one question sops up a majority of the alcohol in my system. My vision clears and the world sharpens.

Tessa pauses a second and then grabs the first shot glass of tequila. Without so much as a *cheers,* she downs the pungent alcohol and grabs for the first lime.

"Turns out, I really am the loser." Tessa shoves the lime in her mouth.

I know she's been hiding Kai's secret now, so that makes me the loser. How long she's been living with what he did to her is going to prove how big a loser *I* really am. I was her best friend. I should have known.

Pat Benatar's "Love is a Battlefield" plays from my purse a second before Thompson Twins' "Lies, Lies, Lies" plays from Tessa's clutch. She fishes out her phone before I can wrap my mind around her ringtone.

She flags down the bartender while downing another shot, no lime. "Coffee," she says. Then grabs the third shot and puts it away like she's drinking water instead of knock-you-on-your-ass tequila. "Thanks." She pushes a hundred-dollar bill to the bartender and a cup of black coffee to me. "Drink up, girl. Hugh's looking for us. They're about ready to announce Halia Surf as an international sponsor. I've worked too damn hard to keep this boat afloat to miss its champagne christening." Tessa tosses back the last shot of tequila and pushes the glass and the lime away.

"Then you might want to lay off the Mexican amnesia."

"Yeah, well, I may still want to forget this night." Tessa shoots me a look through tequila-pinched eyes. "The jury's still out. Can you function?"

I test my legs and push off the barstool. The world tilts, sways, and then seems to settle down. "Yep, all good."

The lights are off in the Ocean ballroom when we walk in. The media package Tessa put together is running. Dad's face and the one-car garage on Toronto Street flash across the screen. I'm thinking I was a damn fool to drink that coffee and stop my world from spinning. Tessa reaches back for my hand and squeezes a moment before a picture of an eight-year-old me and a nine-year-old Hugh, with our arms around our dad's surfboards, swims across the screen.

"You brought me up here for this shit?" I lash out, but my voice doesn't hold any of the venom it should. The opposite: I actually feel something akin to warmth pulsing in my chest.

“Can you make it to our seats?”

“No, I’m supposed to walk on stage with Hugh and Sonia. The Aiónia Agápi seal of approval that Halia can tread the waters.”

Tessa grabs my arm.

“Let me go. I’m buzzed, not drunk.” I glare at her one last time. “Remind me to kick your ass later for the coffee.” I leave Tessa hissing my name and walk to the front of the room where Hugh and Sonia are standing. Hugh has her in front of him, arms wrapped around her shoulders. It’s a stance so familiar, my lungs nearly implode from the sight. They’re a stunning couple, but then again, anyone standing next to Hugh is.

I wipe at my dress, straighten my hair, and put on my best game-face before I walk over and join them. They hardly acknowledge my presence. Sonia’s fingers are wrapped around Hugh’s forearm. As the media package ends, she presses a small kiss to his wrist, and I feel my emotions thrash against the dam of disregard I’ve erected. I remind myself that this is what I want. I want him to move on, because when he moves on, this ache and the jagged fingernails digging into my heart will subside. I scratch at the empty arrow spot on my wrist.

“Keep it together,” I whisper to myself.

“You say something, Jack?” Hugh barely waits for an answer before he tucks Sonia into his side. He works his jaw, chewing on the emcee’s final lines introducing Halia Surf to the vendors. Dad would want me to focus on saving Halia Surf, even if it meant giving up the man. I resist the urge to rub at the ache in my chest by clapping with the rest of the audience when Hugh is introduced.

Still, there is that piece of me that wants to scratch the grin off Sonia’s face when Hugh starts to lead the wrong girl up the three steps to the stage.

Hugh crosses the stage and shakes the emcee’s hand while taking the microphone in the other, while I follow behind like a lost puppy. A second later, E.J. steps next to Hugh and shakes his hand before he settles in next to me. Of course, E.J. would be here on the stage; he's a board member. I try to clear the alcoholic fog from my head. E.J. inches closer, wrapping his fingers around my wrist. Hugh starts the speech Tessa and I wrote for him earlier this week. Still doing the dude's homework. I shake my head.

"You're scratching." E.J. rubs the pad of his thumb across the spot where my last arrow belongs. "Everything okay?"

"Everything's fine. Must be a mosquito bite. You know how annoying those bugs are."

E.J. chuckles, but not loud enough to interrupt the speech Hugh's delivering. "My job to check."

"I didn't realize Eros sent you here to watch over me."

"Did I say that?"

I shake my head. "Then why the concern?"

E.J. drops his hold on me and applauds with the rest of the crowd. "Because I don't think you have what it takes, Jack. I think you're going to wash out like the rest of the niners who get close and fail."

I step away from E.J. "Watch me blow your theory to kingdom come."

"I'll just stop you at the 'watch me blow you.'" He winks.

I turn my focus back to Hugh and Sonia in time to hear him introduce Ai<u>ó</u>nia Agápi<u>i</u> and me.

"With Jack and A.A.'s help, we're certain we're going to show you an event you'll never forget and a summer you'll fall in love with. As many of you know, Halia opened its site a week ago to the public. We wanted to share five epic love stories with our supporters and let them vote on the couple they loved the most. But we didn't want to stop there. Once the visitors voted on that special couple,

Halia wanted to give them a wedding that matched their story. We're so pleased to introduce you to Halia's love story couple . . . *Derrick and Elizabeth.*"

The room erupts into applause as Derrick and Elizabeth's media package runs. Sonia and I put this together two days ago, when it looked like they were our solid front runners. At the end of the package, there isn't a dry eye in the place. I think even E.J.'s wiping something from his eyes.

"Derrick and Elizabeth." Hugh signals to the stairs behind me, and they walk on stage. "At Halia, with the help of A.A. and its subsidiaries, we've defined our brand as the company that not only loves the ocean but is enchanted by the stories of love that happen around our products, which is why I'm going off script. I hope you all bear with me."

I work my molars. Hugh never goes off script. His entire life, he's operated by a script. Even his spontaneous moments are, well—scripted—which means whatever he's doing . . . he's planned it. A knot tangles up in my gut. He reaches back for Sonia and my heart thrashes against my rib cage. My pulse is sloshing around in my ears, roaring so loud I can't hear a word he's saying. Then again, I don't need to hear what he's saying, Hugh's down on one knee.

E.J.'s hands wrap around my waist, pulling me into him. "Be happy. I know this is hard as hell, but be happy. Clap, Jack."

A tear lets loose and trickles down an ancient path all the other tears I've cried over Hugh have carved. It's been so long since I've cried, the salt stings my eyes, I'm almost certain it will burn my skin.

"Will you marry me, Sonia?" Hugh asks.

I bite down on my lip, willing the tears to stop. Despite the ache washing through me, this is what I want. Another rebellious tear lets loose as I watch Hugh put a stunning ring on Sonia's finger. I guess she won't be leaving Halia like she thought.

E.J. pulls me in close. "After this farce of forever is over, we're grabbing Tessa.

Eros wants to speak to the both of you."

"Why?"

"Maybe you were too busy feeling the love, you forgot to look for the glimmer."

I look back at Hugh. He's wrapped Sonia up in his arms, chin resting on the top of her head, when his gaze locks with mine and . . . it's not there. *The glimmer isn't there.* He's put a ring on Sonia's finger, but his heart still belongs to me.

Oh, God, Hugh, what have you done?

"I thought Eros was floating in the Atlantic," Tessa hollers over the wind whipping through my convertible Maserati.

E.J. stole my keys, stuck her in the back seat, lowered the top, and took off faster than a targeted arrow before Tessa could wrap her hair up in a bun. I'll admit it made me laugh until the first light. Then I caught her watered-up eyes plotting all the ways she could maim E.J., and I had to side with my girl. It was a dick move.

"Tessa, darling, he's the god of fucking love. You think a small thing like an ocean hinders him?" E.J. drops the car into first and rolls to a stop. "You haven't learned shit, have you?"

E.J.'s tires squeal against the road and launch us forward as the light turns green, but all the speed in the world can't chase away the tension between these two. The history between them is palpable.

We fly down PCH through the Bolsa Chica Wetlands and near the edge of Sunset Beach, when E.J. pulls the car's speed back and turns at the water tower. Nerves that have no business fluttering start flapping, as we pull into the Surfside

Colony and next to Hugh's house.

"Why are we here?" I ask.

"This is where my dad lives." E.J. jumps out of the car, slams the door, and stalks out the garage's side door.

I open the passenger door and pull up the front seat for Tessa to climb out. "You knew Eros lives here?"

"You didn't?" Tessa undoes the bun she'd finally assembled on one of E.J.'s slowdown stops, shakes out her hair, and reapplies another coat of red lipstick.

"What did you tell your date?"

"What I tell all my dates: it's been fun but I've gotta jet. Call you in the morning." She smacks her lips and plasters on the fake, blonde-bimbo grin.

"You're such a dude, Tessa."

Tessa stops short in the doorway, pinning me with a look that's more serious than playful. More deadly than devilish. "I'm not a dude, Jack. I'm a Cupid."

She leaves me caught between the rancid world of an exhaust-filled garage that holds my future and the sweet scent of Hawaiian Wedding flowers that was my painful past.

We were both Cupids. I just wonder how long it will be before she starts to feel the empty void that is consuming me. I drag my fingers along the greenery, plucking a flower and wanting desperately to go back to the time when Hugh's mom taught me how to string the delicate white flowers into a lei. I know it wasn't Eros who planted the Wedding Flowers; it was the enigma of a man who lived on the other side of the seven-foot hedge. And the part of me I would never allow to live, to dream, wondered if Hugh Halia didn't remember it either.

I chase the thought away. I'm too close to fifty arrows, too close to the god who could take it all away, to be hunting down happily-ever-after what ifs.

Whatever the reason Hugh planted the vines, his mom would be happy he did.

"You coming?" Tessa sticks her head around the corner, nodding to the back of the house.

"Yeah."

The constricted walkway spills into a stunning backyard. At the back of the yard is a pool and spa lit up against the inky backdrop of the ocean. Two canopied sunbeds flank the pool, and a stone walkway cuts through the sand and grass up to the red travertine patio. Fuchsia plants climb up the white columns of the patio cover and dangle from the slats above a teak table. Eros sits at the head of the table, Psyche to his right, and E.J. to his left. Tessa sits next to Psyche, her hands folded in her lap. It's the first time I've ever seen my friend act in reverence of someone.

"Have a seat, Jack." Psyche nods to the empty setting next to E.J.

As I take my seat, Eros starts, "You know why you all are here?"

I'm lead on this assignment, so I speak up, "Hugh proposed tonight."

"Hugh proposed tonight." Eros clasps his fingers and leans his elbows on the table. "Why would he do that if he's still in love with you?"

"He'll lose Halia if he's not married by his next birthday."

"Not a good enough reason to get married," E.J. replies.

I shoot him a look to shut up.

"My son's right. Not a good enough reason." Eros grabs the empty cup in front of him and snaps his fingers. The cups fill with a pink liquid. "Ambrosia?" He nods to all of our now full cups. "You know how we remedy this?"

"I do, but it won't come to that. I'll fix it. There's no need to banish his heart yet."

E.J. snorts. "I told you she didn't have what it takes, Pa." His judgmental look shifts from me to Tessa. "Neither of them do."

A protective surge of heat erupts. "E.J., I get your not liking me, but what has Tessa ever done to deserve your annoyance?" I feel Tessa shift more than see her. Oh, shit. I know that guilty little shift. I try to keep my gob-smacked reaction hidden. When would they have found the time?

Eros clears his throat. "E.J. is learning the family business."

And just like that, the protective surge is gone.

"My son has been training to take over for over a century, Jack."

If surfing and bikini chasing in Australia is training, then he's ready.

"Jack, I think this assignment is so far gone that anything short of you relinquishing your title—"

"I can fix this." I cut off Eros and stand before being dismissed.

Tessa's eyebrows climb up into her hairline. Psyche smiles and puts her hands over Eros's fist.

Through tightly drawn lips, Eros issues his last warning, "I understand this assignment means something to you, but it is just another assignment, and you will respect the protocol as I demand."

"I mean no disrespect, Eros, but this isn't just another assignment. This is my fiftieth arrow. If Hugh doesn't love Sonia, so be it, but I won't lose my shot at immortality over his need to save his family's company. I'll fix it. Now, may I be excused?"

Eros stands. "A.A.'s contract with Halia terminates at the close of the US Open; Mr. Halia has a reprieve until sundown of the Open's last day. Jaquelyn"—I cringe at the formal use of my name, but Eros continues—"You do have forty-nine arrows, but you also have one brand against you; dance too close to the edge and I will be the one who personally pushes you over." Eros nods for me to leave. "I like you, Jack, but I agree with my son on this one . . . you're no Cupid."

I raise a hand in acknowledgement, all too certain if I turn around, Eros will kick me out of the Corps right here and now. And that wouldn't do a single soul any good. I resist the urge to kick open the gate and start the three-mile walk back to my condo.

Hugh'd better get used to falling in love or letting go of his company because I'm not going to allow him to ruin my future again.

Twenty Two

HUGH

I *haven't caught a wave all* morning. Not for lack of swells, but my brain just isn't in it today. I'll blame the night of toss-and-turn on Eric and Pam. My next-door neighbors came home early from their cruise, then had people over until the crack of dawn. I swear—at some point after two in the morning—I heard Tessa's voice. She was talking about Jack . . . and me. I couldn't fall asleep after that, hoping it was reality.

Jack and me, we had our chance. We'd always be the right love, wrong time. Now, with Sonia pregnant and the Open two weeks away, I have to let Jack and the notion of true love go. It just wasn't meant for us.

"You've been floating out here for two hours, dude." Derrick sits up on his board and searches the horizon. "Figure it's about Jack and the wrong girl you proposed to last night."

"Why do you say she's the wrong girl?"

"Because Jack looked like she was going to puke, and not many caught it, but when you slipped that massive rock on your fiancée's finger, you were glaring at Jack, daring her to stop you."

I swallow hard over the lump in my throat. When did Derrick turn into such an observant motherfucker?

"Sonia's pregnant."

"Ahh." Derrick kicks up his prosthetic leg onto his board. "Do you love her?" Dude's still out here kickin' life's ass. And mine.

A swell rolls under us easily, but the answer to his question . . . not so much. If he saw the daring look I gave Jack, he knows the answer.

"She's carrying Halia's future," I finally say.

"Not an answer, dude. That's an excuse. Don't mean to sound like a shit, but people have babies without being married all the time."

I size up Derrick, rolling the next few confessions around my mouth. I know I can trust him, I have since he covered for me when Kai called his house looking for me the night after Jack and I opened the letter with the deed to Mom's secret beach house at Sycamore Beach. The information I'm about to spill would send my legal team into a fit of simultaneous coronaries.

Derrick cocks his head, eyebrows raised like they're saying, *spill, dude. It's me.*

"Kai's put a clause in the company transfer papers that if I'm not married by my next birthday—Labor Day—then I lose the Halia CEO title. It passes on to Mack."

"That's your half-brother?"

I give him a sideways nod.

"I saw the paper." He clarifies how he knows my half-brother. "Your dad always was an asshole. This is what you were talking about when we had breakfast as The Sugar Shack?"

I nod.

Another decent, rideable swell passes under us and the ocean flattens out. I rub saltwater on my face and turn toward the sun. Something has to wash away the menacing feeling I haven't been able to shake since I slipped a rock on Sonia's finger.

"Which has you pulling the marriage trigger: the baby or the company?"

"The company had me thinking Sonia wouldn't be so bad, but when I found out she was pregnant, that kind of sealed the deal."

"I don't mean your baby momma any disrespect, but are you sure you're the dad, Hugh?" Derrick splashes some water on him. The sun is starting to ride high. "Not like you don't have a very public pot of gold sitting at the end of your rainbow."

I chuckle. "The baby isn't mine."

Derrick nearly falls off his board. "One: how do you know that? And two: you still proposed?"

When he puts it so bluntly, I'm as shocked as Derrick is, as Jack was at the dinner—and she doesn't even know the baby isn't mine.

"You remember the press with Randie, Halia's surf star?"

Derrick nods.

"I had to give a blood sample. After they concluded I didn't have sex with the girl, docs asked me to come back because my testosterone levels were low. After a sperm analysis, they let me know the likelihood of me fathering a child was almost nonexistent." I let the disclosure ride away with the next swell under us. "Besides, Sonia's been pushing for me to take things to the next level long before she found out she was pregnant."

"But not before Jack's return, I'm guessing."

"Hard to be in Jack's presence and not feel threatened," I offer up in Sonia's defense.

"Even harder when you're looking at Jack like she's the very air you breathe."

"It's that obvious?"

"Always has been, which is why I'm so surprised Jack's got nothing to say about this."

"She doesn't want me. She's with the Aussie."

"Again, just a new guy's observation, but she can't stand the dude. I can't either. The guy has a serious ego and the chip on the shoulder to match it. If it wouldn't have cost us a spot on the top of Halia's wedding cake, I can say for certain that Elizabeth was two seconds away from dousing him with her drink and then kneeing him in the balls."

"Yeah." I try to think of what Derrick could have seen that I missed. It does no good. All I can think of is all the vicious ways I can fuck up Jack's dude without hurting Halia's relaunch. "I can't stand the fool, but Jack seems sprung on him, and it's not business anymore."

"You can say those words, Hugh, but you and I both know you'll never mean them." Derrick nods off to the horizon at a new set of swells forming. "I'm headed in. Physical therapy day. Oh, Elizabeth wants me to tell you she loves dress and tux option two."

I quirk an eyebrow.

"The wedding site went live today. You should count on me updating you with her choices for the next five days."

Derrick wasn't wrong about the updates. Every day, I received a text or a call, sometimes both, from him and Elizabeth about their preferences. Luckily, the public seems to agree with them on everything except the honeymoon. Halia's couple was hoping to go to my favorite spot, Hawaii, but the public voting seems to be leaning toward a trip to Fiji. When I'd asked Derrick why he wanted Hawaii over Fiji, he'd said it was what they'd dreamed about in high school.

My desk phone rings and I hit the speakerphone.

"Halia."

"You haven't left yet?" Sonia's voice squeaks over my speakerphone, filling the office.

"Yeah, give me two minutes. I promise, I'm walking out the door." I holler *Come in!* at the knock on my door before I can disconnect the speakerphone. "What's up, Jack. I'm on my way out."

Jack walks into my office with a stack of papers and a look of determination in her eyes. I've been doing my best to avoid her and Tessa. I even contemplated paying the old man a visit to get out of an all-teams briefing but opted for a dental cleaning instead.

"Hugh, I don't want to be late, we get to hear the baby's heartbeat," Sonia says through the speaker.

Jack's stack of papers drop to the ground as I scramble to pick up the receiver.

"Right, I'm almost done here." It's a lie. Based on Jack's hand slapped over her mouth and the fact that she looks like she's about to lose the contents of her stomach on my office floor, I'm going to need more than a few minutes to clean up this mess. A couple of sweet nothings and I hang up the phone. I start to walk over to Jack, but she puts her palm out, stopping me in my tracks.

"I'm sorry, I didn't . . . I didn't know." Jack falls to her knees, fishing for her paperwork. "Of course, she's pregnant."

She's muttering in that cute way that would always have me kissing her senseless to shut her up.

"That makes sense," Jack continues.

I follow Jack down and still her hands. They tremble under my touch, and when her eyes meet mine, the raw pain punches me in the gut. God, she didn't deserve to find out this way. She doesn't deserve any of this after everything I've already put her through. I know what must be done. I know my admission stings now, but it'll save her more heartache later. Jack deserves her shot at happiness. So does my kid.

"We're not going to say anything publicly until after her first trimester. I didn't want to take away from the event."

Her eyes dart across my face; her lips pucker and release like she's a fish gasping for air. "And I'm the public."

I know I'm about to ruin her a second, third—hell, I've lost count—time with my answer, but it's time I draw a line in the sand, if not for Sonia or me, I have to do it for my child. "You're not even the public; you're an employee."

I see the words slice through her, and I want to take it all back. Explain all the reasons why we can't be together and then have her tell me they don't matter. But they do, and we both know it. Tears stop filling in her eyes, and her spine snaps into place as she finishes gathering her papers and stands.

"You're right. I'll, um, I'll leave these on your desk and let you get to your family." Her voice cracks around the last word.

Jack drops off the files and walks past me, trying to hide the way her hands are shaking. God, I'm a dick. Her sweet scent is one last reminder of what I'm giving up. She stops at the door, doesn't hold on to it—she just occupies the space like only Jack can do. "I'm really happy for you, Hugh. You're going to make an amazing father."

"If I am, it's going to be by luck and not example." I lean back against my desk, feeling all my shitty choices settle in between my shoulder blades. Jack leaves, taking all the air, all the reasons I'm happy with her. Decimating the girl I love to make sure the girl I'm trying to start a life with sucks balls.

Tessa takes up Jack's place in my doorway as my office phone rings. I'm half tempted to let it go to voicemail, since it's probably Sonia wanting to make sure I'm not with Jack. I wave Tessa in and grab the phone.

"Halia," I answer, but it's not Sonia. "That's me." My fingers dig into the wood of my desk, as my gaze locks with Tessa's.

"Mr. Halia? This is Tender Care Hospice. I'm so sorry—"

"When?" I cut off the caller. I know what they're going to tell me.

Tessa's eyes flare, and she's by my side in less than a heartbeat, palm running up and down my back. My free hand grips Tessa's fingers, and like always, she's solid as granite for me.

"Thirty minutes ago. I'm going to need you to come in. I can handle the arrangements. They seem to be very . . . simple, but I will need your signature."

She has no idea how simple Kai's funeral will be. There are only two souls on this planet who cares if he lives or dies . . . and I'm not one of them.

"Thank you, it'll take me twenty minutes to get to you. No, I'll notify the rest of his family about his passing." I hang up the receiver. Tessa steps away from me, arms wrapping around her chest like that's the only thing holding her together. I should hate the man. My father. The word sours in my throat. I know he did something to make Tessa uncomfortable with even the mention of him. What? She'll never tell, and after this phone call, Kai took it to the grave. Despite everything he took from me and Jack and Tessa, all I can think of is my dad's dead and I'm really on my own.

"He's really gone?" Tessa whispers.

I nod and watch her abandon whatever reason she had for finding me as she slips out my door.

She's finally free.

I'm alone.

And Jack is gone.

Twenty Three

JACK

The *office has been in* a fog of celebration and mourning the past three days. Some even celebrating the mourning. I keep waiting for someone—Tessa—to break out her Dorothy slippers and scream, *Ding dong, the dick is dead.*

She hasn't.

And the oddest feeling is, I don't think she ever will.

This morning, after fighting in a dream with Hugh, his abs, and a surfboard—I'll let my shrink in Sydney deal with that one—I find Tessa sitting on the balcony with a bowl of melted ice cream in her lap.

"You okay?" I ask, leaning in the slider's doorjamb.

"Not sure."

I stay planted inside. She's not the only one. I'm not sure of anything when it comes to Contessa Saint Cloud. "You want to talk about it?"

"Not really. You said you paid the man a visit before he passed." Her big red-rimmed eyes find mine. "I can only imagine what he had to say."

"He told me how good a friend you've been to me." I abandon the game and ease down on the lounge. My first stop after visiting Kai should've been Tessa, but I was too devastated. Shattered that she didn't tell me. Furious for her thinking I couldn't handle myself. I was livid with my dad. How could he have known about Kai and not done anything? And if he had, how different would our lives be today? Now, all I have are what ifs and could haves . . . and even those seem to have a shelf life.

Tessa's red-rimmed eyes steal another quick peek at me. I don't blame her for being so cagey. Knowing what I know now, I'm surprised she didn't beg Eros every day for the last month to allow her to have other living arrangements. I close my eyes and listen to the waves crashing in the distance. They'll be perfect for the US Open next week. The business front of my job is solid. It's the mystical side of my assignment that's in the shits.

"What are we going to do about, Hugh?" I keep my eyes shut, letting the silence stretch between us. It's the first time I've asked her for help in six years. I owe her the courtesy of keeping my eyes shut while Tessa gawks and then flips me off. "Let me know when I've been rightly cursed out in sign language."

She giggles. "Unless you're going to give Ichabod Crane a run for his money, you should get used to me both non-verbally and verbally assaulting you for the next six years."

"Three and we'll call it a deal." I sneak a peek and stick out my hand to shake on it.

"Why three years?"

"Because you should have told me what Kai did. You should have told me

Hugh was trying to push me away to keep me safe. And you should have trusted that we could have handled it together. Does Hugh know . . . about you?"

Tessa lowers her eyes, shoulders slumping. All her sass leaks out onto our deck, and I know Hugh doesn't have a clue. "We probably could have handled it together, but Jack"—she lifts her head and her look cuts right through me—"I wouldn't change a thing. Kai Halia is, was, a monster. He would have destroyed everything that is good and pure in you. Your dad knew it. I knew it. But most of all, Hugh knew it." Her words hang on a breeze before being sucked back out to sea. "He loved you so much. He'd rather you hate him for eternity than risk even the thought of his dad getting his hands on you."

"When this is over, when we've got Hugh's heart safe and sound, you're going to tell me what happened. Not the watered down, what-you-think-I-can-handle version." I swing my legs over and grab Tessa's hands. They're cold and clammy, and I wonder if she's been out here all night. "And Tessa, next time, *you* trust me. You hear me? *You* trust *me*. You owe me that."

Tessa leans forward, resting her forehead against mine. "I don't owe you anything, Jack. But I'll trust you because we're friends. That's the deal."

"Done," I say immediately.

Her look meets mine and the past is put down. It's always been that hard and that easy with us.

"Now, how the hell are we going to save Hugh?"

Tessa's lips quirk up in a grin I know all too well. It's the grin from when we were kids that ended me with either getting a stern talking to or a week's worth of grounding. It's exactly what we need right now.

"We'll bring the baby momma down."

I pull away from Tessa and swing my legs back up on the lounge chair. "I can't do that, not if Hugh's baby is involved."

"Trust me, you can." Tessa mirrors my laidback position. There's a new glow in her cheeks. "She's running a scam, Jack. I just can't figure out what it is."

"Maybe there isn't a scam. Maybe she really loves—"

Tessa cuts me off with a look. "She doesn't love him. I've been there almost eleven months watching the girl. I doubt the baby is even Hugh's." Her eyes roll; I know she's seen mine flare. "Jack, I'd be willing to put all my arrows on the blackness in that wench's heart."

"I see your flair for the melodramatics hasn't diminished."

Tessa snorts. "Like yours has. I'm pretty sure I could get a copy of the Vendors' Dinner and show you your drunk ass nearly passing out when Hugh popped the question."

"I didn't pass out."

"I said almost."

"My ass was drunk because you ordered four shots of tequila."

"Which I drank."

"Whatever." I roll my eyes. The sky is turning pink, and it's light enough I can see there are swells stacking up for miles. "You want to surf?"

"I don't do the water. It's hard on my nails." Tessa examines her fingers to prove her point.

"Put your feet in the ocean and free your soul, Tessa." I stand and smack her leg. "Wetsuits are in the hall closet. You'd better meet me out there, or the three-year deal is off the table."

A few moments later, my stomach tangles with nerves as I carry my board. I haven't been in the ocean in over six years. It makes no sense, but surfing . . . it was something special, sitting out in the water, swells lifting you as you waited for the perfect wave to form. Hugh and I had practically planned our future sitting on our surfboards. Now, Tessa and I need to figure out how to save him. I swish the water and kick my foot up on the board.

"You look like a girl who found salvation," Tessa's voice comes from behind me.

I knew she'd find her way out here. She loved surfing as much as I did. When she was having trouble with her mom, a night at my house and an early morning set seemed to wash whatever problems she had away.

"Have you been in the water since I've been gone?"

Her wet ponytail flops over her shoulder, "No. Seemed almost sacrilegious to be out here when we were all fighting."

"I never asked; why did you stop talking to Hugh?"

"Because I was mad at him."

Tessa's board glides next to mine. I kick my feet up on her board, and she does the same to mine. Six years and we haven't missed a step. I guess that's the test of true friendship.

"Bury the past time?"

Tessa nods.

"You didn't have sex with Hugh?" I ask, but my gut already knows the answer.

"Not even close. I had on my yoga pants and bra. Hugh had on sweats. I figured he'd already seen me in a bikini, so there wasn't any new real estate he'd be checking out."

I think back to the scene burned in my mind. If we'd all trusted each other. I shake the thought from my mind. The past is done. The future, Hugh's future, is what we need to concentrate on.

"You know what happens to a banished heart?" I ask.

"I do. Short story, they're usually dead within a few years of banishment. With no heart, the soul is left in purgatory waiting for the body to die. Heart and soul, not just a piano tune." Tessa nods to a set coming in behind me.

"Next set. Tell me why you're so certain Sonia's running a scheme."

Tessa rolls her shoulders as the swell lifts us up and drops us back down. "This would be easier if I had my notes and something stronger than chocolate malted crunch ice cream in my belly."

"Hit me with the cliff notes version." Another up-and-down motion sends my stomach fluttering.

"She was already in play when I came on as a consultant for Halia. Kai had publicly claimed Mack and was starting his first rounds of chemo two weeks later. I was brought in for crisis management. Given the three hot heads I was going to be dealing with, the emphasis was on management because there were bound to be a shitload of crises. We should paddle away from the pylons."

We break our makeshift raft and paddle away from the pier. My hands dig into the water, up and over another swell, and we settle back into the spot we'd originally had before the current grabbed hold of us.

"So, you weren't here on a Corps assignment?"

Tessa slides sideways on her board and walks her feet across mine. "No, E.A. is Eros's pet project. He's a god. He gets bored. Eros staffs the E.A. with the scabs of the Corps. We run secondary support to Aiónia Agápi. Eros only gives us a shot at a case when there's a potential problem. I always thought the potential was Mack. He was always my bet on who'd piss off Eros. I was wrong about that one."

I didn't know what to say. Here I am going on and on about my fiftieth arrow, and I bet Tessa doesn't even have half a dozen. Once I fix Hugh, I'm going to demand Eros put Tessa on my team. She deserves a shot at immortality. Given the suffering she's endured all her life, I'm surprised Eros hasn't picked up on her potential.

"Here's the thing," Tessa interrupts my thoughts. "Everything I'm finding on Sonia checks out. She's from Podunk, Kentucky, barely graduated high school, did a year in cosmetology school, and then dropped out. Two years later, she shows up in Los Angeles working as the assistant to the Assistant Cruise Director for Hawaiian Cruise Line. She meets Hugh there, and a year later, something crawls up Hugh's ass and he hires her as his personal assistant."

"Wait, what? Hugh's been back to the islands? When?" I nearly fall off my board. We were supposed to go back together. Hike to Waimoku Falls and . . . A wave of sadness washes through me.

Tessa shrugs. She doesn't mean it, but the implied *you've missed so much* cuts me deep.

"He went back the Christmas after you left," she finally offers. "Scattered Alani's ashes like she'd asked."

Something deep inside me breaks. I'd promised Hugh I would go with him. When I came back, I just assumed his mom's ashes had remained in the rosewood box he had made.

"Wow," I whisper. "And Sonia?" I try to change the subject, but the ache of breaking that promise to Hugh makes me . . . regret the choice to be a Cupid. I quickly banish the thought before it ruins me. "I don't like the girl, but I'm not ready to ruin her life if all you've got is a gut feeling."

"Sometimes a gut feeling is all you need." An ocean swell picks us up and floats us down, filling the silence between us.

It's not much to go on, and if we're wrong, this could cost Hugh everything. I'm ready to banish a heart . . . I'm just not certain it has to be Hugh's. My pulse rebels at the thought. In fact, I'm damn certain it won't be his.

"Hey, Jack. I'm loving this bonding ritual we've got going on, but we haven't got a single wave, the sun's climbing, and we're supposed to start breaking ground on the site. I can take over Sonia's duties. We can work this like the kickass team of Cupids we're supposed to be. You can use Sonia's 'delicate way' to soften the blow of taking her off this site."

"No, if there's something in your gut that feels off about her . . ." I pause, thinking really long and hard if I'm ready to take this trip with Tessa again. She chews on her lip like she knows what I'm thinking but she's not going to influence me. She's going to let me come to this conclusion all by myself. Just like she did when we were kids. "I trust your gut, Tessa. I hate to admit it, but your gut's never been wrong. Keep Sonia thinking she's got me hating Team Slutty Tessa. She won't have a clue we're on to her. I know in my heart Hugh doesn't love her, so I'll skirt the flirt line and the risk of my banishment until he's safe." I level her with a look. "Look me in the eyes and tell me one last time—"

"She's running a scam, Jack. I can't prove it, yet, but I know in my core, Sonia's about to ramrod our boy out of his soul."

My heart thumps in my chest.

"And Team Slutty Tessa?" she scoffs before I can answer. "What are we, twelve?"

"Some days that doesn't sound half bad." I kick off her board and nearly send her tumbling off the back. It earns me a double flip-off. "First one in buys the coffee." I dig in to the water and feel my leg jerk back. My board flips me, and when I surface, I see Tessa charging my wave.

"Works for me," she cackles.

Most surfers would be pissed that they were yanked by their leash, but for me, this is normal. This is home.

"Sid!" I holler. Sparks waterfall over the sides of metal scaffolding, nearly drowning out the rhythmic drum of hammers and workers making sure everything is perfect. Everything needs to be perfect, more so now than ever. My stomach

falls away remembering Eros's demand for me to banish Hugh. I shake the memory and continue my pissed-off march from the office to the sand. I blame the slowing cadence on the site of our thirty-foot steel tower. It's ugly, but isn't everything before true beauty is revealed? Yeah, I can't see it yet, but I know this monstrous construction site is going to magically transform into a slice of Hawaiian heaven. Somehow.

Sid, the portly foreman, looks over his shoulder and heads toward me. Sonia is with him, and I saw Tessa park as I tore across the street. I hand Tessa her double-espresso-shot black coffee when she walks up. The girl is going to need it. We're already three hours behind, and the site coordinator for the Open just emailed me new operating hours passed by the city council last night.

"What's up?" Tessa asks.

I hand her a copy of the new hours, the new, six-hours-a-day shorter hours.

Tessa pulls in sip of coffee while reading the document. "This is crap." She hands it back to me like it doesn't matter, doesn't apply.

"What's crap, Ms. Saint Cloud? Good morning, Ms. Alcantar."

"Jack and Tessa will do, Sid." I correct him. "Good morning, Sonia. Early bird getting the worm?"

Sonia nods.

"Did you see this?" I hand Sid the same city ordinance as Tessa.

"Yeah, I got those a few minutes ago. Was working logistics with the team to get some answers for the questions you're about to ask me." He pulls off his hard hat and runs a hand through the last remaining silver strands of hair on his head.

"Sounds like we're not going to like the answers." Tessa chimes in.

"My boys can do it, but it's not going to leave any time for problems."

"Are we going to have any problems?" Sonia chimes in. A ring on her finger, no matter how diluted the proposal behind it, seems to have unleashed some moxie in the girl. Enough pluck that she thinks she can shimmy her way into my shoes. That may have worked in her personal life, but all I have left is my professional life, and I'll be damned if she hip-checks me out of job, as well as love. I feel my eyes flare and push pass the moment.

Sid shoots me a sideways glance and directs his answer to me. Looks like I'm not the only one who can spot a power play for my position. "No, Ms. Alcantar, we won't have any problems. You'll be ready for a wet run in two days."

Sonia bristles next to me while Tessa does her best to hide wide eyes and an untimely giggle. If Sonia didn't know how Tessa felt about her before, she surely does now.

"I'll check in tomorrow."

Sid slides his hard hat back on and looks at Halia's headquarters across the street. "Not like you can't keep an eye on us any time." There's a joking quality in his voice that settles all my nerves. Hugh and Sonia, Tessa and me, how Mack fits into all of this, all these moving pieces, and it's the foreman who gets me to calm down. Maybe he'd like a job in the Cupid Corps. Tessa follows after Sid, probably to get a rundown on all the things that could go wrong so she can catch and hide them from the universe in the back of her project folder. Some things never change.

I giggle.

"I don't think this is anything to laugh at," Sonia chides. She turns in such a way, the wind catches her sundress pulling it tight against her belly, and I can't help the twang of jealousy that lets loose when I spot the tiny baby bump. I didn't think she was this far along. Sonia follows my eyes and pulls the ends of her sweater tight.

"Hugh's not going to like this." Sonia's voice softens. Secrets so close to the surface of exposure have a way of doing that.

"No, he's not."

"So?"

"So, we hope for the best and prepare for the worst." I hand her the clipboard. "Write down all the ways this can go sideways and have the answers on how we're going to make sure that doesn't happen for me before the end of the day." I spy Tessa and Sid glancing our way. "I need to check on security for the site with Sid. I'll meet you back at the office." I walk away, dismissing her. When I reach the foreman's trailer, I know there's only one thing that could make Tessa's eyebrows knit together the way they are. A quick glance back to make sure we're alone and I climb the last few steps.

"Someone's messing with the site already?" I huff.

Tessa hands me the tablet with a grainy picture as an answer.

"This from the security cameras?" I ask.

Sid nods, shifting on the balls of his feet. "Four nights ago."

My eyes meet his and he already knows I'm not happy. "I know one thing that needs to change immediately."

"Yes, ma'am." He doesn't offer an excuse, and given the way the vein on his forehead is dancing, he has a ton of justifications, like security isn't in his contract. But Sid takes the criticism and moves on. "I'll review them morning and evening."

"Twice a day isn't necessary."

Sod touches the tablet, pinches his fingers, and zooms in on the figure. "Ma'am, he's nosing around the return pump. I'd like to think it's a local with a curious mechanical streak, but if your guts as good as mine—and I know it is—you appreciate the malicious intent he's emitting."

I turn to Tessa. I already know the answer before I ask, "Do we have the budget to bring on an extra week of security?"

"I'll crunch the numbers."

My jaw twitches at Tessa's politically correct way of reminding me we barely have the budget for the current plan. Outspending a problem like this one is always easier than outthinking one. I'd totally be up for the challenge if I didn't have to save Hugh's heart from . . . I wince at the thought of banishing the boy I'd loved. Personally, I've seen one heart banished. A job I was tapped to run secondary support on in Sydney. Banishing doesn't look like much in the beginning, a small dulling of the skin's luster, the spark of life dimming in their eyes until they're flat and lifeless. I rub at the dull ache in my heart, hoping to chase away the marrying of that image with Hugh. His eyes, no matter what horror or happiness was happening, always held a spark, a glimmer of hope that had people marching to the future. To imagine that gone, to think I'd have to be the one—I cut the thought off before it can truly form.

"Does Sandpiper have a booth here?"

"You know they do, Jack." Tessa scoffs, but I see the realization hit her square in the chest. "You think they'd be that ballsy?"

"I think you and I need to assume that they are." I turn my attention to Sid, compartmentalizing all the emotions swirling in gut. "Worst case scenario?"

Sid rocks back on his heels, his potbelly a solid anchor he won't tip backward.

"Couple of scenarios. Tampering with the motor means we're dead in the water for three days."

I can feel he's holding back. "And that's worst case?"

Sid pulls a handkerchief from his back pocket and wipes away the sweat beading along his brow. "Say someone gets to the pump and hits the release valve while the machine's running. The water is released; the pump burns through its motor." His clear eyes pin me where I stand. "If the motor isn't shut off within a few minutes, the lack of water would cause friction . . ."

I hate the pause. The pause is never good.

"Sid."

"Ma'am, the friction could cause a fire. With the amount of greenery and decorations we're strapping to the structure. . ."

"We'd go up like a roman torch."

Sid nods.

"Not the spectacle we're looking for," Tessa adds.

"No. It's. Not." The words grind through my teeth while I eye the Sandpiper tent. The organizers were smart keeping us on either end of the massive sand volleyball court. Somehow, I don't think that's even enough space if I find out they're messing with Hugh—Halia. I mean Halia.

"And you're thinking Sandpiper."

"I'm thinking someone knows this is a make-or-break moment for Halia."

Sid's glance ping-pongs between us. "Ladies, I clearly don't need to be here for the who and the why, I need to be prepared for the next time, so excuse me."

Before Sid leaves, I wrap my fingers around his arm. "You're going to need to show me and all pertinent personnel how to shut this thing down in case of an emergency."

"My staff knows, but I'll bring yours up to speed."

"I'll have Sonia email you a list."

"Jack," Tessa pushes. I know Tessa's objection, but if we're going to keep up the façade, then Sonia's got to be front and center for all the good, bad, and ugly. If she's hiding something, she'll be one of the fish gnawing on the bait.

Sid bows out of our conversation, leaving only the wind to whistle through the last of the exposed rafters and me to wonder how else Sandpiper, or someone else, can screw Halia and me out of a job.

"Jack?" Tessa closes the space between us, her eyes glittering with anger.

"Forty-nine is never easy. It's always about prioritizing. If Halia falls, so be it. Hugh has to be our main focus."

I know she's right, but Halia Surf isn't just a surf company—it's the last living piece of my dad. I rub at the reminiscent pain shifting in my chest. "My dad," is all I can get out without my insides imploding under the weight of missing him.

Tessa hesitates a moment before rubbing my arm. "Sometimes the hardest part of letting go is the step before you loosen your grip."

I want to object but I know she's right. If I'm going to earn my fiftieth arrow, I'm going to have to let go of a lot more than my memory of Dad's surf shop. I'm going to have to let go of Hugh to save him . . . and me.

Twenty Four

HUGH

Eight weeks ago, my life was cruising along. The surge of chaos that Tessa's arrival created with Sonia almost a year ago was finally settling into a tolerable swell. I didn't think it possible for Tessa to be even more protective than she was in high school, but after dinner and a carefully delivered ultimatum that I'd need to ask for a different rep if she didn't cool her shit with Sonia, things between the two started to settle. I'll never underestimate my friend again. Six weeks later, that tolerable swell turned into a full-blown tsunami with Jack's presence. Four weeks ago, the three ladies in my life were at each other's throats. Today, they're in the boardroom working together and . . . getting along. And I'm back to counting down menial events to stop an inevitable mental breakdown. Jack lets loose a giggle-snort that has a smile forming on my face; unfortunately, Sonia catches it.

"Glad to see you've worked on your decorum, Jack." I stroll over to Sonia and plant a kiss on her forehead. It's been four weeks since I found out I'm going to be a father, and the notion both thrills and nauseates me at the same time.

"Just keeping it business-like, Hugh." Jack hands a folder to Sonia. Sonia keeps her gaze firmly focused on me, reminding me of all the conversations we've had over the last few days. She's still like a shark that's bit into a fleshy piece of seal when it comes to the idea of firing Tessa. Given the slightly wild look I'm fielding from her now, Jack's name probably isn't too far from being added to that list.

"Sonia, fill the boss in while I deal with Tessa?" Jack doesn't wait for any kind of acknowledgement before she pushes past Sonia.

Sonia grabs the paperwork, stealing a quick glance at Tessa and then me.

"No need to worry," Jack pushes forward. "Tessa, a word." Jack doesn't wait for me to excuse her or Tessa to follow; she's just gone. She's been doing that quick exit a lot lately. I should let it go, let her go, but Sonia's right—if we're going to have a future, then all the pieces of my past need to be dealt with. I never thought of Jack as a piece of anything that needed to be dealt with, let alone my past.

I hitch a hip up on the table and snag Sonia's waistband to bring her between my legs. Something slithers in my stomach. I'm hoping one day it doesn't all feel so forced. Maybe when Jack leaves.

"You don't have to do this." Sonia turns in my arms. "Nobody's watching."

I turn on the charm, level my baby's momma with a look I know will melt her panties where she stands. The shy smile crawling across her face says I'm doing just that.

"Even better." I pull her in for a kiss, but she steps away from me.

"I really do need to fill you in." She pats my leg, but before I can chase after the feeling, Sonia sits at the table and nods to the seat next to her.

Warning sirens fire off in my head. Something's not sitting right. Hormones? I feel my head tilt. Shit, are we playing a game? Is she? What if Derrick's right? I feel everything in me shift as I look for the weakness, the lie I'm not certain I want to find. The deception my heart is desperately hoping for.

"Have you been watching the progress across the street?" Sonia interrupts my thoughts. Her eyes flutter, and I know how to really tell if the girl's playing me. I close the space between us and watch her twitch in her seat as I sit down next to her. The air between us tries to stir. This close, I can watch the dark flecks in her chocolate brown eyes come to life; that's when I know I'm back in control of our relationship.

"I have." I run my hand up her thigh; she moves it away. I can do cat and mouse. It's always been one of my specialties.

"Hugh," Sonia cautions. "I'm serious."

"So am I." I lean in but meet her cheek. "Okay," I hold up my palms. "You need Hugh the boss."

A small grin pulls at her lips. It doesn't light me up, but not all love is supposed to burn hot and fierce. Some love simmers and lasts . . . I hope.

"I need you to know I can do this job."

"I know you can."

A grin lights up her face and reaches her eyes.

"You're already exceeding my expectations, and Jack has nothing but praise. . ." my words trail off as the grin disappears from Sonia's face.

"The stage is built; the waterfall is ready for your final approval." She lays out the progression photos.

The stage is like a slice of Hawaii. Steel scaffolding and girders have been transformed into lush green cliffs. Jack and Tessa split the replica of my favorite waterfall, Waimoku Falls, so it frames the stage before pooling into the lava-rock recycling pond below. Ferns and moss climb the structure with a splattering of birds of paradise and . . . Hawaiian Wedding flowers. Mom's favorite flowers are nestled in the stage, and I can all but smell their scent wafting from the picture.

An ache churns in my heart. "Looks fabulous."

Sonia bites on her lip, assessing my praise before pushing on. "You need to know there are no test runs. Once the waterfall is on, it stays on."

"I have a problem with that."

Sonia's eyes flare. "Why? Why's that?"

I grab the work orders, trying not to physically react when my fingers brush over Jack's penmanship. She still loops her *L*s with a little indent that looks like a heart at the top. "How long will the fall run?"

"Sid says up to two weeks, barring any problems."

"Did Sid say what problems we could anticipate?"

"Um. Yeah, Jack had me give a list to Tessa who said she'd file it . . ." Sonia's words trail off into a mumble before she reaches over and thumbs through Jack's notes. Tessa's writing is in there too. Halfway into the folder, Sonia abandons her search. "He said the water levels could drop and burn out the pump. He also wasn't sure how often we'd need to refill the holding pond."

I lean forward and flip to the problem notes I know Tessa's filed in the back of the folder. Sonia's lip juts out.

"Tessa's been planning events forever," I start to explain, not out of need, but respect for Sonia. She needs to know I respect her, and to do that, Sonia needs to know my past has been formed by the two women she's terrified to turn her back on, but my future is with her. "In high school, Tessa had this superstition that potential problems needed to stay in the back of the folder. The further up in the file potential problems are placed, the more power you gave them to manifest."

"I'm more of a 'confront your problems head on' kind of girl, not a 'bury them in the past—'"

"This has nothing to do with my past and everything to do with our future. That's why *you're* briefing *me*." I pick up her left hand, bringing it to my lips. "That's why *you're* wearing my ring and why *you're* carrying my baby." The last sentence seems to trip on its way out.

"When they're gone—"

"It won't matter any more than the two of them being here." I cut her sentence off. I guess Tessa's rubbed off on me; I don't want the universe to even have a hint of removing Jack or Tessa from my world.

"You say that, and I know you want to believe that, but Hugh, I'm not stupid either."

I pull Sonia's hand to rest it on my heart while I touch my forehead to hers. "Then, trust me."

Minutes tick by, and I swear I'll give her as much time as she needs. I won't be the asshole my father was. This baby she's carrying, this life we're starting, saving Halia Surf, all of it has to be my priority. She pulls a deep breath into her lungs like she's testing the validity of my statement with her soul.

"I'll try," she finally whispers.

"That's all I can ask."

Sonia pulls back, all sorts of contemplation racing across the soft curves of her face. "Sid says we shouldn't turn the pump on until the morning of the open."

"That leaves no time for errors."

"Jack says there won't be any."

"Unless Jack picked up some skills in electrical engineering and waterfall mechanics, there's always room for errors." I skim through Tessa's notes on potential problems. They're all the problems I had assumed, some I hadn't, but one that only I can fix. "Tell Sid we're going live tonight. He's going to have make this fall run for an extra four days."

"You're a stubborn ass," Tessa's whisper catches on the ocean breeze. Her criticism isn't meant for my ears, but it lands like a grenade, hitting squarely the insecure underbelly only Tessa and Jack know about. I am a fraud and just too stubborn to accept it.

"Turn it on, Sid," I command.

Jack shakes her head—is that a smirk on her face?—and gives a nod to Sid. The foreman starts to object, but my look stops any argument from surfacing. I know all the things that can go wrong. I need to see if there's anything anyone's missed. I need to know this part of my life still bows to my will and is still under *my* control. The whine of machinery comes to life. A groan from the return pond sends air bubbling to the surface, and for a moment, my heart stops. Nothing's going to work. I'll have to admit my father was right, I'm a cheap replica, a fail—

A gurgle at the top of the thirty-foot structure cuts off my thoughts. Water erupts from the top and then settles to a steady roar as it makes it way down the rocky structure. It starts off slow and tentative. I close my eyes and a few moments later, hear the sounds of Mom's island paradise. The scent of wedding flowers catches on another breeze. My heart purrs when soft fingers lace with mine.

"You did good, Jack." The fingers pull from mine.

Fuck. Not Jack's hands, Sonia's.

Sonia folds her arms across her chest, and her lip wobbles before she bites down on it. I'm never going to get things right with her.

"Talk to me about security, Sid." The words fly from my mouth as I push us all past my fuck up.

The foreman looks around the semi-circle of gaping girls and throws me a lifeline. "I told Jack I don't have security but recommended a firm."

Silence stretches the moment longer than is comfortable.

"Jack," Sid pushes.

Jack's mouth guppies a second before she finds her voice. "Yeah. I'd scheduled them to start when we'd originally planned to turn the fountain on in four days, not tonight."

The sand shifts as I rock back on my heels. God, I've missed the feeling of sand between my toes. "Probably pertinent information to have shared before we turned the fountain on."

"Wouldn't have made a difference," Tessa interjects.

"So," I prompt the team. "Tell me the solution."

Sonia looks at Tessa. Tessa shoots Jack a quick glance, but Jack misses it. She's too busy sending me to my death a million times over with that look of hers. The look that used to have me finding ways to dig my hands in her hair and bury myself inside her—I cut off the thought and focus on solving problems and balancing the three ladies in my life.

"Our trailer isn't set to move offsite until tomorrow." Sid tosses yet another lifeline into our group's turbulent waters. "It won't be comfortable, but you're more than welcome to it."

"Thanks, Sid." Jack extends her hand, but her judgmental eyes don't leave me. I remember when they'd look at me and fill with passion, pleasure, and ecstasy. "I'll stay tonight."

A smile blossoms on Tessa's face, but Sid rocks back on his heels. He's as comfortable with Jack, and possibly Tessa, watching the site as I am.

"You got anyone who wants to make a lot of cash for a few hours' work?" I ask before bonfires and beach camp-outs root in Tessa mind . . . or Jack's, for that matter.

Jack's eyes lock with mine, and I tumble back, back to the night. . .

Her big blue eyes look black as night when I finally push into her. Her fingernails bite into my back, and I'm willing to take a lifetime of pain if it gives her a second of relief. I know the first time hurts . . . I start to pull out, but her nails are replaced with the soft pads of her fingers, pulling me closer to her, deeper inside her.

Jack swallows hard before a smile pulls at her lips, and I'm gone. I'm hers. I'll walk through hell, I'll sit with the devil himself, promise him anything, give everything if it means she'll be happy.

"Don't stop," she whispers. Her voice is low and sultry as if just this minute moment was enough to unleash the woman inside her. The woman I'm going to love spending forever with . . .

I pull in a deep breath, executing every ounce of mind over memories. Tripping back and falling into the night we'd spent camping on the beach. The night Tessa's mom went into labor and Jack and I . . . My cock starts to harden at the memory of Jack clothed in nothing but silver moonlight and me. God, she was beautiful when she fell apart around me. Her first time. My first time. We'd defied every stereotype and made passionate love, not the awkward three-second fumble fuck every first-time couple experiences. I'd loved her until the world couldn't take anymore.

"Hugh." Tessa helps push me out of the memory. "Sid said his son would watch the site tonight."

"I'll stay too," Jack adds. "Security was my job. It's my fuck up, I'll stay."

"No."

Jack bristles at the put-my-foot-down tone.

"You didn't fuck up. I need my team rested and safe." I turn to Sid. "When can your son be here?"

Sid pulls out his phone, the screen illuminates. "Ten minutes. We're just up Main Street by the high school."

"Fine. I'll take Sonia home and be back to relieve you both. Jack, Tessa, go home. Get a good night's rest." I can see all their lips pursing with objections forming. "I need you all rested for the next week. Now go."

The waves crashing in the distance mix with the artificial waterfall, but no one moves. My father has to be laughing in hell. I chased off Jack only to have two more women join her ranks. Hydra has nothing on these ladies.

Twenty Five

JACK

I *tip-toe out the door before* the pink hues of daylight can touch the ocean, easing the door latch to close softly without a click.

Without waking Tessa.

Normally, the girl will sleep through World War III, but a door latch, signaling a potential sneak out not including her, and Tessa has hearing like a well-trained hellhound. I'd tried slipping out three times last night to check on the site. I trusted Sid, which meant I trusted Sid's son, but secretly, I was hoping to make some headway with saving Hugh from banishment, especially when I saw his eyes fill with memories when Sid offered up his trailer. I knew exactly where he'd tumbled when he looked at me, his jaw grinding on the leftover taste of us.

Our last campout was a first for both him and me. It was far from the last time we explored each other, loved each other. I rub at the now persistent ache in my heart and refocus on the tips of the metal structures jutting up into the air. I finally gave up my attempts to leave when Hugh texted the site was secure and he was climbing into bed. I shudder and pull my sweater tighter. Has to be the breeze dancing off the ocean, not the thump of my heart when I think of Hugh climbing into bed with someone besides me. I steal a quick look at the ocean. At least something seems to be going right.

The swells are really starting to hold their form. The storm down south is going to provide some awesome surf. I walk down the final steps of my condo complex and pull in a deep breath when my toes hit the sand. One of the perks of Dad's house was not only living on the beach, but the Open was only a mile—two, max—from my front door. I round the front of the complex and take in all the vendors and arenas. All the scaffolding and metal has almost been completely transformed into a city unearthed from the sand.

This was the part I loved the most about the Open. Hugh, Tessa, and me—all the times the three of us skipped out early or snuck in late come tumbling back like whitewash trying one last attempt to impress.

Halia's site comes into view and I breathe a sigh of relief when I see the waterfall running. The atrocious metal tower that was there last week is now transformed into a breathtaking site of moss, ivy, ferns, and even the obligatory rainbow coming of the waterfall's spray. The site was gorgeous last night illuminated with the blue backlights, but during the day, it's breathtaking. Given Tessa's reputation for details, it had no choice but to be magnificent. I climb the stage and stop in front of the return pond, reveling at the fresh water spraying off the rocks.

"Figured you disobey me."

I jump at the sound of Hugh's voice.

"Where's Sid's son? I thought you were at home with Sonia?" I hope he doesn't hear the way my voice breaks around her name, the way my heart stutters when I'm in near him. Of course, it could be the way he looks that has my heart panging around my chest.

Sweat pants hang low on his hips, and he's wearing a white tank top that hints at all the muscles I've been longing to see. I drag my eyes up his body and catch Hugh running a hand through his bed-tossed hair, but his eyes trained on me say I've been caught looking.

"Couldn't sleep." He shoots me the impish grin and the offer to help rectify the matter dies on my lips. "Tucked Sonia into bed and came back to meet Sid's son." Hugh continues. "We got to talking. Time got away from me." His shoulders pull like that should be explanation enough. Given our last conversation about my status being "just an employee," it should be. He's my boss, but dressed the way he is and the way my heart is stammering, heat's pooling in my thighs—

"Want to tell me why you're here at zero dark thirty?" He cuts the thought off before it guts me any further. He's not mine to want for anymore. And I shouldn't want to. But damn! Toeing Eros's flirt-line was coming far too easily for me.

I force a giggle past my lips. "It's five twenty. I think we all left at zero dark thirty."

"Jack," Hugh presses, but all my thoughts scatter when he leans against the rail and crosses his arms. The flashback to us in high school and him rooting out a problem I'd thought I'd good and buried is overwhelming. I shift on my heels, knowing that what he wants to uproot is the very thing that will get me banished from the Corps.

So, I lie.

"I really need this to go off without a hitch." I think back to E.J. and the possibility of him taking over the Corps. The possibility of me being stuck at forty-nine forever or worse, being kicked out. With E.J. in charge . . . My stomach drops at the thought and the free fall only solidifies my resolve. I repeat the sentence I've been screaming the last six years in my head: *The only life I can have—I want—is an immortal one.* I pluck my hair from the wind and pull it up with the rest of my hair in a ponytail. I can do this. "E.J. may be my ex-boyfriend, but he doesn't think too fondly of my performance in his parent's company."

Even from this distance, I can see rage light up Hugh's eyes, which means he and E.J. have spoken about me. I bite down on my lip, hoping to chase away any warmth or memories that threaten to surface. The girl I was may have fallen for the protective gesture, the woman I am—even if he *didn't* cheat on me—won't ever be the damsel in distress, but it doesn't mean I can't *play* one.

"Your ex?" Hugh says the same time I ask, "He's said something to you?"

I hate the idea forming. The idea that has me using every good thing about Hugh and warping it to fit my needs. I shift, feeling slimy and gross. None of my other assignments made me feel this way.

None of your other assignments held the key to immortality . . . or were Hugh.

"Your ex?" Hugh asks again, stretching out his long legs. Despite all that previous resolve to stamp down my distressing damsel, a familiar warmth shoots through me when he pins me with *the look.*

The smolder.

I always was a sucker for the smolder.

"Yeah, well. Looks like I can still chase all the boys from the yard."

I inch closer up the steps. Closer to the slimy glimmer of the idea that will save Hugh, save Halia, and get me my fiftieth heart without getting me kicked out of the Corps. Tessa was right. I'm the key to this assignment. I just need to see the sign from Hugh that says he'd still be willing to protect me.

Hugh chuckles, turning the smolder in his eyes to maximum. "He may have said something along those lines. I think it's more that you intimidate him than him thinking you're incompetent."

"Maybe. But . . ." I let my words dangle like bait. Hugh shifts again.

Please don't fall for this.

Please don't make me break your heart.

Please don't make me banish it either.

Please . . .

I kick at the seam in the metal stairs, hating every raw emotion rolling through me. I mean, he could have fallen for Sonia. I chase the thought away as quickly as it forms, but the sickening pit in my stomach grows. I chew on my bottom lip like I'd done in high school, feeling my brow furrow. A few more seconds and . . . yep, there it is, my eye is twitching. I'm using all my bag of tricks whether I like it or not.

What is it with this guy?

After all this time, he should be long gone from my system.

But this is Hugh.

This is the boy who taught me to wish on my first star, left all his friends to teach me to ride my first wave, gave me my first org—

"Jack?"

I jump at how close he is now.

There it is, the warm, low tenor of his voice. That cadence says he'd still do anything for me.

I look up through my lashes, knowing these are the looks the boy I loved can't deny. Hugh wraps his hand around my wrist and gently pulls me up the last few steps and into the office. I'm in a chair with a coffee cup warming my hand and a blanket around my shoulders before I can catch my breath. Nothing's changed, and that only makes the guilty lump in my gut knot cinch tighter. He still cares and if possible, more now than ever. A thick coating of tears slicks my throat. Hugh grabs a chair and angles himself next to me, so close I can feel the heat from his thighs jumping off his body and trying to warm me. I resist every urge to scoot closer. I don't have to; Hugh does it for me, leaning in so near I can see the silver ring around his eyes practically pulsating.

I clear my throat, looking for redemption in the black tar he calls coffee. "Tessa and I met with our boss and E.J. after the sponsors' dinner." I pull a sip of coffee through my lips and that lump in my gut grows. Kona coffee . . . his mom's favorite. My favorite.

"And?" Hugh pushes. His knee touches mine and I nearly lose myself.

"Let's just say you're not the only one who has their job tied to Halia's successful launch."

Hugh rakes his palm across his face before searching for something behind me. Time stretches between us. I fight the urge to squirm at the silence.

"I'm sorry," he whispers to no one, but there's something in me that desperately wants to know who he's apologizing to. And what he's apologizing for.

"What?"

Hugh shakes his head, clearing whatever fog of memories may have rolled in. "I should have never gotten you two involved."

"You didn't—"

"I did," he doesn't let me finish. "Maybe not in Halia's latest fuck up, but I did get you two involved."

"You're talking about the sham of a shag?"

Hugh goes still. All that beautiful olive coloring drains from his face.

I shift in my seat. I'd hoped to escape So. Cal without this conversation, but yeah, we were going to have to do this now—relive the past, so we could move on to saving his future.

"When?" he whispers, and I know exactly what he's asking.

When did I know?

How long had I stayed away?

I want to look him in the eyes when I tell him the truth. Watch every emotion wash through those dark and mysterious orbs, but I can't. I guess in some areas of my life, I'm still too much of a chicken, so I keep quiet.

"When my dad died?" His voices pushes with a sense of urgency that makes me want to fold, give it all up for him.

But I can't.

I won't.

I shrug. "Tessa and I had a come-to-God moment over melted chocolate-malted-crunch and surf wax."

Hugh's eyebrows climb into his hairline. "Tessa went surfing?"

I nod.

"So you two . . . You're . . ." His lips form and flounder around more words, but none have a voice behind them.

"We've reached an understanding."

His eye twitches. If it weren't so utterly heart-wrenching, I'd smile.

But it is.

Shattering, actually.

He lied to me.

Hugh lied to me.

Tessa lied to us both.

"I'm so sorry, Jack. You have to know."

"I do. I have to know why. Why would you do that to me?"

Hugh pushes back in his chair as if I dumped the coffee in his face.

"There wasn't any other way to keep you safe. I didn't know that then, but I know it now."

"You think what happened to Tessa would have happened to me?" I can't stop myself. If he knew what had happened, why did he stay? "I would've never let Kai get that close," I spit at Hugh.

Hugh's eyebrows pinch together. My gut cramps at the way all the remaining color drains from his beautiful face.

"You're not talking about Tessa . . ." My words start as a question and die with whisper sharp enough to gut me. The room sways. He didn't know about his dad. And Hugh would have killed his father if there was even a hint of knowledge Kai killed. . . I can't finish the thought. Not now.

Hugh collapses forward, elbows on his knees, hand shaking as he holds his head. I can hear the sound of bile turning in his gut. I run my hand along his back, hoping to soothe the pain. He looks up at me, the eyes of the boy I'd fallen for in the face of the man staring at me.

I'm utter shit.

"I was talking about Delilah, from high school. I got my dad and Delilah. . ." Hugh wretches out. "My dad got Tessa too?"

I want to say no. I wish to all the gods and jailed Titans that there was another answer than yes.

But I can't. And before I can say anything, Hugh stands and tosses his chair across the room. He stalks the width of the tiny office several times, throwing chairs out of his way before stopping and slamming his fist against the wall. Punch after vicious punch rattles the metal walls.

"Fuck you!" Hugh howls at the heavens before collapsing to the floor.

I'm rooted to my seat, my heart scurrying up my throat only to dive back into my stomach. I've only seen Hugh this enraged one other time—the morning Dad and I came to tell him his mom had passed. I'd hid behind my dad, and when Hugh had finally bloodied his hands enough, we picked him up and took him to the hospital.

"Your dad was right, Jack." Hugh's voice is barely a whimper. "My father would have destroyed every good thing in you. Look what he did to Tessa . . ."

I shake my head, knowing he can read every confused line etched in my face.

Hugh flips himself over. His back up against the wall, hair covering the edges of his face, and knuckles so bloody, I'll be surprised if there isn't a bone *not* broken in his right hand. "You should leave."

My heels dig in, and I know Zeus himself would have to remove me before I'd leave Hugh like this.

"You should leave before I destroy you too, Jack."

"You won't."

A hysterical laugh rips from his chest. "I'm a Halia. It's what we do best. You were smart to get half a world away from me. I'll call E.J. and tell him this wasn't your fault. When he takes over A.A., he'll be a hell of a lucky bastard to have you on his team. I just can't have you in my wake of my destructive life." Hugh pulls back the ends of his hair. The color is back in his face, but there's no life in his eyes. All the beautiful, entrancing sparkle is gone. They're flat black, like a shark before he takes his first bit of flesh. "He's a fucking tool if he lets you go, Jack. I mean that both professionally and personally."

"You're firing me?" My turn to feel all the bile churning in my gut.

"I'm letting you go."

Resignation washes across Hugh's face. If I was a good Cupid, I'd banish his heart here and now. There's no hope for him. But I'm not a good Cupid, I'm a fucking brilliant Cupid, and I won't let my fiftieth arrow go down in flames. If he's given up, then I'll fight for the both of us. I'll poke, aggravate, and agitate him until he has no choice but to fight for his life, and then I'll make him fall in love with love all over again.

"Fuck you, Hugh." I hiss.

His head snaps back against the wall.

"You heard me. Fuck. You." I point a judgmental finger at him. "I'm not some little girl who needs your protection. I sure as hell was a much stronger woman than you and Tessa gave me credit for." I kick his foot and relish the shock registering on his face.

"This is who you are?" I wave my hands at the destruction in the room, at the coward huddled up on the floor. "A man who shrivels up and dies at the realization his father was a slimy motherfucker who should have been castrated the moment he was birthed? Newsflash: We all knew your dad was a dick. Shame on Tessa for not telling us, but I get why she kept quiet. Shame on you for thinking I couldn't protect myself." My turn to look to the heavens. A weight settles in my stomach at the knowledge the man who loved me most was responsible for my unhappiness. "And shame on you, Dad, for not having faith in me . . . or Hugh." I sink into the only metal chair that hasn't been caught up in Hugh's tirade tornado. "You should have trusted me, Hugh." My voice wobbles. I fight to find the armor that's protected me the last six years, but it's a thin as a morning fog hanging on the coast. Maybe I've never been able to protect myself when it came to Hugh.

He's still sitting on the floor, elbows on his knees, with a shocked look of love on his face. "I loved you, Jack. I'd still do anything to make you happy."

"Then don't fire me. Let me see this through."

Hugh scrubs his face with his palm. He never could say no to me, not when I really wanted something. And by the way his shoulders slump, he's not going to start now.

"Please," I beg.

He shoots me a look, and I know he sees the glow of hysteria lighting my eyes. *If you fire me, I can't save you.*

"What do you need from me?"

I'm about to tell him when the sound of metal on metal squeals through the silence. We both jump to our feet. Hugh has the door open, and I'm following down the metal stairs, but the smell of burnt rubber nearly knocks me over.

"We're burning the motor from the pump." I point to the structure. "Shut off valve is in the back!"

Shit! There's smoke billowing up from the reserve pond. The sand is wet, which means—I take a quick peek while I round the corner—the pond is dry as a bone.

"Where?" Hugh's ripping vines and ivy from the metal infrastructure. If we don't shut it down, soon the entire thing will go up in flames. I pull in a deep breath and push Hugh out of the way. I find the control panel just to the left of the hole Hugh's plucked and hit the stop button. I hold my breath, stealing a quick glance at Hugh to see he's doing the same, while we wait for the motor to whine down.

"Where's Sid's son?" I ask.

"I sent him home."

"Why?"

"Because I couldn't."

My feet move toward him like they have a mind of their own. "You couldn't what?"

"I couldn't go home, Jack." He steps into my space, forcing me to tip my head back. I'd forgotten how much taller than me he really is. I'd forgotten how standing this close to him can be as intoxicating as shooting shots of José Cuervo. I guess I'd banished everything exciting about Hugh from my memory. My breath catches in my throat when he wraps his arm around me, pulling me into him. "She's not you."

Warmth explodes inside me. He's already there. I just need him to call off the wedding and follow his heart.

"No." I swallow hard over the word. "Sonia's not me."

The hint of a smile tips his lip. My pulse races in my ears as he bends down. The tingling sensation dances across my lips, and without meaning to, I wet them, readying for. . .

"I told you the next time I kissed you, you'd have to ask me."

I blink, feeling the cold ocean air rushing past my teeth.

Hugh's heated look imprisons me. I know if I ask him now, it will be breathy and full of need, and the very words that will kick me out of the Corps. But there's something about being held by this man, held in a way that taunts and pleads with me to take a chance—

"What the hell is going on here?" Tessa's voice destroys the moment. "Seriously, what is it with you two and sand?" She saunters past me, grabbing her phone and hip-checking me closer into Hugh, as she turns her focus to the smoldering electrical panel. "Next time you two want to get hot-n-heavy, could you not ruin the company's last chance at survival?"

I open my mouth, but Tessa holds up a finger before a sound escapes.

"Sid?" Tessa's voice sings out like she's tattling. "Jack and Hugh broke the waterfall." She shoots me, then the panel, a look that snaps all my senses back to reality.

"Is he on his way?" I ask, straightening out my sleep tank, suddenly realizing I'm not wearing a bra and my nipples are standing at attention. The site isn't lost on Hugh either. I pull my sweater tight.

"Tessa?" I push.

"Sid's in the parking lot."

"Wrong." Sid's booming voice comes around the structure before his belly and then his body. "Sid's here." He takes off his hard helmet, wipes back the last remaining wisps of silver on the top of his head, and mumbles. I'm pretty sure there are a few curse words in there.

"How bad are we?" Hugh sidles up next to Sid.

"Jack"—Sid looks back at me—"you remember the worst-case scenario?"

My stomach flops to my toes as I nod. I can't even form the words I need to. I've specialized in client crisis management for six years at A.A., and this is the one I eff up?

"No hope?"

Sid chews on the inside of his cheek. "Give me a second." He opens the trap door further down the structure and disappears into the greenery. Tessa hides a giggle behind her hand at Sid's continuous string of mutters. Hugh wipes away a grin at the blatant curse. But I stand there hoping not to hurl chunks. It's one thing to hit and miss with my recruits. When they wash out, it's not because of me. It's not because I fucked up or made a bad choice. That's not the case with my day job. A.A. is all me. It's where I reign supreme. It took me a while to become a badass Cupid, but I've always been A.A.'s best crisis consultant.

Always!

"Sid." I cringe at the hint of hysteria in my voice. "We could use more words, less profanity."

Sid emerges from the trap door. Even though it's a cool morning, sweat trickles down his face almost in the same path our fountain did. I push the thought aside and rock back on my heels. Clearly, I'm losing my shit.

"Relax, Jack." He holds up a shredded rubber belt. "You stopped it in time. Only damage is the belt to the pump for the recycle pond."

"And you can fix that . . . when?" Tessa asks.

Sid pulls a handkerchief from his back pocket, swiping it across his face. "It's a special-order part, but once I have it, two days? You'll be wet by the end of the second. You were damn lucky."

Tessa claps her hands together.

"Yes," Hugh growls, and before I can thank Sid, I'm wrapped up in Hugh's arms twirling through the air.

"Knew you were the best for a reason, Jack." Hugh's breath dances across my face. This close to him, I can't help but smile. I can't help the way my lips pucker. Hugh's eyes darken in a familiar way. The thrill of it rocking me to my core. His grip tightens around my waist, and it's everything in me not to wrap my legs around his hips and pick up where we'd left off all those years ago.

"Say it, Jack," he whispers so quietly, I know Tessa and Sid can't hear.

I feel the words forming in my heart, working their way up my throat one pleasurable heartbeat at a time.

"Hugh," I murmur, reveling the way his name tastes on my tongue, wishing this was for real and not just a job to save his heart.

"The early bird really does get the worm," Sonia's voice suddenly cuts into me, halting all my thoughts as I slide down Hugh's body. "You said I could trust you. You're just like the rest of them."

I'm not sure who Sonia's talking to, but it doesn't matter. She's turned on her heels and making a beeline to the parking lot. Even though my gut says it's me, my head knows it could be Hugh.

"I can't do this with you, Jack."

I feel the push in Hugh's arms and pull him in close to me. All the warmth in his eyes bleeds out like the water from the recycling pond. Only there's no emergency stop button for me to push to stop Hugh from drifting out of my arms. I'm losing him, and the ache is nearly as painful as the brand that will give me immortality and a life without him.

Twenty Six

HUGH

"What part of no disruptions are you all failing to comprehend?" I hiss at my closed office door. The heavy wood eases open, and I pray to God it's Mack. Ever since the vendor's dinner last month, he's made himself scarce. Which means he's up to something. I feel my lips tip, hoping it is him who walks into my office. My fingers curl, biting into my palms. I can feel the itch of fury coursing through my body. Hell, he's probably the one behind the fountain's sabotage yesterday.

Maybe?

"Hugh?" The distinctly male voice has me pushing away from my desk and closing in on the door like a man about to let loose years' worth of pent-up kick ass. I nearly rip the door off its hinges, and Derrick tumbles onto the floor of my office.

"Shit! Derrick." All my pent-up kick ass turns into guilty son of a bitch as I scramble to help my legit war hero friend up off the floor. "I'm so sorry. I thought—"

"Dude, whoever you thought I was, I'm glad I'm not." Derrick grabs his cane and waves off my help to get him on his feet. "I haven't seen that look on your face since Vivanco said he made it with Jack on the make-out mover at Disneyland."

I want to laugh, but my nerves are so raw, even that memory has me ready to track *that* dick down and pummel on his face a little more. For old memories' sake.

"You see what mood I'm in, Derrick. You sure you want to dance on that nerve?"

Derrick walks past me, and the punk even lunges at me like he's about to throw a punch. "All day long, Halia. Even a half a man, I can whoop your ass all day long."

I chuckle. "You live in that fantasyland."

He doubles over, pretending to laugh. "Touché. Touché. Now what's eating your ass?"

I cringe at the visual. "Who says—" The look Derrick hits me with stops me from continuing with that lie. I shut the door and stalk over to my desk. Derrick's already sitting in my seat, ballsy motherfucker, so I take the uncomfortable guest chair. "You didn't come here to listen to me bitch. What can I do for you?"

"Hugh, you always bitch, and besides that fact, you're my friend. You obviously need an ear to chew on—one that isn't tied to your past or your payroll," he clarifies. "I'm your friend, dude. Spill."

I know I'm sitting statue-still, but that doesn't stop my insides from twisting. It'd be nice to have a friend like Derrick around. One with no hidden agenda and only my best interest at—I cut the thought off, because there were only two people who were friends like that, and I destroyed them both. I shift in my chair, and I know Derrick knows the conversation is finished before it ever began.

"What can I do for you and Elizabeth?"

Derrick shakes his head before standing up and walking from behind my desk. "We're friends, right?"

I nod.

"When a friend asks what's wrong, don't take that tone with them."

I don't say anything. Derrick dances from foot to artificial foot, slapping me with a *fuck you* look.

"Trust me, you don't want me as a friend. I'll only hurt—"

Derrick rubs his fists to his eyes, fake crying like he did when we were kids making fun of one another. "Dude, I thought Jack was full of shit. You really are all 'woe is me.'"

I lean forward, slightly amused at the small way he jumps. "Jack sent you?"

"Yeah?" Derrick curls his lip in that "duh, moron" look he mastered at our seventh grade, third-period English teacher's expense. She never underestimated a jock, and Derrick never underestimated the way a sonnet could make all women pliant, again.

"Why?"

"You really are stupid." He walks around my desk and sits down in the other chair. "The girl loves you, never stopped."

I lean back, stretching one leg out and hanging my arm off the back of the chair. I want to take back the lounge look I mastered in high school the minute it sticks. For a man who is in control of every aspect of his life, the boy I'd thought long disappeared sure has a way of rearing his ugly Neanderthal head when it comes to all things concerning Jack.

"She told you this?"

Derrick shakes his head, more in disbelief than confirmation that I'd have to ask. Jack may not have come right out and said it, but after this morning, the way her eyes flooded with need when I dared her to ask me to kiss her. . . The memory has my cock twitching.

"You gonna write her a 'check yes or no' note, do that girly origami folding, and have me pass it to her in homeroom?"

"You're an ass, you know?"

"Right back at you." Derrick leans forward, his elbows on his knees, his fingers folded under his chin. "What's the problem?"

I shake my head, knowing there are so many problems, I don't know where to begin, but I also know the only one he's interested in is tied to a leggy blonde with killer blue eyes and can shred a wave—as well as a man's heart—with a skill that has you coming back for more.

"I can't."

"Baby momma?"

I pinch the bridge of my nose, feeling the headache forming.

"Did you get the paternity test?"

"There's no need."

"Beg to differ, dude." He shrugs his shoulders. "There's a lot of—"

"There's no money, Derrick. This is Halia's last stand. You literally are our last leg. If our relaunch doesn't go off without a hitch. . . Someone's already tried to sabotage the stage. . . And there's Jack and Tessa." My head floats like all the problems are helium and it's slowly ripping my mind from my body. "Jack and me. We have to be the last thing I think about."

"And how's that working for you?"

The pain inside me bubbles up in a chortle. "Like a bitch."

"Then pay Jack a little attention, and see if she doesn't unravel some of the other problems."

Mom's face flashes across my eyes. I remember the way she waited for Dad, waited for the sliver of attention. She never complained, always covered. My stomach turns. She had to know about Dad's extracurricular. Maybe even the underage girls. I fight down the need to vomit. Mom deserved better. I deserved better. The moment, as painful as it is, breaks and on the horizon is my future.

A future without Jack.

Not because I won't love her until my last breath, but because I won't repeat my father's mistakes. I won't be the father he was.

"I can't." I finally whisper.

"You won't." Derrick grabs his cane and stands up. The thread of our friendship pulls tight with each step toward the door he takes. The man he wants me to be for Jack, and the man I need to be for if I choose Sonia and her child, they can't both exist in me.

He winces when he looks back at me. "Don't kid yourself, Hugh. Love really is a cruel bitch when you don't treat her right."

If I was a betting man, I would double down that the pain that just flashed across his face isn't from his leg, it was something else. I'm a shit friend for not asking what's wrong, but I'm failing at my own lady problems. My mind tumbles back to last night. Sonia packed up all her things and walked out the door, leaving only an ultimatum taped to my front door when I got home.

Me and the baby, or Jack and Tessa.
You can't have us both.

She was right. Jack was gone after the Open. She made that abundantly clear the night of the high school reunion bonfire. While I could reason with Jack, the guillotine hanging over Halia Surf's future . . .

"I'll keep Halia's secrets, Hugh." Derrick pauses at the now open door. "Elizabeth wanted me to let you know she really wants Hawaii."

"I know."

"I guess we all know what we really want. Who knows? Maybe the universe is in a generous mood and will give it to us, despite what we deserve? I'll shut the door." Derrick leaves, and the latch of my door clicking shut sounds like a death sentence.

The room seems to quiet with Derrick gone, allowing the weight of yesterday morning's events at the site to hang heavy. I'm not sure how long I sit staring out my office window, watching the waves break against the pier's pylons. Every thought I chased of a future with Jack only crashed with the thought of my son or daughter growing up and looking at me like I did my dad.

"Hugh?" Jack's voice drifts into the room, and on cue, my heart triples its beat. If I hadn't just been thinking of all the times Dad let me down, how I knew in my heart we were always second—Mom was always second—I'd pat myself on the back for still loving the shit out of this woman, but I had, and now I have a chance to be that dad for my kid. I turn my chair slightly. Jack clears her throat, stopping that thought and any other thoughts that don't include her in my life.

"I knocked but you didn't answer."

I keep my chair still. Afraid to see her face. I can't. Not when the woman can read every emotion, every thought, from a simple glance at my face. For a man who prides himself on self-control and the world bending to his will, I can't seem to channel any of that when Jack is near.

Never could—I pull in a deep breath and finally turn my chair to face Jack and feel my heart stutter—never will.

Jack closes the door behind her but doesn't walk into the room. I can see the concern etched into her face. She knows I'm dancing on a ledge, what she doesn't know is that how far I'm willing to fall for her to look at me the way she used to is the same depth I'd fall to make sure my kid never knows how much I love her and not his mom.

"What can I do for you, Jack?"

She takes a tentative step forward and then another. By the third step into my office, she's striding like the kick-ass professional who'd stepped right over the pieces of my broken heart to get to the job she'd been hired to do.

"Sid called."

Now she has my attention.

"The belt he needs is in Santa Barbara."

"Great." I lean forward, waiting for the other shoe to drop.

Jack pulls the pen from her wound-up bun, letting all that gorgeous blond hair tumble free before she bites down on the tip of the pen.

Fuck.

"You might as well tell me. You only eat your pens when shit is about to hit the fan."

A smile pulls at the edge of her lip before she pulls the ballpoint pen from her teeth. "Guess not that much has changed."

"Everything's changed, Jack. Everything."

The charged declaration hangs in the air. I watch every syllable hit her body, her heart, over and over again.

She clears her throat and shoves the pen back in her mouth, then flips through her clipboard. "Yeah, well. The piece is in Santa Barbara. The company doesn't have a messenger to bring it to us until Monday. Sid doesn't have anyone to make the two-hour drive up, and—"

"Send one our couriers."

"I can't. It's four thirty on a Friday."

Four thirty? I'd spent the entire day staring out my window? God, I was a fool.

"I can go and grab it," Jack offers. "But I'm going to need a second body for the carpool lane if I'm going to make it up there by seven thirty."

"Take Tessa."

Jack shakes her head. "Tessa's meeting with the florists to see if we can repair the damage."

"Take Cassidy."

"She's overseeing the wedding prep."

"Take her assistant."

"What part of wedding prep are you not getting?"

I rip my hand through my hair, and growl, "Sarah."

"She's handling media."

"Why isn't Tessa?"

"Because she's with the florists?"

"Fuck, Jack. Take Sonia."

"I can't take your pregnant girlfriend. Not after yesterday morning. And most certainly not after the 'stay away or I'll tell your boyfriend/boss' threat."

"What?"

Jack waves it off with a brush of her hand, but the way she's gathering her hair back up into a bun tells me Sonia rattled her.

"Hugh, four days before the Open, everyone is stretched tight. Everyone but you. So, you're my second body." She turns on her heels and heads for the door, only stopping to toss me her set of keys as she says, "Meet me downstairs in ten."

I pluck the keys out of the air and swear I see her smirk as she shuts the door.

Jack's right. I am the only body available. I just wished it didn't mean I had to betray my honor.

I hate everything about this situation. I steal another glance as Jack shifts in the passenger's seat, taking her skirt on a ride another inch higher up her thighs. A rocket of unwanted heat knees me in my balls when I notice she isn't wearing pantyhose. I shift in my seat, pretending not to notice the way my pants feel a whole hell of a lot tighter. Jack moves again and I smile.

"When did you get all antsy in a car?"

Jack shoots me a sideways glance. The skin between her eyebrows is puckered, which means she's got something in that beautiful brain of hers. I chuckle at the two of us, earning me another glance; this one has a little more bite.

"Jack," I push when she doesn't answer. "Antsy and quiet." I nearly cluck my tongue like Mom did when she was determined to pry some nefarious secret out of the two of us.

"I'm not antsy." She fidgets. "Okay, I'm anxious."

I check her then the road. "About?"

Jack squirms in her seat, rolls down the window, and sticks her head out like she did summer I got my license. I wipe away the smile and watch her hair catch in the wind. Watch all the memories rush into the car along with all the regrets. I almost forget what I've asked her when she brings her body back in the car and turns sideways. Despite the skirt—or maybe in spite of the skirt—she pulls her leg up underneath her and leans against the car door, making my heart grab hold of my balls as they climb up into my throat. I hated when she did that. One wrong bump and I could see the door jarring open and her flying out.

Gone.

She levels me with a look. "You're not anxious? There's seriously a million things that could go wrong. Even down to Derrick and Elizabeth getting cold feet."

I scoff. "Derrick won't get cold feet. If ever two people were meant for each other…" The thought trails off, following the small frown of Jack's lips. Yeah, we were *that* couple. "Fine. What's *not* in the back of Tessa's binder?"

Jack stiffens and I know I'm on to something.

"You two have been tighter than a new surf leash." I wipe another smile off my face when the color bleaches from Jack's face. "That means you two are up to something or about to be."

"Just doing our job," she forces through the fakest smile ever.

A laugh rips from deep inside me, catching me, and Jack, off guard. "Try. Again."

Jack leans back, resting her head on the open window. I signal and maneuver the car through the LA traffic, knowing downtown, despite all its bumper-to-bumper cars, is Jack's favorite. She belonged on a movie screen. Fuck, she deserved to be the center of every story ever written.

As if she's reading my mind, she says, "You remember when your mom brought us up here for that casting call?"

I nod.

"We were . . ."

"Fourteen and fifteen."

She lifts her head and smiles at me. Really genuinely smiles at me. Like she did when I was her everything. Before I ruined it all.

"We were going to be the next big thing. The next 'it' couple," I add, relishing the pain slicing through me.

"It was all so simple back then," Jack whispers.

She shifts again in her seat, turning so all I can see is her back and all she can see are the high-rise buildings of downtown LA. Coming or going, I'd have been a happy man watching her the rest of my life. Hot pain pulses through my body, knowing that dream, that vision, will never happen.

"Bottega Louie is there." She points to one of the ornate 1920s buildings. "You know that was one of my fondest memories of your mom?"

I grip the steering wheel like it's the past's neck and all I want to do is wring it free of all the memories. Good or bad, it hurts too much to relive this part of my life with her.

"Jack." She turns at the raw pain cutting my voice, and there it is in her eyes. The girl I fell for in the eyes of the woman who's sworn to hate me forever. Before I know what's happening, her cool palm slides across my cheek, awakening parts of my soul that have no business aching for her touch.

"I remember everything about that day." I hate the way my voice thickens with nostalgia, the way my body turns without thought into this woman and her touch. "You'd snuck in my room the night before and made me watch *Titanic* until I'd memorized all of the DeCaprio lines. You fell asleep in my arms, and I swore to God that there would be nothing that could take you away from me."

I pull my gaze from hers and check the distance between me and the next car. I can't *not* look back. When I do, her eyes are filled with water and want.

"We heard the garage door open and thought for sure Kai'd caught us," she whispers. "I've never been so scared in my life when your bedroom door handle turned."

"Mom always did have a unique way of saving us."

Jack chokes out a pain-filled *ha*. "She packed us up in the car and took us to the LA theater. How the woman knew where every iconic movie was playing still stumps me."

"Then lunch at Bottega Louie. I could have sworn with all that white marble and proper manners, we were on the Titanic."

"Until she took us to the Queen Mary in Long Beach." Her voice drifts away, and I know she's reliving the day just like me.

Quiet fills the car again. The uncomfortable silence of memories long gone, moments I'd kill to have back. We travel the next hour through downtown in silence. We merge onto the 101 freeway and finally make our way out of the LA corridor and onto open highway.

"Are you and Sonia fighting?"

"Yes." My answer is so automatic, it catches me off guard.

"Is it because of yesterday?"

"Yes." I don't turn to see Jack. I'm not sure I'd have the resolve to not be my father if I see even an ounce of possibility in her eyes. "She gave me an ultimatum: her and the baby or you and Tessa."

Jack snorts.

"I know. Shouldn't be a hard choice." I steal a glance and regret the minute I do. The wind's blown Jack's hair over her shoulders and into her face, and I swear she looks the same as the first day I dared to kiss those beautiful pink lips. Her cheeks are flushed, and if I were a bastard of a man, I'd pull the car off to the shoulder and kiss those lips until they were red and moaning my name.

"When you look at me that way, I can see why it's not quite so easy." Her voice is throaty and in no way condemning. If anything, it's an invitation and one I'm fighting with every ounce to not accept. "So, what are you going to do, Hugh Halia?"

If I missed the subtle invitation in her voice, she pulls her bottom lip in between her teeth to make sure I know she's not talking about Sonia and waits for my answer.

Twenty Seven

JACK

My *palms shouldn't be sweating* as much as they are. It's not like I haven't sat in a car with a man before. Hell, I used to live in a car with this boy, but this man . . . I watch his gaze ping-pong between me, my own ultimatum, and the open road in front of us.

"Do you remember the Point Mugu surf trip?"

I blink about a gazillion times, earning me a brilliant smile.

What about my ultimatum?

"The one after Mom's secret beach house delivery?" Hugh pushes when I don't answer.

I nod, not sure where this is going. "The three of us told our parents we were staying at each other's houses . . ." The thought drags on, hoping Hugh will pick it up and take me where his mind has wandered off to.

"I told Kai I was at Derrick's." His voice softens, turns almost regretful. "I never told you, but I caught Kai in bed with his secretary that day. We'd just buried Mom earlier that week, and the only thing he could do was stick his . . ."

Defeat starts to kill the bud of hope I'd had blooming in my gut. I want to reach into the grave and drag Kai back to life so I can kill him again. Maybe I could put in some vacation time for a trip to visit Hades. I quell the anger and focus on the wounded boy next to me. Muscles undulate under his bronzed forearms. Most would see it as anger, but they don't know Hugh like I do. Those ripples aren't from fury, they're from pain. A pain so deep, even your bones don't know how to react to the ache.

My gaze holds onto the parts of Hugh not hidden behind his hair, but isn't that Hugh? Always only showing me the pieces he wants.

"I didn't know that." I finally answer.

Hugh stays quiet. I hate that's what he remembers about our trip. We'd gone to Point Mugu to celebrate his mom. She loved Sycamore Cove Beach, said it was the closest thing to her backyard in Oahu, and then left a hidden piece of herself for only Hugh's eyes.

"You know you're not your father, right, Hugh?" Even I can hear the hurt in my words. "You're the farthest thing from the man. If anything, you're the spitting image of your mom." I weigh the next words with my heart. I need him to hear them, feel them in his soul. I need him to know that he can be a dad and not have to condemn his heart. "She'd be proud of you, whatever you do and however you choose to be present."

"Maybe." He wipes back the black locks from his face and shoots me a devilish look that would make any girl wet and ready, but I know it's just a ploy to get me off our current subject. My heart lurches, sending a ripple of ache to my toes and a need to soothe this look from his face.

"Gotta wonder though, Jack. Maybe she'd be proud of you for walking away." By the cold tone in his voice, he really believes the woman who only saw love in this world would be pleased her only son stopped fighting for it.

"You never knew her, then," I whisper and turn back to watch the highway flying by. Maybe Eros was right. Maybe Hugh was too far gone. And if he was, how could it not be my fault? And how could I ever forgive myself?

We drive silently the rest of the way to Santa Barbara, pick up the part, and grab dinner before hitting the road back to Huntington Beach. All in the uncomfortable awkward silence of two people who have a lifetime of love that seems to have bled them dry.

Hugh places my keys in the palm of my hand, standing so close to him, his hand holding mine, I can't help but look up and wonder: if I'm debating all my own life decisions, how could he not be? His jet-black eyes grab hold of me, and I can see every lost night of sleep etched into his face.

He's tired.

Not just tired, he's beaten, and nobody knows it.

Nobody but me.

Nobody has ever known him the way I do . . . or did. I chew on my lip, realizing how utterly useless to do anything about it I am, except to try and break him some more. It's sadistic. Hugh's lips pull into a tight smile, deepening the nauseous ball in my gut.

"You mind driving home?" he asks.

The wind kicks up off Pacific Coast Highway, pulling the edges of his hair back and exposing all the sharp, hidden planes of his face. All the places I would devour with my kisses. I shake the thought loose before it roots and earns me my last bolt. This is the life I chose.

The life of a Cupid.

"Be my pleasure to chauffeur your ass back to Huntington Beach."

The hint of a genuine smile ghosts across his lips before he walks to the passenger's door. Across the top of my car, his look meets mine. "You know you'd do anything for my hot ass."

"You wish," I mutter and slip into the driver's seat. A giggle rips from my belly, shattering the tension for a few brief seconds as Hugh folds his six-foot plus frame into my seat's setting. His knees near his ears, he shoots me an exasperated look before the hum of the seat motor kicks in. It only adds to the tension and unspoken need between us. Stretched out, he nearly takes the entire length of my car. Hugh folds his arm under his head, letting his t-shirt rise. I can't help but stare at the exposed band of bronzed skin and think of all the ways I could—

He looks up at me, somehow moving my heart from its natural place in my chest to my throat. "You don't mind?"

If I lick that delicious piece of skin you've got on display? Nah, it's only my immortality.

I can't speak, just shake my head and turn the car on. Before we hit the first stoplight, Hugh's fast asleep. I stop and watch the steady rise and fall of his chest. Wonder if he still babbles in his sleep. I mean, I know he's said my name, but the babble about baseball and surfing. I wonder if Sonia's . . . I let that thought die while another one bubbles to the surface.

A honk from the car behind me jolts me in my seat but does nothing to stir Hugh. I flip off the driver for no other reason than it's California and you've got the ocean on one side; paying attention to a green light is the least of your concern. A few lights later, I pull over, change the navigation route, and smile at the first very clever idea I've had all day. I just hope the place is still standing after all these years.

With the help of the full moon and maybe a few promises, I'll spend my soon-to-be immortal life repaying Artemis (the Greek goddess of the moon, hunting, and nursing; all of which I may need if Hugh wakes up). I find the dirt road that leads to another sand-dusted mountain to climb. I lean forward, wrapping my arms around the steering wheel as I navigate the dips and turns in the road.

"Where's my freaking full moon, Artemis?" I mutter. It feels like we've been climbing this side of the rocky seaside forever. Either time or my memory have eroded the smooth trip this was six years ago. Hugh stirs next to me, bringing his palm up under his chin like a young child instead of the multi-million-dollar surf mogul he is. My Maserati hits another pothole and jerks my attention back to the road. Poor Italian GranTurismo was definitely not made for navigating rocky seaside dunes. I crack the window and pull in a deep breath of salted air. I swear I'm a junkie and the ocean is my dealer. The road starts to flatten out, and as we traverse the last bit of the sand-dusted cliffs, the silver rays of moonlight glint off the swells of the ocean. The whitewash turns iridescent as it hits the sand, and the only thing that could sever my hold is the sleepy voice next to me asking, "Where are we, Jack?"

Adrenaline dumps into my system, a rush I haven't felt in years. I steal a glance, afraid of the emotion on his face and regret the moment I do. "Navigation directions must be off," I whisper.

The seat motor hums to life next to me, and few seconds later, Hugh's leaning on the center consul, his face so close to mine, I'm certain he can see every lie I've told, or am about to tell, twitch my lips.

"That's why you should drive American cars."

I can't help the grin. "I love Italians."

A devil-may-care glint shimmers in Hugh's eyes a moment before he tucks a strand of my hair behind my ear. "You love Hawaiians; you drive Italian."

My cheeks heat under his touch, my stomach tumbles, and a wave of desire squeezes an ache-filled beat from my heart. My head says I'm dancing to close to the edge, but my heart says I'm not close enough.

"Why are we here, Jack?" The husky tone of Hugh's voice has nothing to do with sleep.

I clear my throat and hopefully my head. "I wanted to see if it was still here."

"It's an ocean, Jack. Where would it go?"

I turn my focus back on the road and navigate the last bits of the worn asphalt. "Not the ocean."

Hugh stills. The clouds pull away and a silver spotlight from the moon seems to light the pale-blue beach house nestled up against the cliffs.

"It's just a beach shack."

"That's like saying she was just a woman." My words hit him hard, but not hard enough to shake his gaze. "You never came back, did you?"

Hugh shakes his head.

"She kept this place hidden from your dad, left it to you, and you couldn't be bothered?"

"It hurt."

"Life hurts." I park the car at the edge of the sand and kill the engine. "Doesn't mean you give up."

"Worked for you."

"I didn't give up. I just knew your game was too rich for my heart." I shake my head. "Besides, isn't that what you wanted? Me gone?"

Hugh nearly kicks the door open. "Don't kid yourself, Jack. If we were going to make it, you would have stayed and fought. . ."

"You were testing me?"

"I gave you the out and you took it! You got your perfect shiny life, jet setting around the world on A.A.'s dime. All the luxury, none of the risk. You should be thanking me."

The door slam shuts. Hugh stalks to the front of the car and stops. My headlamps cage him in, but the anger rolling off him is tangible. He throws a glare back at the car, then plants his hands on his hips. "Are you coming or what?" Hugh turns on his heels, and the Neanderthal hikes toward the beach house.

Anger courses through my body. He's wrong on so many levels. And who was he to *test* me! I'm the one who . . .

I pull in a deep breath, trying to remember this is what I want: him so pissed he remembers what it's like to fight for something. But I'm not sure it's enough to get him to fight for his heart.

A Cupid never loses control. I chant seven more times before I ease out of my car, fighting every fiber in my being to resist the urge to run up next to him and keep fighting. Instead, I slip off my high-heels and relish the feel of sand between my toes. By the time I reach the bungalow, yellow light pours out of the windows like a puppy happy its owner is finally home.

Hugh stalks back out; he's ditched his shirt and my breath catches when the moon shines off the planes of his chest. Muscles ripple as he slams two surfboards into the sand, points a finger at me, and says, "There's a wet suit in the closet, but I dare you to do it naked." He walks right up to me, shimmies out of his pants, and based on the wicked way his eyes are dancing, I'd say his undies too. "I fucking dare you, Jack." He pushes past me, grabs a board, and—yep, his two well-toned and never-seen-the-sun naked cheeks taunt me as he walks to the water.

When he dives into the water, I turn, catching my breath, and walk into the beach house. I pull up short, take in a deep breath, and I swear I can still smell Tessa's coconut baby oil perfuming the air. It's like time stood still here, unwilling to change. Pictures of the three of us growing up still hang from the pale-yellow walls. The couches are still covered with the dustsheets we'd used six years ago, but they look as fresh as the day we covered them. The hardwood floors are swept, and there's no hint of stale musk in the air. I run a finger along the dark polished-wood breakfast bar as I walk to the closet and inspect. There's not even a hint of dust. Hugh's taken care of the bungalow like a mistress ready and waiting for her lover's visit. I pull open the closet door and freeze. I'm not sure how long I stare at the three wet suits. A dare from Hugh used to have me biting at his heels to prove him wrong, and where did that get us?

The cuckoo clock on the wall chimes ten, breaking the hypnotic trance neoprene seems to be capable of holding me under. I pull the black wetsuit with the purple hibiscus on the shoulder off the hanger. *I'm not sure what he was trying to accomplish.* I rip my blouse from my skirt, only hesitating a moment to think about snagging the silk on my zipper as I let my skirt puddle to the floor. *Did he really think an* I dare you, Jack *and a well-leveled look would get me fired up?* I look at the mound of silk on the floor, shimmy out of my G-string, and unhook my bra while eyeing my wetsuit. I know that look that flashed in his eyes. It was the one that always dared me out of my comfort zone and had me questioning to what depths would I follow Hugh Halia. I grab the scrap of purple fabric on the floor and slip it on. *It's even tinier than I remember.* I pull in a deep breath before shutting the closet door and looking at myself in the mirror. It's not smaller, I'm just not the naive girl who used to wear it. A smile ghosts across my lips.

Nearly naked and a smile, let's see how it feels, Hugh Halia.

I dare him to not fall tongue over dick if he saw me looking like a moment from his past and a glimpse of his future. Warmth pools in my belly at the thought of Hugh slick with ocean water, his eyes flaring when he sees me. I shift on my heels. I swallow hard at the thought of the fire sparking to life in his eyes as he takes me in from foot to forehead.

Silly, Hugh. Some treats are best left to the imagination.

I turn on my heels, leave the wet suit on the back of the couch, and shut the door behind me.

"Your move, Halia."

Twenty Eight

HUGH

For a dude engaged to another lady, my heart is pounding out of my chest to see if Jack will take my dare. I'm not even sure why I dropped my drawers and taunted her to take a look.

I'm engaged.

Liar.

Okay, my heart may not have caught up with my head, but not all marriages are made in love and happily-ever-afters, despite what Derrick says. My stomach drops, and I blame it on the swell that just rolled under me, and not on the girl I'm desperately hoping swims out here and shoves my dare down my throat. I splash some water on my face; the cool liquid only stirs up more memories of Jack and me when we were a "Jack and Me." I pull saltwater through my hair, letting go of the nervous breath I've been holding from my lungs.

Who'm I kidding?

The Jack Alcantar from six years ago is not the woman who took her sweet-ass time to walk to the bungalow. She sure is hell not going to dive in the ocean and prove me wrong by getting naked. Although I wish she would.

God, I really wish she would.

I look out past the jetty and catch the full moon bouncing off the crests of the waves, making them glow a magical white. I shake my head. My girl's back and she has me thinking of glowing magical waves and full moons. I smile, remembering how we spent one of our last nights under a full moon.

"Just like old fucking times," I mutter and glance back at the shore in time to see Jack surface close to me, too close, from the last swell. I can't help the shocked smile crawling across my face. And then I wish I could.

Jack wipes the water from her face, the tiny saltwater streams race down the curves of her face, over her bare shoulders, and then meet to dribble down her . . . I swallow hard. I've never been so jealous of water as I am at this moment. She's not naked, although she's about as close to it as the tiny purple bikini she's wearing will allow.

She left that scrap of swimwear here ten years ago. It looked amazing then, but now, on the woman she's become, it's fucking perfect. More perfect than any memory of her could do justice. Breasts that beg a man to admire and pay homage, and hips that demand a firm but gentle hand to maneuver into positions of ecstasy. The primal urge to claim her rumbles awake.

I want!

"I'm here," she tosses my way, like there's no big deal that she's out here *not* naked, but close enough to it. To prove how here she is, she sits up on the board, leaning back to give me a better view of all the ways the years have been so fucking kind to her. And if the universe wasn't done rubbing my face in all the ways I fucked up, Jack kicks a foot up on her board and my ability to breathe is gone. Wet and looking like a fucking playboy centerfold. A smile pulls at her plump lips. I bite back the groan and every desire to dive off my board and bury myself in her.

"Mermaid got your tongue?" There's a laughter in her voice my soul has craved for years, lifetimes maybe.

I splash some more water on my face. "She's got something."

Even in the darkness, I don't miss the blush staining Jack's cheeks. Maybe not everything has changed.

Jack's focus shifts to something over my shoulder, but I can't take my eyes off her. She left me a girl, but holy shit is she a woman now.

"We going to surf, or you going to stare at my tits all night?"

The image of her rises and falls in time with another swell, taking along my smile.

"There are worse things to have to endure for an evening, but actually I'm reveling in the fact that you still walk away from a dare." I splash water on my face, hoping to calm down all the primal needs in me. "You've gone soft, Jack."

Jack shakes her head; wet blond hair flips over her shoulder and splays against the sun-kissed swell of her breast. It's like a fucking arrow directing my mouth where it needs to land. A few more waves ride underneath us, but neither of us breaks the silence of the night. There's so much I should say, so much I want to do. None of it compares to the need to know what her game is.

Jack Alcantar has always been a "think three steps ahead" kind of woman. Which means whatever change of heart she's got happening, it didn't happen spontaneously on the way home, it probably didn't happen the morning of the sabotage. Maybe the night I proposed?

I try to recall her face, but all I remember is her lithe body silhouetted by the back light of the stage, and E.J. wrapping his arm around her waist. Which leads me back to my original question. One she better damn well get ready to answer.

"Why'd you bring me here, Jack?"

Her eyes flare. "I wanted to see if it was still here."

"That's a reason, but it's not *the* reason. So, I'll ask one last time: Why'd you bring me here, Jack?"

"I'll answer your question if you answer mine." She smiles and pushes back on her board, arching everything I want to taste again to the heavens. The woman is going to be the death of me. I'm all but certain of it now, but not before I know what the real play is here.

"You had a question?" I push.

Jack leans forward on to her belly and kicks her legs behind her. The view of her backside is as stunning as her front. I never knew how she could balance on her board like that. I never complained either, not when I can see every muscle flex and release as she keeps her balance.

She looks up at me; the moon glinting off the water hits her eyes like it was the spotlight into her soul.

"What does your heart desire?" she finally whispers.

I gasp like a freaking chick. Why does she want to know? It's not like she doesn't already know the answer to that question. My heart starts, and I swear it's the first time I've felt a flush overcome my body in six years. All my walls come tumbling down, and I'm certain she'll know the answer when I speak. My heart's desire is her. It's always been her. Instead, I keep my gaze locked on Jack's, hoping to find the hint of laughter at the question, but there's none. She's dead serious. I cup my hands and try to drown the answer from my lips in seawater before pulling in another deep breath and start a dance I know will leave one of us shattered.

"That's a big question."

"Seeing where you are"—Jack lets all my responsibilities, present and future, hang in the air with the statement—"don't you think it's about time you take a moment to think about an answer?

"Who says I haven't?"

"I do."

When did she get so bold? So in-your-face? And when did her body become my greatest weakness?

When you were fourteen, you dumb shit.

"That's what I thought." She bites down on her lip. "You don't know. So where does that leave us?"

Us? Yes, I want an us.

"You're not going to answer?" Her shoulders rise in a familiar way of irritation nearing ire. Jack slaps the water, trying to get my attention, but I'm still stuck on the realization that the only person I *want* to have a relationship with isn't the person I'm going to *have* to spend the rest of my life with. Not if I don't want to end up like my dad.

"Fine, let me answer for you. It leaves one of us naked"—she nods to me—"one of us not, in the ocean with you wanting to surf like old times. And if you're too much of a pussy to really look at what your heart wants—what makes your soul burn—then that leaves us with 'last one in being a rotten breakfast burrito.'" Jack turns her board and starts paddling toward the shore.

"Knew you were a chicken, Jacquelyn Alcantar," I holler after her and the wave she's chasing. A smile forms the minute she pulls off the wave, turning her board toward me. I know her so well—My heart stops. Even at this distance, I can see a new look dance across her face. The ocean seems to quiet. Hell, even the mermaids might break the surface to see what my siren of an ex-girlfriend has to say.

Jack's surfboard comes right up next to mine. Her leg tangles with mine under the water, and I'm all but certain she's going to take my chin in between her fingers like a two-year-old being scolded. Instead, she shakes her head before cupping my face in her tiny, delicate hands and pulls me so close to her, my lips start to pucker out of habit.

Her eyes dance back and forth across my face. "You think me not biting at your dare proves I'm a chicken?"

I nod. There's something about watching the fire light her blue eyes to the point they're glowing. It was one of the things I loved best about getting under Jack's skin. That is, until I was inside her and watched the raging fire temper into embers of lust that could only be stoked by my touch.

Jack laughs like she's been listening to the voice in my head.

"Hugh, the only chicken I see is the one who's too afraid to admit what he really wants. The only chicken I see"—her voice is low, so low, it's down near feral—"is out here with surf wax scratching his balls raw. You let me know which one you want my help fixing."

She winks and then pushes my face from her touch before turning the board to start paddling in. I can't help the pull of a smile at my lips, even if it is at the cost of defaming my balls.

"Chicken!" I holler again.

Jack keeps paddling, not even breaking her rhythm to check and see if I'm following. She finally catches a small swell and rides it into the sand. She picks the board over her head, and I lose myself watching the sway of her hips mark the trail to the beach shack. But something has shifted.

Something . . .

My mind floats back to the conversation I had with Derrick this morning. Why can't I be a good father and have Jack? Maybe *I* was the chicken? Sonia knows what's happening. She even told me to choose, so why not both? If I marry Sonia knowing I love Jack, doesn't that make me just as bad a fuck-up as him? What would I be teaching my kid? The questions bob through my mind in time with the water I'm floating in.

By the time I make it to shore, my hands are pruned, my balls are probably raw—because Jack is right, surf wax is not kind to my delicate man skin—and I'm no closer to solving the riddle of Jack Alcantar than I was the moment I saw her standing in Halia Surf a couple of months ago, except to know: I want her. I've only ever wanted her.

Brown-sugar sand gives way under my feet as I follow the path Jack's made, and for the first time in six years, I feel like my feet are on the right path. A path the girl I've always loved carved in my heart years ago. I smile when I near the shack. She's wheeled out the fire pit that looks like a stripped-down trashcan and somehow managed to get a low-burning blaze going. I pull in a deep breath and close my eyes. There's something about burning firewood and salted air that calms me down to my soul. Could be because every good thing that ever happened to me had one, if not both, of those scents attached to the memory.

I jump out of the memory when a piece of terry cloth slaps me in the face.

"Cover up." She nods casually, but the look that just flashed across her eyes says she's anything but. "Shrinkage is never an attractive place to start."

An evil chuckle rumbles in my chest as I quickly catch the towel before it hits sand and wrap it around my waist. When I look back her way, I go as still as she has. She's found my work shirt, and her long, tan legs seem to pour out from underneath the fabric. My shirt covers a lot more than the bikini did, but for some reason, seeing her in *my* clothes, hair wet and piled up in one of those messy buns on the top of her head—she looks like she could've rolled out of *my* bed—that's all the more enticing. As if she can read my mind, Jack jumps when

I shift her direction.

"You made a fire?" I ask.

"I did."

I take a step closer to her and feel my body rejoice at the first *right* decision I've made in a while. "Did you find the fridge?"

"I did." Jack takes a step away from me, but her eyes say *come and catch me.* "If you haven't been here in ten years, why do you keep it stocked?"

My shoulders pull involuntarily, answering her question. I shift my focus to the sand, resisting the urge to "aw-shucks" kick at the answer like I did when we were kids.

"Hugh?" Jack pushes before taking another step away from me, now on the other side of the fire pit.

The air ripples from the heat of the fire separating us, making the woman I love look more like a mythological apparition or mirage.

"I hoped. . ." The rest of my thought trails off.

"You hoped?" There's so much optimism in her voice, it rocks me to my soul.

"Someone would make me want to come back?"

Jack's shoulders fall a little, and I know that's not the answer she was hoping for.

"Would you have brought Sonia here?"

I shake my head without a second thought. This place didn't belong to anyone but the three of us—the two of us, if I was truly being honest. Honesty. I forgot what that felt like in a relationship.

"She's going to be your wife, the mother of your child, and you wouldn't have shared this?" She steps out from behind the waves of heat, toward me, not stopping until her toes are touching mine in the sand. "Hugh, your mom would have wanted you to share this with someone you loved."

"I did. I shared it with you." My words wash over her. I see each syllable erasing years of inked-in doubt, years of ache I'd tattooed on her heart. I wish there were more I could do. More to say that would show her I'd take back the moment I ruined us—

"Why would you say that?" The skin between her eyes crinkles as she bites down on the tiny piece of the corner of her lip. No one knows this is Jack at her most vulnerable, no one but me.

I can't help but smooth out the skin with my thumb.

She reaches up on the tips of her toes, eyes holding onto mine like a lifeline to something I'd trade a million souls to give her . . . a second chance.

This woman, she's every breath I've ever taken, she's every memory I want to create. All I've ever wanted is her. I wrap my arm around her tiny waist, pulling her to where she's always belonged, next to me.

"Ask me, Jack. I'll give you anything."

"Would you give me your heart?" Her hands splay against my chest, but her fingertips pull at the skin on my chest, drawing me closer. I wouldn't have expected anything less from my fierce girl. She won't let me waltz in and sweep her off her feet, not after I shattered her.

With my free hand, I flatten her palm against the place only she's ever claimed. "It's always been yours." I pull her fingers to my lips, revel in the small gasp, and place a tiny kiss on her knuckles. "You don't have to fight this anymore."

"Neither do you."

"Ask me, Jack. Ask me to kiss you. Let me love you like my soul was fashioned to do."

"And what about Sonia? What about the baby? I don't want you to make a mistake . . ."

Her question fades into a million thoughts. What about them? Why couldn't I be good dad and love Jack? I pull in the first deep breath of freedom.

"No," I say. Jack's shoulders slump a little. "Wouldn't I be making an even bigger mistake if I marry Sonia knowing my heart has only ever belonged to you, Jack?"

She ducks her head away from me, but I notice the small tear dribbling down her cheek. It slices right through me. I caused this hurt, and I'll take it all away, she just has to ask me and I know—

Jack wraps her hand around my neck and pulls my forehead to hers. Her eyes are wild, unsure, like what she's about to do could cost her everything. She closes her eyelids again and I'm dying inside. Praying that she'll be courageous enough for the both of us. One long blink later, she opens her eyes and firmly plants her lips on mine. Our eyes lock, shock lights up my insides. My heart stops at the timid but firm kiss. There's so much caution, so much hesitation, so much hurt. I wrap my arms around her, lifting her up off the ground, her legs dangle until I slide my tongue across the seam of her lips, begging her to give me another chance. Let me in one more time. Her lips harden but she doesn't pull away.

Too fast.

I let her body slide down the front of me, a little shy about her feeling how fucking hard she's made me with a couple of simple kisses. I keep my forehead against hers as her feet settle on the ground, my arms wrapped around her waist. Even if I wanted to let go, my body is home when she's in my arms, I can't.

"It's always been you, Jack. Only. You," I whisper against her lips; her eyes shimmer and then she places the softest kiss on my lips. It's sweet and innocent, like we used to be. Cautious and careful, like we should have been. Another pass of her lips against mine and I lose myself. I thread my fingers into her hair. I'd never forgotten the silky texture, but wow, had the memory dulled the sensation.

Slow.

Jack angles her lips, deepening the tentative kiss. I want to dive in, but this is her show. She didn't ask me to kiss her, so I won't take this from her. She's in charge; she always has been. The ache in my chest grows, fills with the need building up in me, but I stamp it down. If I go too fast, this will all end. If she's ever going to trust me again, this has to be . . .

I suck in a year's worth of air as her lips slip down my jaw, along my throat, and to the spot on my neck that only she knows about. Her tongue glides along the sensitive patch of skin where my neck and shoulder meet, spilling all of me out onto the sand. I curl my head into her hair and suck in the sweet smell of plumeria and sea salt. The scent so unique, it seduces my senses. *Yes!* Everything about Jack seduces my senses.

"Hugh," Jack whispers against my shoulder.

"Yes?" *I'll give you my soul if you ask me to, whatever you want, just don't leave me again.* The words catch on the emotion in my throat.

"What am I doing?"

My lungs nearly collapse at the hesitancy in her voice.

"Letting me love you," I murmur.

She pulls back; the hint of a smile tugs at the edges of her lips. Her eyes dart back and forth across my face, searching for an answer to a question she hasn't asked, a question she's too afraid to know the answer to.

I cradle her face, willing every ounce of who I am with her to flow through my fingertips. I need her to *feel* what I'm about to say because it's the only way she'll ever believe me. My words are hollow, but my love . . . it's the only chance I have of making my world right. My gaze latches onto her wide eyes.

"Jack, it's always been you. Only you." I swipe away a tear I know she doesn't realize she's let loose. "I've loved you since you were twelve, loved you when I pushed you away when you were seventeen, and will fight heaven, earth, and anything that dares comes between us again."

The last remaining edges of the cold woman I've made of her melt away. Something glimmers in her eyes a second before she jumps into my arms, wrapping her legs around my waist. I pull her into me, reveling the feel of her skin against mine.

"Jacquelyn Alcantar, you're not wearing any panties," I croon.

She giggles into my neck. The sound mingles with the heat of her core washing through me, healing the broken man I was and making me new. And when her lips meet mine, all the hesitation, the worry, the years of neglect disappears like sun melting a fine mist that's hung on the ocean for too long.

Sand sinks under every step I take as I walk us back to the porch. I still want to take this slow. Love her the way I should have the last six years. I make sure this is everything Jack wants, because my heart couldn't take having to say goodbye to her again.

"Hugh," she whispers, but there's so much need laced in her words, I know *slow* is going to have to wait.

I walk us past the porch swing and carry her over the threshold. My heart nearly stops at the thought, the image of us living here. Making our lives here—Her tongue flicks mine and any sane thoughts left are eviscerated. Jack threads her fingers into my hair. I nip at her bottom lip, she assaults mine. In the span of a few steps, I'm willing to give everything to her. I'm not sure who's taken the lead, all I know is that I'll follow wherever she takes me. I pull her closer into me as I walk us down the narrow hallway to the master bedroom. I haven't been here in ten years, but I know every turn, every corner of this house—just like I haven't had my hands on Jack, but I know every inch of her body, her soul. As if she's reading my mind, Jack bites her fingernails into my shoulder, pulling me closer, fastening my soul to hers. This is how we were. This is how love should be. I angle my head and dive deeper into everything that's Jack, rejoicing when a small groan rips from her throat.

"Me too, Jack. Me fucking too," I mutter, against her lips, but she's not done. Neither am I; I'll never be done with her. I was a fool to think we could ever exist apart. Not when this Jack tickles my nose with hers, not when we're this damn good together. I lay her down on my bed and revel in the primal triumph coursing through my body, before burning this memory into my mind. With her blonde hair splayed across my pillows and a look in her eyes that promises me forever, she bites down on her lip, trapping her words. She loves me too. I know she does, and if she can't trust her voice, then I'll let her body talk for her.

I join her on the bed we've shared once before, mesmerized by the silver moonlight washing over her. I watch the sheen of lust cloud her eyes. She's so goddamn beautiful, it hurts. I push back the small blond wisps of her hair dancing along her forehead.

She licks her lip before whispering, "It's always been you." She slides her palm along my face, down my neck, and finds her rightful resting spot over my heart. "Only you."

I'm gone.

I'm done.

Signed.

Sealed.

Delivered to anything and anywhere Jack wants me. I cage the only woman I've ever loved between my arms, settling in between her legs, and revel in the fact that it took six years, the near loss of Halia, and a wrong turn to finally make my life right again.

I dance my fingers down Jack's leg, grabbing her knee, and hooking her leg around my hip, loving the way my shirt on her slides open. How'd I miss that she'd only fastened the top button. The same way I'd missed everything about this woman. She was right. Everyone underestimated her, but I would never make that mistake again. Tracing the curve of her leg, I beam at the shiver I coax her body to release when I skim the hourglass shape of her belly. And lose myself when I push back the cloth covering her breasts.

"God, you're beautiful."

I place a small kiss at the side of her breast and when that rosebud of a nipple puckers, I pull it into my mouth and swear this woman will never know a day without my love.

"Hugh," Jack gasps, arching up from the bed. Her fingers wind their way into my hair, pulling me into her. "It's been so long."

I pull back, hearing the tears in her voice.

"Why are you stopping?" There's panic in her voice.

"I need you to ask me, Jack." I shake my head. "No, I need you to tell me this is what you want. This is where you want to be."

She nods, pulling herself up against me, then twisting us and pushing me back against the mattress. Time stands still as she hovers over me. My heart in my throat, fear coursing through me, afraid I've shattered whatever spell we'd fallen under.

"Jack?"

She unbuttons the top button of *my* shirt and lets the fabric slide down her arms and pool around her waist. I flip her over, kiss her until I feel her lips plump from my assault. Her eyes meet mine, warm blue waters, kissed by the haze of love. I run my hand up her belly, smile when she gasps as I roll her nipple between my fingers, and nearly end our reunion when she reaches down and grabs hold of me. Right then and there, I make it my goal to reacquaint myself with every inch of this woman. Remind her of all the ways I undo her, like she does me. We tangle ourselves in the sheets, wrapping up all the old memories, all the tragic mistakes and burying them in the past.

Winded from just foreplay, Jack straddles me, I can feel the warm and wetness so close to everything that make me a man. She runs her hands up my chest, eyes lost in a distant memory before she asks, “Do you believe in love?”

“I believe in you.” I kiss her cheek. “I believe in everything that makes our love story. I believe in loving this freckle on your neck that looks like Oklahoma.” I kiss it. “I love this white patch of skin that never tans on your shoulder.” Another kiss. “I love every inch of you. Every freckle, every fold, every potential wrinkle I get to discover with you. You’re my future.” I look up at her. The doubt swirling in her eyes guts me. “My God, Jack. What’s it going to take? I love you. Hell, I even love this scar that looks like a Harry Potter lightning bolt over your heart.” I go to kiss it but Jack sits up.

“Jack?” I run my palm down her spine, but instead of melting into my touch, she stiffens. “What’s wrong?”

She runs a hand across the scar and lies back down. “Nothing.”

My gut turns. She’s lying to me. “Jack?”

“It’s nothing. I’d forgotten it was even there.” She puts on a smile, and if I didn’t know her as well as I do, the lie might have worked.

“Tell me about it?”

The fake smile deepens. “It’s nothing.”

I feel the skin between my eyebrows crinkle.

“Just a scar.” She runs her hand over the jagged puckered skin.

I still her hand. “Did this happen in Australia?” What I really want to ask is, is that asshole, E.J., responsible?

“No, actually. It happened here.”

I drop Jack’s hand. “When?”

"Not too long ago?"

"How many times have you come back to Huntington Beach?"

She doesn't answer, which means a lot more times than my heart can bear. My grip tightens around her waist.

"Jack?"

A breath passes, even though I can't pull air into my lungs, before Jack unravels herself from my arms. Everything in the room seems to shift and pull under the strain of Jack's silence. She walks to the window, moonlight pouring in, and I know I need to remember the way she looks at this moment, because Jacquelyn Alcantar is about to rip my heart out of my chest and serve it up to me under the moon we'd first made love to.

"Jack," I whisper. "You were never going to stay, were you?"

Her shoulders square and I have my answer. All the hurt I'd thought I'd long since buried the first time she left floats to the surface. I'm not a man, I'm the boy she had no problem leaving. I'm the asshole who pushed her out the door. And she's not the girl who left my bedroom shattered; she's the woman who will never allow anyone into her heart. And I did that.

There's nothing else to say.

There's nothing else to do.

She was mine to love and I fucked it up . . . like everything else in my life.

I untangle myself from the sheets, committing the past few moments to my heart before I feel it harden. I guess some of us really are never supposed to know what a lifetime of love feels like. So, I'll stop. I'll let her go. Because I can only fight for something both of us believe in.

I swipe my shirt from the bed, afraid to breath in Jack's scent, certain I'll never launder the fabric.

"I'll be in the car." I walk to the door, feeling the strain of my forever slipping from my fingers. It burns like a wildfire scorching my soul. I stop at the door, holding onto the doorjamb like it's a lifeline to my very existence. I taste the next few words in my gut before I say, "Lock the door when you're *finally* ready to leave."

Twenty Nine

JACK

I *pace the hallway outside Hugh's* office, hoping to catch him before everyone comes in for the day. If I keep moving, maybe the crushing sensation of loss won't consume me. My nipples pebble at the memory of his lips on me, his fingers—I banish the thought. He hasn't spoken to me in three days, I haven't even seen him the last two. I thought for sure I'd be able to steal a few minutes with him at opening day, but we'd stood on stage with only inches separating us and I'd never felt so distant from him. He looked right through me, like I never existed, and . . . I didn't think I could live in a world where that was a possibility. I was okay with him hating me, but completely ignoring me? The ache I've felt since we left the beach shack flares, gripping my heart and stealing my breath. I stop in front of his door again, my fist hovering over the door while I listen for the velvet tone of his voice. I'd give almost anything to hear that reverence in his voice. Almost. The door opens, and I'm face to face with Hugh.

"Yes?" His voice is cold, distant, dismissive.

"I, um, I . . ." I stammer over my words. "We need to talk."

"You said all you needed to—"

"I didn't say anything." I cut Hugh off, grabbing his arm to make him stop. I want to make him understand all the reasons why I can't give him what he wants, but the way he looks at my fingers wrapped around the fabric of his shirt, it's clear I'm too late. The ache I've felt since we drove home turns into a throb that threatens to undo me.

"And yet, your silence said so much." Hugh peels my fingers off him and then places my hand by my side like a two-year-old told not to touch. His eyes level with mine, cold and nearly void of life. I've never witnessed the days leading up to a banishment's beginning until now. The shiny black onyx in his eyes is dulling, the life that used to evoke a million responses from me now seems to just be a flat black. Hugh's heart is dying in front of my eyes, and there's not a damn thing—short of a miracle—for me to do.

"Message received, Jack. You're not interested." Hugh steps around me, starting for the elevator. "Finish the job you were hired to do, and be on your way. Now if you'll excuse me, I have a doctor's appointment with Sonia." He opens the door to the lobby and passes Tessa.

I feel the quiver in my lip; taste the salty tears clogging my throat. The pager on the waistband of my pencil skirt vibrates.

I know who it is.

I know what it says.

I grab the archaic device and read Eros's message:

He's gone.

DO IT, NOW.

"I have three more days, Eros." I whisper to the face of the pager, knowing the God of Love can hear me.

My Cupid pager vibrates again:

When the last "I DO" falls,

SO DOES HALIA.

I grip the pager, pushing down the need to throw it against the wall. Why is he so hell bent on Hugh's banishment?

"Fifty is never easy." I jump at Tessa's voice as she reaches for the pager, prying it from my Kung Fu grip.

My eyes lock with hers. She has no idea hard fucking hard fifty arrows is. I can't see her arrows, another one of Eros's "focus on the job, not on the rewards" clauses. Cupids can't compare, not even mentors, but I'm certain she's nowhere close to fifty. I'm also certain she's never witnessed a Cupid attempt fifty. I bite back the contempt and vitriol swirling in my gut.

"I have a plan," Tessa drapes her arm across my shoulders.

"That's my line."

"Yeah, well." She looks over her shoulder where Hugh just left. "Your plan sucks. I'm not sure what you were thinking taking him—"

"You have a plan?" I cut Tessa off. I don't need her to relive my near banishment play by play. I'd felt the warning warmth of the second branding over my heart. I'd almost mistaken it for my nearly petrified, immortal heart coming back to life because of Hugh. I was wrong. Oh, it was my heart and it was because of Hugh, but it was nearly the death of my existence. My pulse races with just how close to the edge I'd danced. After I'd gotten dressed, found Hugh sitting in the driver's seat of my car, and made our way back to the land of cell service, my phone nearly exploded with texts from Tessa. Fifty "call me, now!" texts gave me a hint, but when I walked in the front door, Tessa ripped my blouse, buttons raining down on the tile like plinks of hail as she checked for the pink puckered skin of my second brand. She'd collapsed to the floor in a heap of sobbing, surfer-girl mess, muttering *I can't lose you too.*

I knew what she meant. It would be Shakespeare tragic if both Hugh and I ended up banished. Tessa'd be left here alone . . . with E.J.

She'd slept in my bed like we used to do growing up. Usually when she'd been tortured by the mean girls or had a psyche-damaging fight with her mom. I wouldn't tell her, but those moments were some of my fondest moments. We'd drifted off to sleep somewhere between her telling me I owed her for distracting E.J. and Eros and my questioning whom she'd lost.

"Jack." Tessa squeezes my shoulders, pulling me out of my memories. "Are you in or out?"

I don't have a moment to think, but when it comes to Tessa, from here on out, I know I'll always be in. I nod, committing the memory of the smile blossoming across her face.

"Good, now let's go save our boy."

Thirty minutes later, I didn't know what I had agreed to when Tessa asked if I was in, and given the get up I'm in, I'm pretty sure I'd have said hell no. I adjust the string bikini top and pull the Brazilian cut bottoms out of my butt.

"Why are we reliving our worst teen mistakes?"

Tessa giggles next to me. "C'mon, Jack. Some of our teen mistakes were the most fun we've ever had."

"Right, but where are we going?" I sink into the sand as I hurry to keep up with my friend. We've walked past Halia's site and under the pier. The men's surf heats are over, and the women don't start until after lunch. The shore is pretty empty with everyone concentrating on the BMX arena. But "pretty empty" during the Open just means there aren't people standing shoulder to shoulder.

"While you were playing hide the s'more stick with Hugh, I was watching Sonia." Tessa smiles at a group of preteen boys that may have lost their virginity by just looking at Contessa St. James.

"And what did you find?"

"That the girl isn't as squeaky clean as she portrays."

"You need to tell me something we don't already know."

"How 'bout I show you."

We stop a distance away from the Sandpiper tent. Okay, tent is a loosely used term for the three-story structure on the beach. The area is fenced off, and they've laid down blue AstroTurf so their models' feet don't get sandy when they jump out of the three hot tubs and head into the "house" past the white gauzy curtains. On the third floor, there's a DJ with every single hot dude and drop-dead gorgeous girl in the state dancing. They've partnered up with MTV to do a spotlight on the colorful company and their marquee surf star. My blood starts to boil at the thought of the girl who accused Hugh of slipping her a roofie.

"Sonia's at the Sandpiper's tent?" I ask.

Tessa lays out a couple of towels and plants her body. "Not just Sonia." She nods to the side entrance.

I follow her gaze. A man in a suit at the US Open stands out like a stripper in church. I squint, wishing I had a pair of binoculars, but even at this distance, it's not hard to make out the familiar stature. Not when the memory of his half-brother's body is still making my fingers tingle. It's Mack, and he's talking to one of the security guards. Mack throws his head back in an over-exaggerated laugh. The security guard claps him on the shoulder and then lets him into Sandpiper's tent.

"What the hell?"

Tessa hands me a pair of binoculars. "Wait till you check out the second story privacy cabanas."

With the binoculars, I scan the second story. More white gauzy curtains flutter in the wind. Half-naked bodies spill out from almost all the four privacy cabanas, except for one. You wouldn't think mousy brown hair would stand out in a crowd, but when a handsome Hawaiian in a suit walks in and tangles his fingers in that mousy brown hair, then fiddles with the strings of her bikini, it makes a difference.

"Holy shit?"

"Yep."

I push the binoculars closer to my eyes, hoping the view changes. No such luck. "And why the fuck is she kissing the wrong Halia brother?"

"Because she's a two-timing, back-stabbing, conniving, bedroom-hopping whore?"

I welcome the snort because I'm certain I'd be banished if I let the rage lose. I pull my gaze from the binoculars and look at Tessa. Her sun-kissed skin looks pale, like she's going to hurl.

"How long have you known?"

"I told you, my gut is never wrong." She continues, not acknowledging my eye roll, "I never trusted Mack, and Sonia's good girl doe-eyed routine always rubbed me wrong. You know I never trust a person who doesn't have at least one or two skeletons falling out of their closet." Tessa steals a glance back at Sandpiper's tent. "I just didn't know Sonia was hiding a Halia in hers, not till last night when I followed her to Mack's hotel room."

"But this is flat out ballsy. I didn't think Sonia. . ." My words trail off. How could I have been so wrong about her? And what if I'd been wrong about everything when it came to Hugh?

Tessa wraps her fingers around my wrist like she knows the rabbit hole I'm falling down. "You've noticed the shift in Hugh, he just doesn't care anymore. If you've picked up on it, then it was only a matter of time before Sonia did."

"But she's pregnant with Hugh's baby. How could she?"

"Is it Hugh's?" Tessa pulls her knees up to her chest. "This is her out in the open, how long has she been messing around closed doors?"

I shake my head. "How do we prove it?"

A set of waves crash, filling the silence my question's produced. Tessa has a plan; the girl always has a plan. And the calmer, quieter she is, the more I know I'm not going to like the plan.

"Tessa," I push.

"She moved out of Hugh's house a couple of weeks ago. I can tell you with all sorts of certainty she hasn't gone back to her apartment."

"She's at the Hilton?"

Tessa shrugs.

"With Mack?" I add.

A stillness washes over Tessa, one that reminds me of the time we snuck into the principal's office to dig up dirt on him and dirty Delilah when he tried to sue Tessa's mom for custody of her sister. That's how we'd found out Principal Can't Keep It In His Pants knocked up Delilah too. I'd wanted to blast her dirty laundry, but Tessa had stopped me. Seeing Delilah's face fall at the bonfire had been worth the eight years we'd sat on the secret.

"You're going to make me break into a hotel room and watch them do the dirty, aren't you?"

A smile ticks at Tessa's lips. "No, sweet Jack. That's what cameras are for."

I start to relax.

"We're just going to break in and retrieve the cameras."

"Tessa, the President of the WSL is staying in that hotel, not to mention the celebrities. Sweetie, security is going to—"

Tessa stands, cutting me off. "Trust me, I called in every favor I have and I owe a few to some extreme undesirables." She reaches for my hand before hauling me out of the sand. "Time for sweet Sonia to see what happens when she messes with our guy." Tessa shakes out our beach towels and starts for the Waterfront Hotel. When she notices I'm not following, she turns, walking backward in the sand with all the grace of a ballerina on polished wood, and says, "Well, hurry up, who knows how long their porno pet fest will last. Maybe twenty minutes if Mack is lucky." Her snort catches on the wind. "The girl talks a good game, but she's got no stamina."

"I think I just threw up in my mouth."

"Puke and rally, Jack. Puke and rally."

I've gotta give it to my girl. The door to Mack's suite opens without much fanfare. Tessa turns and wiggles the "donated" key card between her fingers. She definitely hasn't lost her charm when it comes to getting men to do what she wants. I slip past her and the grin that's certain to be plastered on her face long after the Open is over. The suite is the size of a small one-bedroom apartment. I wrinkle my nose. It smells like Mack has definitely made it his own.

Tessa steps next to me, her hand covering her nose and mouth. "Gross, it's called maid service, Mack."

"Not sure he got the memo that's a free amenity. Damn shame." I walk further into the room, over the mounds of clothes, and past a several room service trays. "He's murdered this room."

The Waterfront is a gorgeous hotel; Hugh and I spent a few days in a suite similar to this one. I run my flip-flop-covered foot over the lush sand-colored carpet that's rippled to look like the shore has rushed out; warm earth-toned paint softens the walls. There's a small dining room, or should be if you can find it under the clutter of papers, napkins, and takeout bags. The fast food carnage bleeds into a kitchenette, left out to stink and spoil. I cover my nose at the stench of the overflowing garbage. I'm pretty sure the hotel is going to have to HAZMAT it after Mack's stay.

"Is Halia Surf paying for this?" I ask.

Tessa shakes her head; she hesitates a moment, then pushes the door to the master suite open. "Gods, I hope not." Her body revolts like she's about to throw up for real this time.

In the bedroom, polished driftwood planks decorate the wall behind a California King bed. The sheets are twisted, the comforter pushed into a wad at the foot of the bed, and the mattress is skewed and bending where it's fallen off the box spring. Clothes litter the floor, thousand-dollar suits are tossed like they're scraps of cheap swimsuits. I spot the empty box of condoms on the floor by the trash can, a filled one dangles off the edge of the wastebasket, and I nearly hurl myself. I can't take any more, so I turn and walk to the balcony. Tessa's behind me, following every careful step I take.

"Think I know why the maids aren't invited in." I nod to the coffee table and the mirror covered with white powder. "He'd have to hide his party favors."

Tessa's nose wrinkles. "How sure are we he's a Halia?"

"Ninety-nine point nine percent, according to Eros's Springer paternity test." I look out the balcony slider and find Hurricane Mack's destruction here too. I look over my shoulder and find Tessa climbing a chair against the wall. She has a screwdriver in between her lips and is teetering perilously on the back while she fiddles with the air vent. I should offer to help, but Mission Impossible spy shit is her thing, not mine. "You're a brave soul to traverse this hot mess twice."

"As if!" She pulls a small camera from the vent and tosses it my way. "I had the front desk move him into this room when I came on with Halia Surf." Tessa jumps off the chair, landing like a graceful cat. "After I set the cameras up in here, of course."

"How many favors did that take?"

She shoots me a wicked smile.

"Really?"

"I'm a Cupid, I'm not dead. I mean, not technically." She walks into the master suite and sticks her head out a second later. "Dude, I'm not clearing this room by myself."

I tiptoe over a few more discarded pieces of clothing, ignoring the scrap of hot pink lace. Sonia really is a tramp if she's leaving her undies here. I walk into the master suite where the stench of old sex and sweat hits me hard.

I cover my nose with the back of my hand. "How many did you put in here?"

"Three out here. Two in the bathroom." Tessa peels off a square film from the mirror across from Mack's bed. She turns and shows me the back. There's a black dot the size of a pinprick.

"Is that a camera?"

She smiles. "No audio, but the picture is crystal fucking clear!" She pulls out a metal business card holder and carefully places the deceptive camera into it. "Do me a favor. There's one of these in the bathroom on the makeup mirror." Tessa tosses me another metal case. I pluck it from the air as she says, "I'll grab the other two and meet you in the shower."

My stomach churns. "You have a camera in the shower?"

"Kinky shit happens in hotel showers, Jack. You should know that."

"I've never gotten kinky in a hotel shower."

Another wicked grin pulls at her lips while she crosses the room and grabs the alarm clock. "I know a boy who can rectify that universal tragedy."

I turn on my heels before she can see my cheeks flare. "You're crude and unusual, Tessa. Crude and unusual."

Her giggle chases after me as I enter the bathroom. I flip the light on, expecting to see the same gross filth in the bathroom, but instead the tile is a pristine white, the towels have been changed, and the only evidence of Mack's use of the space is the still wet toothbrush dangling on the side of the basin. Who knew he had a sanitary line that wouldn't be crossed? I find the vanity mirror, tilt the face, and easily spot the rise of the small translucent square camera. I'll be checking all hotel mirrors in the same fashion from here on out. Maybe even utilizing some of Tessa's tech on future Cupid missions. A flush of adrenaline races through me. At the end of this mission, I'll be a Cupid with fifty arrows. I won't have any more missions to complete; I'll just oversee them. My heart won't beat. My soul will be immortal.

The memory of moonlight dancing over Hugh's face from the other night releases an ache I haven't felt in years.

This is why we're doing everything for fifty. I'm rubbing at the pain in my chest when Tessa walks in.

"You good?"

I nod and concentrate too hard on putting the camera in its case.

"Jack?" Tessa drawls.

"Grab the shower camera. Last thing we need is Hugh and Sonia coming back."

"You mean Mack?"

I hand Tessa the metal wallet. "What?"

"Mack. Mack and Sonia? Because you said Hugh." She slips the wallet into the bag she's dropped by the side of the shower/tub and climbs in. I don't miss the knowing glance she gives me. "Somebody on your mind, Jack?"

"Nope."

Tessa unscrews the shower nozzle and hands it to me. "There's another nozzle in my bag." She nods to the beach bag. "No shame in washing out at fifty."

I fish out the nozzle and trade her the standard sprayer for the covert one.

"Let's chat when you have forty-nine arrows on your wrist." I zip up the bag, expecting Tessa to be done, but she hasn't moved an inch. She's so still if she hadn't just been yammering, I'd have thought maybe she'd snuck a peek at Medusa. That bitch is crazy.

"Tessa?" I push. "I'm sorry. Shitty thing for me to say. Once I'm at fifty, I'm going to help you—"

"I don't want your help, Jack." Tessa cuts me off.

My heart scurries down to my toes. I'm an asshole.

"Tessa."

"I don't want your help, Jack." She shakes her head like she's hoping to rattle something loose. Her gaze collides with mine; blue eyes glitter with something I've never seen before. The solid, impenetrable walls she's kept fortified by a lifetime of hurt and determination aren't just down, they're completely eviscerated. Tessa, raw and unguarded, is so devastating, so heartbreaking, it kicks me in the gut, taking all the rebuttals I have along for the ride.

"You just don't get it," she starts. "Once you give up on love, really fucking kick it to the curb . . . it never comes back." She screws the nozzle back into place. Each twist punctuated with something I've never seen from Tessa. Anger. "Never. The world is a little duller. Life is a little more monotonous. There's just no . . . sparkle. Not even the potential."

I stare at her, stepping back when she climbs out of the tub and yanks her bag from my hand.

"Fifty." She looks away like she has so many thoughts on Eros and the fifty-arrow finish line. "Be careful, Jack. Don't confuse the chase for the finish line with running away from living."

I'm not sure how long we stand there, sizing up each other's hidden demons. She knows who sent me to the Corps. What I don't know is, who landed her here? Who pulverized Contessa Saint Cloud's heart?

The unmistakable sound of the front door's lock opening makes sure I don't have a chance of asking that question. Tessa's eyes flare like mine. She grabs the bag and my wrist and tugs us both toward the master bed. We come up short. Mack, with Sonia wrapped around him like a cheap baby Bjorn, is in the bedroom doorway. His hands are busy assaulting her ass, eyes closed, and the slick, smacking sound they're making rolls my stomach.

Tessa yanks me down to the ground and starts army crawling through the floor of filth. With no other way to escape, I follow. I pause when Tessa slips under the bedframe but scurry to follow when Mack starts for the bed. The bed skirt flutters as I pull my feet under and Mack hits the bed with Sonia.

I fish out my cell and switch it to silent mode, breathing a massive sigh of relief when my screen lights up the area. The bed is the second cleanest place in the suite. Tessa's switched her phone to silent and dimmed the screen. Not that I think Mack will notice, but a bed with a lit skirt probably should only be on fast cars.

"Oh, baby!" Mack croons. "Let me see your tits."

Sonia giggles.

"They're so fucking big!"

My body gags at the mental image Mack's voice is creating. The slippery smacking picks up again. When Sonia moans, I start reciting random math facts in my head to try and distract me from what part of her body is being attacked. The mattress rolls. Tessa's hands fly up to protect her from the creaking box springs.

Oh! My! God! She mouths. *What a bitch!*

I nod.

"Mack."

Smack, slurp.

"It's because of the baby."

"I don't care why," he growls. "They're definitely much more fun to play with now."

A twinge of pity releases in me. Poor girl. No matter how crazy devious she is, no girl deserves that kind of backhanded compliment about her body.

Sonia clears her throat. "Speaking of, we really should talk about the baby."

Everything stills. My eyes latch onto Tessa's.

I knew it! She mouths, fist pumps the air, then fishes out her cellphone. Tessa turns it to me. She's got the voice memos app open and the red microphone is flashing. My stomach flops. This is going to kill Hugh.

"What's to say? Hugh thinks it's his. He's got all the money—"

"But what about after?" Sonia cuts Mack off.

"After. . ." Mack lets the word trail off.

"After you dismantle Halia. What happens then? I mean, the baby will be here by then."

I know I should do something, say something, but I'm frozen, paralyzed at the thought if the Corps doesn't get Hugh, then his brother will. The mattress rolls again. I scoot closer to Tessa when Mack's feet touch the ground.

"Babe, we've talked about this. We can't be seen together, ever."

Silence creeps into the room.

"Don't pout. You knew this was the deal."

"No, me getting pregnant was never part of *the deal*."

"Condoms aren't a hundred percent foolproof." Mack's feet turn, toes pointed at the bed like they're about to tell we're hiding under here. "Babe."

"Don't babe me. You said to trust you. I've trusted you for five years. Five years, Mack!"

"I know, so why are you questioning me now?"

"Because I'm pregnant, Mack. I'm. Pregnant!"

"Even better."

"Better?" Sonia spits. "How is that better when you're telling me we won't be together? Ever! This entire farce was so we could be rich and *together*! Now you're telling me not only am I going to be a mother, but you're leaving me?"

I cringe at the hysteria in Sonia's voice. That hysteria attached to a key phrase has gotten many a lady drafted to the Corps.

"Babe."

"Stop it." Sonia hops off the bed, her toes meeting Mack's. "You promise me right now, that me—alone!—isn't how this story ends." Her foot is tapping so hard against to the floor, I'd be surprised the Joint Training Center in Los Al doesn't pick up a trace of Morse Code.

Mack turns and strides toward the bathroom. My heart stops, my stomach falls, and I'd pay almost anything for the ability to be invisible, because, from this angle, I can see the black screw we've forgotten like a Hollywood Premiere spotlight on the gleaming white tile.

"Mack!" Sonia hollers; this time, the threat of tears replace her anger. Mack shuts the bathroom door behind him, and we all hear the door's lock slide into place.

My breath catches in my throat when Sonia crumples to the ground. Her hands roam across her blossoming belly. Tears plummet to the carpet, and I almost feel sorry for the girl.

Almost.

She turns toward the sound of the shower about the same time a buzz from the bedside table starts.

My phone lights up with a text from Hugh. Tessa turns her phone and I see the same notification.

"Son of a bitch," Sonia spits, now standing. The phone clatters on the bedside table while she starts getting dressed from the clothes she left in the dresser. A few minutes later, she grabs the cellphone, pauses at the bathroom door, then leaves.

Air rushes from both Tessa and I when we hear the front door shut. Who knows how long we'd been breathing shallow, holding our breath that we wouldn't be found? The shower is still running, so we scramble out from under the bed and rush to the front door. After a quick check through the peephole, Tessa eases back the front door while I watch her six.

I'm in the Cupid Corps. Some of our jobs are just as dangerous as a Marines' mission. We're hustling to the service elevator when my phone notification vibrates again. It's Hugh's original text:

Beach Talk scored an exclusive.

Photos too.

Wedding is off.

Get your asses to the office.

"Oh, shit," I mumble, clicking the link in the second text message.

"*Beach Talk*," Tessa spits. "Stupid wannabe tabloid."

I hold up my cell. "Yeah, well, this isn't so wannabe now." The picture is grainy, but that's Liz half naked on the sand. And the man, whose face is buried between her legs, has two legs himself, and one isn't a prosthetic that should be attached to her fiancé.

Tessa's face pales. "Holy, shit. Liz cheated on Derrick?"

"They've tagged Halia Surf, the Open's governing board, and the A.S.P." My stomach knots. This is really bad. The service elevator opens at the valet station, and while Tessa grabs us a cab, I search the web to see if the story shows up anywhere else.

"Any of the other trash outlets pick up the story?"

I scroll through the search results, feeling my pulse slow, my stomach turns as I count. "Eight of the small ones. Two of the big ones. And . . . oh, shit."

"Not the Mirror."

"Yeah, London has it too." I turn the screen for Tessa to see the headline:

Halia's Surftastic Couple:

Down for the Count?

Her eyes lock with mine and I see the same thought crash in them: We're so screwed.

Thirty

HUGH

I *let my eyes adjust as* I walk into the Ocean Blvd dive bar in Long Beach. Stale beer and a fine mist of old beer nuts hangs in the air. I scan the bar looking for Derrick but find two old timers already tipsy at one in the afternoon. My focus shifts to half a dozen empty pool tables sitting in the middle of the room, and I finally find my friend in the back corner.

"Grab ya something?" the bartender asks while he's wiping down the polished bar. The blue from the neon beer sign hits his thinning, silver, shoulder-length hair just right; it looks like the silver ocean whitewash. Jack naked on my bed at the beach shack flashes behind my eyes. It's so intense, only the darkest place in my mind can handle the image, the place where all my tortured memories hide

"Dude?" the bartender bites with a little more force. "Drink?" He scans me up and down while he waits for an answer. I know the judgment that is forcing his features to harden as he takes in my laced-up, wing tip, leather shoes: too good for the world, never good enough for my father. What none of them know is I've only ever been perfect for one person, and she doesn't want me.

"Gin and tonic with a wedge of lime."

The bartender shrugs like he's got a lot to say about my drink order and me, but I'm not worth the energy or the waste of his breath. I walk over and slap a hundred on the bar.

"This should cover the drink, and my friend's tab." I nod to the corner where Derrick exists. "Keep the rest."

His surly demeanor changes instantly. Money has a way of doing that to people. Everyone softens when you wave a hundie in their face.

Not Jack.

I ram a hand through my hair, hoping to wipe the memory of her from my mind, and make my way back to Derrick. As I near the table, he's hunched over his drink like it's the only thing keeping him alive.

"Doc say you could start up again?" I nod to the half empty glass in front of Derrick.

He doesn't start at my voice. It's almost like he expected me to find him here, and by the way his shoulders tense, he's irritated it took me so long.

"Seltzer water. The lime is for flavor. The rocks are so dumbasses don't ask."

I pull out the barstool, slip down, and wedge myself into the corner like we did when we were in high school. Yeah, I remember the bartender even if he doesn't remember the surf rat kid he'd let run the tables and hustle the losers.

"Place hasn't changed," I muse.

"Nope." Derrick runs the pad of his finger around the rim of his glass, sparing a glance at the bartender, who's shown up to personally deliver my drink. Like I said, money changes everyone.

"Talk to Liz?"

Derrick nods. "Right before I put her on a plane to Fiji for our honeymoon."

Shock replaces whatever feeling I had simmering inside me.

"Why?"

"Because she doesn't deserve to be in the middle of this shitstorm."

I feel my eyebrows crawl to the back of my head. "She doesn't?"

A silent chuckle shakes Derrick's shoulders.

"Nah, she doesn't."

I rake my hand down my face, hoping whatever parallel universe I've crossed into will right its self. "Hmm?"

Derrick chuckles. "Your hmms say a lot more than any other person's full-blown temper tantrums."

"That obvious?" I growl.

"You're so fucking obvious, people wonder if you're for real." His eyes pin me to the wall. If he weren't hurting so bad, I'd return the favor, only not with my eyes but with my fists.

Tension stretches between us until it's so tight, I'm surprised the universe doesn't shift a little. I lean forward, anger bubbling just under my skin. I don't bother moving the strands of hair obscuring my vision of Derrick. Hell, maybe it'll help bring what he's seeing into focus.

"So, great and mighty Derrick. You want tell me how Liz getting photographed providing a late-night meal for some random dude between her legs gets her a tropical pass and you a broom and dustpan to clean up her mess?"

There's a small tick of warning in Derrick's lip, while his eyes zero in on mine. "Not some random dude. My cousin. And because I fucking love her. That's what earns her a pass."

I shove the table away from me, clattering our drinks and earning us a cautionary glare from the bar owner.

"Your cousin?" I hiss. The image of the scrawny, tweaker, douche of a cousin who was always sniffing around Liz in high school flashes like a lightning strike in my brain. The only reason I didn't take him to the moat was because he *was* Derrick's cousin.

Derrick nods. "It started six months into my second tour."

"How long have you known?"

"She came clean when I got back. The forces prepare us for Dear John letters; this one we had to figure out on our own."

I shake my head. I'm seriously looking at this guy for the first time. When did black-or-white Derrick decide his heart could live in the fucked-up world of gray?

"We were good on my third tour and then . . ." His words trail off. He didn't have to tell me about the third tour. The tour he was nearly blown to kingdom come. "We've been solid for two years. I don't know what happened. She says it was just the one time Delilah caught her on camera." He wipes his hand down his face like it's going to erase the memory. "I love her," he whispers, but I can tell by the tortured lines etched around his eyes, nothing will ever erase the image of that grainy picture from his mind, which makes my blood go from boiling to volcanic.

"So it's all seashells and mermaids because you fucking love her?"

The man I thought I knew, the one who said once a cheater always a cheater, is gone. I'm not sure what to do with the person in front of me.

"I don't expect you of all people, Hugh, to understand."

"What the fuck is that supposed to mean?"

"It means you've never stayed and fought for a damn thing in your life."

"Fuck you."

Derrick shakes his head. "Tell me you fought for Jack." He smiles and before I can answer, says, "Yeah, you think what you and Tessa did was fighting for her, but it was you being a pussy and pushing her away. Don't give me that death glare." He points a judgmental finger at me. "Jack told me everything. At first, I was like, hell no, but you know what? You never could walk through a shit-storm, Hugh. You always found a way to walk around"—his eyes narrow in on me—"or someone like Tessa to wear as a raincoat so you came out smelling fresh as a daisy."

Something in me snaps. I wrap my fingers around his shirt and pull him across the tiny table. "Fuck you."

A sinister laugh escapes him. One that makes my blood run cold.

"Fuck *me*, Hugh? Dude, you fucked yourself six years ago when you kicked Jack out of your life. You've been a corpse existing until the undertaker comes to claim the body."

"Because we're friends and because I know you're hurting, I'll give you the last hundred and twenty seconds, but no more." I shake him before I push him back into his chair. "No more."

Derrick adjusts his shirt, runs his hands through his hair, and then tosses back the reminder of his drink.

I'm not sure how long we sit there in silence. Long enough that the waves of fury and tension rolling off both of us seem to flatten. Long enough that we've polished off both our drinks and the ice cubes are melted.

"You want another round?" the bartender hollers. Even he's smart enough to keep his distance. So why wasn't Jack? Why wasn't Tessa? Why the hell would they come back, knowing all the ways I made their lives hell? All the ways I could decimate them.

As if Derrick's reading my mind, he says, "You always thought you were saving Jack, didn't you?"

There's not much rage left in my bones, and just the sound of Jack's name has always been the balm to my anger. I nod.

"That's the thing about love, Hugh. We hurt the ones we love the most, and if we're lucky, they love us enough to forgive us, and we try again. But here's the fucked-up thing about it all, Hugh. We have to forgive ourselves. Otherwise, we're doomed to repeat it all over again."

I rake my hand down my face. "Just that easy for you, Derrick? Liz comes back from Fiji, new tan, new chance, and you'll forgive her?"

"Not that easy. There's a lot of hard work to get us past this. Look, I know she fucked up, Hugh. I'm no saint and I know I wasn't marrying an angel, but if we're going to get to the next chapter, then one of us has to carry the other. I have to forgive her even if she can't forgive herself."

"How? She cheated on you *again*. With your family, dude!"

"Blood doesn't make a person family. You of all people should know that." Derrick leans back in his chair. Legs stretch out, and I'm jealous of the peaceful way he can breathe. There's no hitch in his chest. There's pain in his eyes, but it's not anything that'll consume him. Not like the pain I'm feeling. Not like the fatal-sized hole in my chest I've been walking around with since I realized Jack and I . . . I can't finish the thought.

"When I finally came to in Ramstein, I couldn't remember Elizabeth's name, face, or the fact that we were engaged. I broke everything off, slept with anything that wore a bikini. Liz was always there to pick me up, sober me up, and loved me through the hell I put her through. She loved me until I remembered. I guess it's my turn to love her until she remembers why she fell for me."

I sit, stunned into silence.

"Elizabeth and I, we'll walk down the aisle. Some loves are just too great to fight the evil in the universe. I've already forgiven her." He rests his chin on his hand and focuses on something past me. "And I'll be here when she forgives herself. What I am sorry about is the jam we left you in."

My thoughts tumble back to the three women I left fighting in the Halia boardroom. One I love more than life itself. One I've loved like a sister my entire life. And the third I'm supposed to love for the rest of my life. Something painful sits on my chest. Somehow, I've nearly destroyed all three. The cold hard fact is: there isn't one of them left who would fight for me the way Derrick is willing to fight for Elizabeth. I fish my keys out of my pocket as resolve settles in my chest. He's right. It's time I give something a fighting chance in my life. I slip my free hand into my breast pocket and grab my cell. The girls are probably still fighting over how to fix this mess. Jack's pissed as hell, and given the look in her eyes when I walked out the door, I totally saw where the cut-throat nickname came from. I'd left Sonia there to face their fury. It was a dick move, but maybe this would make up for it. The blue light from my cell illuminates our little corner of the room.

"Hugh?" I can hear Derrick's concern wrap around my wrist as I pull up the group text all three girls are on.

"You were right, Derrick. I never have fought for something, certainly not for someone. Don't worry about Halia. I think I've got the perfect solution."

"That glint in your eye tells me I'm not going to like what happens in two days."

I finish my message and hit send.

"Probably not. But I guess we all have to grow up, don't we?"

Thirty One

JACK

"He's fucking out of his* ever-fucking loving mind!"

Tessa catches the front door I've nearly ripped off its hinges before it bounces off the wall and smacks me in the face.

"Jack, pretty sure *ever-fucking loving mind* isn't—"

I cut her off with a look.

"He's all but banished, you get that, right?" Fear and rage twist in my gut and the ache of failure sits on my chest, making it hard to breathe. The weight of the catastrophe *I made* buckles my knees until I'm sliding down the entryway hall, fingers tangled in my hair and no options bleeding from my soul. I've totally failed him. Hugh needed me to save him and . . .

"What I get is that you're more upset about Hugh being banished than you are about your fifty arrows."

"What?" I shoot Tessa what can only be the wild-eyed look of a caged animal. "Fifty *is* what I'm upset about," I quickly correct her.

But Tessa's knowing eyes cut right through all my bullshit. Bullshit that's assured E.J. and Eros and the Corps I was a Cupid through and through.

Tessa wraps her hands around my wrist and yanks me off the floor. She presses her finger to my lips to shut me up, her eyes wide and equally as wild as mine have to be.

"Grab your suit, you need to cool off."

I look at her sideways.

"Trust me?"

A few minutes later, I duck under a six-foot wave before it crests. The roar of the wave echoes its fury all the way down to my soul. I pop up on the other side of the swell and keep paddling after Tessa. When we're far enough from the shore, she turns, sits back on her board, and waits for me to come along the side. My feet land on her board and our makeshift pow-wow raft is completed.

"What's up with the secret lips and trust mes?" I finally ask.

"I've already got one friend dancing on the ledge of banishment. I don't need you chasing after him."

I bite back any denial, knowing she's right.

"You've already got one lightning bolt—"

"How do you know that? You can't see it."

Something short of shock passes through Tessa's features. "I was on the phone with E.J. when you were branded. He was quite pleased you were proving to be a 'complete and utter waste of time and energy.' Besides, we're in Poseidon's realm now, and Eros has no ability or business listening in when we're talking about Hugh."

I start to question Tessa, but she's right, Eros has been too anxious to have Hugh wash out and watch me fail. I get fifty is an elite number. There are only fourteen humans in the history of time who have achieved immortality. I was going to make it fifteen.

"Talk."

A smile pulls at Tessa's lips. "Truth time. You love Hugh."

I nod and counter the observation that's too close to the truth with, "As do you."

"Not the same way, but, yes, I do."

"He's going to marry her in two days, Tessa."

"I know."

"So, we pull whatever we can get off the tapes and show it to Hugh."

"That's not the only—"

"Tessa." I cut her off because I know the way she wants to handle this has me professing something that will either get me kicked out of the Corps or banished. And neither will save Hugh.

I kick off her surfboard, breaking the friendship raft.

"We're going to his house tonight, Tessa. I want the footage ready to roll." I lie down on my board and welcome the burn my muscles digging into glass water creates.

"Did you ever trust him?" she hollers at me.

My arms seem to react to the spasm in my heart. "I trusted you both. Now, we're doing it my way."

The video Tessa's pieced together of Sonia and Mack makes my stomach roll even at the memory. I threw up when she first showed it to me. It wasn't watching all the lecherous ways they fucked that made me sick, it was the pillow talk—the way they had methodically set out to destroy Hugh and the company. Five years they'd plotted the downfall of Halia. Five years. Mack hated Kai for leaving him and his mom in the slums of Waikiki with only a small stipend, but he hated Hugh all the more for having lived the life he felt he was deserved. From what we could tell, Mack's mom only fueled the anger by making sure Mack knew it was Hugh's fault Kai couldn't be with them. I wasn't sure how, but somehow hell had spit out a carbon copy of Kai Halia. His name was Mack, and he wouldn't be happy until Hugh Halia spent eternity in purgatory. My foot presses down harder on the accelerator as I fly past the Huntington Beach wetlands.

"You know, there are speed traps, Jack." Tessa's knuckles are white from the way she's gripping the door.

"You know, Tessa, for someone who's had no problems breaking every rule life's thrown at her, you need to shut up."

"See, you're still raging-bitch mad."

I spare her a quick glance before I gun the engine and blow through a yellow light. "And you aren't?"

"Hugh and you were the only family I had left. I mourned losing you two a lifetime ago. Welcome to my world, Jack."

She pulls her gaze from me, as well as any emotions I can try to decipher.

It seems like I couldn't get to the Colony fast enough, but as I pull into Hugh's driveway next to Sonia's car, it seems like time has turned to molasses and I'm the fly caught in its slow pull.

"Are you coming?" Tessa calls from the front of the car. "Stupid question. Of course you are." She turns and disappears down the walkway.

Was I ready?

Ready to destroy Hugh?

Ready to banish him if need be?

It won't come to that.

I scratch at the spot my fiftieth arrow is meant to occupy, pull in a deep breath, and join Tessa on the front landing. She's already rung the bell. Sonia opens the door, and Tessa wraps her fingers around my wrist. I hadn't even realized my hands had balled into fists.

"Hugh home?" Tessa asks.

"We're having dinner."

Tessa steps into the house pulling me past Sonia. "Yeah, well, it's important."

"Don't scurry off. This concerns you." My low murderous tone makes Sonia's eyes flare. She never leaves my sight, so I know the exact second she realizes we've uncovered her dirty little secret. "Hugh!" I holler, but my glare roots Sonia to where she's standing and steals the color from her perky pink cheeks.

I feel Hugh enter the room before he speaks. I'd never noticed before how he shifts my center of gravity. He is my epicenter, my universe. And I hope he forgives me having to shatter his world.

"There's something you need to see." I turn, reveling in the pea green Sonia's turned.

"You've still got your big screen, right?" Tessa chimes in.

Hugh watches all twenty minutes of the filth Mack and Sonia created the past eleven months on Hugh's eighty-inch HD TV. Thirty seconds in, Sonia tries to escape, but Hugh wrapped his fingers around her wrist, and there she still sits a full minute after the video goes black.

Time ticks by. Two minutes turns to ten, then thirty. Then Sonia finally breaks the silence.

"I can explain."

"There's no need." Hugh says with a calm that chills me to my core. "I've never treated you very well." He shifts in his seat, and something rolls in my stomach. His eyes are dull, there's no rage in his face, no fight in his features.

"Oh shit." Tessa whispers.

Oh shit is right.

Hugh pulls his gaze from Sonia. "You two can leave now."

"Hugh?" I whisper.

"Jack." I hate how cold my name sounds from his lips. "I get what you tried to do. You and Tessa. . ." His thought fades as his eyes focus on a what I can only imagine is a time when we were a you and Tessa and Hugh. "You two have your lives to live. I appreciate what you tried to do for Halia, but I think it's best I take over."

Sonia wraps her fingers around Hugh's wrist and something murderous breaks free from my chest, but Tessa's the one who finds her voice first.

"You're firing us?" Tessa asks.

"I'm letting you go."

His meaning isn't lost on Tessa or me. He's done. All that's left is for me to do is put my hand on his heart and say the words. Utter the phrase that will seal the fate he's chosen.

"But you get that the baby isn't yours." The wrong words rush out of my mouth. I can feel Eros watching. How couldn't he be?

"I know."

"You know!" I feel every ounce of hysteria in my voice. "She's been lying to you. She's been sleeping with Mack. You know you're not the father, and you're still going to marry her?"

"Why do you care, Jack?"

I look at Tessa for back up. She's nowhere to be found. She may be physically standing next to me, but she's gone.

Hugh stands and takes my elbow in his hand. I fight his forward motion. My hand hovers over his heart. I know what I'm supposed to do.

Say it! A tiny voice in my head screams. *Banish his heart and claim your reward. Two words: Sas exorísei, and immortality is yours!*

"Sas . . ." I fist my hand and pull it back.

Not yet.

Eros gave me until the last *I do,* and it hasn't happened. I step in front of Hugh, but he towers over me and keeps us moving forward.

"It's time we grow up, Jack." He's guiding me to the door, and I'm powerless to stop him. "It's time to let go. I'm letting you go." Hugh opens the door and it doesn't even register that I'm outside until he shuts the door and turns off the porch light.

"Eros wants us next door." Tessa whispers.

I can't move.

He's gone.

I can't breathe.

"Jack." Tessa pulls at the hem of my top. "We have to go now." She's rubbing at the spot over her heart where I witnessed her receive her first lightning bolt. The minute movement breaks whatever trance Hugh had held over me.

We round the wall of wedding flowers that separates Hugh's house from Eros and Psyche's. Cold tendrils of fear and regret grasp at my ankles and I'm certain if I stop, I'll fall into a place I won't be able to recover from.

"Just keep your mouth shut," Tessa warns. She stops a moment and grabs my hands. "Damn it, Jack, your hands are freezing. You're in shock. Look at me." She dips down and grabs my attention. "Keep your mouth shut. Nod at anything Eros says. Jack."

"Nod. Got it."

Tessa pulls in a deep breath. "Shit. You two really are going to my undoing." She rubs her hands up and down my arms and taps some color into my cheeks with the back of her hand. "I'm really going to need you to push past what just happened and concentrate on the next ten minutes."

"Why ten minutes?"

"Because if we're here longer than ten, we're never leaving."

My eyes flare as the threat of not just my banishment, but Tessa's too, knocks me out of my stupor.

"You with me?" Tessa holds out her hand.

I slip my palm into hers. "I'm with you."

"Great. Let's survive this storm."

"So we can save Hugh next," I add as she pushes through the wrought-iron gates.

Eros is sitting at the back of the property on one of the chaise lounges next to the outdoor fireplace and the lap pool.

"Ladies," E.J. greets us as we pass the patio.

I scan the yard, looking for Psyche. Nothing bad happens when Psyche's present. Just like nothing good happens when she isn't.

"Mom has business in Hawaii." E.J. drapes his arm around my neck as we walk down the travertine tiles to the lower level of the yard. A small chuckle rumbles from his chest. "Ya sure fucked this one up, Jack."

"Shove it up your ass, E.J."

He pulls me in close. "I'm game if you are."

"Son," Eros calls out as Tessa breaks E.J.'s hold on me.

"You're a right son of a bitch, aren't you?" Tessa mutters. We both see E.J.'s eyes flare a bit, which is blood in the water for Tessa. I almost feel sorry for him. Almost.

"What? Hit too close to home?" Tessa finishes with E.J. and turns her charm toward Eros. "Hi ya, Eros." Her voice drips with bubble gum sweetness. "Where's your beautiful wife?"

"Tessa," Eros croons as he walks to us. "No amount of personality is going to change the fact that I'm extremely disappointed." He points to the lounge chair opposite his.

"You said the last *I do*, Eros," I say, which earns me a look from Eros, E.J., and Tessa. All of a sudden, I feel like the petulant child who wasn't invited to speak up. "Well, you did."

"I know what I said, Jack." Eros wipes his hand through his hair, and I swear the gold strands grow in front of my eyes. His voice drops an octave to sound eerily familiar. Almost like my dad's. My heart triples its cadence. My palms sweat, and my head seems to float. No, it's not my head—it's my soul. My soul is being ripped out of my body.

"Jack." Tessa wraps her fingers through mine. "Eros, stop!" she pleads, but my heart only beats faster.

Black dots prick the corners of my eyes, and I know even if I wanted to scream, I couldn't. I'm not in control of anything, and the only thing keeping me in this realm is Tessa.

"What's happening?" The voice uttering the words doesn't sound like mine, but I know it is.

"Don't let go, Jack." Tessa whispers in my ear. "Eros"—I think that's calm in her voice—"You did say she had until the last *I do*."

"You want to join her?"

I know I'm not drunk, but the way my body is suspended, the way my head sways, it makes the world seem hazy. Sounds are long and muted. I giggle. I'm losing my soul. I giggle again. He was worth it. Wait. I didn't save him yet.

"You know I don't." I turn toward Tessa's voice. It's so smooth, so fresh, so calm. "Just like you know Jack's going to make an amazing immortal. C'mon, Eros. Not all of us get an easy fifty."

I want to say something. I should, right? But I know I can't even if I try.

Whatever Eros has done to me . . . I look at Tessa's fingers wrapped around my wrist. The arrows around my wrist glimmer brilliant gold. So do Tessa's. That bitch. I snort. She has a wrist full of arrows?

"Dad." E.J. sits next to Tessa.

Did she just flinch?

What did that Australian playboy do to her when I wasn't looking?

Tessa gives me a motherly "sit still" look. And I do.

"Fine,. Eros's stern voice snaps me out of the stupor. I gasp, pulling fresh air into my lungs. I hadn't even realized I wasn't breathing. "Jack?"

At the sound of my name, blood seems to rush through my system; every nerve ending, muscle, and capillary seems to rejoice.

"Jack," Eros says again. He's inches from my face now. I don't know how he moves so fast except I do. He's a god and I'm a mortal. "I'm never wrong." His threat hangs between us, binding us together in such a way my stomach rolls.

"You don't know Hugh like I do," I whisper.

Eros's lips pull into a snarl. This close, I can see the edges of his teeth are sharpened like tips of deadly knives. "I think one of us will be right, and one of us will be banished." He snaps his fingers and the world folds in on itself. All the air is wrung from my lungs and my vision fades to black.

"Waaack." A garbled voice bangs around a blackness I can't seem to shake.

"Wack?" I jump at the cold fingers wrapping around me. "Wan you hewwwr meeee?"

I feel what has to be a smile pulling at my lips.

"Jack?" It's Tessa's voice. "Girl, you're gonna need to open your eyes. We've got about twelve hours before that last *I do* falls."

I sit up so fast, my head swims, launching a wave of nausea that can only rival the worst hangover . . . ever. Tessa slams a glass of dark, cold liquid in my hand.

The scent of rum and . . . "Is there egg in here?"

She snorts. "Yeah, I learned it in Vegas from a recruit." Tessa pushes the glass toward my face. "Best to do it all in one big shot."

"Clearly, she hated you."

Tessa's look hardens. "Didn't like me when I banished her, that's for sure."

My eyes flare.

"Story for a different time." Tessa pushes the glass again. "Drink. We don't have a whole hell of a lotta time; Eros knocked us both out. You're lucky it's not my first time getting on his bad side."

I'm so lost in the fact that Tessa's banished a soul, I don't think, I just drink. The milkshake-like consistency slips down my throat. Surprisingly, I don't gag. I guess it smells a lot worse than it tastes. I wipe at the remnants on my lip.

"Give it thirty minutes and the nausea will go." Tessa stands, pulling me with her. "Take that time for a shower. I'm going to need you to live up to that cut-throat nickname."

I stop in the doorway. "Last thing I remember was Eros's house."

"Yeah, you're not his favorite right now." Tessa starts pulling at the sheets on my bed.

"You're not going to tell me what happened?"

She stops and regards me through a veil of gold hair. "The abridged version: you pissed the God of Love off. He was in the midst of banishing your soul when I grabbed hold of you." Her words hitch.

"Only true love can rescue a soul."

Tessa nods. "I mourned losing you and Hugh years ago. Doesn't mean I stopped loving you two."

Warm tears fill my eyes. "And why'd I black out?"

"Because even the God of Love has a vengeful streak. A rescued soul needs time to recuperate. He walked you right to the gates of purgatory."

"And you pulled me back."

"Let's hope it's not so I could join you." Tessa nods to the door. "Go shower. The ceremony is at sunset."

I step out of the shower feeling a million times more me than when I stepped in. I'd let the hot water beat on me, driving in the fact that Tessa had banished a soul, and the wrist full of arrows I remembered. When the water turned warm like the ocean water in the harbor, my thoughts turned to Hugh. He was marrying the wrong girl today. And our souls were tied to his wrong decision.

The smell of chilaquiles drifts down the hall. By the time I pull on my skirt and tank top and round the corner to the kitchen, my mouth is watering.

"Last meal?"

"Ha, ha." Tessa spares me a quick glance before dishing the eggs and tortillas onto the plate. "You look better."

"Thanks," I say as she slides the plate in front of me. I nod to the brown milkshake remnants in the glass next to her elbow and shovel some eggs in my mouth. "That stout yours or mine?"

"Mine." She grabs the dirty glass and rinses it out for the dishwasher. "You really pissed Eros off. We're lucky this wasn't my first walk of banishment."

I nearly choke on my eggs. "He's a fan of yours."

"Yeah." Tessa's thoughts seem to wander a moment.

"So, what do we do to make sure this walk isn't a permanent one?"

"I'm deferring to you."

I pin Tessa with a look. The gravity of how serious our situation hits me. I don't need to remind her about her soul being tied to mine.

"So, what's it going to be, Jack?"

I think back over the past couple of months Hugh and I've had together. There'd always been a glimmer of hope in his eyes, even if it was the size of a grain of sand. The way he watched me. There was a heat in his eyes, an ember that would roar to life if I smiled at him, touched him. The tips of my fingers tingle at the memory of his skin under mine. He always held back, kept a piece of himself from Sonia. A piece of him that was only mine. I knew it from the way he would walk into my space, force me to acknowledge the magic between us. A shiver of pleasure releases from deep inside me as my thoughts tumble back to the night at the beach shack. He'd walked away from Sonia. Gift wrapped his heart in a beach towel and laid it at my feet. And I ruined it. The realization hits me hard, knocking the very breath from my lungs. My grip tightens around the granite counter top.

"What've I done?"

Tessa's hand covers mine. "You love him."

I pin her with a hard look.

Was it really that simple?

Was it really that hard?

Everything inside of me screams, yes, I love Hugh. Everything except my mind. I can't stop the endless loop of Hugh in bed with Tessa. Even knowing it wasn't what it seemed. Even knowing they did it because they loved me. *You always hurt the ones you love,* Dad's voice whispers in my ears.

He was right, and I loved Hugh more than the air I breathed. Dad was banking on the fact that Hugh loved me as much. The realization hangs like noose around my neck. We were all so busy protecting each other in the name of love, we forgot to trust in that love. No wonder Eros was furious. We were hurting each other in the name of love.

My body shudders under the realization for the second time in as many days: to save Hugh, I have to leave the Corps. I want to leave the Corps . . . for him.

"He'll never forgive me."

"Yes, he will."

Tessa grabs my mother's old suitcase from under my bed. I'd hidden it when Dad was getting rid of her things after she died. After she was killed. It was a dumb thing to hold onto, but it was so her. Hot pink with silver levers that locked the lid closed, kept what was inside safe. When I left, it seemed fitting I bury my heart in there too. Tessa walks over to my dresser and opens the drawer where I stashed the key. The girl knows all my secrets. Every. Last. One. A second later, she pulls out the white sundress. It was a simple dress with white lace flower overlays. I loved the way it would catch in the wind. I loved the way Hugh's eyes would darken when the spaghetti strap would slip off my shoulder. I rub at the memory of his fingers on my shoulders, his lips on my neck.

"You definitely don't play fair, Tessa." I carefully take the dress and head to the bathroom.

"All's fair in love and war," she mutters before I shut the door.

"Let's hope so."

The sun is riding low in the sky when we finally leave the house. The baby-blue sky darkening with each step we take. We've got about forty minutes before the sun sets. Forty minutes to save our souls. Butterflies flap against my stomach and turn into raging pterodactyls by the time we reach the Halia site.

While Tessa was doing my hair, I read the spread the *Register* did on Halia and the innovative team bringing the surf company into the next era. Conveniently, Tessa and I were left out of the write up. What wasn't left out was the hint of a wedding despite the scandalous fall of the Halia couple. Sonia was quoted as saying the people had spoken and Halia had listened. There would be a wedding. Given the size of the crowd we were navigating, everyone was more than curious to watch the trainwreck than witness a wedding. I swallow over a bundle of nerves one of the pterodactyls kicked into my throat.

"He'll be in the groom's tent." Tessa nods to the small white tent to the left side of the stage. As if Tessa's reading my mind, she nods to the other tent. "Don't worry. I've got her."

Tessa disappears into the crowd, and for the first time in a long time, the ache of being alone invades me. This was what my life was a few short months ago. Alone, looking for the next recruit. Counting fallen hearts to reach my goal. Hugh was right; I wasn't living, not really. But that's what I'd needed to survive. Now, I want to live. I want Hugh.

I start to pass the authorized access gates when a security guard steps in front of me.

"Authorized personnel only."

"I'm Jack—"

"I know who you are." I recoil at the tone in his voice. "Mr. Halia has given explicit instructions neither you nor Ms. Saint Cloud be allowed access."

"What?"

"You're going to need to leave the area or—"

"I gave no instruction." Hugh cuts off the guard. Even from this distance, even in this light, I can see his eyes darken as he takes me in. The dress, the hair. I can even see when he catches the sweet scent of perfume. Everything is exactly as they were the day we started down this path

"Not you, sir. Your brother."

"Half," Hugh and I reply at the same time. Hugh steps in front of the guard and sweeps his arm toward his tent. "She's a cunning lady. Given that jagged little set between her eyes, she would've found me, one way or another."

I try to hide my smile as I walk to the tent and slip inside. There's a temporary polished wood floor laid on the ground. Hugh's tuxedo jacket hangs on a valet next to the floor-length viewing mirror. I pull in a deep breath of orchids that make up Hugh's Maile lei, the wedding lei for royalty. And he was. He was royal to me in all ways. This was nothing what Tessa and I had planned, but it's everything I would have wanted for our wedding. I touch the green Maile leaves. I'm not sure how they got these here; California agricultural usually forbids their entrance.

"Mom grew them in a greenhouse in Laguna," Hugh answers my silent question. "The horticulturist contacted me not long after you left."

"She was full of surprises, wasn't she?"

I feel how close Hugh is before I see his shadow overtake mine. I want to lean back into him, but I've done too much damage. A simple gesture won't even come close to setting things rights. Maybe there's nothing that will . . .

"Why are you here, Jack?"

I turn and revel when I see his breath catch. His eyes dart across my face. Whatever we had is still there. I can feel it just like he can. That ember of love . . .

"You can't marry Sonia."

Hugh turns from me and heads to the chair in front of the vanity mirror.

"I'm not going to do this with you, Jack." He runs his hands through his hair once, then twice. I smile because he's frustrated. Frustrated is good. Frustrated is better than defeated. Better than banished.

"Why?" I push.

"Because." The words die on his lips.

I walk over to his chair. Hugh pushes back in the seat when I slip between his legs. "Talk to me. You know you're not the father." I pull his face back to look at me. "Hugh." He has to hear the urgency in my voice. I want to tell him how close he is to the end. How we've risked everything for him. But I can't.

"I know I'm not the father."

"What?"

"I had the doctor run a paternity test after our last appointment." Hugh runs a hand down his face. "The results came back the day after we almost . . ."

I blush, knowing when he's talking about. The night after we almost made love. "Then why?"

"It's the right thing to do. The baby. The company." The words hang around Hugh's neck like a noose tightening its hold.

"No. It's not." I cradle his face in my hands. "This is bigger than doing the honorable thing. This is about your heart." I ignore the warming sensation over my own heart. It'd be easy to mistake it for love and not the warning it's meant to be. A warning from Eros that I'm toeing too close to his line of anonymity.

My hand slips to Hugh's chest. His heart thunders under my palm. This close, I take stock in all the things I'd missed before. The curve of his lips, the weight he carries in the wrinkle between his eyebrows. I miss the ferocity that would light his eyes on fire. I can bring it all back. I know I can.

Hugh wraps his hands around my wrists and pushes me away from him as he stands. "What do you know about matters of the heart?"

A strangled laugh escapes my throat. "More than you know"

Hugh pulls up short. He works his jaw like he wants to ask me what I mean but knows it shouldn't matter.

"Five minutes, Mr. Halia," a voice warns from outside the tent.

Hugh shifts, grabs his jacket, and starts for the flap in the tent. "I've got to go."

"Don't do this." I fish for his arm, for any piece of him that will listen to me and when I grab hold, I know he's already gone.

"I'll lose Halia."

I tighten my grip on him—trying to stop him—to the point my knuckles ache. I ache for this man. "They're going to dismantle Halia after you're married."

Hugh stops and for a brief moment, a ray of hope slices through the fog of doom surrounding us. "I know they were. Sonia told me after you and Tessa left." Hugh rests his hand on his hips, and I know there's nothing I can do to make him change his mind. But if he knows what Sonia was capable of, knows he isn't the father of her child, then why?

"Sonia told me everything," Hugh starts. "Gave me the accounts where Mack is stashing the money. Sonia was just another tool in Mack's game of revenge. He never planned on marrying her. He certainly wasn't going to be a father. We came to an understanding. He won't be able to scuttle Halia."

The room spins. A small streak of concern flashes in Hugh's eyes as he steadies me. Wrapping his arm around my waist, my hand splays against his chest.

"Sonia and I need each other, Jack." His fingers tangle with mine on his chest, but he's telling me goodbye. "She needs a father for her child, and I need a marriage certificate to keep control of Halia."

"A marriage of convenience?"

Hugh tilts his head like he's trying to pacify an upset child. "An understanding."

"And you trust her."

"No." He bites down on his lip. "But she's all I have left."

"That's not true!" I dig my fingers into his tuxedo shirt. He's marrying the wrong girl!

"I know what you're thinking, Jack." He taps my nose like he did when we were kids. "I've already taken too much from you. You love the life you've made for yourself. I can't ask you to give that up. I won't. Not for me." He slips my hand into his. "You were happy before you came back to Huntington. You'll be happier once you're gone."

Hugh kisses my knuckles and slips out of my grasp, out of the tent, and out of my life.

I'm not sure how long I stand there. My heart crushed on the ground. The sound of the wedding procession begins and I pick up what shattered pieces of me I can and rush out of the tent. The crowd roars. I push through the staff, trying to catch a glimpse of the wedding, and try to climb the stairs to the stage, but Mack steps in my way.

"Let it go." He wraps his fingers around my arm and pulls me down.

"Stop!"

The minister's voice echoes through the speakers, "Any person knowing just cause . . ." My pulse rages in my ears. This is my only chance. I dig my heels into the sand and claw at Mack's grip on my wrist.

"What is it with you?" He yanks me up and forward. The muscles in my shoulder scream as I slam into his chest. "Why can't you give it a rest?"

My toes dig back into the sand. "Because I love him."

"Fuck love."

The space behind Mack shimmers, the edges of the universe fold back, and I know the irate god who is about to step through the split. I brace for the site of Eros, but E.J. appears behind Mack. His eyes glow, and for the first time, I see the air of the demigod ripple around E.J.

"Fuck you," E.J. hisses. Mack takes E.J.'s punch on the chin and then hits the sand, pulling me with him. I scramble to my feet and rush the stage. There's only one reason why he'd be here. Eros knew what we were doing and sent E.J. to finish the job I refused to complete.

My feet slow as I pull in a deep breath. Hugh and Sonia are standing in front of the waterfall facing the crowd. The minister in front of them. There's no bridal party. Of course, Sonia would want all the focus on her. I start to step out on the stage when Sonia looks up at Hugh. I look for the glimmer. The telltale sign that true love gives off, but it isn't there. After everything, she's still using Hugh.

I step on to the stage and hear the wave of whispers ripple back. Sonia catches sight of me first. Her face pales. Hugh looks over his shoulder. Is that a smile pulling at his lips? Please, God, say yes.

The minister's eyes finally find me. "I'm sorry," he starts. "Do you have something to say?"

"No, she doesn't," Sonia spits.

Hugh pats Sonia's hands before he leaves her side. Hugh starts my way. Long confident strides eating up the space between us. I smile when he wraps his arm around me, but it falls as quickly as it came when Hugh looks down at me.

"Not today, Jack." He's moving me back to the recesses of stage. "Whatever you're going to say—"

"I love you." The words rush out.

I watch my declaration fall at his feet. The way he looks down at the ground, I'm almost certain it was too little and I was too late. Something inside me dies. It's not painful; it's an all-consuming ache. One that I know only the boy I love can take away. Something I know the man in front of me has given up on.

"Jack." My name comes out strangled by Hugh's voice. He steps toward me. This time, my world is tied to his movements. Not because Eros owns my soul, but because Hugh owns my existence. He owns me to the core of everything that makes me. Every breath. Every smile. Every second. They're his. They always have been.

He gives me a glance, grief etched into every plane of his face. "I love you too. I always have."

"Then don't do this."

Hugh runs the pad of his thumbs across the tears I didn't realize were falling down my face. "Don't cry, baby."

"Don't do this." I wrap my arms around him, burying my face in his chest. His heartbeat is so slow. "Hugh?"

"Sometimes love isn't enough." He pushes me away from him. "We had our shot. I'll always love you, but sometimes we have to do the responsible thing. Sometimes love has to lose." He steps away from me. A cautionary look washes over his face before he turns his back on me and walks back to the wrong girl.

The space next to me warms, and I know Eros is standing next to me, but I still jump at his voice.

"Jaquelyn"—he sounds exactly like my father—"it's time."

"No," I whisper. Everything inside me crumbles. Hugh takes Sonia's hand back in his, not even sparing a second glance my way.

"You've always been my favorite, which is why I'm giving you this last chance." Eros steps in front of me, severing the link I have with Hugh. "Do it now, or join his banished soul."

I shift my focus to Eros. His gold hair is cut short on the side, long on top. The strands flop into his face like my dad's did when I was a little girl. When I did everything he asked.

I swallow over the lump in my throat. It's not from fear of banishment; I've lived in exile the last six years. This is fear of knowing I had the right love and threw it away. Not this time.

"Jack."

"I'm sorry, Eros, but some loves are bigger than even you."

I step around the God of Love and walk back out on stage. This time, the wave of whispers is like a tsunami, gaining speed and turning into all-out groans.

Hugh looks over his shoulder while Sonia gives me a withering glare. I rub at the burning sensation over my heart. My legs start to tremble, my knees shake. I'm being banished.

"You said all I had to do was ask."

"He doesn't love you, Jack." Sonia hisses.

"Yes, he does." The words rip from inside me like they're the last few I'll ever speak.

The minister's look bounces between the three of us. "Is this true, Mr. Halia? Do you love this woman?" He gestures to me.

My heart sputters. I can feel it taking its last few beats.

"I'm asking you, now, Hugh. Show me all the things we've taken for granted. Choose me."

I wince at the intense heat burning my chest. A dribble of sweat shoots down my spine. "Hugh?" My head spins like it did the other night, only this time there's no one to keep my soul in my body, my heart in my chest. I risked it all for him. I'd risk it all again. The world around me starts to dim, darkness closing in. "You were worth it." I whisper. I feel myself falling. The ache where my heart used to be spreads, leaving a bitter cold in its wake.

"Jack?" Hugh's voice washes over me. "Are you asking me to kiss you?"

I try to focus on his face. "I'm asking you to do a lot more than that. Spend forever with me?"

"That's my line." He dips down, lips hovering over mine; I can feel the electricity arc between us. "It's only ever been you, Jack."

I pull back, but Hugh's arms keep me tight against him. It might be hazy and altered because of my brush with banishment, but there it is . . . the glimmer.

And it's because of me.

Hugh sweeps his lips over mine, sealing my fate and his. A rush of warmth crashes into me. Like a rubber band rebounding against flesh, my heart careens back into its rightful spot. I wrap my arms around Hugh's neck as he sweeps me up into his arms and leaves the stage. The cheers turning into groans doesn't register. Nobody likes to see a girl in a wedding dress jilted at the altar, not even a bride like Sonia. I snuggle into the crook of Hugh's neck as he carries me past two men hidden in the stage—I'm not sure why they seem familiar, must be their blonde hair reminds me of Dad's—and down the steps. It's not until my feet hit the ground in Hugh's tent and he's cupping my face, making sure I don't go too far, that it hits me what we've walked away from.

"Why are we here? We can get married now and—"

Hugh cuts my thoughts off with a kiss, his tongue sweeps against my lips, and I open up for the only boy, man, I've ever loved.

"When I marry you, it won't be to save a company." His thumbs rub circles along my cheeks.

"But Halia?"

"Means nothing if I can't have you." Hugh closes the distance between us.

"But I can save Halia."

A smile spreads across his face. One that I know I'll never get tired of seeing. Especially when there's that mischievous sparkle in his eyes. "You already have." He whispers. "You saved me." He presses a kiss against my lips. Soft and urgent, full of hope and the promise of a future.

"Knock, knock." Tessa's voice invades our space.

"Go away," Hugh mutters against my lips. He captures my giggle with his tongue before righting me. Sunlight slices into the tent, but that doesn't steal the attentive look from Hugh's eyes. He brushes the palm of his hand across the side of my face and into my hair. Like he's making sure I'm not going to disappear on him again.

"Can I borrow your girl for a minute?"

"No." Hugh barks, but there's never been any bite when it comes to Tessa.

"Two minutes, then she's all yours." Tessa cocks her hip and is armed with an all-business look in her eyes.

My heart drops. I know what's coming. I look down at my wrists. All my gold arrows have vanished. I'm not a Cupid anymore. I swallow hard. Hugh threads his fingers through mine and tips my chin up with his other hand, and all my fear subsides. He's always been able to do that . . . when I let him.

"Two minutes." He punctuates his demand with a soft kiss. A second pass of his lips and all my thoughts scatter.

"Okay," I whisper.

Hugh places one last kiss on the tip of my nose. "Hurry back."

"God, you two are disgusting," Tessa mutters and wraps her hand around my wrist. She pulls me away from Hugh. Already I miss his touch. How have I lived without him for six years? We slip out of the tent into the warm summer sun. I shield my eyes. The haze must have burned off because I don't remember it being this bright. I pull in a deep breath, and the flowers . . .

"It'll take some time to get used to the unmuted sights and smells," Tessa offers. "Six years." She walks me to the temporary office we rented from Sid. "I envy you. I can't fathom what you're seeing . . . what you're feeling." The ache in Tessa's voice is nearly tangible.

"You lied to me."

Her eyes lock with mine and follow my gaze to her wrist.

"Yeah, well, you always did better when you thought you were in charge." Tessa smiles. "Sorry."

We round the corner and climb the metal stairs outside Sid's office. I used to make fun of Cupids like her, Cupids who envied their . . . It hits me what we're doing when the door closes behind me. Tessa has to swipe me. I'm out of the Corps, which means she's out of my life. The thought strangles me. Life without Tessa?

I watch Tessa wince. She steadies herself but is doubled over in agony. I know the look. I know the pain. She's getting another arrow. Even though I'm certain it's well past her fiftieth, her face flushes and beads of sweat dot her forehead.

"What about you?" I choke on the words.

"Don't worry about me. I'll be around."

"Will I remember you?"

"Try and forget about me." She smiles, but I know it will be different. We'll be those friends who were inseparable in high school but seemed to drift apart in time. In the real world. I can tell by the way her eyes shimmer, we won't be the same; nothing will. All the Corps conversations, I know they'll be vague recollections, ones that make me happy but I can't recall why. The pain I'd run from the last six years throbs in my heart. Before I can say anything, she asks me the question. The one I've asked forty-nine other souls.

"Do you love him?"

I nod. "With all my heart."

She swipes a finger against the cooling perspiration along her forehead.

"Make it a good one." I whisper as Tessa wraps her fingers around my wrist and presses her pheromone-laced finger to my forehead.

"The High Jack swipe," I mutter before my world goes hazy.

"I heard it's failsafe," Tessa's voice garbles and twists, and before her words turn into gibberish, she says, "Love him always. Love him forever."

A bright light explodes and my world goes black. The last words I hear as a Cupid are Contessa Saint Cloud's: "Your name is Jack. Don't let the masculine nickname fool you. When it comes to matters of the heart, you are thoroughly loved by your high school sweetheart, Hugh Halia. Make it a life all other love stories are compared to. You've been wiped."

Epilogue

TESSA SAINT CLOUD

I *leave Hugh and Jack in* a tent that should count itself lucky it doesn't have a cot, although that chair won't be so fortunate—it's definitely going to see some action. I snort.

"Proud of yourself, I see." E.J.'s voice slices through some of the joy I've found today. He'll pay for it. I don't find much to smile about these days.

"Go away," I sing, turning my face to the sun.

"You know you haven't been able to feel the real warmth of those rays in about nine years."

A giant frustrated breath rushes from my lungs.

"Aww, feeling nostalgic?" E.J. tickles my side. "Fifty arrows sit hard on a petrified hopeless romantic heart, doesn't it?"

I elbow him in the gut, relishing the umph. "Go away, E.J. My two best friends finally found their happily ever after." I spare him a quick look over my shoulder. "You of all people know how rare that is."

I watch a set of memories wash across his face. Oh yeah, he knows how rare it is. He also knows how exceptional it is for two people to be at the same place in life for that lighting-in-a-bottle moment to happen. I step out of the mental whitewash before it can get my toes wet with memories that have taken me years to bury.

"Ever wonder about us—"

"No," I cut him off before he can drag me back in. "I don't wonder about any of it." I shift so he can see his words, his charm, even that cute little dimple that still plays on his cheek has no effect on me. "Neither should you."

E.J. wipes a palm across his mouth. Most guys run a hand through their hair, grind their teeth, or work their lip, but not E.J. It's almost like he has to physically wipe whatever he wants to say from his lips. And gods be damned, those lips.

"Eros and Psyche want us back at the house." E.J. turns from me, taking the unwelcome memory with him. He starts for Pacific Coast Highway before I can ask him why. Before I can wonder what I've done now to piss off the God of Love or his wife, E.J. shoots me a quick grin. I flip him off, hoping the you-don't-bother-me message is received by him and the flutter in my stomach.

Ah, shit on a stick, whom am I kidding? Watching E.J. leave still has the same effect on me as it did when I was sixteen. White linen pants that scream endless summer stretch and pull across his fine ass with each step. I pinch myself. I've been doing a lot of that lately—nearly bruised my immortal skin the night he walked into Villa Nova and surprised Jack and me. My life was so much simpler when he was in Australia and I was seventeen hours away from any memory he could wiggle out of me. I start for Jack's condo. I'm glad I packed last night and wrote her my move-out note. I won't be too far away, I try to remind myself. I still have three months on my contract with Halia Surf. The wind pulls at the edges of my white skirt as I climb the stairs to the condo. The fabric's touch across my leg releases a renegade memory of E.J. and I climbing an abandoned lifeguard tower a lifetime ago. If I close my eyes hard enough, I can feel his palm on my calf. My heart lurches.

"Enough, Tessa." I chastise myself. "Even if E.J. had wanted you, Psyche made it very clear you weren't good enough for her spawn." I grab my suitcase, do a quick make-up check, and leave my note. It's going to be hard not living here, but Hugh and Jack, they've waited long enough for their hit of happy. They don't need a third wheel like me slowing them down.

I pull the door shut behind me, hating the way it feels more like an ending than the next chapter, and try to shake the sinking feeling.

Why would Eros *and* Psyche want to see me?

Acknowledgments

This page is always the hardest for me to write, because there are so many people who walk beside me, pick me up, kick my butt, and make this piece shine. Each time one of my books makes it into your hands I'm in complete awe of the process.

First and foremost, thank you—yes, you holding the book!— for taking this adventure with me. You continue to honor and humble me.

Misty Provencher - my alpha reader and overall writing conscience. I would still be huddled up rocking in my mental writing corner with out you. Thank you!

Molly E. Lee - my #PitchWars mentor who became my friend, my go-to, my champion. I'm thrilled you allow me to tag along on your adventure. I'm honored you let me borrow your brain on a moments notice. You'll never know how you altered my life. Thank you.

Rebecca Yarros – overall badass. Seriously, the woman needs her own Marvel Comic. Your stories inspire me and your graciousness humbles me. We need to get your Superheroes and my Pieces together. It's the only way the world domination will begin.

Rachel Harris – Who I want to be when I grow up one day. Her grace and poise and acceptance and talent … see the list really can go on. I'm so blessed to call her my friend.

Hope and Beth and Megan, my friends from the beginning of this adventure, I love you.

Italia Gandolfo – my agent who totally understands my "all who wander are not lost" way of writing. Thank you for hanging with me.

Janet Wallace – my mentor, my friend. Thank you for being there in ways you'll never know this last year.

My HeartBreakers – Hanging out with you guys is seriously the reason why I do what I do.

Sara Meadows – my PA who makes sure I'm chasing the right rabbit down the right hole. I can't wait to see what we do together!

To my family who has put up with my "sauce on the taco" stories for decades, I love you.

Special thank you to my #RuizesPieces.

Always be weird.

Embrace the nerd in you.

Always love yourself first.

And forever know Mommy loves you to the moon and back.

To the boy who stole my heart with a box of Valentine Conversation Candy Hearts: Twenty some years later and you still make my toes curl, my stomach flutter, and my heart race. Thank you for loving me, Mark Anthony.

About Mindy

Mindy Ruiz lives in a sleepy Beach Town in Southern California. When she's not writing, she spends her time chasing after three boys, making flirty eyes at her hunky husband, watching fantasy television shows, cheering for the Dallas Cowboys, and hanging out at the beach with her very large and loud Italian family.

Her career in publishing started in the 4th grade with a story about a magic, museum-hopping, chair. Now, Mindy writes young adult, new adult, and adult paranormal romance. Her books always include tormented heroes, snarky heroines, and lots of escapades that will make your heart swoon.

Because Love is Always an Adventure.

Mindy is the lover of a good romance, the underdog and John Hughes' 80s teen movies.

When her toes aren't in the sand or her mind isn't in the clouds, Mindy loves hearing from readers.

BECOME A HEARTBREAKER:

www.Facebook.com/groups/HeartBreakers4Ever

FOLLOW HER ON:

www.Facebook.com/MindyRuizBooks

www.Twitter.com/MindyRuiz

AND LOOK FOR HER ON:

www.Instagram.com/MindyRuiz,

www.GoodReads.com/MindyRuiz,

www.Pinterest.com/MindyRuizBooks.

FOR EXCLUSIVE SNEAK PEEKS, JOIN MINDY NEWS:

http://bit.ly/mindynews

Made in the USA
San Bernardino, CA
11 February 2017